NEVER REALLY MINE

AN IVY RIDGE NOVEL

ALICE DANIELS

Never Really Mine

ALICE DANIELS

CONTENTS

To all the readers who love a good surprise pregnancy romance.
If you don't like that trope, then you probably shouldn't read this book.

PLAYLIST

All I Ask- Adele
Almost Lover- A Fine Frenzy
Call Your Mom- Noah Kahan
Chasing Pavements- Adele
Clean (Taylor's Version) -Taylor Swift
Dead Sea- The Lumineers
Down Bad- Taylor Swift
Ends of the Earth- Lord Huron
Everything Changes- Jesse Mueller, Kimiko Glenn, Keala
Settle
exile- Taylor Swift ft. Bon Iver
invisible string- Taylor Swift
Just a Friend to You- Meghan Trainor
Mary's Song (Oh My My My)- Taylor Swift
Mess it Up- Gracie Abrams
NEVER REALLY MINE- The Lumineers
Not Over You- Gavin DeGraw
The Roads- Jonah Karen
Say Don't Go (Taylor's Version) (From The Vault) -Taylor
Swift
She Used to Be Mine- Jessie Mueller
Slow Burn- Kacey Musgraves
Treacherous (Taylor's Version)- Taylor Swift
Unstable- Zak Abel
You Matter to Me- Jessie Mueller, Drew Gehling

To view the whole playlist, follow the link!
https://open.spotify.com/playlist/
3DaEBGq5mQwqE7zOVKVeKo?si=ad3ca6860ac64205

Dear Reader,

Never Really Mine contains subjects that may be triggering to some. This book is not meant to be dark, but it does include scenes depicting depression, and suicidal thoughts and ideation. This book also includes on page scenes of labor and delivery, and an infant not breathing after delivery. Other triggers include a mild lactation kink, breastfeeding, postpartum anxiety and depression, and graphic sexual scenes. There is also brief mention of a drug overdose of a teen in the context of a police investigation.

Take care of yourself. Your mental health matters more than a book.

"You told me I was like the Dead Sea,
    You'll never sink when you are with me."

"DEAD SEA" BY THE LUMINEERS

MARLEY

AGE 18

The needle of the tattoo gun pierces my skin in a precise cadence, but it doesn't hurt. If anything, it feels good, like relieving an itch that I just can't quite reach. The leather chair underneath me is becoming uncomfortable the longer I sit here, but there's only so much I can do about the position I'm in.

"How's the pain, Mar?" my best friend, Beau, asks. He's wearing a devilish grin, like he's anticipating me to whine about how bad it is. He's sitting on a stool next to me, watching the tattoo artist work.

"Not bad," I answer truthfully. My right arm is laying out on a padded armrest, while the artist, Nina, does her job. Months ago, when Beau asked me what I wanted for my birthday, I didn't hesitate. As soon as the suggestion left my lips, I was worried he'd think the idea was stupid, but when he took the leap and made the appointment for us, it made it all worth it.

I thought my heart would beat out of my chest when I watched Beau get his tattoo done first. He made it look so simple as he leaned back and gave me an easy smile. His tattoo is on his right bicep, the same spot as mine. His whole upper arm is covered in a thin film wrap, the skin underneath red and raised from the inflammation of repeated needling.

Nina listened to our ideas of what we envisioned and drew up a sketch for us, and it's everything I could have wanted. Two hands clasped together, one in the water, one out. It symbolizes a lyric from the song "Dead Sea," by our favorite band, The Lumineers.

Beau has been my best friend since the age of eleven. My family moved into the house next door to him, and we became fast friends, despite my initial hesitancy. When I found out the next door neighbors had four boys, I was devastated. I was convinced that they would only be friends with my older brothers, Kenny and Prescott. They're four and five years older than I am, and they wanted nothing to do with hanging out with their eleven year old sister. Beau proved me wrong. Until we moved to Ivy Ridge, all the neighbors were my brother's age, and they all played together. I was the annoying little sister, always ignored, always in the way.

Shortly after we moved into the new house, I was reading a book on the front lawn when Beau and his younger brother, Andrew, rode by on their bikes. Beau noticed me first. He stopped, calling out to Andrew who had zoomed by, not even realizing that his brother had stopped. Andrew kept going, saying something about meeting him at the baseball fields, but Beau waved him off. He dropped his bike onto the lawn, and strode over to me. A heavy feeling of nervousness made its way through my body. Was he going to tell me to stay away?

His brown curly hair flopped over his eyes and he pushed it back off his forehead. Wearing an Ivy Ridge Baseball tee and basketball shorts, he looked ready to head to practice. I wore a bright yellow sundress that mom always said made my brown eyes pop.

He introduced himself, asked what book I was reading, and promptly declared us friends. Ever since that summer day, Beau has been my rock, my one person I know will always be there for me. He was the first person I told the day I started taking antidepressants. The first one I called the day my mom wasn't home, and I was slipping toward the edge of a cliff with no return. He's helped me through some of my darkest days, and I'll never be able to thank him enough for it.

Pulling me right out of my memories of Beau, Nina swipes the towel across my aching skin and clicks her tongue. "Done," she sings. I look down at my arm, at the artwork that was now permanently on my skin. A smile grows on my face, and I look up, meeting Beau's eyes. His smile mirrors mine. "What do you think?" Nina asks.

"I love it," I say. It's perfect.

She finishes cleaning my skin, covering the tattoo with a thin layer of ointment and wrapping it in gauze and tape. I meet Beau over by the counter at the front of the shop, pulling out my money from my back pocket.

"I got it," Beau says, pushing my hand with the money out of the way. "My birthday present to you."

I scoff, trying to slide in and pay. "Then I should pay for your tattoo," I say.

"Nope," Beau says with a sly smile. "I already paid for both of ours while you were getting cleaned up."

"Beau, seriously?"

"What, am I not allowed to treat my best friend on her birthday?"

"Not when it's a tattoo, and you paid for your own, too! You should have saved that for your college fund."

He shrugs. "It's done now. Besides, you can just buy our next tattoos."

"Ugh," I grumble. "Fine. Thank you," I begrudgingly say, but on the inside, I'm giddy. I can't wait for this new chapter in our lives, to start this new tradition for us.

"You're welcome." Beau catches my eye, winking quickly. My heart flutters, not for the first time today. Things with Beau have been... different lately. To the point where I think something more might be evolving between us. At graduation, he hugged me for just a second longer than normal, and it didn't feel like our normal, platonic hugs we share so often.

In a few weeks, I'm off to one of the local community colleges, where I plan to study photography. Beau's heading off to business school in the city. Sure, we will only be an hour from each other, but I can't help but worry that things will change.

I climb into Beau's truck, a hand-me-down from his Gramps. It's a '97 Chevy Silverado that used to be used as the company truck for his woodworking business, but has since been retired to each of his grandsons. Beau starts the forty-minute drive home, but instead of taking a right into town, he turns left, heading toward Cinder Valley. "What are you doing?" I ask.

Beau shrugs. There's a sort of scheming glint in his eye, but I don't question it, he's always up to something. He drives us through the small town, heading to the river landing. He parks, then jerks his head toward the river. "C'mon."

I get out, following him. The rocky gravel crunches beneath my sandals, and the landing is surprisingly calm, despite the late summer day. There are groups of canoers heading down the river, but I don't really pay them any mind. Beau sits down on a log, patting the spot next to him.

I sit down, and he wraps his arm around my shoulders, pulling me into his warm chest. He smells of his cologne, clean, and sharp. I chuckle when I think about the phase he went through with AXE body spray. He sprayed that shit everywhere, seemingly coating his skin in a layer of the potent stuff.

"What's funny?" he asks.

I tilt my head to glance up at him, admiring his chocolate brown eyes and mussed hair. "Just thinking about your AXE body spray phase."

He groans, squeezing me tighter. "That wasn't nearly as bad as your Warm Vanilla Sugar phase from Bath and Body Works."

I gasp, pulling away from him. "Hey, I smelled like a cookie, which is much better than... whatever you smelled like."

"Alright," he chuckles. "You've got me there. You did smell like a cookie." He pulls me back into his side and I relax into his touch. A lot of the time, people assume we're dating, because of the way he holds me, or hugs me sometimes, but we're both quick to correct them. Beau's just a physical touch kind of guy, and he's a great hugger, so it's a win-win, in my opinion.

"I feel like things are going to change when we go to school," I murmur. I gaze off into the distance as I speak, too afraid to meet his eye. I know he's going to tell me that it won't, but I can't help but feel like he's just saying that to appease me.

"They will," he says. I whip my head off his shoulder to look at him. He's grinning maniacally.

"Beau," I squeal. "You're supposed to tell me that things aren't going to change!" I smack his chest lightly.

"They are, though!" He tries to defend himself. "Just because things in our lives are changing, doesn't mean that *we* have to change."

I nod, hearing what he's saying. "I guess. I'm just so scared I'm going to lose you. You're the best thing in my life, Beau." I squeeze him tightly.

"Marley, you could never lose me." He grips my chin, tilting my face upwards. "Eventually, we're going to get married to someone, have kids, grow old, but I will *always* be there for you. You're my best friend."

I don't know why, but his words feel like a knife straight through my heart. Leaving me aching and bleeding for everyone to see. I nod, words failing me.

His eyes stray from mine down to my lips. They dart back up when he realizes what he's done, but it's too late. I saw, and I know what he's thinking. He pulls away from me, shifting slightly. I straighten so I'm no longer tucked under his arm, trying to shake off the embarrassment that is currently forcing its way through my body.

When I'm confident I have my breathing under control, I turn back to Beau. "You're my best friend too, Beau. You're right, we'll always hav-"

I'm cut off by lips crashing onto mine. *Beau's* lips.

Holy shit, is Beau kissing me?

I pull away, gasping for air, trying to process this new feeling. "Beau, what-"

He stops me, tucking a hair behind my ear. His eyes are wild, breathing ragged. "I just couldn't go another moment without knowing what your lips feel like."

My eyes flick down to his lips, where his tongue is darting out to wet them. He notices, and his hand slides down my jaw to cup my cheek. "What do they feel like?" I ask.

"Otherworldly."

I nod, my heart fluttering in response to the unexpected kiss, and the way he described it. "And that's good?" I ask.

"So flippin good." He presses a softer kiss to my lips, lingering there for a long moment. I've been kissed before by one other guy, but he had braces. When I tried to make out with him, my tongue got caught on one of the wires. Talk about embarrassing.

Beau's tongue slides between my lips, tasting me, teasing me. I wrap my arms around his neck, holding him to me. He skillfully moves our tongues together, the hand not on my cheek sliding around my neck. I begin to lose myself in the kiss, the alarm bells screaming at me that this is *Beau*, and we shouldn't be doing this, starting to quiet in my head.

Someone wolf-whistles from the river, and we spring apart like someone shocked us with a live wire. I hold my breath for a moment, scooting away from him. I release it, trying to calm my pounding heart. "So..." I start to say. Does this change literally everything I thought I knew?

Beau stops me. "I... I don't know how to say this."

Was my heart pounding before? Because now it's not even beating. Blood drains from my face, because I know what's coming. I'm not girlfriend material—at least not for Beau. I'm just the best friend.

I resign myself to this fact, taking a deep breath before I interrupt him. Saying what I know he's going to say. "We can't do that again. Not if we want to keep our friendship."

Beau nods, blowing out a breath, running his hands through his hair. "Yeah." His jaw tightens, and I see a flash of something in his eyes, some new emotion I have never seen in him before. It worries me, not knowing what that emotion is, or what kind of ripple effect this will have on our friendship.

"Good." He doesn't say anything, but he doesn't need to. I just single-handedly saved myself from the inevitable heartbreak of hearing him say the words that I dreaded hearing from him. I mean, sure, there's been tension leading up to this moment, but that's all it was. We are teenagers, after all. And you know what they say about hormones.

Beau pulls me in close again, and I let myself pretend for just a moment that things could be different, that I could be his, and he could be mine. But I know it's just a silly dream. If I want to keep him, I'll never get to have him in the way I really want.

2

———

BEAU

PRESENT DAY

"It's because of her, isn't it?" Ashley whines. My eyes widen as I stare at her from across the small table. The restaurant is dimly lit, and a few couples at other tables glance over as Ashley's voice rises in pitch.

Sighing, I run my hands through my hair. In retrospect, I should have done this a long time ago. "No, it's not," I mutter. *Liar.* "I... I don't see this being long term."

Tears stream down her face, black streaks from her mascara lining her heavily made up cheeks. "Why are you doing this to me?" she cries. "I thought you loved me. I thought we had something amazing."

I hold back my scoff at her words. I know I seem like a dick right now, but I don't exactly know where she got the idea that I loved her. I've kept her at an arm's length for the last six months we've been together, if that's what you could even call it. I've been her emotional punching bag, and she's been a distraction for me. We've never even slept together.

A distraction for what, you might ask? My best friend. The very person Ashley is accusing me of breaking up with her for. She's not wrong, but she's also not right.

9

Marley will never be mine. Not in the way I need her to be.

I've loved her since we were kids, playing in the treehouse in the backyard or pretending to be detectives solving a murder mystery. I'll never tell her, though, not after I tried to take things further with her when we were eighteen. Not after my dad, and her dad shot down any ideas I had of making her mine.

I kissed her, and it was the best fucking kiss of my life. The most intoxicating thing I've ever felt was having her lips on mine. But she shut me down. Shut any concept of *us* down. It hurt. I was ready to give her my all, to give my heart over to her on a silver platter, but between her shutting me down, and our dads telling me no, I was done. All hope shattered of a chance at a future with her.

I had a taste of her, just one, and I was going to fight for her. I was. Two days after that kiss, I went over to her house when she was working.

I knock on the old wooden door, a giddy excitement coursing through my veins. This is it. I know Marley said she didn't want to risk our friendship, but I don't think she sees just how amazing we could be.

Heavy footsteps make their way to the door, and I tamper down the small burst of anxiety. It's fine. Gabriel isn't going to disapprove of me, in fact, I think our parents will collectively be excited for us, for this new chapter.

Gabriel opens the door, a soft smile on his face as he greets me. "Beau, what are you doing here?"

My mouth goes dry, feeling like someone shoved three cotton balls in it. I clear my throat, hoping my voice doesn't crack when I speak, when my own father strides up to the door. "Beau? What's up, kiddo?"

Shit, this is already not going how I planned. "I- uh-" I cough. "I just wanted to talk to Gabriel about something."

Both Gabriel and my dad's brows lift in confusion. "Come on in," *Gabriel says, gesturing for me to come through the door. I kick off my sandals, following him inside.* "We were just having a drink."

He leads me through the living room to the kitchen table where they were clearly sitting. Two cans of beer sit on the otherwise empty table. Gabriel pulls out a chair for me to sit in.

I follow their lead, sitting when they do, my body stiff and uncomfortable. I don't know whether or not to continue with my plan since my dad is here, or what to do. I don't know when I'll get another opportunity before I leave for school to see Gabriel without Marley nearby, so maybe I just have to do it.

My palms sweat, and I rub them up and down my thighs, attempting to dry them off. I take a breath, ready to say what I came to say, but Gabriel shocks me by speaking first.

"Beau, I think I know why you're here," he softly says. He glances over to my dad, who nods.

"You do?" I murmur, raising my brows. Am I really that obvious?

"You want to ask Marley out, don't you?"

Seems like I really am that obvious. "Yes, sir," *I say.*

He cackles with laughter, easing some of the panic I feel. "You have never called me sir, and I think we should keep it that way."

"Noted," I say with a small laugh.

My dad shakes his head, eyes bright as he tries to hold in a laugh. His once dark brown hair is starting to gray at his temples, hair thinning as well. He looks more and more like Gramps everyday.

The mood changes in an instant as Gabriel speaks. "Beau... You know I love you like a son of my own, right?"

I nod.

"With that being said... I don't think," he pauses. "I don't know if this is the right thing for you two."

My heart stops beating. I never could have anticipated this. I thought... Well, I thought he'd be happy for us.

"I disagree," I say through gritted teeth, trying to mask my pain. I need to stand up for her. For us.

Gabriel sighs. "I thought you might say that. Hear me out," he says. "It's not because I think you aren't good for her. I just... I think you both need to focus on school and where this year is going to take you. Who knows, you might end up three states over and in a long-distance relationship. Your friendship is too important."

I inwardly scoff, my annoyance growing with each passing second. They don't understand. I need her to breathe, to be the person that I am. "We could make it work. I know we could," I argue. "I can come home every weekend, and we will talk all the time. She's worth it."

My dad shakes his head. "You're not getting it, Beau. What happens if you break up? Or she shoots you down? What if you meet someone else at school? We are trying to protect you both, and the friendship you already have."

He continues, ignoring me when I try to interject. "We know how close you two are, and we don't want you two to lose each other. We aren't saying never... just maybe think things over really hard before you dive in." Dad winces slightly, as if he knows they've just ripped my heart into a million pieces. What they don't know is that I'm capable of reading between the lines.

We don't want you to ruin your friendship, *which actually means* you're not good enough for my daughter.

I'm too much of a flight risk. She needs someone steady, who knows where they're going in life. I don't even know what day of the week it is, or what classes I'm taking this fall. But I know Marley. I know her life story. I know her favorite color, down to the exact shade. I know that she prefers tea over coffee, that her favorite tv show is Friends, *but only until season eight, because then she knows the end is coming and it makes her sad.*

I know how to pull her out when she's sinking and can't see the light at the end of the tunnel.

I know that she can't sleep without music, and I know that I will love her until the day I die.

I shove away from the table, trying to hide the sheer agony. I never want to feel this embarrassment ever again. Two people I look up to most in the world just told me not to ask my best friend out, to not take things further, so maybe... maybe that is my sign to live with the pain of knowing I'm not good for her. With the pain of knowing what her lips feel like on mine, never to feel it again.

"Are you even paying attention to me?" a shrill voice brings me back to the present.

I wince, running my hands through my hair as I glance around at the other people in the restaurant. "I'm sorry, Ashley," I say. "I enjoyed our time together, but I think we need to move on."

The tears in her eyes dry immediately, and she straightens her back, adjusting her platinum blonde pony-tail. "If that's what you really want."

The sudden change in her demeanor sends a chill down my spine. She's done this a few times with me before, but I've never seen it happen so aggressively, so cold and collected.

I nod, ignoring the emotional whiplash from her, and spare another glance in her direction.

"Don't come crawling back to me when she rejects you, Beau Cunningham." Ashley points a finger at me. "Because she will. She will never love you the way I do."

At a loss for words, I nod again, watching as she scoots her chair back and stands, twiddling her fingers at me. She spins, her ponytail flying at the aggression, as she hikes her massive purse over her shoulder. The contents inside rattle, as she heads to the door without giving me a second glance.

A weight lifts from my chest as she exits the small restaurant. I feel like a free man, though Ashley's words sting a bit. I'm never going to be good enough for Marley, no matter how hard I try. She deserves so much more than me. More than the kid who has never been able to confess how much he really needs her. More than the kid who allowed his dad to convince him he wasn't right for her.

3

———

MARLEY

6 MONTHS LATER

"You know, we wouldn't be here if it weren't for you, Marley," Josie says.

I wave her off, taking a sip of the dry wine, the flavor bursting over my tongue before sliding down my throat. "Yes you would," I scoff. "You of all people know that Andrew would have moved mountains to find you."

Josie shrugs, her cheeks pinkening as she takes a sip of her wine. She glances over at her soon to be husband across the room, and he must feel her gaze. He turns, winking before turning back to his conversation with his brother, Beau, and best friend Isaac.

Just over a year ago, Josie and Andrew met when she was the working florist for Isaac's wedding to his wife, Megan. They hit it off immediately, but Josie left before Andrew could get any of her information.

Lucky for them, I was able to convince them both to be my first test subjects of a blind date photoshoot, for my studio, Chrysalis Photography.

Anyone could see that it was practically love at first sight for them. Now, a year later, we're here at the place

15

they first met, ready to celebrate that love. Josie has become one of my best friends, even more so now that we work next door to each other.

I purchased my own studio space last summer, and have moved my business from weddings and events, to more intimate sessions, like boudoir, single or couple, and engagement sessions. I've done five or six additional blind date photoshoots, and they always are a hit on my social media.

The wedding is at Meadow Grove Winery, where Josie is contracted as their florist for events, and where they first met. Andrew's best friend, Isaac is the new general manager after his parents retired last summer.

"I suppose that may be true," Josie says, her eyes full of mischief. "So…" she drawls.

"So?" I murmur, a smile that I fear may turn into a grimace on my face. With the look on her face and the way her eyes keep darting between Beau and me, I have a feeling I know what she's going to say.

"Have you talked with Beau lately?"

I withhold the painful sigh, my chest tightening in anxiety. Josie knows everything. She witnessed the fight Beau and I had months ago, and knows that things have not been the same between us.

"Not really. I mean, yes, we talk, and we hang out, but it's surface level. Neither of us wants to rock the boat. And, he's got that girlfriend that none of us know anything about." I push my bangs out of my eyes, and take another long sip of my wine.

She solemnly nods. "Do I need to say it?"

I shake my head. "Nope. Besides, this is your weekend. We aren't going to dredge up my emotional baggage." *And there's a lot of it.*

Beau's been dating a girl for probably a year now, and

no one in the family has met her. We don't even know her name. Anytime I bring her up, he shuts down and won't say a word about her, though I probably bring that upon myself. I can't help it.

He walked in at the tail end of my boudoir session with Josie. I was wearing a set of lingerie that I felt incredible in, dark green lace that accentuated my ample curves, even allowing a bit of a glimpse of my nipple piercings through the fabric.

I haven't worn it again, not since that fight. He started spewing some bullshit about how he didn't want guys to see me wearing the lingerie, and I called him out on it. I don't regret it, he had no right to say that, but I fear it was the final crack in the armor we've been wearing for fourteen years.

Falling in love with your best friend is not something I'd recommend to anyone. Loving someone you can never have is a pain that I'd never wish on anyone. Watching him love someone else? That's a rare form of torture. Over the years, I've watched him fall in love, get his heart broken, and been there every step of the way to put him back together.

I've loved Beau Cunningham since I was eleven. He's my best friend, and has been since the day we met. I swore that I would never let myself lose him over my feelings for him. The one time we kissed, I knew he was about to tell me we couldn't be more, so I beat him to it.

Beau is my person. He's the only one who really knows me. The deep, dark, and gritty pieces of me. He's the one who has put me back together time and time again. He's saved me from myself, more than I'd care to admit.

"Is his girlfriend coming this weekend?" I ask, because I have to know. I try my best to mask my emotions, but I know Josie sees my ulterior motive. I have to mentally prepare myself for the inevitable pain.

She winces slightly, shaking her head. "I asked him a few weeks ago. We gave him a plus one, but he declined."

Some of the tightness in my chest eases, leaving me breathless for a moment. At least I won't have to see him happy and in love this weekend. I give myself one more glance in his direction, finding his dark brown eyes on mine. My face flushes under his stare, but I don't pull my eyes away. His curls are long, resting on his shoulders. He has them styled so they aren't a frizzy mess, remembering the days when he didn't know how to do his hair, so it was just pure fluff.

Beau offers me a soft smile, and I give him one in return before turning back to Josie. "I wonder why, I mean, they've been together about a year now, right?" Josie chatters, not noticing that I wasn't fully listening.

I swallow the thick lump in my throat. Reaching over, I fix one of the red curls hanging in her eyes. "Yeah, I think so," I reply.

"Why hasn't he brought her around? Is it not serious?"

I shrug.

"You might not realize it, Marley, but I'm rooting for the two of you," Josie says quietly.

I shake my head, ignoring the burning of tears in my eyes. "You shouldn't. I can't let anything happen between us, or ruin our friendship. I need him."

"I'm not saying this to be mean, but..." She hesitates. "Haven't you already done that?"

"What do you mean?"

"After that fight... things haven't been the same, right? Didn't you already mess up your friendship?"

I sigh, because she's right. I know she is. I just don't have the balls to say it out loud, to admit it to myself.

"I am saying this because I love you, Marley, and I want

you to be as happy as I am. I wouldn't be as happy as I am without you, so I'm making it my own personal mission to get you two together."

I'm not going to try and convince her not to, not tonight at least. I don't have the energy to fight it tonight. Tonight... I can let myself give into the fantasy that maybe, just maybe, I could let myself love him the way I want to.

4

BEAU

S he looks stunning.

It's not that she isn't always beautiful or stunning, but tonight, she's taking my breath away. Marley stands across the room with my future sister-in-law, Josie, talking in hushed whispers.

Marley's long brown hair is pulled back into a high ponytail, the ends curled loosely. Her makeup is soft, muted colors, lips painted a sultry maroon. Her emerald silk dress clings to her every curve, a high slit up her right leg, baring her smooth skin. The cut is a low V, showing off her cleavage, leaving little to the imagination. If I look close enough, I can just barely see the outline of her nipple piercings, leaving me trembling, aching for more, to see them bare. To see her laid out before me like my last feast, eager to be touched, claimed, finally made mine. My mind drifts to the day I fucked up worse than ever before, but... fuck, I couldn't help it. Seeing her in that lingerie? Nearly killed me dead.

Driving through town with the windows down, I slow as I pass by Marley's new photography studio. I helped her with the purchase, and from the sounds of it, she's getting settled well. When I see her car in the spot out front, I halt, pulling in next to it without a second thought.

I get out of my vehicle, heading toward the front door. I peek in the front window, noting the small glimmer of light I can just barely see. I tug on the front door, unsure of how to feel when I learn it's unlocked. She should have the door locked if she's here alone. You never know what kind of people are out there, even in a small town like ours. Just ask my brother, Thomas. Just a few months ago, he was telling us how there is word of sex traffickers in the drug circles. He's been working on a case for nearly a year, trying to bust them, but can't seem to track it down.

Giggles fill the air, and I recognize Marley's laugh, and another vaguely familiar voice. I don't want to scare them, so I call out her name. "Mar?"

Her slightly irritated voice calls back. "What are you doing here?" I know she's been upset with me since I announced I was going on a date a few weeks back, and I want to clear the air.

I stride through the small studio as I speak. "I was in the area, so I figured I would stop by and see if you needed help with anyth—" My words cut off with an audible gulp, because when I see Marley, my Marley, standing in front of me wearing the world's sexiest lingerie, I nearly swallow my tongue.

We stand there in an epic staredown. Her body is just barely covered, leaving not much to the imagination. The deep green lace is nearly see through. If she turned around, I'm sure I would be left with an incredible view of her ass, one that I've fantasized about for years. My eyes trail up her stomach to the curve of her breasts, stopping when I see the outline of her nipples through the sheer fabric.

Holy hell. She has nipple piercings? Kill me now. I'm done for. I suspected that she did after years of faintly seeing something on her chest, but I never had the guts to ask, and now that I can physically see them, I have to fight the blood that is making an effort to rush south.

Her tattoos are on display, and I note one I've never seen before on her ribs: a vine covered in a floral pattern with little butterflies flying from the stems. God, I love this woman so much, every inch of her. Every piece of her soul is so woven into mine that I don't think I can live without her for another moment.

Words fail me, and I realize I need to say something. "Wha—" *I clear the lump from my throat.* "Why are you in lingerie?"

Her hands settle on her hips as she gives me an irritated look. "I read up on it. Clients can feel more comfortable when they're not alone in being half naked." *Her voice is strong, unwavering.*

My mind can't process thoughts, but I ask, even though I heard someone else earlier. "You did a session today?"

"Yes. The client is still here actually, so can we make this quick?" *she snaps, her voice growing increasingly irritated. It softens ever so slightly when she says,* "Why are you really here, Beau?"

She has always seen right through me. "You've been ignoring me."

She scoffs, pinching the bridge of her nose. "I haven't been ignoring you, I'm busy."

Now it's my turn to get irritated. "You sure? Because the minute you found out I was dating someone, you shut me out. Why is that, Marley?" *I try to rein it in, but there's a haze over me now, fighting to make her see that I'm just trying to survive, trying to make my way through life without* her as mine. "You're my best friend. I don't want to live without you. We're in our thirties, it's normal to date."

Marley stiffens, not breathing, not speaking. My chest heaves as blood pounds in my ears. Is this it? Is this the final nail in the coffin of our friendship? Or is it the opening to more?

I seal my fate with nine words. I don't know why I say it, some sort of caveman urge settles over me. "I don't want guys to see you wearing that," I mutter.

My heavy statement falls like lead, landing and exploding like a nuclear bomb.

I run a hand through my long hair, knowing that I just fucked up. I ruined everything.

Marley lets out a wicked laugh. "Oh, that's real fucking rich, Beau. Why, might I ask, don't you want guys to see me wearing lingerie? I'm going to go out on a limb and say it's not because you think I don't look good in it."

I try to speak, but she interrupts me, holding up a hand. Her dark eyes fall to the floor, her entire posture turning defeated. "No. Just... go. I don't want to do this with you. You have a girlfriend, and I'm just your best friend." She pauses, and my heart splits in two. Doesn't she see that she's so much more? That she is literally everything to me? That the only reason I've lived with the pain of not having her for this long is to protect her?

Marley continues, "The one to hold you while you cry, the one to make sure you're okay after she inevitably breaks up with you."

Anything I were to say now would fall on deaf ears, so I offer one final apology. "I'm sorry. I'll go." I turn, heading to the door, but I can't leave without saying one more thing. "I'll talk to you later, Mar. I hope you'll forgive me for being an ass."

She says nothing as I push the door open, leaving her behind me.

I don't know where to go from here. I hadn't planned on dating Ashley for long—she's simply someone to distract me from the aching hole in my chest in the shape of Marley's heart—but now, I fear we may never break through the barrier holding us apart.

Marley coyly glances over where I'm sitting alone at the bar, her eyes widening when she realizes I'm already watching her. I take a long sip of my gin and tonic, letting the cool liquor slide down my throat. It eases some of the anxiety churning in my gut. Her eyes dart away within a second, returning to her conversation with my other brothers, Jason and Thomas.

The glass of wine in her hand is empty.

I raise my palm, signaling the bartender. "What can I get for you?" He eyes my nearly full drink.

"See that girl over there?" I subtly point to Marley. "Any chance you remember what she's drinking?"

He nods. "Oh yeah, she had the special wine for the event. Dry as shit, but I guess everyone likes it."

"Give me a glass of it, please."

The bartender smirks, leaning down to grab the bottle from below and filling the glass with the proper amount. He hands it to me. "On the house. Good luck, bro."

I chuckle, throwing down a ten-dollar bill as a tip. "Thanks."

With that, I take her drink in my right hand, my own in my left, and make headway toward Marley. Her eyes are light with humor, cheeks flushed. Her lipstick is just barely smudged on the corner, and I fight an urge to use my thumb to swipe it clean. I stride to her side, holding out the glass of wine. "I got you another, Mar."

She tries to hide her surprised look, but fails. "Thanks," she says with a squeak. She takes the full glass, trading me the empty. I set it down on a table next to us, turning my attention back to my brothers. I stand close to Marley, watching my older brothers' eyes as they watch me.

"Feeling ready for tomorrow?" I ask, the question not directed at anyone specific.

"Oh yeah," Thomas says with a chuckle. "I've got it all planned out. Lennie and I are going to kill the flower girl job."

I laugh, glancing across the room where my four-year-old niece sits with my and Marley's parents, smiling as she colors. I feel bad that she doesn't have any cousins her age, but hopefully soon she'll have some to play with.

"You just have to remember not to take Lennie's thunder," Marley says with a smile.

"That girl is going to run the show. Did you see her practicing tonight?" he asks, completely serious. "She was telling me exactly how to throw the flowers, even correcting the angle of my arm. I think she's got it down. I'm just the cool uncle."

"That you are," Jason mutters. His eyes stray to the wedding planner, Fallon, standing at the table by Lennie with whom I assume is her daughter. The young girl sits down next to Lennie, and the two of them seem to get along instantly, giggling and smiling as Lennie hands her a coloring sheet and crayons.

"Looks like Lennie made a friend," I say.

"Yeah," he says, his brows furrowing as if he's not sure how to feel about it. It has me curious, as I've never seen my brother look at someone with such intent, but I opt to let it go for now.

I take a step closer to Marley, focusing on her reaction.

She tenses, adjusting herself so she isn't beside me, only to change her mind, and move closer to me, our arms nearly touching.

Marley relaxes after a moment, and I follow suit. No matter what is going on between us, I feel at home at her side. The conversation flows easily for the rest of the evening, the members of the bridal party slowly dipping out one by one, as we have to get a lot of sleep before the big day tomorrow.

5

MARLEY

Beau has been clinging to me all evening, and I don't exactly know why. He's weirdly chipper compared to his normal grumpy attitude. The rest of the bridal party made their way up to the shared suite about fifteen minutes ago, but I wanted to stay back and make sure things got cleaned up and ready for the reception tomorrow.

Beau hung back, watching me move and direct the staff, offering his assistance now and then. Now that things are settled and ready for tomorrow though, I have nowhere to hide, nowhere to escape his haunted gaze.

"I'm going to head up to the room," I say awkwardly, jerking my thumb over my shoulder to the elevator.

"I'll walk you up. I'm on the same floor."

Of course he is.

I wordlessly nod, turning to head toward the elevator. My heels click on the wood floors, my emerald green dress swishing at my ankles. I press the button, and the elevator arrives at the main floor with a *ding*. Beau extends his arm, gesturing for me to go first. I step across the threshold and head to the far corner of the small space, though I doubt it will deter him. Beau seems hell-bent on being within five inches of me at all times this evening. I'd be annoyed, but he's always been like this. Always wants to be close to me, to make sure I'm okay.

Sure enough, he steps in, turning to hit the button for the third floor and watching the doors slide shut. Once the elevator dings, moving upward, Beau steps back, standing as close to me as possible without physically touching me, though I can feel his body heat on my arms. Goosebumps flare down my arms, my body betraying me.

I take a deep breath, trying to ignore the scent of his cologne. Beau clears his throat. The air is thick with words unsaid. Anxiety churns in my throat, and I need to get out of here.

"Crazy that tomorrow's the big day," Beau says, his voice gravely and low. I glance up at him, watching as he pulls a ponytail off his wrist, pulling his long curls into a half pony on the back of his head. I've never found long hair, or man buns, for that matter, particularly attractive on men. But on Beau? It's divine, the perfect look for him, somehow making him even more attractive than he already is.

I drop my gaze when he catches me staring, clutching my right forearm where my newest tattoo is—a butterfly with one perfect wing and the other illustrating a transition into flowers, then fading to dust. I got it shortly before Andrew and Josie got engaged, one of the only tattoos I've ever gotten without consulting Beau.

The elevator shudders as we reach the third floor, dinging our arrival. I realize that I never responded to his statement.

"Hard to believe it," I reply. I step forward when the doors open, looking to my right for the bridal suite. I hear the sound of a popular song and giddy laughter down the empty hall, and point down the hall toward it. "Sounds like they're having a good time."

Beau chuckles. "Don't let my mom get too tipsy. You know how she is."

I laugh. "Pretty sure she's already tipsy. Tipsy Nikki is my favorite, so I won't be the one to stop her. She can't wait for one of her boys to get married."

He groans, his dark eyes crinkling at the corner.

"My bet is on Thomas being next," I say, instantly regretting it. Beau narrows his eyes, his jaw clenching. For some reason, I continue to poke the bear. "Though, you've been dating your secret girl for a while, so who knows, maybe you're ready to pop the question, and you haven't even introduced us to her." Bitterness laces my tone.

We used to tell each other everything. I don't understand why things changed. Why we are so tense with each other, when before, he was the person I relied on for everything. The person I called when I was at the lowest of lows.

Beau tenses, shoving a hand into his pocket. He slowly nods as if agreeing with me, and my heart splinters just a bit more. "You're right, I haven't introduced you to her."

I don't speak. Not that I'd even know what to say right now.

Beau doesn't stop though, barely giving me time to process. "I haven't introduced her to anyone, because I don't have a girlfriend. I haven't, not since April."

I blink, not saying a word as I process what he's telling me. He's kept this information from everyone, his family, his friends, *me*? All for six months?

He steps closer to me, resting his warm hand at the small of my back. My brain is screaming at my body to react, but I'm frozen in time, standing in the hotel hallway.

Pulling me in close, my hands fly up, resting against the warmth of his chest. Through his dress shirt, I can feel his heart pounding, but I don't look up. If I look at his face, into those brown eyes, it will be my ruin. I will never be able to return to the way we were before this moment if I cave into the things I want to say. The things I want to do.

Words finally tumble out of my mouth. "Well, now I feel like a fool. Am I the only one who didn't know you broke up?" Rationally, I know that's not true, as Josie was just talking about it earlier, and yet that's what my mouth says anyway. He shakes his head.

I step out of his arms, needing a clear head. "Why did you lie?"

Beau shrugs, eyes cast to the floor where he kicks an invisible rock. "I just... I don't know, Mar. I did. It's not like I planned on lying to everyone... to you."

He steps closer to me, reaching out for my hand. I let him take it, trying to ignore that zing of electricity that happens every time he touches me. Just because he's single... it shouldn't change anything, but the way my heart is pounding, and my brain is fantasizing about us, something tells me that it is changing.

I look down at the floor at our feet, my satin dress wrinkled at the bottom after hours of wear. "Marley," Beau whispers. His voice is thick, strained, pleading. I shake my head. I can't give into this. If I give into this, he's going to regret it, and hate me forever.

God, I want him so bad, I need him, but I'm so fucking scared of losing him.

I can't lose the person who has been with me since day one. The person who fought Joey Swenson in grade school when he compared me to a cow. The one that held me in my college apartment when I had lost the will to fight, the will to live. I can't lose the person who has helped me survive.

Beau drops my hand, resting his warm hand on my waist. His fingers tug at my chin. I shake out of his grasp, trying to step away. "Look at me," Beau murmurs.

"No," I whisper. "I can't."

"Why can't you look at me?"

I take in a shaky breath, my lip trembling. "Because if I do, I don't know what will happen."

He exhales sharply, his fingers again trying to tilt my chin to his gaze. This time, I let him. His brown eyes swirl with emotion, pain, love and so much heat. Those little flecks of gold in his eyes that I love so much are practically burning a hole in my chest.

His thumb slides over my trembling bottom lip, leaving me aching. It's so irritating that he has this effect on me after all this time. His eyes flare with a look that I recognize as the one from all those years ago at the river landing when he kissed me.

I squeeze my eyes shut, trying to wake up from this dream. Did I drink too much at dinner tonight? Because this can't possibly be real. Beau can't possibly be telling me he's been single for months, and looking like he wants to kiss me. It's just not realistic. He doesn't want to kiss me. The mess of a girl, hiding behind a confident façade. I've seen and met some of his girlfriends in the past, and I'm nothing like them. They're all blonde, thin, with no personality.

Beau rests his forehead on mine, and it feels so right. The world around me stands still until it's just us two, no fear of losing him, no fear of a broken heart. His nose brushes mine, and that one moment before lips meet, has me crashing back to earth. To the reality of this.

I gasp, stepping away from him, from the almost kiss.

Beau's hands drop to his sides, shoulders hanging low. I'm breathing heavily as if I just finished a marathon. My eyes prick with tears and I pray they won't fall.

"This can't happen, Marley," he says through gritted teeth.

Throat tightening, I say, "If it can't happen, then why are you the one that started it?" I shake my head, ignoring the tears burning my eyes, forcing them back. "Goodnight, Beau."

I turn, rushing down the hall to the bridal suite, trying to shake off the rollercoaster of emotions from the last five minutes. I can't even begin to process it, and I need to get it together. This weekend is not about me and my bullshit. It's about Josie and Andrew.

I suck in another breath, risking one last look at Beau, standing in the same spot at the opposite end of the hall. His fingers are running through his hair, his eyes glassy, face flushed. He steps forward when he sees me looking, but I shake my head, opening the door to the suite with the key Josie gave me.

I shut the door behind me quickly as if running from a ghost. All eyes are on me as I try to control my emotions. Josie's brow furrows, her eyes widening after I stand still for a long moment. Dammit, she can see right through the façade I'm trying to put on. Everyone is dressed in matching pajama sets, glasses of wine in their hands. Nikki Cunningham, Andrew and Beau's mom, slowly rises from her spot on the plush couch.

My mother eyes me from her corner of the room, where she's laying cucumbers over Lennie's eyes. Lennie's thick brown hair is swept back with a bow headband, and she has a goopy face mask on.

"Gotta pee!" I shriek, darting right into the bathroom

and slamming the door. With the door closed, I glance at myself in the mirror. My eyes are wild, cheeks flushed red, hair falling out of my ponytail as if I just had a weekend long fuck fest. I spot a set of satin pajamas hanging on the hanger behind the door, my name written on the tag. The color matches my dress for tomorrow, a marigold yellow that Josie says perfectly accentuates my skin tone. Thankfully, my makeup remover is still in here from earlier when we got ready. I wash my face, taking my time, giving myself a long minute to calm down.

I've just changed into my pajama set when there's a soft knock on the bathroom door. "Marley? Can I come in?"

I shouldn't be surprised that Nikki is the one to come to my aid, and even though I love her with my whole heart, she is the last person I want to talk to right now. She's the one who raised the man of my dreams and has been a second mom to me since I was a kid, the person I would run to when I needed someone to talk to about things I was too embarrassed to discuss with my own mother.

Flinging open the door, I'm met with her kind eyes. "Sorry, I just figured I would change while I was in there," I say, gesturing behind me. My dress is in a rumpled pile on the counter, waiting for me to put it on the hanger.

Nikki nods, her blue eyes taking in my appearance. "Are you okay, sweetie?"

"I'm just fine, I drank too much, so I'm feeling a little flustered!" Even I can hear the lie in my voice.

Thankfully, she drops it. "Josie wants to go over her plans for tomorrow, if you're okay with that?"

"Oh, yes! Let me hang my dress, and I'll be right out."

Nikki reaches out, squeezing my hand softly, then turns to head into the room. I take a deep breath and turn to grab my dress and hang it. I take a final glance into the mirror and decide I'm as good as I'm going to get.

The small group of women are scattered around the room. Nikki and Josie sit on the couch with Josie's older sister, Jess, in the middle. She's around eight months pregnant, and looks utterly miserable. She's spent most of the day trying to hide her discomfort, but I've seen it.

Josie and Jess have grown much closer in the last year once Jess moved back to Minnesota. She and her husband were in Missouri for a long time while he was stationed at a military base. She told me once she had no ill will toward her, but they just weren't close. I'm happy that has changed. I always wanted a sister.

It makes me wish that someday Jason will find someone so Lennie doesn't grow up without siblings. At the very least, maybe Josie and Andrew will pop out kids sooner or later so she has cousins to play with.

I'm not especially close with my older brothers. Kenny works as a PA in the ER a few towns over, and Prescott lives his own life. I don't see either of them often, and sometimes I wish we were closer, but that's just the way it is for us.

Megan, Isaac's wife and now Josie's close friend, sits on one of the queen-sized beds. She pats the empty spot next to her, and I nearly launch myself at her. I've always been close with Megan, but having Josie has helped us grow our relationship even further. She's a few years younger than me, the same age as Andrew and Isaac, but we all grew up together.

Megan pulls me into her side, and Josie gives me a little side glance. Her eyes say the words she can't. *You okay?*

Even though I'm dying to talk to her about this on the inside, I will not take her attention away from her wedding weekend. I refuse to. I nod at her, hoping she buys the lie.

Josie's mom, Lori, stands from the other bed, heading to the small desk covered in empty paper cups and bottles of wine. She fills a cup and hands it to me. Her smile is kind. I swear, moms have a sixth sense about things because she reaches down, clasps my forearm, and gives it a gentle squeeze.

I smile softly up at her, and turn my focus to my friend. Josie clasps her hands in front of her as she sits cross-legged on the couch. Her red hair is neatly pulled back into a loose pony, her face glowing from the moisturizing products used on her skin.

"The next twenty-four hours are going to be pretty crazy, so I wanted to touch base and see how everyone is doing," she says. Her blue eyes scan the room, stopping as she glances at each of us to assess.

Jess lifts her hand off her pregnant belly, wincing as she tries to scoot herself to a better position. "I have a question."

"What's up?" Josie asks.

"What if I have to pee in the middle of the ceremony?" she asks. Her brows are furrowed, and her face so serious, that I can't help but snicker slightly.

Josie's stunned silent for a moment at the unexpected question. "Uhh," she starts.

"I know where da bathroom is, Miss Jess," Lennie says, rising from her relaxed position in a loveseat.

"Thank you so much, Lennie," Jess coos, a smile quirking on her full lips. "I'll let you know if I need help getting there. How does that sound sweetie?"

"Okay," Lennie replies. She's grown so much in her speech in the last year that I can hardly believe she's the same little girl who called me Auntie Mawey for the longest time.

Jess turns her focus back to her sister. "I am serious

though. It's... been an issue lately. This," she points to her round belly, "has been causing lots of bathroom misery."

"I think we can attest to that," my mom chuckles. "At the end of my pregnancy with Marley, if I had to go to the bathroom, I had to go *now*. No waiting."

"She's right," Lori replies with a chuckle. Nikki laughs in agreement.

Josie smiles. "If it comes to that, you can just sneak out the side and to the bathroom. I don't care. A girl's gotta do what a girls gotta do."

"Oh thank goodness." Jess heaves a sigh, her hand rubbing her belly fondly.

I eye her stomach with a hint of... jealousy? I definitely don't envy this stage of pregnancy, but I've always wanted kids. I also thought I'd already have them by my age, but life has had other plans.

Doing newborn sessions in my studio for the last year has been so fun, and has definitely given me a hint of baby fever.

Okay, a lot of baby fever.

Maybe Josie and Andrew will have kids someday, then at least I can love on them, since who knows when I'll have one of my own. Or maybe Megan will have one soon.

The sadness creeps in, the same kind that I always have when I think about this. I want to find someone, to have a family of my own. Watching my friends slowly get that for themselves hurts, despite how much I love it for them.

Soon enough, I'm sure I will have plenty of babies to love up, and they say the best part of being an aunt is you can give the baby back at the end of the day, and get your full eight hours of sleep. So, hey, that's a perk. Right?

BEAU

It takes remarkable effort not to rip my hair from my scalp as I watch Marley close the door to the bridal suite behind her. I just fucked up so hard. It's like I took all my plans for our future and threw them out the car window while driving eighty down the freeway.

Crash and burn.

I curse under my breath, spinning on my heel to head toward my room. On second thought, I should check in on the guys, make sure Isaac, Andrew's best friend, is doing his job and not letting Andrew get too drunk.

I head down to the opposite end of the hall, hearing the rambunctious laughter of my brothers and friend. I knock on the door, and like a group of teens, they shush each other, before one of them stumbles to the door, loudly.

The door flies open, and Thomas is the one to greet me. His eyes are glazed. "Little bro!" he nearly shouts, smiling like a lunatic, showing me the gap in his teeth. I shush him, glancing behind me, worried someone is in the hall.

"Dude, we're in a hotel, you gotta be quiet."

"Pffft," he scoffs. "We aren't that loud. It's just 'cause you're standing right next to me."

"Right," I murmur, sidestepping him into the suite. The three men—Andrew, our brother Jason, and Andrew's friend Isaac—sit on the floor cross-legged in a small circle, a pile of poker chips and cash in the middle of them.

"Shhhhh," Thomas hisses. He pushes around me, nearly throwing himself onto the floor as the heavy door falls closed with a *slam*.

I pinch the bridge of my nose, thankful they aren't completely shitfaced, just happy drunk. Isaac seems to be the only sober one.

Well, besides me.

I sit down next to him, offering him a chin tip. I spot Jason across the circle, catching him laughing at Thomas as he flops back down onto the floor.

It's been a while since I've seen Jason let loose like this, probably since before the birth of his daughter, Lennie. Being a single dad has been hard on him, but he's done it amazingly, all while starting up his own brewery.

My heart rate is finally starting to slow after the near kiss with Marley. I use the bed behind me as a back rest, sitting diagonally and crossing my legs in front of me. All the other guys are in t-shirts and sweats, or basketball shorts, while I'm still in my suit from the rehearsal dinner.

"Beau, my man, where have you been?" Andrew asks, his words slurring ever so slightly.

"Just helping Marley with a few things downstairs," I answer, taking the beer Isaac offers me. It doesn't really look like they're actively playing poker, more so getting distracted with every turn of hand.

Andrew's brows twist in displeasure. "You know, I really don't get you two," he mutters.

"What do you mean?" I ask, though I know what he's talking about.

"You're obviously meant to be together. Obviously in love with each other. Why not make it official? I love Marley, like a sister of course, but fuck man, you are hurting her."

Irritation flares in my chest. "Don't you think I know that, Andrew?" I spit. I instantly regret it when his face falls. I sigh. "I'm sorry. I didn't mean to snap at you. That was uncalled for."

Andrew's smirk returns. "You know I love riling you up man."

I scoff. "Yeah, I know."

"I don't get it though. I've let it slide for as long as I have because I know it hurts you, but I'm not going to, not anymore. If it weren't for Marley, who knows if I ever would have found my girl, and the thought of letting Josie go, and watching her live life, maybe with some other dude, makes me physically ill. I love her so much. So why are you purposefully doing this to yourself? Is it this other girl that none of us have met? Is she really that special if we've never met her?" He finishes his speech, taking another drink of his half empty beer.

Jason pipes in from across the circle. "He's right, you know. How come we've never met your girlfriend?"

The irritation rises in me again, and I know that it's not fair to them, they don't know, but I can't help but shut them out, shut everyone out. It's easier than feeling right now, and I don't have the capacity to deal with it. I need to change the subject, but I at least need to give them something so they get off my back.

"I'm only going to say this once, and then we are taking

the focus off me. This weekend isn't about me." I glare at my brothers and Isaac. They nod eagerly.

I fidget with my fingers. "I don't have a girlfriend. I did, for about six months, though I'm not sure you could even call her that. She was a distraction. I've been single since around the time you and Josie got engaged, Andrew." His eyes widen at my confession. "I've been told before that I'm not right for Marley, and I'm not about to go through that again. Got it?" I scan their faces, watching as one by one, nod.

Andrew's eyes are glassy as he presses his hand to his chest. "Oh my god. If I wasn't marrying the girl of my dreams tomorrow, this might be the best night of my life." He pauses, scratching at his scruff. "No, scratch that, the night that Josie and I fu-"

"Annnnd, you're done," Isaac interrupts, taking the beer from his grasp.

Andrew bursts into laughter. "Just saying, this is awesome. Marley's finally going to be my real sister, after all these years."

I shake my head. "Don't say things like that. I just said I don't want to be told again that I'm not right for her. I can't lose her."

"You're not going to," Jason says. His face is serious, all traces of humor from earlier gone. "I won't push this anymore, we've pushed it for years, but the two of you... It's time for you to be together. It's either that, or lose her to someone else."

The thought alone makes me nauseous. Yeah, I've seen her with guys through the years, just like I've been with girls, but that was when I was fighting tooth and nail to deny my feelings. I'm done with that now, and if what she wants isn't me, I'll have to respect that.

I won't like it, but I will do whatever I can to keep her in my life.

7

MARLEY

"Marley, can you help me with this?" Josie calls from the dressing room.

"Coming," I call. My marigold yellow-colored dress swishes at my ankles as I make my way over to her. I knock on the wooden door once, then let myself into the small room. Josie's facing the mirror, hands on her hips as she stares at her reflection. She's wearing a lacy, low-cut white bra that makes her tits look fabulous. I helped her pick out her undergarments about a month ago, and we did a mini boudoir shoot in them. I've printed off the photos for her in a book that is currently en route to Andrew at this very moment.

"You look incredible," I say. Her cheeks flush, freckles popping with the color.

"Thanks," she replies. "I can't get this to feel right." She points to the back of her bra, and I immediately see the issue.

"Oh, you're all twisted." I slide my finger under the hem, unhooking the clasp and righting it. Once she's all put back together, I rest my hands on her shoulders. "Feeling ready?" I ask.

Josie nods enthusiastically. She spins to face me. Tears well in her eyes and I point a finger at her. "Nope, no tears. Not today," I say.

"But I'm happy," she blubbers. "These are happy tears."

I wrap my best friend into a tight hug, holding her close. I pull away, grabbing a few tissues from the side table and blotting under her eyes softly. "There, still perfect," I say.

She smiles before her expression grows more serious. "I'm going to ask you this, because I knew something was not right when you walked into that room last night. What happened?"

Nope. I will not get all weepy and act like a tween who just got her heart ripped out of her chest today. "Nothing," I try to say, but Josie narrows her eyes, her brows raising. She's calling my bluff.

Stepping back, I slump into the soft couch. "You aren't going to let me get off that easy, are you?"

"Nope," she says, popping the p. "I know Beau stayed back to help you get things organized, and I also know that he was glued to your side all night and was giving you moon eyes."

I clasp my arm, brushing the slightly raised skin of my "Dead Sea" tattoo. "Fine. But I'm okay now, and this day is not about me, so I will tell you, and then we drop it, 'kay?"

Josie nods. She sits down onto the couch next to me. "I... I think he was going to kiss me last night."

Her eyes widen, mouth gaping open, but she doesn't speak.

"I stopped him before he did, but... yeah. Oh, and he doesn't have a girlfriend, and hasn't for six months." I take a deep breath. "That's all I'm going to say. When you get back from your honeymoon, we can analyze it, and every word and touch."

I can tell she's about to burst, trying to hold in whatever emotion is bubbling to the surface. "Can I ask one *teensy* tiny question?"

"Fine, but consider it a second wedding gift," I tease, shoving her shoulder gently.

"Why didn't he tell anyone he wasn't dating her? He made it seem like they'd been together this whole time." Josie's voice drops low, tone confused.

"I really don't know. I keep asking myself that same question." I shift my attention back to her. This is *her* day. "Enough about me." I stand up from the couch, feeling like a slight weight has been taken off my chest with just a short conversation. "Ready to get into your dress?"

I gesture to the dress bag hanging from the wall, and Josie blushes a deep pink. "Yeah. Can you get the photographer, and my mom and sister?"

"You got it," I say. I slide out of the room, heading back to the small sitting room where everyone else is. Megan sits at the small table, coloring with Lennie, while my mom fusses over a piece of Nikki's hair. Lori and Jess sit on the couch, Lori's hand on Jess's belly, feeling the baby kick.

The wedding planner, Fallon, knocks on the door right as I'm about to grab Lori and Jess. She glides in, the picture of effortless beauty. Her blonde hair hangs in long waves down her back, half of it pulled up off her face. She wears a deep maroon top tucked into a pair of high-waisted dress pants that cuff at the ankle, showing off her shiny black heels. She has thick curves accentuated with the top that fits her perfectly.

Behind her is her daughter, Presley. She's about six if I remember correctly. Her sandy blonde hair is in one long braid down her back, and she wears a sage green cotton dress that buttons down the front and has pockets on the side.

"How's the bridal party?" Fallon asks.

I offer a quick thumbs up. "Great. I was just grabbing the mother of the bride and sister. She's ready to put on her dress."

"Perfect, we are right on time then!" Fallon pushes a hair that has fallen in her face off and looks back at Presley. "Sweetie, do you want to ask Lennie?"

Lennie perks up at the mention of her name, kicking her feet under the table. "Hi, Presley," she calls. One thing about Lennie is that she will always make a friend wherever she goes. Probably something she gets from Jason. While a bit of a grump, he's always known how to talk to people. Fitting for a brewery owner to be good with people.

"Lennie, I brought a coloring page for you," Presley says, her small voice gaining confidence with each word. "Do you want it? It has a princess with pretty flowers on her dress, and a frog that she has to kiss." Her mouth forms a grimace as she mentions the frog.

"Can you color it with me?" Lennie asks. She glances around the room until she meets Nikki's eyes, searching for her approval.

Nikki smiles. "If it's okay with Presley's mom, then it's just fine with me."

Fallon looks down at Presley and grins, giving her the go ahead. Presley rushes over to the table and Megan stands, moving out of the way to give Presley her seat. She steps over to Fallon and hugs her tightly.

Fallon and Megan are friends from college. Fallon was the maid of honor in Megan's wedding where Josie and Andrew met. It's weird how small of a world it is.

I guess she moved here shortly after her ex-husband up and left without a trace. It's like he vanished out of thin air, only sending her signed divorce papers with no return address, but rather a note to drop off at a specific lawyer's office.

As far as I know, she hasn't heard from him since. She was living with her mom for a while, but was able to move out when she got the job as the wedding and event planner for Meadow Grove Winery.

Lennie shrieks with delight as she sees the coloring sheet, her cheeks turning a rosy hue. I notice Fallon and Megan talking in hushed tones. Fallon's brows are pinched together like she's distressed. I don't want to pry, but I also don't want anything to go wrong today. I gesture for Lori and Jess to head to the dressing room while I step over to Fallon and Megan.

"Hey, everything okay?" I ask.

Fallon sniffs, turning her face away from Presley's point of view. "Oh yeah, just... life. I know it's so unprofessional to bring Presley with me, but my mom has a stomach bug, and my backup babysitter has a volleyball tournament. And... well, anyone else I feel comfortable leaving her with is here. So, I'm low on options. Isaac is probably going to fire me for being so unprofessional," she babbles, her pitch growing higher with each word.

I reach out, clasping her arm. "You have nothing to worry about. We get it. And you know Josie and Andrew won't mind. And, if Isaac fires you, I'm pretty sure this one," I jerk a thumb in Megan's direction, "will divorce him."

Megan laughs. "She's right, you know."

Fallon solemnly nods, then stands up a little straighter, taking a deep breath. "Alright, no more of that. I've got shit to do. Can I leave her with you for a bit? Or... " she drags, furrowing her brow as she thinks.

"Leave her," I say. "She's got plenty of people to look out for her. We'll bring her along to photos and the first look. You'll just have to grab her before the ceremony. Right?" I say, looking at Megan. Fallon probably won't feel convinced unless her best friend says so.

"Right. We've got her," she agrees.

Fallon gives us a more determined nod. "I've got my cell, so just call me, but... shit, I have to go. The cake people are here." She calls out a goodbye to Presley, and she's gone with a gust of air and sweet smelling perfume. She definitely is good at compartmentalizing if she needs to, it seems, and puts on a killer brave face.

There's a creak, and the door to the dressing room opens, Josie's head peeking out. "Get in here," she whispers.

I turn around because she's probably looking for Nikki. I'm about to call her over when Josie raises her voice. "No, dingbat, *you*! Get your sexy ass in here!"

I glide over, and she yanks me by the hand, pulling me into the room. Marissa, the photographer, stands in the corner, already snapping pictures. Marissa used to work with me at Chrysalis Photography before branching off and starting her own studio just over a year ago. When Josie asked me to be in the wedding, she asked me for a recommendation since I wouldn't be able to do photos and also be her maid of honor. Marissa was an easy recommendation.

Lori looks gorgeous in a navy blue floor-length gown, her slightly graying hair curled and pinned loosely at the nape of her neck. Her makeup is tastefully done. She's pulling Josie's gorgeous dress out of the bag.

Jess helps, making sure the dress doesn't snag on any zippers. Her deep emerald colored dress accentuates her bump and contrasts with her strawberry blonde hair. Her hair isn't nearly as red as Josie's but it still has a soft red hue to it.

Josie releases my hand to step into her dress. I subconsciously reach up to my right bicep, trailing my fingers over my tattoo yet again. Goosebumps flare over my skin at the touch, the same thing that happens every time I touch it.

The dress fits Josie like a glove. A wide, over-the-shoulder neckline, with delicate lace across the bust in a criss-cross. The fabric hugs tight to her thick curves until it flares at the waist, trailing with lace flowers scattered to the floor.

Lori zips the dress and takes a step back, covering her mouth with her hand as her eyes shine with tears. Jess smiles softly, her eyes sliding up and down Josie's body in awe.

"Don't cry, please," Josie begs, her own eyes filling with tears.

"I'm not," Lori blubbers, turning her head down and patting at her eyes with a tissue.

Marissa snaps photos in the background as I adjust the layers of Josie's dress so it lays perfectly. When I rise, Josie throws her arms around me in a tight hug. "Thank you," she murmurs, words thick with conviction.

I nod, my throat tightening. I never would have guessed that by setting her up on a blind date with Andrew I'd gain a lifelong friend, but I'm so thankful that I did.

With a few finishing touches to her makeup and hair, we head back into the sitting room to wait the few minutes before taking pictures. Initially, Josie wanted to do the first look in the more traditional way—when she walked down the aisle—but I came up with the idea to do something similar to their first official date.

The blind date photoshoot.

Andrew will be blindfolded. Josie won't, as we don't want to mess up her hair and makeup, but she's promised to keep her eyes closed.

I lift the train of Josie's dress as we walk onto the dirt path. Josie's eyes are pinched shut, and thankfully, Andrew stands only five or six paces off the path. Both of their families, as well as the rest of the bridal party, are scattered in a half circle behind Marissa. I don't take the time to see the specific people, my focus on Josie. I adjust her positioning, feeling a warm sense of deja vu as I turn her so her back is pressed against Andrew's, watching as their hands find each other.

Andrew starts bouncing on the balls of his feet and I chuckle under my breath, pressing down on his shoulder to stop his movements. He did the exact same thing during the first photo shoot I arranged for them. I turn around and offer Marissa a thumbs up. She nods gratefully and I skurry off to the side where Megan stands.

We count down from three, and the pair turn around. Josie's eyes open. Andrew yanks off the blindfold from his face. His brown eyes comically widen as he takes in his bride-to-be.

Of course, as a florist herself, Josie insisted on creating her own bouquet and Andrew's boutonniere, but left everything else up to her trusted assistant, Kenzy. She's done an amazing job with the flowers and the glimpse of the arch I got as I walked around the reception and ceremony area earlier.

My gaze strays from their initial reactions, catching Beau's attention from across the circle. His shoulder length dark curls are neatly pulled back into his signature man bun. The groomsmen all wear khaki pants, crisp white button down shirts, and terracotta-orange ties to match the flowers. Beau's brown eyes hold mine, never wavering until I turn away first.

I do what I do best for the rest of the photos—ignore Beau. I've ignored the pull I automatically feel when I'm around him for years, so what's another day to add to the list?

8

BEAU

To be honest, I always thought Andrew would be the last of us siblings to settle down and get married. Though, when he met Josie, I had a feeling almost immediately she was the one for him. She matches his chaotic energy, all while being her bubbly self.

I watch Marley from across the small room we're all huddled in before the ceremony starts. Voices carry through the closed doors, signaling the arrival of guests and nearing ceremony. Marley sits at a small table with Jason and my niece Lennie. Lennie has always had a special bond with Marley, probably because she's the only young girl she's been around until Josie came around.

Marley fixes a hair that has come loose out of Lennie's curled hair, tucking the pinned flower back in place. I watch her closely, dreaming of how good of a mother she will be someday.

The lingering thought is cut off by Gramps sitting down next to me, huffing a little as he adjusts in the chair. He sets his cane so it rests against the table next to me.

"Give me a few crackers, would you?" he says, skipping over the pleasantries of a greeting.

I chuckle under my breath, reaching over to grab a handful of crackers for him from the snack platter. "Hungry?" I ask.

"Your mom keeps stealing the snacks from me. She's worried I'll get crumbs all over my suit. But like I told her, I'm not a toddler."

"No, you're not," I reply. Gramps had a head injury over a year ago now, and he hasn't gotten back to where he used to be. He has to walk with a cane now, and the shaking in his hands hasn't quite resolved. He goes to physical therapy and takes good care of himself, but it's been hard to see the man my brothers and I look up to so much decline. It's been even harder on our dad to watch his own father deteriorate like this.

I glance over at Marley again, telling myself it's just to make sure she's okay, but I know it's because she looks like a literal angel from heaven today. Her dress hugs those thick curves I love so much. The sleeves are short on her shoulders, giving me a full view of all her tattoos. She reaches into the center of the table to grab another crayon for Lennie, and I spot the familiar tattoo on her inner arm which matches the one on mine—two hands clasped together, pulling one out of the water. No matter what happens, that tattoo will always tie us together, and I'm proud of it. A melancholy feeling washes over me, and I'm almost wary to dive deeper into it.

"If you keep lookin' at her like that, Thomas might have to arrest you for stalking," Gramps says, bringing my attention back to him.

I narrow my eyes. "I'm not looking at her like anything," I mutter. "I wasn't even looking at her."

"Sure," he chuckles. "And I was just doing jumping jacks. I don't think I'll ever understand you two." He pats my knee. "You deserve to be happy, Beau. She's your happiness."

I nod, my throat tightening as a wave of insecurity drops on me like a bucket of cold water. "I don't think I can be her happiness."

"Why not?" he asks, more sincere than sarcastic.

"Because... I'm not the right person for her. I've been told it before, and I never want to hear it again."

"Who told you that?" his voice is irritated, dancing on the verge of anger.

"Doesn't matter. They told the truth, and I need to keep that boundary up."

Gramps shakes his head, muttering something under his breath. I think I catch "damn fool" though, I'm not sure. He sits for another minute, thankfully dropping the conversation, then saying he's going to check in with the bride and groom.

He grunts as he tries to stand. I help him out of the chair, watching him walk toward where Andrew and Josie sit together at another table. Probably off to impart some wisdom, or something like that.

It's actually pretty cute, Gramps has called Josie *Cindy* since the day he met her. Andrew considered her his missing Cinderella until Marley set them up on their blind date, which in turn gave Gramps the idea for the nickname.

To be honest, if Jason and Thomas ever get married, the women they marry have a lot to live up to between Marley and Josie. Even though Marley isn't *technically* family, all my brothers consider her their sister.

She's never been like a sister to me.

Fallon claps her hands together as she enters the room,

her blonde hair still perfectly curled, despite her running around all day, doing all the last-minute tasks. "Showtime, ladies and gentleman!" she calls. We all rise, making our way out of the room and into the spots we were designated last night.

I make my way over to where Marley stands, fidgeting with the large bouquet of orange flowers in her hand. It's like the world quiets when it's just me and her. The background noise fades, leaving me staring into those chocolate brown eyes, the ones that hold so many secrets and so many truths about us.

"Ready?" I ask. My throat tightens when I realize that this might be the only time I get to walk down an aisle with her on my arm. The sadness from earlier returns, this time with a vengeance.

I offer out my arm to her, and Marley nods. Slowly sliding her arm into mine, I relish this feeling of closeness to her, wondering if this is as close as we'll ever be to something more.

9

MARLEY

"For the very first time as husband and wife, please welcome Mr. and Mrs. Andrew and Josie Cunning-ham!" The DJ announces. Andrew stands, pulling Josie to her feet and away from the head table toward the dance floor. Josie's dress is bustled now, the train no longer dragging everywhere. Once they reach the middle of the dancefloor the song starts to play. "Butterflies" by Kacey Musgraves. It's honestly the perfect song for them. Happy and uplifting, and so fitting to their relationship.

They sway, both of them smiling at each other, their foreheads tipped together. My heart clenches at just how happy they are. I'm so happy for them I could puke, so happy that they have each other.

The song ends, the entire room breaking out into cheers and clapping. I take a long swig of my champagne as the music switches to a bouncing pop song. The party is officially starting and it's time for fun.

I stand from my chair, heading to the bar. The cute bartender from last night is working, so I move to the side he's tending. I'm single, slightly sad, and sure, maybe I'm *slightly* tipsy, but I think that just means that I get to flirt a little.

"Hey handsome," I croon as I step up to the bar. I prop my elbow up, resting my head in my cupped hand.

His green eyes widen, brows raising. "Uh," he coughs. "Hey, what can I get for you?" I don't miss the way his eyes watch me closely.

"I want a vodka cranberry with a splash of soda," I say. "Ooh, and a lemon drop shot, please!" My excitement rises. "I love those."

"You got it," he says with a wink.

Maybe he's flirting to get a bigger tip, but I can't find it in me to care. He's flirting, and so am I. I haven't flirted with anyone in a long time, and I deserve to live a little.

The bartender—*I should really learn his name*—makes my drinks, setting them on the counter in front of me. I slide them to the side, pulling out my phone from the pocket of my dress. The whole tap to pay thing is so convenient.

I pay, and finally catch his name on his nametag. With a glance behind me, I see no one is waiting, so I have time to chat him up a bit more. "So... Matt," I say once I confirm his name again. "What brought you into the wonderful world of bartending?"

Matt chuckles, pushing his slick blonde hair back. The more that I look at him, the less attractive he seems. And he looks... young. Definitely younger than me.

"My cousin is the GM here, and he needed an extra hand this weekend. Enter me," his low voice says. He leans forward on the bar, mimicking my stance.

"You're Isaac's cousin?" I ask.

"Sure am."

"Huh. Well, cool." I adjust my stance, pressing my breasts forward slightly. Sure, he's not my type, or even someone I'm interested in long term, but I need the practice. I'm about to say something flirty when a hand slinks around my waist, sending a shiver down my spine. Lips caress my ear, a low whisper giving me goosebumps.

"What are you doing?" Beau's recognizable voice, laced with—possession?—makes me stand up straight.

I sheepishly grab my drinks, stepping away from the bar, and the conversation with Matt. I feel like I've been caught doing something bad, like a kid stuck with their hand in the cookie jar. I know it's absurd, but Beau makes me feel like this.

"Why do you care?" I ask, my tone clipped and defensive. He always has to interrupt me, has to stake some sort of invisible claim on me. I stride from the bar, focusing hard on my footsteps. The last thing I need right now is to trip. Talk about embarrassing. I do, however, swish my hips a little more than normal.

I sit down at my spot at the head table, and take my lemon drop shot. The sweet and sour flavor trickles down my throat, and I can't help but shiver at the intensity. The liquor warms my blood almost instantly.

Beau drops down in the seat next to me. "I care, because..." He runs his hands down his face, as if he's overwhelmed. His eyes narrow on me. "Do I really need to say it, Marley?"

"Seems like we've been leaving things unsaid for this long, what's one more thing?" I say bitterly. My tipsy state is allowing me to say things completely uninhibited, and the freedom is thrilling.

The dance around us is starting to ramp up as the music does, the beat bumping, reverberating in my chest in pace with the rapid beat of my heart.

Beau groans. His lips are set in a firm line, eyebrows knotted as he tries to come up with the words to say. "Just…"

"I'm going to dance," I say, interrupting him. My brain buzzes with the mild exhilaration of being so bold. It's time to celebrate with my friends.

OKAY, so I *probably* shouldn't have had that last shot of fireball, but I couldn't help it. When the bottle got passed around the circle, it was too tempting. It seems that it was Thomas's goal to get me drunk tonight, and he succeeded. Not that it was hard. I was a completely willing party.

I grab Josie's arm as another upbeat song starts to play, and we spin in a circle, dancing and laughing together. Andrew is standing on the outside of our little circle of people, watching his bride with a smile.

I'm sure I look the opposite of attractive right now. My back is damp with sweat, my bangs plastered to my forehead, not that I care. My flirting idea was tossed out the window as soon as the brooding Beau interrupted me. Now he stands on the outside of our circle, watching. He's not *not* dancing, but I personally wouldn't consider bouncing up and down and swaying side to side dancing. He's had quite a few beers, and the hazy glint in his eyes lets me know that he's just as drunk as I am. The liquor appears to have relaxed him, though there's still the furrow between his brow. I hate how attractive he looks right now.

Jason brought Lennie up to their room about an hour ago to take her to bed, with promises to come back and finish out the night with us. Then Nikki showed back up at the edge of the dance floor, instead of Jason, and we all knew that he had crashed right along with his daughter.

Megan and Isaac bounce up and down, singing the poppy love song to each other as they dance. It's so sickeningly cute I want to puke.

The song slows to a ballad, Ellie Goulding's cover of "How Long Will I Love You". Josie drops my arm in search of her new husband, and they gravitate to each other, slowly swaying to the beat. Josie's head rests on his chest, Andrew's cheek tilted to lay atop her head.

Couples in love make their way to the floor, holding each other close, murmuring sweet nothings to their partner as they sway. A sense of longing runs over me, as I watch. Walking down the aisle today on Beau's arm felt so... right. Despite the pain thrumming through my veins at the knowledge that I can never let it be us, I gave into the fantasy, dreaming for just a moment.

Thomas escapes the dance floor, heading to the table to drink a glass of water. I start to follow him, since clearly this is a moment for all the couples, when a hand wraps around my wrist.

"Wha—" I start to say, but when I turn to see who's grabbing me, I'm shocked, but also not at all surprised to see it's Beau.

"Dance with me," he murmurs. I can barely hear him, but somehow I know that's exactly what he said.

I'm nodding, not giving myself a moment to think. I'm short of breath, but I'm not sure if it's from dancing or from the feeling of Beau. He pulls me in close, one hand moving to rest on my hip, the other clasping my hand as he starts to sway us to the beat.

My head drops to rest on his chest, my ear pressed where his heart thumps loudly. Just hearing his heart soothes the piece of mine that was cracking at the proximity to him. I let myself feel this moment, enjoy this time with him. I don't want to let him go, and yet I know I'll have to. Let this dream of us go. I love my best friend. He's always been my person, but lately, I can't seem to separate my love for him with the pain I feel of keeping things platonic. Everytime we're out with our friends, I'm struggling not to think about how natural things could be if I just gave in. But what if I break down the barrier and he rejects me? What if he just wants one night? One taste of it?

The song reaches its crescendo, beginning to slow and fade into another slow dance. I start to pull back. We had our dance, and now it's time to let him go.

Beau doesn't let me go though. The hand on my hip squeezes tighter, keeping me connected to him. "No," he mutters. "Not yet."

I relax into his hold. What's one more song going to hurt? Well, only my heart. But I guess it might be worth it.

He continues to sway us, and Josie and Andrew catch my eye. I pull back, offering her a small smile. She returns the gesture, her eyes flicking up to Beau's face. She nods slightly, and Beau squeezes me gently. He rests his head back on mine, and I swear, I feel his lips gently caress my head. But maybe that's just my drunkenness imagining things, right?

He pulls back, dropping my hand to use his finger to tilt my chin up, meeting his eyes. If he didn't have his arm wrapped around my waist, I'd stumble at the intensity of his gaze. He glances away to Andrew and Josie for a moment, before glancing back. "Did you ever think that would be us?"

Just like that, my heart stops, and my blood runs cold. "What?" I say, my voice breaking.

He looks at them again, then back at me. "I always…"

Tears burn behind my eyes as I process his words. Because I did think that would be us. Dreamed every night that someday I would walk down the aisle in a beautiful white gown, to see him at the end, waiting for me. To slow dance with my best friend, and the love of my life, at our wedding. I can't let myself dive further into my dreams, or I'll crack right here on the dance floor. "Beau, don't."

He furrows his brows. "Don't what? I don't want to fight, not tonight," he says.

I'm shaking my head. "We can't," I reply, though my heart is screaming at me, *we can, we can!*

I step back, and this time he lets me. Anger burns through my veins, mixed with the pain and sadness my heart is feeling. The song ends, and I spin, heading off the dance floor to the table. I grab my clutch and the glass of tepid water, chugging it down quickly.

"Alright gang, I've got one more song for you, then it's time to call it a night," the DJ calls over the loudspeaker. The beat bounces, and I decide that's my cue. I glance around the room, catching Josie's eye, giving her a smile and wave. She furrows her brows for a moment, a questioning look in her eyes, but I just shake my head.

Before anyone can stop me, I turn, heading down the hall to the elevator. I need to get out of here. At Beau's statement, I feel like I can't breathe, and the anxiety starts to pound in my veins.

"Marley, wait," Beau calls when I hit the elevator button.

"Beau, please," I cry, the tears finally spilling over, running down my cheeks non-stop.

"Please, what?" he taunts. The elevator doors open, and

I step onto the cart. Beau follows, slamming the close door button, and the button for the third floor.

The tears never stop as the doors close, and Beau follows me to the far corner. He lifts his arms, caging me in. He takes long, deep breaths. His brown eyes stare deep into my own, but they don't give anything away. I can't read what is on his mind the way I normally can. He looks as if he's in pain, his brows furrowing deeply, before he mutters under his breath.

"Fuck it."

And then he's slamming his lips onto mine.

Like the first time he kissed me, it's abrupt, unexpected, and literally everything I've dreamed of. His tongue parts my lips, a hint of the spicy whiskey from earlier on his tongue. His hands drop from the wall of the elevator, one clutching my cheek, the other resting at the base of my throat.

His fingers tap at my rapidly thrumming pulse point, like he's needing the proof that I'm feeling this as much as he is. My palm rests on his chest, feeling his own heart beating so fast and untamed. My fingers clutch at the fabric of his dress shirt, pulling him closer, while also knowing I shouldn't really be doing this.

I can vaguely hear the ding of the elevator as it moves up the floors. It dings one last time, and the doors open with a *swish*. I break away from his deft lips, gasping for air and coming up short. With every beat of my heart, I push my feelings down, further, further, further.

I push back on his chest, escaping him. I rush down the hall toward my room, digging my key card out as I do. I don't think about the fact that Beau just kissed me, or the fact that we have both had a little too much to drink.

10

MARLEY

Footsteps follow close behind me, and Beau's voice calls my name. I fumble with the key, pushing the door open as soon as the light flashes green. Of course, I'm not fast enough, and Beau storms in behind me, pushing through as I try to close the door on him.

"What the hell was that?" I ask, my breath coming in short spurts.

"I mean, *I* know what it was," Beau responds with a smirk as he closes the door behind him.

"Stop it." I smack him across the chest with my clutch.

Beau sombers. "I don't regret kissing you. Not now, and not when we were kids."

I rub my temples. "Beau, we're drunk, this... we need to stop." *Oh my god, is this really happening?*

"I'm sober enough to know what I want, Marley. What I've always wanted." His eyes are blazing, but no longer hazy like they were on the dance floor.

I take a step forward, my tummy fluttering with butter-flies. Because he's right. I'm drunk, but I'm also sober enough to give in, to *let go*. Beau does the same, his eyes trailing from my eyes to my lips. His hand reaches up, cupping my face. The other hand reaches out, gripping my waist tightly.

"Tell me to stop, tell me that this isn't what you want, Marley. It all ends now if you say the word." His voice is low, breathy.

God, this might be the worst decision I've ever made, but yet, I don't see myself stopping him. Stopping this. I need to see this through, even if it breaks my heart. I need to know what it feels like to have his unbidden touch. His complete and utter devotion, even if for just one night.

"Don't stop," I say, and his lips are back on mine. His hand drags up my chin, sliding around to the nape of my neck, gripping my hair at the scalp. The tug of hair gives a bite of discomfort, but enough to keep me sane, so I know that this is real life.

His hips press into my stomach, and I can feel the hard bulge through his pants. I have to stifle a giggle, because the thought of Beau being hard, for me? It's laughable. I'm the complete opposite of any girl I've seen him with. I have wide hips, an apron belly, and thick thighs. I'm nothing compared to the skinny girls he's been with before.

He pushes me backward, into the large bathroom. The light flicks on automatically, and Beau pulls his hands from my hair. I'm pressed against the bathroom counter, one palm flat on the cool surface to keep my balance.

He breaks the kiss, smiling down at me. "You're fucking perfect, love."

Love.

I don't have time to read into him calling me that, because his hands are sliding down to cup my breasts through the fabric of my bridesmaids dress. He kneads one, the other continuing a path downward, finding the long slit at my thigh.

Beau's mouth descends on my neck, placing soft, soul-sucking kisses there. The hand at my thigh slides up between the slit, feeling the layer of shapewear I have on. He groans against my neck. "Why are you wearing that?"

I chuckle, feeling lighter than I have in ages. Something about this feels so right, yet so forbidden all at once. It's exhilarating.

"Because I have to keep the muffins in the tin, Beau," I explain, gesturing to my ample rolls.

He snickers softly, but not in a mocking way. "I love muffins." He raises his brow ever so slightly, a silent question.

I nod and turn so I'm facing the bathroom mirror. My eyes are red rimmed from my earlier tears, but my face is alive with emotion, hair falling out of its perfectly placed curls and pins. I pull my hair over my shoulder, giving Beau access to the zipper. His fingertips trail up the length of my back until he reaches the base of my neck. The zipper clicks down the tracks slowly, and I hear Beau's slow intake of breath with every inch of skin that is revealed. I'm wearing a black bra that does good things for my cleavage, all while having a little extra padding to cover the bars from my nipple piercings.

The warmth of his fingers makes me shiver, my mind whirring with thoughts. I pride myself in being confident in my body. It's taken me a long time, but I love the body I'm in. Muffin rolls and all.

Yet, for just a moment, I worry. Beau has known me since we were kids. What if he doesn't like what hides under the fabric?

The dress slides down my arms and to the floor, leaving

me in only my black bra and the nude shapewear. In the mirror, I watch Beau's reaction carefully. His eyes slowly rake down my body with so much heat and lust that I'm surprised I haven't spontaneously combusted.

I slowly turn so my back is to the mirror, my ass pressed against the cool counter. My hands slowly glide up to Beau's chest, fingering the silk of his tie. "I feel like you should pinch me," I murmur.

"Why would I pinch you?" Beau asks, his voice low and sultry.

"So I wake up."

"This isn't a dream, Mar. This is really happening."

A frenzy stirs inside at his words, and I'm yanking at his tie, fumbling my fingers to get it loose and off his neck, then moving down his shirt, unbuttoning them as fast as I can. Once I reach the bottom, Beau throws the shirt off his shoulders, tossing it to the floor, leaving him in a plain white t-shirt, and his trousers.

He whips the shirt up and off, revealing his bare skin. His arm is covered in tattoos that are so familiar to me, as I was with him for every single one. I held his hand in solidarity while he sat for hours. I'm momentarily distracted when the "Dead Sea" tattoo on his inner arm calls to me, and I trace it with my pointer finger. I trace the hands, then the water, before moving on to his other tattoos.

Beau's hand reaches up to clasp mine, the other caressing my cheek before he leans down, kissing me. I lose myself in the kiss, entangling my fingers into his tousled hair when he drops my hand.

He plays with the edge of the shapewear, tugging it slightly. I softly chuckle against his lips. I drop my hands, taking over for him, yanking the shapewear down to my knees, shimmying it off to my ankles and kicking it across the bathroom. I'm left in only my bra and black thong.

Our kiss becomes more ravenous as we touch, our bodies melting into each other. I dig into the skin at his hips, searching for the belt buckle. It opens with a click, and I slide it through the loops as Beau kisses down my chest. He finds the curved barbell of my piercing through my bra, giving my nipple a soft pinch.

Beau shoves down his pants as I gasp, coming up for air. He's in a pair of gray boxer briefs that outline his hard cock. I zero in on it, seeing the small circle of wetness where the tip rests. I swear to god, my mouth fucking waters. When I lift my gaze, I notice that Beau is watching me, watching him. His hands slide down to my hips, gripping hard.

My hands reach out, pulling his face to mine so I can kiss him roughly, putting every pent-up feeling and emotion into my kiss. I don't know what will happen after tonight, but I don't think we can ever be more than this. The thought sends a twinge of pain into my heart, but I ignore it because I don't want to be distracted. I need to be present for every moment of this.

Fingers curl around my back, sliding up to unhook my bra. Or, rather, *attempt* to unhook my bra. He groans into my mouth as he fumbles. I laugh softly, dropping my hands from his hair to help him.

I unclasp it, letting the straps slide down my shoulders. My breasts fall to my chest, no longer held up. They sag, the opposite of perky. Beau doesn't care though. He hones in on my piercings.

"Jesus," he says with a groan. "You're so fucking sexy." His fingers coast down my chest to pinch one of my nipples.

I gasp at the sensation. Since I've gotten them pierced, I haven't been with anyone, so I don't know what it feels like to have someone other than myself play with them. "Beau," I breathe his name.

Beau lowers himself, his mouth descending onto one of my peaked nipples. His tongue flicks at it, teasing me with every movement. His teeth gently bite around the barbell, tugging until I nearly fall on the floor. My hands catch myself on the counter, and I feel my thin panties dampening with each passing moment.

His other hand is tugging and playing with my other nipple, sure not to leave it out. He pops off one side, switching to the other, and each tug and twist sends a zing of pleasure straight between my legs.

I buck against his touch, my body going haywire with everything he's doing to me. He stops for a moment, and I immediately feel irritated.

"Up," Beau says.

I look down at him, confused. "What?"

He gestures to the counter. "Up." He rises back to his full height, hands reaching around behind my thighs. Beau helps me up onto the counter, and for a brief time, we are at an equal height.

The counter is cold against my ass, and I suck in a sharp breath at the change in temperature. Beau reaches to hook his finger under the hem of my underwear. He looks up at me, eyes questioning.

"Yes," I murmur, leaning back on my palms, shifting my hips so he can slide them out from under me and down my legs. The cool air tingles my soaked pussy, and I sit forward, fighting an urge to cross my legs and hide.

I didn't expect Beau, *or anyone for that matter,* to be between my legs tonight, but I can't say I'm upset about it.

"You have no idea how long I've dreamed about doing this," Beau says, his voice low and gravelly. Unexpected heat forms in my stomach at his words. Does he really mean that? Has he really thought about doing this with *me*?

His eyes flick up to mine, a look of pure sin in them. A finger trails up between my thighs. He slides it between my slit, gathering the warmth and wetness from me. I shiver involuntarily, my head falling back on a gasp. Beau drops to his knees before me, and the feeling of looking down at him between my thighs is something powerful, something I never gave into imagining. He looks up at me, eyes hazy and glossed over.

The soaked finger taps at my entrance, gently sliding in as his mouth lands on my clit. He eats me out with everything he has, and I'm climbing toward a heavy release in mere moments. My heart pounds in my chest, my mind swimming with thoughts and emotion. What is going to happen after this? Will we ever be the same? I know these thoughts are important, but yet, this feels right at the same time. I reach out with one hand, leaving the other on the counter to hold my balance, and sink my fingers into his thick curls.

"Shit," I gasp, as he flicks his tongue over my now sensitive clit. I tug on his hair, pulling him back off my clit.

Beau groans. "Not done yet."

He holds me down by my thighs with one hand, the other sliding another finger inside me, pumping in and out slowly. He curls his fingers, and the motion has me crying out his name, jerking my body toward him.

My orgasm burns like a fire in me that has been building from embers for years. Beau fans the flame, fucking me with his fingers and mouth, harder and deeper until I'm exploding all over him, my wetness covering his bearded face. I breathe heavily as he continues, carrying me through the aftershocks, my cunt twitching around his fingers.

The drunken haze settles over me again, exhaustion heavy on my limbs. I let go of his hair, using my other hand to hold me up on the counter.

Beau stops his gracious touch, standing up, a boyish grin on his face. "Now I don't have to wonder anymore," he says as he pecks my lips softly. I can taste myself on him, but it doesn't turn me off, it only makes me crave more. His eyes are glassy and lust filled.

"Wonder what?" I ask, leaning forward to rest my head on his chest, my arms wrapping around his shoulders. He smells familiar, comforting, *right*. I can feel his heart beating under my cheek, rapid and hard. I'm ready to crawl into the bed in the other room and sleep for twelve hours.

"What you sound like when you come. What you taste like." His voice lowers nearly an octave, the rumble deep in his chest.

Suddenly, I no longer feel like crashing into the bed that was calling my name a moment ago to sleep. Now, I feel like crashing into it for a whole other reason. Beau's erection presses against my center, still covered by his briefs, but my legs latch around his hips, keeping him close to me.

"Now it's my turn," I brazenly say, reaching between us to grip him.

"Not here," he mutters, his voice shaky as I feel him for the first time. He pulls my hand away, guiding it up and around his neck. He grips under my thighs, lifting me off the counter.

I shriek, gripping him tighter. "Beau, put me down!"

"Absolutely not," he says. He walks with ease out of the bathroom, into the small room with a huge king size bed in the middle. He drops me onto the middle of the bed, immediately climbing up between my legs, caging my head in with his arms, like he did in the elevator. He kisses me hard, like making up for lost time. He grinds his pelvis into mine, meeting my movements as I press into him, so eager to feel him. The fabric is rough against my sensitive clit, spurring the growing ache inside me a second time.

"Need," I gasp. "Beau!"

"Mmmm," he moans into my mouth. My nipples are pressed up against his warm chest, the friction from his movements giving my belly flutters. He stands, climbing off the bed and shoving his briefs down.

It's my first time seeing him completely naked, and I can't help it. I stare. I stare, and ogle, because he is everything that I could have possibly imagined and more. Sure, he's not cut and muscled like a bodybuilder, but... he's Beau. He's soft, but hard in all the places that matter.

His cock juts out from him, hard, with a drop of precum spilling out the tip. He strokes himself a few times, his shoulders trembling with the touch.

He kneels back on the bed, and I scoot backward so my head rests on the pillows. A strange sense of euphoria mixed with anxiety settles deep in my chest. If we do this... If we really do this, it changes everything. Who am I kidding, things have already changed, but... this makes it real.

Who knows what tomorrow will bring, but for now, I'm going to enjoy the ride. I don't stop the giddy smile, or the giggles that burst over my lips. This is... god I don't think I've been this happy, this free-feeling in a long time.

Beau settles between my legs, hovering his body over mine. I feel his length against my wet pussy, and I shift so he's even closer. Beau locks eyes with me, all heat and rampant desire from earlier gone, in its place is... something I've never seen. Something I can only describe as... love.

I shake off the thought though. My heart will already

break come morning, there's no need to speed up the process.

"Kiss me, Beau," I say with a sigh. He obliges, pressing his lips to mine in a soft and gentle kiss, so different and unhurried than before.

My legs wrap around his hips, one of my hands cupping his cheek while the other slides around his back to hold him closer. His cock nudges at my opening, and I gasp, a burning building in my stomach again, just from the simplest of touches.

"Are you ready?" he asks. I nod. I'm ready to indulge in this one night, this one taste of something bigger that I never thought I'd get. I'm so ready to feel him, feel what we are as one.

He slides into me, filling me so deep with every thick inch of himself. We both gasp at the new sensation, something I never would have dreamed of happening between us.

Slowly, he slides out, almost completely, before thrusting back in, *hard*, hard enough to jolt me slightly.

"Fuck," Beau groans, and I mimic the expression, because this feels unlike anything I've ever felt before.

He pulls out though, not giving me any more of him, and my heart sinks. Did he already realize our mistake? I don't think I can take the rejection. Beau scrambles off the bed, mumbling to himself. He runs into the bathroom, emerging only a second later with something between his fingers.

"I forgot to put on a condom," he says, breathing hard.

I nod, words failing me.

I watch as he opens the crinkled packet, sliding the condom over himself. I feel stupid, forgetting all about that side of things, only focusing on how good he felt, but at least one of us came to our senses.

"I'm so sorry," he mutters, cupping my cheek, kissing me softly. "I promise, you have nothing to worry about."

I freeze, trying to convey my thoughts with a glance. "What abou—"

"You have *nothing* to worry about, Marley." His voice is thick with conviction, and his brown eyes stay locked with mine. "Do you want me to stop?"

I shake my head abruptly, realizing what he means. "No. Please, I need you to keep going," I say, nearly whimpering. "It's okay. I didn't realize either. You don't have to worry about it on my end either. I thought you were panicking, regretting this." I place my hand against his chest.

"Never," he says, leaning down to notch himself in my pussy, sliding in deep again without a moment wasted. Like before, we gasp in unison.

I feel so full, and not just from him. From this, from finally connecting as one. Emotion clogs my throat, as Beau gently thrusts his hips, moving us together. My hands twine in his hair, legs around his hips again.

"Oh," I cry. "Oh my god."

"I've got you, Marley. I won't let you go," Beau murmurs. Sweat beads on his brow, his hair falling into his eyes. I push it back, kissing him hard.

My pussy flutters with his every movement, squeezing him, unwilling to let this moment between us end.

It has to though.

Beau reaches between us, finding my clit with his fingers and circling it in a fast motion. His thrusts become unpaced and fast, as he gets closer to his release. I pant against his mouth, my own climax surprising me with its eagerness and intensity.

I can tell the moment Beau finds his climax, because he shudders, his breath choppy against my lips. At the same moment, my own orgasm peaks, causing me to clench and tighten, my fingernails digging into the skin of his back.

Coming together is so fucking cliché , like something out of a romance novel or movie, and yet, it happened, and I feel whole. I feel content for the moment. Beau places kisses up and down my cheek, my neck, my chest, over and over, giving us a moment to catch our breaths.

Like clockwork, the gut churning anxiety creeps in. What now? Do I ask him to leave? Is he going to leave? Do I want him to? I shake slightly under Beau's touch, and he slides his cock out of me, quickly taking off the condom and throwing it into the nearby trash. He reaches out a hand to me, and I take it.

He squeezes my hand three times. I calm instantly.

Beau leads us into the bathroom, turning on the faucet, and grabbing a washcloth from the rack. "Let me clean you up a bit, and then you can go to the bathroom," he murmurs, squeezing the excess water from the rag. He kisses me quickly before bending down.

I stand awkwardly, as Beau cleans between my thighs with a delicate hand. He's done only moments later, rinsing out the rag and hanging it over the towel rack. "Are you okay?"

I nod, because that's really all I can do right now. He tips his chin, leaving me alone in the bathroom. I take my time using the restroom, washing my hands, and then wiping the makeup off my face. With each passing minute, the lump in my throat grows, the knot in my chest tightening.

I glance around the bathroom, cursing myself for not grabbing clothes, or something to put on so I don't have to walk out there naked again. I'm just about to do the walk of shame back to the bed, when there's a soft knock on the door.

"Mar, I have some pajamas for you. I hope you don't mind that I grabbed them."

I sigh with relief. Beau always knows what I need before I need it.

I crack open the door, taking the clothes from his outstretched hand. A few minutes later, I'm in an old t-shirt, and cotton sleep shorts. Beau sits on the edge of the bed in his boxers. His hair is tousled, and there's marks on his skin from my nails, and mouth. I didn't even realize I'd scratched him so bad, but the proof is there.

"Sorry," I mutter, gesturing to his chest.

Beau absentmindedly reaches up, feeling at his skin. When he notices the tenderness, he chuckles. "I had no idea. Trust me, I don't mind."

My cheeks heat. I don't know what to do now, but thankfully, I don't have to say anything. "Get in bed, I'll be back in a moment." Beau points to where he's pulled down the sheets, and plugged in my phone. He heads into the bathroom, closing the door behind him.

I do as he says, cuddling under the blankets as I wait. My thoughts run with every moment of the last hour, from dancing, to kissing, to... oh my god.

I just had sex with my best friend.

I curl tighter within myself, shutting every door I let open in the last hour. I lost control, lost sight of what is best for us, for our friendship, and I gave into my feelings. I wasn't strong enough, and I gave in. Now, he's going to toss me aside like he did every other girl before me. I *can't* be that girl. I need to get away before he can do it.

Beau exits the bathroom, climbing into the bed behind

me. He pulls me in close, wrapping his arms around my hips. He's the big spoon. I'm spooning with my best friend after I had sex with him.

"Stop thinking, Marley," Beau says, his voice low and rumbling against my neck. One hand slides up my body to my chin, turning so he can press one more gentle kiss to my lips. It's chaste, as if we've been doing it for years. Familiar.

Beau's held me before, and hell, we've cuddled before, but never like this. Never so intimately.

"I can't," I whisper back.

"Give in to tonight," he replies. "Tomorrow is a fresh start."

A fresh start. A fresh start... without him. This is just a one night thing. It has to be.

I've fought so long to keep him, I can't let one night ruin it all.

11

MARLEY

My head pounds, the sunlight streaming through the open curtains of the hotel room. Arms are banded around me, holding me close and warm. Memories of the previous night flood my brain, and I remember all the realizations I had as Beau held me as we fell asleep.

I've never been one for confrontation. As a kid, I had my older brothers to do it all for me, and as time went on, Beau, and the rest of the Cunningham boys were the ones to help me fight my battles. Now, I have to be the one to do the confronting, in what may possibly be the most awkward moment of my life.

So, I do the only thing I know how to do in a situation like this, I run.

12

———

BEAU

Eight fucking weeks.

Marley has been avoiding me for eight fucking weeks.

Déjà vu settles itself on my shoulders as I walk up the front steps to Marley's parent's house. I've wrestled with myself over the last eight weeks. Do I let this go? Say it was just a one-night thing, something to burn off the heat that's been brewing for years? Or do I fight for her? Fight for her like I should have done in the first place.

I've gone back and forth. Regretting ever kissing her, to having sex, to... everything. Then, deciding it was the best thing I've ever done, drunk, or sober. Sure, do I wish our first time was when we were both of clear and sound mind? Obviously, but I don't regret that both of us had lowered our inhibitions enough to give into what we wanted.

I've sent her countless messages, called her just as much, and I've gotten nothing but silence. I sent her two bouquets of flowers, which was a difficult task, seeing as I had to go to my new sister-in-law to order them, and she had an abundance of questions. I need to prove to Marley how much I want this, want her in my life as more than just my best friend. I have to do one thing first. Sure, we've seen each other in person, but only at Sunday Brunches, and it's not like I'm going to bring it up as we sit across the table from both our families.

I can't help but think about the way my last attempt at a chance with her went. When I asked Gabriel for the go ahead and was shut down. I still don't think I will ever be good enough for her, but now, I don't care. I need to prove to him that now, I'm not an eighteen-year-old kid. I've thought this through, and even if he tells me no, this time, I'm not going to take no for an answer.

My decision is clear to me as I knock on the door.

It's time to fight.

It opens with a click, Marley's mom, Jane, on the other side. "Well hi, honey, what are you doing here?"

"Is Gabriel home?" I ask.

"Sure, come on in," she says, opening the door wider. "How are you? We haven't seen much of you lately."

"Busy," I answer. I've seen her at the weekly Sunday Brunches that Marley and my family have, but haven't seen her otherwise. "Lots of houses on the market, so lots of showings."

She leads me into the family room where Gabriel is sitting in his recliner, watching *Law and Order*. "Gabe, Beau is here," Jane calls, getting his attention.

At the mention of my name, Gabriel chuckles. He turns the TV off, standing from his chair with a low groan. "Took you long enough," he mutters.

I step forward, offering him my hand. "Sorry?" I ask, a little confused.

"You know, when we told you it wasn't your and Marley's time, we didn't mean forever." He squeezes my hand tightly. "You guys weren't ready back then, but we thought that if after college you were both still single, you'd ask again. But you never did."

My heart pounds furiously in my chest. Is this a joke? "I... so what are you saying?"

"Well, I thought you would've turned around and asked her out that day when you walked out of the house, but you never did. We had your best interests at heart, but when I think about it now, I realize we probably were in the wrong. We could've voiced our concerns and then moved on. I just hope it's not too late."

My jaw drops slightly. "So... you don't think I'm not good enough for her?"

Gabriel chuckles. "Son, you are the best person for her. We can all see that."

I clear my throat. I'm angry that I wasted all this time without her, but now... now I can go get her. "Thank you, Gabriel," I say, my voice breaking slightly. I've forgotten that Jane is in the room still, until she speaks.

"What the hell are you two talking about? What happened back then? Oh my god, are you going to marry Marley?" Her voice increases an octave with each sentence. I turn, pulling her into a tight hug.

"That's the goal," I say, my heart light, tension relieved in my body for the first time in a long time.

We chat for a while longer, until I decide it's time to find Marley.

13

MARLEY

Missing Beau has me feeling physically ill. I haven't slept, can barely eat, and I'm nauseous all the time. I've been avoiding him. Even at our worst, things were never this... awkward. Nevermind the fact that he's in my dreams every night, doing unspeakable things to me and my body.

I've woken up more than once with my panties wet and my heart pounding. Only now, my dreams aren't a fantasy. They're based on real life. I know what it feels like to have Beau hovering over me, his lips on mine, feel him thrusting in and out of me.

I shake myself out of yet another daydream as the door to my studio opens. The bell on the door rings, and my client walks in. Since I've started focusing more on boudoir, I've met some incredible women.

I greet her, and get to work right away. She had her makeup and hair done at the salon down the street, a part of the package I offer. She picks out the lingerie she wants to wear, and we discuss poses and the vibe she wants for the shoot.

An hour later, we're finishing up the shoot, and I'm

feeling like I'm about to vomit. I am at the point where I'm not even going to clean up the studio when she leaves. I can deal with it tomorrow. My bed is calling me.

Another wave of nausea roils through me, and I have to swallow down the extra saliva gathering in my mouth. My forehead is clammy, a sign of impending doom. The only perk right now is that I'm currently wearing a thin bodysuit, so at least I'm not sweating through my clothes.

We finish up, scheduling a time next week to go over the images, and decide which ones she wants to have printed. After saying a quick goodbye, she's gone.

As soon as the door closes behind her, I'm dashing toward the small bathroom, heaving the measly breakfast of a banana and toast I was able to eat into the toilet. My stomach clenches and my eyes water as I get sick, cursing my own existence the whole time. I fight the urge to lay my head down on the cool tile floor, because, gross. My eyes start to drift close as I hold myself over the toilet, threatening to give into the overwhelming exhaustion I feel.

"Marley?"

I shriek, immediately flinging my arms out in front of me in an attempt to hit this unknown person. Am I being kidnapped? This is not how I wanted to go. A hand rests on my forearm, and I kick out my leg in an attempt to break free. I know I should have locked the door behind my client, but I had other, more pressing needs.

Hopefully, my kidnapper likes an overly exhausted, sick girl, cause that's what they're going to get.

The kidnapper grunts, but I don't open my eyes.

"Marley, it's Beau!" he shouts. "Open your eyes!"

At the sound of his familiar voice, I do what he says, immediately opening my eyes and halting my attempt to maim him. "What are you doing?" I ask, my voice hoarse.

"I came to talk to you," he says, slumping down on the floor next to me. He leans his head back against the wall, tugging at the roots of his hair. "What's going on, are you sick?"

I nod, leaning back against the wall again. I realize I'm still in the deep purple lace bodysuit, but honestly, I can't find it in me to care. "I think so. I've just been really tired and nauseous the last few days. I probably just have a bug or something."

Beau's dark eyebrow raises as he glances at me. "Let's get you home. I'll drive. I don't think you're in a good place to be behind the wheel." He stands, offering me his hand. I grasp it, glancing down at the toilet with a groan. I quickly flush it, even though I know Beau has more than likely already seen the mess of vomit.

I nod, feeling slightly grateful for his presence. Driving right now sounds like the very last thing I want to do. "I need to change." I steer myself in the direction of my office, and grab my leggings and sweatshirt off my desk. Beau follows me in, standing at the corner of my desk.

"Can you... Can I have some privacy?" I ask.

Beau hesitates. "I don't want you to get sick or something again."

"Beau, I'm fine."

He raises that brow at me, silently calling me on my shit.

I groan. "Ugh, fine. Just, turn around, please?" I beg, using a swirling motion of my finger. He does, shoving his hands in his pockets, and kicking the door shut. Once I'm sure he's not looking, I throw my sweatshirt over the body suit, and then work on pulling it down from underneath it. Now that I'm feeling a little better, I'm cold as hell, and thankful I have something cozy to climb into.

I shimmy the bodysuit off and snatch my leggings from the chair I laid them on, tugging them up my legs as quickly as humanly possible. I jump, hiking them up and over my stomach. Sudden dizziness causes me to break out into another clammy sweat, and I drop down into the office chair. "Woah, head rush," I murmur.

Beau rushes over, clasping my head in his hands. He pushes my bangs out of my eyes, his own eyes searching into mine, with such concern and care, I fear I might burst into tears.

What the hell is wrong with me? I can't regulate my emotions for shit, feel like utter crap, and I'm so tired I could sleep for a week straight. Though, this doesn't feel like a normal stomach bug. What could possibly be going on that I feel so crummy?

My chest grows hot, stomach turning for a completely different reason. Beau must reach the same realization as me, because both our eyes widen, and Beau's cheeks pale of any color.

But... no. There is no way I could be. I mean... he wore a condom, and I'm on birth control. My eyes flit back and forth over his face, watching for any sort of reaction. He stands up straight, clearing his throat.

"Marley," he grits out. "Are you," he coughs. "Are you pregnant?"

Blood drains from my face. "I don't know. I hadn't thought about it until just now. You wore a condom, right?"

He nods. "Yes, but... not right away, remember?"

"Oh god," I say, dropping my head down to my hands. I shake my head in my hands. "I can't be. I mean, I'm on the pill. I never miss a day."

"You could be," he says.

"No. I'm just sick, that's all. We're overthinking this,

having second thoughts about what we did." I lift my head, frantically waving my hands back and forth. My heart is pounding in my chest, a sense of panic overwhelming me.

"I have never had second thoughts. You're the one that ran that morning. You've avoided me for two months, Marley." His voice is strained. "Are you late?"

"I don't have a regular cycle." I don't have the mental means to try to explain to him that I only get a period once every three months due to the birth control I take. Tears well in my eyes. "I need to go home. Sleep this bug off."

Beau nods, but I can tell he wants to say more. He watches me closely as I lock up the studio, turning the lights off as we leave. Instead of fighting him on letting me drive, I let him open the passenger door to his vehicle, helping me in and making sure I'm buckled before he closes the door.

The uncomfortable silence drags as Beau drives. I lean my head back against the headrest, letting my eyes close. I'm so fucking tired.

I feel the car slow to a stop, and my eyes flutter open, expecting to see my small twin home in front of me, only to see the glowing lights of a chain drugstore. "What are we doing here?" I ask, turning my gaze to Beau. He stares straight ahead, face a blank slate.

"I...would you take a pregnancy test? I was already planning on stopping to get you some ginger ale, and other things, but since we are here..." He takes a deep breath. "All the symptoms and timing add up, so I thought maybe it might be a good idea. You can say no. I trust your judgment. You know your body best."

I nod, knowing he's completely right. "Yeah. I'll take one."

He nods in response as he climbs out of the car. Panic

squeezes my throat, fear that he might see someone we know in the store. "Use the self checkout!" I call.

Mind whirring, I try to think back to the last time I got a period and if the timing would line up. Then I think about my birth control, did I really take it every day? Did I miss any days?

I wrack my brain. When I got home and unpacked from the wedding, I couldn't find my birth control pack, but I shrugged it off, and opened a new one. Where did the other one go? The fact that I can't remember is startling. I am always on top of my pills.

Tears begin to stream down my face, because I really could be pregnant. With my best friend's baby.

The man himself strides out of the small drug store, a plastic bag in his hand. He looks as cool as a cucumber in his flannel jacket and jeans, not minding the late fall cold. The only thing that gives away the potential stress he feels is his hair. He must have pulled it into a bun during his time in the store, but it's already falling out in places, likely from being tugged on.

I'm full on crying now, because I don't want to cause him any more stress than I already do. I know that I've avoided him since Josie and Andrew's wedding. But I've also avoided everyone. I've dug myself into a deep hole, only ever being this low once before.

I don't let myself think of that night though. Instead, focusing on now. Whatever that test says, I need to man up and talk to Beau. I need to apologize for blowing him off like that.

Beau hops into the car, instantly seeing my tear streaked face. "No, don't cry, Mar. It's okay. Whatever it says, it's going to be fine." He reaches over, cupping my cheeks, wiping away the tears.

How is it possible that even after treating him like shit for two months after we had sex, and being rude as hell to him in the time before, that he still cares for me?

I shudder, dropping my head to his chest over the center console. "I'm sorry."

"Stop," he murmurs. He kisses my cheeks, the top of my head, anywhere he can. He takes my cheeks again, pulling me off his chest. "Marley, no more running from me. I can't take it."

I nod, gasping as he holds me close again.

"Let's get home, yeah?" he asks. Shakily, I pull away from him, settling back into my seat as he drives out of the parking lot toward my house.

If it wasn't an inanimate object, I'd swear that the box inside that plastic bag was mocking me for my errors, and certainly losing the best person I have in my life. What will happen if I'm pregnant? What will happen if I'm not?

I can't think about all the plausible outcomes now. There isn't enough time in the world for that.

Beau reaches his hand across, grabbing mine from where I was gripping my sweats in between my fingers. He doesn't say anything, just squeezes my hand three times.

When we get to my house, I get out of the car, and try to dig through my bag for my keys, but Beau is already unlocking the door with his extra set. I've locked myself out of my house a few times, so I've made sure that he, and my parents all have an extra key.

Walking into my quiet house, I flick on a few lights, immediately running to the bathroom as another bout of nausea overtakes me. Beau runs after me. I attempt to close the door behind me, but he beats me, pushing through it as I crouch down, trying to hold my hair back as I vomit.

Nothing comes up, just bile, and the bit of water I'd

drank in the car. I startle when Beau's hand rests on my back, the other gathering my hair in his hands. He soothes me softly, all while rubbing my back. When I'm done, he gets a washcloth from the drawer, wetting it with cool water and placing it on the back of my neck.

I take my time standing, allowing myself time to catch my breath. Beau speaks before I can. "I think that before you take the test, we should talk."

"Okay," I murmur. "I'll meet you in the living room."

I wash my hands, and instead of heading right to the living room, I take a detour to my second bedroom where my suitcase is stored. I have to search it and see if the old birth control pack is in there. I have to know.

I grab it from the closet, immediately unzipping it and digging through the inside pockets. When there's a crinkle of plastic, my fingers start to shake. I grab the packet, pulling it out of the zippered pocket. Inwardly, I die a little, because the packet isn't empty. There's four pills left. I have the twenty-one day pack, so it's not even like I've missed four days of placebos, which wouldn't mean anything. I missed four actual days.

This is all my fault. I'm ruining Beau's life, all because I somehow forgot to take my pills over the wedding weekend. I rise to my feet, leaving the suitcase in the middle of the floor as I head toward the living room, pill pack in hand. Beau sits in the middle of my couch, hands folded as he leans forward, elbows on his knees. He doesn't look upset, more... contemplative.

I clear my throat. "I think you might be right," I say with a shaky voice. I offer out the pack to him. He takes it, looking at those four pills, his emotions masked.

"Sit down," he says. "I still want to talk." He sets the pill pack to the side without another glance at it. I sit down cross legged, pulling a blanket off the arm of the couch, and covering my lap with it.

"If you are pregnant, this may not be the way either of us had planned on things going, but it's not going to change my plans for the future, for *our* future." He pauses, reaching under the blanket to take my hand.

"I don't regret that night. If anything, I regret that it didn't happen sooner, that we lost out on all that time. I gave you time, but I'm done. I'm about to become the clingiest motherfucker you've ever met."

I chuckle softly. "Beau," I start. "You don't have to lie. I should just take the test, and we can go from there." I take a deep breath, saying words I don't want to say, but know he needs to hear. "I haven't been with anyone else. If I am..." I trail off.

"Stop," he interrupts, holding his hand out. "I never questioned it, nor would I. The test doesn't change anything for me. Either way, I'm not stopping until you're mine."

His words make my pulse thready, because these are the words that I've been dying to hear for years, only now, it feels... tainted. Like he's only saying it to be the good guy. Nevermind the fact that I had no idea I could possibly have been pregnant until we realized it at the same time.

I don't respond, simply stand from the couch and grab the plastic bag on the kitchen counter. With confidence I definitely don't feel inside, I pull the box from the bag, noting that Beau bought not only one, but three different kinds.

He sheepishly walks over. "I wanted you to have options in case you didn't want to believe whatever the result is."

"Thanks," I say. I grab two, the digital, and one that is the classic two pink lines. On second thought, I grab the third one too. Never can be too sure.

14

BEAU

My stomach is churning. Marley went into the bathroom just a moment ago, promising to let me in as soon as she was done and to not look at the results before I was with her.

I'm standing outside the door to the bathroom, trying to give her privacy, but also not willing to go too far. I never expected the day to end up like this. I thought maybe I'd find her at the studio and finally tell her how I feel, how I want our future to be.

The toilet flushes, and the sink turns on. Marley opens the door a moment later, her beautiful eyes red and glassy. "It's okay, Mar. I'm here," I say. I pull her into a hug, noting three tests laying face down on the counter top.

My heart thumps rapidly in my chest as anxiety, excitement, and so much more run through my mind. I hold Marley while we wait. This will be a life changing moment, regardless of the result. I don't know what I have to do to prove to her that either way, I'm hers. I'm not letting her go.

The alarm on her phone goes off and she pulls away abruptly. I let her go, but stand behind her as she faces the mirror, setting her hands palm down on the counter. I slide my arms around her waist, holding her close to my chest, needing to feel her in this moment. "Whenever you're ready," I say.

Marley takes a deep, long breath, and flips over two of the tests at the same time. These two are dye tests, one a bright bold blue plus sign, the other two dark pink lines.

With shaking hands, she flips over the digital test and I hold my breath.

15

MARLEY

Pregnant.

All three tests state the glaringly obvious. The test that has two lines even has one line darker than the other, to the point where it's pulling dye from the other line.

The digital one reads *Pregnant, 3+ weeks*. My breaths come in short stutters as I try to process. Beau's arms are tight around me, and he's whispering in my ear, but I can't hear him, can't understand what he's saying. His arms are the only thing keeping me from collapsing.

He didn't want this. He wanted one night with me, one night to get our feelings out in the open, and now he's stuck. Stuck with me, stuck with a baby that he probably doesn't want. He's going to feel obligated to be with me now, to care for me. That's not what I want. I wanted him to want me for me, not because he has to.

"Marley, listen to me. This is okay." His voice is the opposite of how I feel. Strong, steady.

"How is this okay?" I shriek. I rub my face, pushing my bangs out of my eyes. I'm sure they are skewed all over my sticky skin, but I really can't find it in me to care. "I just trapped you for at least the next eighteen years of our lives!"

"You act as if that's a burden." I can't bring myself to look in the mirror, to see Beau's face in the reflection. "If anything, I'm the one that trapped you. I got so lost in the moment, in being with you *finally*, that I forgot to put on a condom."

"I forgot my pills!" My voice is at an ungodly level, my ears ringing.

"Marley," Beau coaxes, spinning me so I face him, cupping my cheeks in his hands. "Stop it. Neither of us are at fault."

Breathing heavily, I stare into his eyes. Inside of his gaze I see no fear, no anger, just pure adoration. The same look he gets on his face when he tells me he's proud of me.

"We're having a baby," he murmurs. His eyes shine and his lip trembles.

"We're having a baby," I repeat, the words finally sinking in. The reality hits me, and it's no longer the sheer panic of what might happen between Beau and me for our future, but the panic of realizing I'm carrying a baby. Beau's baby. Tears freely fall from my eyes, down my cheeks and fall to my sweatshirt. "I don't know whether to laugh or cry," I admit.

"I'm right there with you. Fuck, Marley. I... wow."

I press a palm to my sweaty forehead. "What do we do now?"

Beau leans down, kissing my lips with the gentlest of pressure, our salty tears mingling together. "Now, we talk. Really, really talk."

16

―――

BEAU

I push Marley's hair back behind her ear, and stare into those gold-brown eyes which are so captivating, so torn between emotions.

"Come on," I say, pulling her out of the bathroom, leaving the positive pregnancy tests on the counter. I bring her back to the couch, opening the blanket for her to sit. "Stay," I order, pointing my finger at her. If she wasn't feeling so crummy, I'm sure she would fight me, but thankfully, she's content to lean back, and wrap herself in the fluffy navy blanket.

I head into the kitchen, monitoring her at all times, satisfying an inherent need to make sure she's okay. I take a glass out of the cupboard, fill it with ice, and grab the ginger ale from the bag. I pop the tab open and pour it into the glass, listening to it fizz.

I grab the other things I purchased at the store, a pack of ginger candy and saltine crackers. Heading back to the couch, I take in Marley. The direction of our lives has changed so drastically in the last hour, but yet... I don't feel panicked. I don't feel out of sorts or a mess. I feel... steady, like I have a purpose. To take care of Marley and our baby. To care for them and keep them safe.

"Here, try this," I say, offering her the glass. "It might feel good on your stomach."

She takes the glass, and sips it cautiously. "Thanks."

I sit down beside her, resting my hand on her thigh. "How do you feel?" I ask.

"Mentally? Or physically?" she asks in return.

"Both," I suggest, offering her the lead.

She tilts her head down, her hair covering her pale face. "Physically, I feel like I got hit by a truck. It makes sense. I've been exhausted, and well... you saw the vomit." A hint of color makes its way back to her cheeks at the last comment. "Mentally, I have no idea. I think I'm numb. Or maybe dreaming."

I reach over, squeezing her thigh. "You aren't dreaming. Waking up to find you gone... I thought maybe *I'd* dreamt the whole thing. Marley... this isn't a one-night thing for me." I put all my emotions into my words. "I'm here for the long haul. For us."

Tears stream down her cheeks again, and she swipes them away with irritation. "I don't know what to say," she murmurs, voice breaking.

"Say we can give this a try." I wipe her tears with my thumb, tilting her head up to look at me. "I've wanted this since we were kids. I was too scared to lose you, scared of other people's reactions, but I realize now that never having you is worse."

Marley is silent for a long moment. "I don't think I can give you an answer right now," she says. "My mind is so all over the place, thinking of all the things we have to do, and the fact that I'm pregnant. I can't focus on anything else right now. I don't know whether to be happy or terrified."

I nod. "I can understand that. I just need you to know that I'm here. That I'm not letting you go."

I pull her in for a hug, swearing to myself that I will do anything for this woman, anything for her future, for the future of our unborn child, and for our future together.

"What are we going to tell our parents?" Marley cries. "My parents always talked to me about the importance of safe sex, how teen pregnancy could be an uphill road."

"Marley..." I chuckle. "We aren't teens. We're thirty-two."

She stiffens. "It feels so scandalous, pregnant, from a one-night stand? What will people say?"

"First off," I say, squeezing her gently. "We aren't a one-night stand." I don't let her interject, even when she tries to, putting a finger over her lips. "I doubt people are going to be surprised. Everyone assumes we are together, anyway."

Marley thoughtfully nods. "Yeah. They do."

"As for telling people, we can tell them whatever you want. We can tell them nothing at all. It's all up to us."

"Can we wait to tell people? At least for a bit?" Marley bites her lip, a hint of uncertainty in her eyes.

"Of course. However long you need."

"Thank you," she says, leaning her head on my shoulder. "I guess I need to find a doctor."

"Yeah," I say. "I want to come with to appointments, if that's okay."

"Absolutely. I don't think I would want to go without you, anyway." My heart thumps proudly at her confession. "Promise to stay at my head, though," she says with a laugh.

"You got it," I say, kissing the top of her head. I may not have all of her yet, but I'm one step closer. That we are having a baby together makes it that much sweeter. I hold her close as she slips deeply into a sleep that she needs.

17

MARLEY

The click of my camera is soothing, something for me to focus on, as my stomach tries to rebel against me for the third time today.

I can't keep anything down. Water is even a struggle. Beau has texted me no less than five times today, asking how I'm feeling. I was able to call this morning on my way to work and make an appointment with a doctor in Cinder Valley in a few days. The gal I talked to on the phone seemed to understand my urgency in wanting an appointment.

Beau put up a valiant fight, wanting to stay at my place last night. After I told him I just needed a little space and time to mentally process the new direction that life has taken me, he agreed, but made me promise to text him if I needed anything.

In a weird way, I almost feel more at peace today than I have in months. I have my best friend back, something I haven't had in a long time. I've missed having him by my side, being the person I feel like I can conquer the world with. And not only that, I'm having a baby. Something I've wanted, well... always. I always hoped I'd be a mom.

I snap a few more photos of my client, thankfully finishing up the session. It was an amazing session, but with how exhausted and nauseous I am, I'm ready to be done.

An hour later, the studio is clean, the client is gone, and I'm ready to call it a day. The bell on the door jingles, and I cringe. I don't know if I have it in me to do more small talk today. I plaster on a fake smile, ready to greet the person as I walk toward the entrance.

Beau rounds the corner, wearing his work clothes. He had a few showings this morning, and then we had plans for dinner, and to make a loose plan for things going forward. I guess I'd forgotten that he said he would pick me up.

His long hair is loose around his shoulders, and my belly flutters with just how attractive he is. He's always been the hottest man in the room, at least where I'm concerned, but now, it's like my body is hard-wired to want him even more.

"Hey," he greets. "You look pale."

"Such sweet words you speak to the mother of your future child," I say, waving him off with an attempt at sarcasm. I turn, ready to head back to my office and grab my things, only as I turn, my head spins.

"You know I don't mean it like that," he refutes. "I'm trying to make sure you're okay." I hear his footsteps following closely, and with each step I take, my nausea and dizziness grow.

"I know, Beau," I say, trying to hold back the vomit threatening to make its appearance. "I'm really not feeling good. I haven't been able to eat or drink anything all day. I can't even keep down water."

A hand clasps around my wrist, pulling me back. "You

haven't eaten all day?" Beau's gaze is intense, his face etched with worry.

I slowly shake my head, noting that even that small motion makes me dizzy. "I can't."

"Let's go find you something to eat."

I turn back to the office, telling him I need to grab my bag, but suddenly, I can't speak. My words are muffled and slurred. My body grows hot and clammy, black spots and stars dance across my vision. My body sways as I lean into the too-warm body of Beau. I hear him shout my name before everything goes black.

"Marley!" I shout as she slumps into my arms, face ghostly white, eyes falling shut. I hold her tightly to me, sliding us down to the floor. "Marley, wake up, butterfly," I say over and over, trying to get some sort of response from her. Nothing happens. Her chest rises and falls with steady beats, relieving the slightest amount of anxiety.

With no idea what could be wrong, I panic, doing the first thing I can think of. Without moving Marley, and watching her the entire time, I grab my phone from my pocket and call Thomas, hoping he is on duty.

"Hey man," Thomas greets, his voice ever so cheery.

"Thomas," I grit out. "Marley passed out, I'm at her studio, I don't know what to do."

"Shit," he murmurs, and the sound of his cruiser picking up speed, and sirens echo through the call. "I'll send out a dispatch for EMS. Is she breathing?" His tone has changed from playful to all business.

"Yeah, but she's pale as fuck." I place a hand over her chest so I can feel the steady beat of her heart, and the rise and fall of her chest. She's still breathing. She's still here. She's okay.

"I'll be there in five. Keep talking to her. She might just have low blood sugar or something."

I swallow down my words, because I don't know whether or not to tell him she's pregnant. "Yeah." I drop the phone from my ear, keeping Thomas on the line, but I do what I can to wake Marley. I fan her with my hand, say her name, anything. I can't lose her. I can't lose *them*.

What feels like hours pass as I wait for help to arrive. As the ambulance and Thomas's police cruiser pull into the parking lot, Marley's eyelashes flutter, a low moan falling from her lips.

"Wha—" she mumbles.

"Marley, oh thank god." I push her hair back from where it fell over her eyes, leaning down to press an urgent kiss to her lips. "Are you okay? Are you hurt?"

Her eyes widen as I kiss her, and she tries to sit up, but I don't let her move. She gives me an irritated grunt but doesn't fight me. "I'm not hurt. I feel really gross, though."

"Okay, help is coming," I reply.

"Help?" her voice squeaks, brows furrowing. "What do you mean, help? I'm fine." She tries to sit up again as the bell on the front door goes off.

"Beau?" Thomas calls, his footsteps heavy.

"Back here!" I call back. "She's awake."

"Oh thank god," he says. Other voices fill the room as Thomas directs the paramedics to us. When he comes into view, he takes in our position, me sitting on the floor with Marley draped across my lap, her arm strewn across her face, covering her eyes. "Hey, Mar," Thomas says with a small chuckle. "Felt like causing some trouble today, huh?"

Marley doesn't move her arm from her eyes, only uses her free hand to flick him off.

Thomas chuckles. "You still have your sense of humor, so I think you'll make it."

"Why did you call them?" Marley groans. "I'm fine."

I lean forward so my mouth is at her ear. "You're pregnant, Mar. I'm not taking any chances." When I pull back, I raise my brows. She nods in response.

A young paramedic kneels down next to us, pulling some items from her medical bag. "Hi, Marley, my name is Hannah," she says. She looks young, probably in her early twenties, with blonde hair pulled into a slick bun and bright blue eyes.

She gets to work, taking Marley's blood pressure, and sticking her finger to test her blood sugar. She asks her all about what symptoms she's experiencing and reasons she could have passed out.

Marley gives her all the answers, except for probably the most important one, being that Thomas is here. He's hovering over us, listening closely to every answer Marley gives. I can't really blame him for sticking around, I called him in such a panic, and he loves Marley like a sister. He wants to make sure she's okay. I, however, want him to get the heck out so Marley and I can be truthful about something major.

We move Marley into one of the loveseat chairs she has in the front waiting room of the studio while they check her over. I refuse to be over five feet from her at all times, so I'm sitting in the chair beside her, holding her hand.

Thomas meets my eye from where he's sitting, and I give him a grateful nod. "I think we're good, Tommy," I say, looking down at Marley. "Unless you want him to stick around."

She shakes her head. "Thanks for everything, Thomas," Marley says emphatically. "I appreciate it."

Thomas steps over, leaning down to pull her into a tight hug. "You let me know if you need anything, okay?" He points a finger at her. "You know I'm here for you, anytime."

Marley nods. "Thanks, I will." Thomas kisses her cheek and offers me a chin tip. He heads toward the front door, and once the click of the door behind him sounds, Marley lets out a deep breath, tears rolling down her cheeks.

"Are you in pain?" Hannah asks, fretting over her. Her co-paramedic has been less than helpful, mainly standing behind and watching Hannah work.

"I'm fine, just really overwhelmed," Marley replies. "I didn't want to tell you this while Thomas was here, but I'm pregnant."

Hannah's mouth forms a little "o" of understanding. "Alright. I'm going to ask some different questions then," she says, rattling off a whole new set of questions.

Ten minutes later, it's determined that while Marley doesn't need to ride in the ambulance, she should still go to the hospital. She's been able to keep down some water and orange juice now, and her color is getting better. If Hannah hadn't suggested going to the hospital, I would take her, anyway. I'm too worried something is wrong with her, or the baby not to.

Hannah finishes up, and she and her partner say their goodbyes before heading out the door. I stand from the chair next to Marley. "Stay here. I'll grab your stuff." She nods, and god, she looks so exhausted.

I run back to her office, grabbing her bag, phone, and keys. When I arrive back in the front, Marley is sitting with her head tilted back on the chair, eyes closed. "Hey, you okay?" I ask, nerves bubbling up again.

She opens her eyes slowly. "Yeah. I think I'm overwhelmed. Hannah was so sweet. I want to be her friend."

"I'm sure you do, she was very nice. Come on," I say, offering her my hand. "Let's go get things checked out."

She takes her time standing. She leans down, grabbing the blue puke bag that Hannah left for good measure. I hold on to her hand, making sure she doesn't get too dizzy. We walk to my car slowly, giving her time.

I'm pulling my car out of the lot and heading down the road to the emergency room when Marley pukes into the blue bag. I do my best to make sure she's okay, but also focus on driving so we can get to the ER. I squeeze her leg as she heaves into the bag, thankful she isn't looking at me.

I can't help but gag a few times at the noise and the lingering smell, but I know I'm not the one who needs sympathy right now. We're only at the beginning of this pregnancy, and if it's already this rough? I'm quite nervous for how the rest is going to go.

I retch bile into the bag once more as we finally arrive in the parking lot of the emergency room. Beau gags yet again. I can tell he's trying to be secretive and not bring attention to it, but he's failing. I feel a little bad for him, but also, he's screwed once this kid starts spitting up and pooping all over.

He parks, and thankfully, the lack of motion seems to have helped with my nausea. Beau runs to my side of the vehicle, taking deep breaths as he does. When he opens the car door, I can't help but tease him a bit. "Feeling alright?" I snicker.

Beau narrows his eyes. "I'm fine, worried about you."

I pat his chest as he helps me from the car. "I'm alright, promise."

"You don't sound alright."

I shrug. "Puking in pregnancy is normal."

"Yeah, but passing out isn't," he retorts.

I say nothing, just let him lead us into the ER, dropping the near empty bag into a nearby trash can. The hospital smells clean, but not in a good way. Like someone just poured bleach all over the floor. It makes my nostrils burn.

"Go sit down. I'll get you checked in," Beau says, guiding me over to the waiting room. I want to fight it, say I can do it myself, but I'm too tired. I sit, watching him walk toward the U-shaped desk where various personnel sit. He runs his fingers through his hair a few times, leaning over the desk and resting his head on his palm as he speaks to the employee.

She's attractive—thin, young, and blonde. All things I am not. Anger and jealousy bubble up in my chest as I watch him talk to her. Is he flirting? Seriously? The girl laughs, waving a hand at him as he steps back.

Beau frowns as he strides toward me, shoving his hands in his pockets. "What's wrong?" he asks when he's close.

"Nothing," I mutter.

"Don't lie to me, Mar."

"I'm mad at you," I say. I know I'm being juvenile, but I can't help it. I'm pregnant with *his* child, and he has the audacity to flirt with someone mere hours after he was telling me he was all in? Yeah. I'm irritated.

"Why?" His voice is concerned, and thick with worry. "What did I do?"

"Marley?" A voice calls my name. A nurse in neon pink scrubs waits for me at the double door entrance. I stand, striding over to her. I've never gotten in at an ER this fast before, but I couldn't have asked for better timing.

"You can stay here," I say to Beau. Am I being petty? Sure. Do I care? Nope. Beau stands, following behind me. I turn, glaring at him. "I don't need you back there."

"I'm coming," he says roughly. His jaw clenches. He's clearly irritated with me, too.

Ignoring him, I greet the nurse. "Hi, I'm Marley."

"Great, my name is Lily. I'll be your nurse today." She eyes Beau behind me. "Can I ask who you are?"

I start to say, "He's just a friend," when Beau speaks over me.

"I'm her husband," he says confidently.

My jaw drops in shock. *What the fuck?* I swear, this man is giving me whiplash.

"Great!" Lily says, leading us through the double doors toward an empty room. "I'll give you a minute to get changed, but can you verify your name and birth date for me?"

I do as she asks, and then she's spinning on her clogged heel, heading out the door.

"My husband?" I hiss as soon as the door is closed.

Beau has the nerve to look sheepish. "If I said I was your friend or something else, they probably wouldn't have let me back here." He has his hands in his pockets, rocking back on his heels. "You didn't want me back here for some reason, but Marley, I think I have at least a little bit of a right to be here, don't you think?"

"Why were you flirting with the front desk lady?" I accuse, figuring we might as well get it out in the open now.

His eyes widen at my words, and he stalks toward me with purpose. "I was not flirting. She was being nice. I said hopefully the wait isn't too long, or you'd throw up in the waiting room, and she laughed. That's all." Beau cups my cheek in his hands. "Not only do I have no interest in anyone that isn't you, I would never flirt with anyone else. I said it yesterday, and I'll say it again. I'm all in. I'm here for you, for us."

My eyes sting with tears, and I curse myself for being so emotional. "Okay," I say, turning out of his grip. "Can you turn around so I can have some privacy?"

Beau nods, but doesn't move right away. Instead, he leans down, pressing a tender kiss to my forehead. As soon as he's facing the other direction, I whip my shirt over my head and push down my jeans, leaving me in my sports bra and undies. I tug the scratchy gown up my arms and try to tie the back. When I fight to find the ties for a moment, I give up. "Can you help me?" I unwillingly ask.

Beau spins around immediately, a look of concern marring his beautiful face. I spin, showing him the open back. He inhales sharply and ties the gown for me. With shaky legs I head over to the bed, and slump down onto it.

When my head hits the pillow, a wave of exhaustion hits me like a truck. My eyes fall shut as another bout of dizziness and nausea overtakes me. "Beau?" I ask.

"Yeah, love?"

"I think I need another puke bag."

"You got it," he says. His footsteps rush toward the door, opening it and calling for the nurse. She rushes back with a crinkling bag and promises to be back in just a moment.

Beau comes back to my side, setting the bag in my left hand, sitting down in the creaky chair next to my bed and taking my right hand in his. He squeezes it three times, and I squeeze back three times. "Thank you," I whisper.

"Anything for you."

20

MARLEY

I know she doesn't mean to, but this nurse is making me feel all sorts of stupid. She's shocked that I don't know the day of my last period, or how far along I am down to the day. Beau and I did a little mental math, counting out eight weeks since the night of the wedding, but I guess that wasn't a good enough answer for her.

She got me hooked up to an IV with some good anti-nausea meds that have helped a ton. I feel better than I have in days, and have even kept down a turkey sandwich they offered.

There's a knock on the door, and a woman in a white coat enters. She's tall, with curly dark waves and black scrubs on. I thank my lucky stars that Megan isn't working this week. She and Isaac are visiting extended family in Florida. Megan is a family medicine doctor, but occasionally picks up a shift in the ER to help. I'm not ready to own up to this yet, to escape from this little bubble of denial, and if Megan were here, I'd have to do just that.

"Hi, Marley," she greets, reaching out to shake my hand.

"I'm Dr. Carmichel. Sounds like you passed out, and are having some severe nausea?"

I nod. "Yeah. I feel better with the meds, but today has been the worst. I thought I had a stomach bug with how gross I felt until last night when I took a pregnancy test."

"I'm glad the meds are helping. Who do you have with you?"

"My—" I start to speak, and yet again, Beau interrupts me.

"Her husband." Beau stands, striding over to shake the doctor's hand. I glower at his back, all while trying to ignore the flurry of emotion that word brings.

Dr. Carmichel nods, shaking Beau's hand. "Nice to meet you. Marley, had you eaten or drank any water before you passed out?"

I shake my head. "No, the paramedic said my blood sugar was super low."

She nods again thoughtfully and scribbles some notes on a clipboard. "Likely what happened is your blood sugar dropped, and you were just so dehydrated that you passed out. I'd like to run some labs, and do an ultrasound and check on baby just to cover all of our bases."

"Yes," Beau interjects. "To all that. I want to make sure everything's okay with them."

"Of course," she says through a laugh, probably used to overbearing fathers-to-be. "I'll get an order in and they'll come get you soon. Shouldn't be too long of a wait."

She takes a few more notes before she leaves me and Beau to ourselves.

"So much for having dinner together and talking," I say with bitterness. "I'm sorry I've made such a mess of things." I don't look at Beau when I speak, afraid of his reaction. He hasn't let go of my hand through it all, but he's been uncharacteristically quiet.

"You have not made a mess of things, Marley. It's important that both of you are healthy." He pushes my hair back, pressing a kiss to my temple. He's been so physically affectionate this evening. I don't know what to do with myself.

My phone buzzes at my thigh, Josie's name lighting up the screen.

> JOSIE
>
> Thomas said you passed out??? Are you
> okay? Do you need me to come over?

"That didn't take long," I say, showing Beau the screen. "I guess we won't be able to keep it a secret for much longer."

"We can keep it a secret as long as you want, Marley."

I type out a quick response.

> ME
>
> All good, just getting over a stomach bug
> and was dehydrated. I'm good now. Beau
> was there, thankfully.

> JOSIE
>
> Beau was with you? Does that mean things
> are better? He never would tell me why he
> was sending you flowers.

> Things are good. Long story. Coffee soon?

> You got it. Seriously though, if you need
> something, call me. I can be to your house
> in five.

> Love you.

> *Heart eye emoji* Love you most.

"I feel bad lying to her," I admit. "She's my best friend. Well, besides you."

"You aren't lying. Trust me. You know that as soon as she knows you're pregnant, she will tell Andrew, and that man cannot keep a secret to save his life. The entire town would know in about an hour."

I chuckle at the truth about his brother. Ever since we were kids, we had to keep him in the dark on a lot of things. It's not like he would purposefully tell the secrets, he would just get so excited that it would spill out. "Good point," I say.

"When we're done here, I figure I'll drop you off at your house, and run home and grab some things," Beau says, subtly changing the subject.

"Why?" I ask. "I'm fine. The doctor even said so."

"I know she did, but I can't help it. I'm going to stay with you for a while."

"Beau, seriously, I'm fine. You don't need to move in with me," I scoff.

"That's an even better idea," he responds, and I can already see the wheels turning in his head.

"I said you *don't* have to move in with me!" I reiterate.

"I know, but why wait? I mean, I'm going to live with you once the baby is born. Might as well start now."

I throw my hands up in exasperation, letting them drop to the bed with a heavy thud. "You're killing me, Beau."

"I'm trying to take care of you. Quite the opposite," he says.

I ignore him, laying back and closing my eyes. Thankfully, he lets me rest for a while, though my brain is doing the opposite of resting. It's running at high speed in a state of panic.

I was exercising plausible deniability until now, but

soon we will see proof I am, in fact, pregnant with Beau's baby. Where will we live? My house certainly isn't big enough for Beau, a baby, and me. Beau's place isn't much bigger than mine, but I can't afford to buy a bigger house. I'm just scraping by as it is. I make a living just fine, but adding in a baby? They're expensive as hell.

My heart beats harder as I think. I'll have to get baby gates, and baby proof the house. Oh, god, will I need one of those toilet locks? They're nearly impossible to get open. I'll probably pee my pants before I open it, and then my kid will think it's normal to pee your pants. That's going to be a pain in the ass.

My mom is probably going to set up camp in my living room, and try to move in, too. That's three adults and a baby in my tiny house. And I'm sure Beau's mom will join in, too. I love them both, but all in my house? I don't think I can do it. I like my space, my alone time. Fuck, will I resent my baby? I won't get any alone time for the next eighteen years. I'm so fucked.

"Marley, breathe," Beau shakes my arm slightly. "Your heart monitor is going wild."

I can vaguely hear the beeping through my state of panic, but I pay it no mind. There are other things to worry about right now.

"It's okay," Beau murmurs, touching me softly, rubbing his hands up and down my arms soothingly. "Breathe, sweetie, breathe."

"I'm so scared," I say, speaking the honest truth.

"I know. I'm scared too," Beau tells me. "We've been scared before, but we've gotten through it together, yeah?"

"Yeah," I say. "We have."

"We can do this. One thing at a time, one day at a time.

I'm here for you, and you're here for me, Marley. We can do anything if we have each other."

"Right," I reply as the door opens.

"Hi there!" A woman's voice calls. "Ready to see your baby?"

I nod, my entire body shaking. I sit up, scooting into the wheelchair she brings over to me. Beau rounds the bed as she lays a warm blanket in my lap, moving the IV bag from one pole to the one connected to the wheelchair. He reaches out, taking my hand in his.

The tech wheels me down a long, white hallway, and then brings us into a dark room. She helps me onto the exam table, moving the IV bag again and adjusting my body so I can see the large screen in front of the bed.

She pulls out a large wand looking thing, sliding what appears to be a condom on it. Beau grimaces, still standing at my feet.

"Psst," I hiss. "Get your ass up here. Remember?"

He rushes up to my head, shuddering as the tech drops a glob of lubricant onto the wand.

"Alright, have you had a trans-vaginal ultrasound before?" the tech asks.

I shake my head.

"This is going to go into your vagina and show us your uterus. It shouldn't hurt, but there will be a lot of pressure, and more than likely discomfort. I'll put it under the blanket and pass it off to you so you can insert it, and then I'll take over. Ready?"

"As I'll ever be," I say.

She chuckles, directing me to lift my legs up as she lifts the blanket just enough so she can slide the wand under. I reach down, taking it from her and inserting it into my vagina. I nod when it's in, and she takes over.

"Alrighty," she mutters to herself, clicking a few buttons on her screen, and displaying the black-and-white picture onto the bigger screen in front of me.

I don't see anything at first, just movement and the whooshing sound of the machine, and then I hear it.

A rapid thumping sound. Our baby's heartbeat. It whooshes, filling the room with its steady, strong beat. "Oh my god," I say, tears filling my eyes as I see a little blob on the screen. Beau leans down, wrapping his arm around my shoulders. He shakes as tears stream down his cheeks, his hand squeezing mine tight.

"There's baby," the tech says sweetly. She adjusts the wand slightly, giving me some of the discomfort she mentioned. The screen moves from our baby till it's just a blur again. "Hmm," she mumbles under her breath.

"What's wrong?" Beau asks, his voice tight and anxious.

"I think..." she pauses. "Yes. I was right." I'd be more worried, but her voice is steady, almost happy. She moves the wand again, pointing at the screen for us. "There's your baby." Letting us take in our little blob again, she holds there, but moves away too soon. I want to yell at her for moving, for not giving me enough time to admire my little bean. "And there's your other baby."

21

MARLEY

Other baby?

"I'm sorry, what now?" I question.

"Baby A." She moves the wand. "Baby B," she says, as if that explains everything. "You're having twins."

"Twins?" I shriek.

Beau's completely still next to me, his eyes wide and focused on the screen where our baby, no, *babies*, are displayed side by side. Two little beans.

Two.

Not one.

Two.

Beau squeezes my hand, and my heart races with each breath I take. "Holy shit, okay. I don't," I stutter. "How? What?"

"Twins can run in families. Do either of you have a set of twins in your immediate or extended family?" The tech is so calm, as if she didn't just change my life even more than it already was.

I shake my head, and Beau does the same. "No, no one

in my family is a twin." I pause as I realize that, in fact, is not true. "Oh my god, my grandma was a twin," I breathe.

"Twins usually skip a generation, so that makes sense." The tech does her thing, moving her wand around, showing us different angles of the babies.

She takes measurements and when she's done, has me head into the bathroom to clean up, letting us know she will be right back to bring us back to our room, and then she's gone.

I use the restroom, cleanup, and watch as Beau paces back and forth in front of the bed. I climb back in, still mindful of the IV pole I've been dragging around. Once I'm comfortable and covered, he speaks.

"Twins run in your family?" Beau asks incredulously, using his free hand to run over his face and beard. He grabs hold of my hand, and we both squeeze tightly, holding onto each other. "You didn't think to mention that?"

I scoff in irritation."Yes, Beau, tell me. When should I have mentioned that twins run in my family? Before, or after, you mauled my face?" I imitate myself. "*Oh, by the way, Beau, if I somehow get pregnant tonight, there's a chance it might be twins since they run in my family.*"

He huffs out a sigh, leaning down to rest his head against my forehead. "I'm sorry, that wasn't kind of me. I'm just... very overwhelmed. Going from one baby to two is a lot."

"Yeah, you're telling me. I'm the one that has to push two babies out of my vagina."

Beau grimaces. "I can't believe there's two." He looks back at the screen where the tech froze a photo of them.

I'm suddenly overwhelmed by it all as I realize one thing. Tears careen down my face. "I forgot to ask for a picture," I cry, lifting my hand that's still entwined with

Beau's to wipe away my tears. "Now I'll never get to see them this little again, Beau. They're going to grow."

"Oh, my love," Beau croons, pressing a gentle kiss to my forehead. "I'll ask for a picture of them. And I took a video with my phone." He points to his phone sitting on the small desk in the corner. "We have it all on video. Their heartbeats, finding out we have two babies, everything."

Now I'm crying for a whole other reason. "You did?"

He nods, lifting my hand to his lips to press a soft kiss to the back of my hand.

"Thank you," I cry.

He leans down as if he's going to kiss me, but there's a knock on the door, interrupting us. Beau steps back, clearing his throat and scratching at the back of his neck.

"Alright, I'll take you back to the room, and then Doc should be in," the tech says, her face light and happy. "How are we doing?" She guides me off of the table and into the wheelchair.

"Overwhelmed," I say with a shaky voice, my mind still unable to process anything else.

"I'm sure," she replies, squeezing my shoulder. She lays another blanket across my lap, moving the IV over, and then pushing me out the door. I want to walk, as I'm feeling a lot better, but I know it's probably some policy that I have to be in the chair, so I don't bother asking. Beau walks next to me, hands in his pockets, face unreadable.

22

———

BEAU

The woman who took the ultrasound helps Marley get in bed back in the ER room, making sure she's comfortable and warm enough. My heart is racketing in my chest, thumping hard and strong with each passing second. Marley lays back onto the pillow, closing her eyes as the tech exits.

I stride over to her, not willing to be apart from her for any longer than necessary. I sit down in the chair next to her, scooting it as close as I can, reaching out to take her hand again. I've always been a physical touch kind of guy, but really only with Marley. Growing up, I'd always hug her as often as I could, or cuddle platonically while watching a movie. I know she said she isn't ready to give me an answer on us, but I'm all in, full steam ahead. I love her, have loved her for a long time, was just too chicken to say it, out of fear of more disapproval from our fathers, or fear of rejection by her. I didn't want to ruin what we had, or lose her, but now I am determined that will never happen. Regardless of the fact that she's pregnant, I will stand by, or take things however slow she needs, for as long as she needs.

Marley's eyes stay closed, but a small furrow in her brow lets me know she's thinking about something.

"What is it?" I ask.

"Nothing," she murmurs.

"Marley," I start.

"No, it's nothing. Just a lot to think about," she says. Her eyes are still closed, but one hand is now laying over her stomach where our babies are. I rest my hand over hers, hoping to give her some sort of silent reassurance.

Dr. Carmichel comes back into the room, a beaming smile on her face. "I heard we are having twins!"

Marley opens her eyes, nodding softly.

"Congratulations," the doctor says. "The on-call OB took a look at your labs and the scans, and everything looks normal with you and the babies, so once we get your discharge paperwork done, you'll be out the door toward home. You already have an OB appointment set up, right?"

"Yeah," Marley replies.

"Great. I'll go get your paperwork started, and I'm also going to write you a prescription of Zofran, which hopefully will help your nausea."

Before she turns to leave, I hold up a hand. "Can we get some hard copies of the ultrasound photos? And do you know what the due date is? They didn't tell us."

"Oh!" she says with glee. Shuffling through her notes, she pulls out the little strip of photos, handing them over to us. "Due date is approximately June 21st, but that will vary with twins. You will probably deliver sooner."

"Thank you," Marley says, her voice thick with emotion, and I can't tell if it's excitement, or some form of sadness..

"I'll be back in shortly," Dr. Carmichel says, turning to leave the room.

I can't help it, I slide into the small hospital bed next to Marley, holding her to my chest. She shudders with silent tears, clutching to my shirt. I know she has to be terrified, and to be honest, I'm a little scared too. I've never been around many babies, but I can learn, right? They say a lot of it is instinct, and I just hope that's true. "I know," I murmur, kissing the top of her head softly. "It's a lot."

She nods into my chest. "How am I going to afford two babies, Beau? How are they going to fit inside my house? I always thought when I got pregnant I'd be in a different house, not living alone in my bachelorette pad."

"Hey," I reply. "You are not alone. This wasn't your plan, but you will never walk alone. I am here with you, and lucky for you, you have a baby daddy who knows his way around the housing market."

She sniffles, chuckling a bit. "I guess."

23

MARLEY

"What are you doing?" I ask when Beau turns right at the stop sign instead of going left toward my house.

"Going to my place," he responds matter of factly.

"Why?"

"Need to grab my clothes and a few things."

"Again, I ask, why?" I pry.

"I told you I would stay with you for a while," he replies.

"And I said you didn't need to. I'm fine, Beau."

"This isn't a conversation, Mar. I'm going to stay with you. You passed out today. What happens if you pass out again, only this time, I'm not there to catch you, and you fall and crack your head open?"

I huff out an irritated sigh. "You can't be with me every waking moment, Beau. I don't need a bodyguard, I need to drink more water. Just because I'm pregnant with your kids doesn't mean you have this sudden obligation to me."

I let myself build the wall, keeping him out from seeing

how I'm truly feeling. "We had sex once, and these are the consequences. You don't have to move in with me to ease some of your guilt, or whatever it is you're feeling."

He can't stay with me. It's already going to be hard enough for me to keep my distance, keep my head on straight when it comes to him. There's no way I can do that if he's staying with me and sleeping in my guest bedroom.

His jaw ticks. "I don't feel an obligation toward you Marley. And this isn't a consequence, this is a change in plans. I'm staying with you. At least temporarily while we figure out a plan for when the babies are born."

My head drops back to the headrest. "Fine," I say, knowing he's just saying that. There's no way he could actually mean it. "I have to put fresh sheets on the guest bed."

Beau doesn't respond, but I see the slight tightening of his jaw as we pull into his driveway. "I'll be back in ten minutes," he says. His mood has shifted in the last thirty seconds, leaving me confused.

I spend every second of the next ten minutes anxious and overthinking to the point that my nausea returns with a vengeance. He feels like he has to stay with me, because I'm pregnant. Not because he wants to. I'm an obligation, no matter how many times he tells me I'm not. He's going to do the right thing, because that's who he is, he's a good person.

The nurse gave me a stack of those blue bags, and I worry I'll have to use one now.

The backseat door opens, and Beau tosses in a large black duffle bag, as well as a pillow. Beau climbs into the vehicle, shifting into gear and backing out of the driveway without a word. The rest of the drive to my house is silent. The street lights illuminate Beau's face every few moments.

I can sense myself slipping, falling into a hole that I'm

quite familiar with, and I have no way to stop it. I try to make myself smaller, to be less of a burden, less of a hassle. I tuck my head down into my chest, letting my hair fan over my face. My hand rests over my stomach, knowing what is inside, and feeling completely lost. Where do I go from here?

We pull into my driveway, and I remember that my car is still at my studio.

"Can you bring me to work in the morning?" I ask, my voice meek, timid.

"Of course," Beau replies. "I don't have to be in office until ten, so whenever you want to head in, let me know."

I nod, opening the car door and sliding out. I'm exhausted, both physically and mentally. This day has been filled with so many highs and lows that I feel like I've been put through the wringer. The exhaustion of the day, then passing out, waking up to Beau's scared face, the insecurity of thinking he was flirting with someone in front of me... Finding out that I'm carrying twins... I just want to shut my eyes and wake up from this insane dream.

Beau follows me inside, kicking off his shoes and striding through my small kitchen.

"Hold on," I say, stopping him as he walks down the hall toward the guest bedroom. "I need to change the sheets, remember?"

"I can do it myself, Mar," he replies, not letting me stop him.

"God, you're irritating," I grumble, following him into the room. I grab the sheets from the closet, tossing them on the top of the dresser. Beau sets his duffle down, and starts pulling the quilt down. I pull the other side down, following his steps.

With the bed stripped down to the mattress pad, I throw the fitted sheet on the bed. Beau and I work together to get the bed made, and with every movement, I grow even more tired. The bed is finished, and I can barely keep my eyes open.

"Marley," Beau says, rounding the foot of the bed to reach out and grab my arm. "You okay?"

"Tired," I reply. I can't offer him more right now, because to be honest, I don't know if I'm okay. I don't want him to try and pry my feelings out of me, something he's always been good at, because the way I'm feeling right now is something totally new.

"Okay, let's get you to bed." He slides his arm around my waist, guiding me out of the guest bedroom.

He follows me into the room, and I ignore him, grabbing my things and heading to the bathroom to change and wash my face. When I finish, Beau is sitting on the edge of my bed, picking at a loose string on his jeans.

"How are you feeling?" He glances up at me, his eyes insightful. His forehead is wrinkled in deep thought.

"Alright. Currently not sure if the churning in my gut is anxiety or the need to vomit." I sit down next to him, noticing that he pulled back my blankets for me. Not that I made my bed this morning, but still, it's the thought that counts. It just goes to show how good he is, how perfect he would be for someone. Even though he's doing it for me right now, I don't know how long it will last.

Beau chuckles softly. "I guess I'll let you get some sleep." He pats my knee awkwardly and stands. "I'll be right across the hall, just... please promise you'll yell if you need something?"

I nod in agreement. "Yeah. I will, promise."

He holds out his pinky finger. "I'm holding you to it,

Marley Bell." He winks slyly. "Might have to bet some Superman ice cream to make sure you do it."

"Or," I tease, "You could just buy me the ice cream anyway, because I'm your best friend."

"You got it, Mar." He walks to the door, giving me one final glance before pulling the door shut behind him.

24

———

BEAU

A knock on my office door startles me out of my Google search. I quickly minimize the screen showing home remedies for morning sickness. In the week since the ER visit, Marley has continually gotten sick, and not only in the morning. Apparently morning sickness doesn't just mean she'll only be sick in the morning. Sometimes, it's an all day thing. Her first official appointment is tomorrow morning in Cinder Valley, and I'm looking forward to joining her. I've made a list of all the things I've noticed about her pregnancy so far, and I plan to ask if there are things we can do to ease her discomfort.

My gaze lifts from the screen after I lock it, and in front of me stands Josie, my new sister-in-law. "Hey," she says. Her red hair is pulled up in a ponytail, and she's wearing a pair of black leggings with a Cunningham Bespoke Woodcraft shirt on top. "I dropped off a bouquet next door, and figured I'd stop by, say hi!" Her voice is cheery, much like her personality.

Josie's an incredible person, and I truly couldn't imagine someone better for my little brother. I stand from my chair,

128

rounding the desk to give her a quick hug. "How's the day going? Busy?" I ask.

"Yep," she says, dropping down into the chair I have for clients. "But it's a good kind of busy. Not too stressful."

"Good."

"How's Marley?" Josie asks, arching an eyebrow. "She's been so busy this week, too, I haven't even seen her since she passed out. Lucky you were there."

"Hmm," I mutter noncommittally. "Yeah. She's good though, I've seen her a few times since." I'm not about to tell her that I've pretty much moved in with her, cause not only is she pregnant with my child, but she's pregnant with my *children*.

One thing about Josie, though, is she's extremely perceptive. I know she knows something is up. Especially since she's watched Marley and me interact for the last year and a half. She's seen the tension and mutual fighting of feelings between us. For things to suddenly be so chill, she has to know something is up. I also suspect she didn't have a delivery next door. Andrew probably put her up to this.

I'm pretty sure he's been conspiring to get Marley and I together for years. It feels good to know that I don't have to fight things between us anymore, even if I do have to take things at her pace. I don't have the pain of not knowing if she will ever be mine anymore.

"How are things between you two? You stopped begging me to send her flowers..." Josie trails off in a slightly sing-song voice.

I clear my throat, running my hands through my hair. "Things are fine."

"Just fine?"

"Just fine," I say. I will not crack, I will not tell her. "We're working things out."

Josie's eyes light up. "Working things out... as in.... *working things out?*"

"You just said the same sentence twice." I point out. "How am I supposed to know what that means?"

"Oh shush," she replies. "You know what I mean."

"Not really," I reply. I'm totally playing dumb right now, but I can't break. "We're fine, same as always."

Josie groans. "Ugh, you're like a freaking brick wall. All three of your brothers fold within a second of interrogation from me, but I don't think I'll ever get you to crack."

"Does that mean you'll stop trying?" I ask hopefully. I don't care that she likes to interrogate me, I think it's funny. I just can't tell Marley's secret right now, and especially not to her best friend. Well, her best friend besides me.

"Never," she states.

I chuckle. "As fun as this has been, I need to get going. I have a showing in thirty minutes."

She huffs a sigh, standing from the chair she was in. "Fine, but this conversation isn't over, Beau Joshua Cunningham."

"That's not my middle name," I reply as we walk toward the glass doors of the realtors office.

"Yeah, it didn't sound right even as I was saying it."

I walk her over to where her car is, and give her a quick hug. She murmurs something into my chest that has my heart squeezing. I've never had a sister before, but having Josie in our lives has been amazing. "Are you really okay? You'd tell someone if you weren't, right? Or if Marley wasn't?"

Her strong confident voice from before is gone, insecurity in its wake. The knowledge that I'm lying to her, that I have to keep this secret from her hits me hard. This is Josie's best friend, and my sister-in-law. I know she means well, but

I can't think of a way to let her in on this without betraying Marley's trust in me.

I squeeze her tightly. "Promise. I'm good, Josie. Really."

She nods, and we say our goodbyes.

"STOP BOUNCING YOUR LEG," I say, reaching over and pushing down on the top of Marley's thigh. She's sitting on the exam table, dressed in one of those scratchy hospital gowns. She looks like she's ready to hurl, but from nervousness, rather than morning sickness. Her chestnut brown hair is curled in waves, but pulled into a half ponytail with a clip.

She glares at my hand. "I can't help it."

"I know, but you're going to shake all the sterile tools off the table." I point to the small rolling table with various items on it. It rattles with the bounce of her leg.

A knock on the door stops her suddenly. In walks the nurse who roomed us, a young woman with short blonde hair and plum colored scrubs on, as well as Dr. Ness. Dr. Ness is a middle aged woman who exudes confidence, but not to the point where it's obnoxious. She just knows what she's doing. "Hello hello," she greets, a broad smile on her face. "It's so nice to meet you!" She shakes my hand, then Marley's. Marley smiles, her face relaxing immediately.

They get the basic introductions out of the way, and then it's time for business.

"I got your notes from the ER and the ultrasound imaging. Both babies look great. What kind of symptoms are you having, Marley?" Dr. Ness asks.

"Um, just like overall tired, nausea," Marley says. I wait

for her to continue, tell her how she throws up pretty much non-stop, but she doesn't. I narrow my eyes at her, and she waves me off.

"And you went to the ER because you passed out?" she asks, writing on her yellow notepad.

"Yeah. I couldn't keep anything down and I must have gotten dehydrated," Marley explains.

Dr. Ness nods. She goes over the basic dos and don'ts of pregnancy, followed by an exam, and a pap smear. I do as requested and stand at Marley's head for that part.

At the end, Dr. Ness does a breast exam. Marley widens her eyes, and I take the hint, turning around, facing the corner while she has her gown open.

Dr. Ness fills the silence with small talk, and I tune it out, until she asks, "Do you have any concerns about the piercings, or any other questions?"

Marley coughs. "Um, I guess I'd forgotten about them. Do I have to take them out?"

"Up to you. If you plan to breastfeed, we suggest taking them out sooner rather than later, but otherwise, it all depends on what you're comfortable with. Some women experience a lot of sensitivity and discomfort in their nipples through their pregnancy."

Fuck me, I never thought about the sensitivity of Marley's nipples, but now, it's all I can think about. If they were sensitive that night, I can only imagine what they might be like now. I will my hardening cock to knock it off, because there is *nothing* about this moment that is sexual. Except for the fact that I've totally zoned out their conversation, and I can't stop thinking about the way Marley moaned when I sucked on the piercings.

"Beau?" Marley's voice pulls me out of my daydream. "You can turn around."

I whip around, eyeing her up and down quickly. The constant urge to make sure she's okay hasn't lessened, especially not since the ER visit. I'm constantly checking up on her, to the point where I've peeked through her open bedroom door more than once when she's sleeping, just to make sure she's breathing. I've sat outside the bathroom while she's sick, there in case she needs help. I need to know that she's okay. It's probably not healthy, this anxiety, but I don't see it going anywhere for a while.

"Everything okay?" I ask, raising my brow.

"Yeah," she murmurs, her cheeks flushing pink as if she's embarrassed. I step over to her, holding out my hand. She takes it, and I notice how clammy her hands are. I look down, catching her eye. She nods again, soothing some of my momentary anxiety.

Dr. Ness gives us a few pamphlets with pregnancy resources, as well as another prescription for the anti-nausea medication. "Any other questions?" she asks. "Oh, I forgot to give you my briefing on sex."

I gulp, my throat suddenly feeling tight. My cheeks burn slightly.

Marley shakes her head maniacally. "No, we don't need that," she says hurriedly.

Dr. Ness apologizes. "I assumed you two were together, things seem so natural between you."

"Yeah." Marley chuckles awkwardly, dropping my hand like it's burned her. "Long story. He's my best friend. Drunken wedding, you know." She fans at her flaming cheeks. "Now he's stuck with me forever."

I want to clamp my hand over her mouth to make her shut up. I get so frustrated when she says these belittling things toward herself, toward the change in our relationship. I'm not about to duke it out with her in the exam room though, so I settle for taking her hand back, squeezing it three times.

"Best friends since we were kids, just took us a long time to get our shit together," I say with intent. How long will it take to get it through her thick head that I'm in this, that I want her for more than just my best friend or the mother of my babies?

The nurse in the corner smiles sweetly. "You two are adorable. Couple or not, you're going to be amazing parents."

Marley's eyes turn glassy. "Thanks," she murmurs.

Dr. Ness strides over, patting Marley's thigh. "We will leave you to get dressed, and then we will see you in four weeks, sound like a plan?"

Marley looks down at where our hands are tangled. "Yep."

Dr. Ness walks by us, patting me on the shoulder. The nurse, Peyton P., who's name tag I'm just now seeing, smiles again, getting a pump of hand sanitizer from the machine by the door.

When the door latches behind us, Marley slides off the exam table, dropping my hand, and using her other hand to hold the blanket around her body. "Could you?" She makes a spinning motion with her head.

I dramatically sigh. "I suppose," I tease.

"Thank you," she mutters. I can hear her shuffling around behind me, grabbing her clothes and undergarments. In record time, she's dressed, and we're heading down the hall to make her next appointment.

MARLEY

I can't rid myself of the awkward tension in my body as Beau pulls into my driveway. It wasn't Dr. Ness's fault, she was just doing her job, but as soon as she brought up sex, I felt like I was a teenager in health class getting sex-ed. Obviously, she knows we had sex, otherwise I wouldn't be pregnant with his kids. Though, I suppose there are plenty of other ways to get pregnant, but still. *She knew.*

"I think I'm going to lay down," I tell Beau. Who knows, maybe I can sleep away the awkward.

"Sounds good, need anything?" he asks, grabbing an electrolyte drink from the fridge.

"No," I say. Beau has the most beautiful hands, and in those hands, is the blue electrolyte drink, which suddenly I would kill to have.

Beau watches as my gaze slides down from his face to his drink, and I can tell I've been caught. "You sure?"

"Positive," I say, spinning on my heel and heading to the bathroom. I don't need a stupid drink, just because Beau was holding it. Only, my mouth starts to water, and I swear, I'll die if I don't have that stupid drink right fucking now. I use the bathroom, cursing myself when all I can think of is the drink. I even brush my teeth, doing anything to get the mouthwatering taste out of my mind.

I climb into my bed, covering myself with my blanket, and start scrolling through social media. I can do this. There is no reason why I need to go out there, and make a fool of myself over a drink.

A soft knock on my door startles me. "Yeah?" I call.

I sit up in my bed, and watch as Beau strides in, bottle in hand. "I know you said you didn't want this, but I think maybe it's a good idea to drink it. I mean, Dr. Ness did say that you need to stay hydrated."

I let out a strangled sob, because she did say that. "I don't know why I'm crying," I say, tears streaming down my face. Beau cracks open the drink, handing it to me and sitting down on the bed. I take a long gulp of the drink, sighing in relief as the flavor permeates my taste buds. When I've downed nearly half of it, I pause to breathe. "Thank you."

"No problem. I could tell you really wanted it."

"I really did," I blubber. I wipe at my tear stained face.

"Hold on," Beau says, reaching out to my face. "Your nose piercing is crooked." With gentle fingers, he fixes the hoop in my nose, and dries my tears with a swipe of his thumb. "There, that's better."

He leans in slowly, his brown eyes melting into something sweeter, something darker. He's kissed me more than once in the last few days, but each time, I write it off as something he feels compelled to do, because of the heat of the moment, not because he wants to. But right now, Beau looks like he really wants to kiss me. It's the same look he had the night of the rehearsal dinner. My head spins, seeing that look in his eyes. I blame the pregnancy for the fact that

I want to bury myself in his skin. There has to be some sort of biological reason for that, for why I find him so attractive right now, more than ever before. Or maybe it's the way he's been so sweet and so forthcoming with me.

He leans in, darting his tongue out to lick his lips, and just like that night, I'm the one to break the spell. I've already given into the natural touches and seemingly unconscious movements that draw me to him, but now, I need to be the one to stop this, to maintain the distance, despite how much I wish I didn't have to. "We can't," I murmur. "I... I can't. I'm not there."

Beau leans back, nodding. "Yeah. Okay."

"I'm sorry," I say, guilt eating at my heart. Inside, I'm screaming, *"please, hold me, I need you."*

"Hey, you have nothing to be sorry about," Beau says, resting his hand on my thigh. "Get some rest." He stands from my bed, giving me a gentle smile as he leaves my room, shutting the door behind him.

God, I wish I could call Josie right now and tell her everything, but I'm not ready. I'm scared, not of her judgment, but scared that telling everyone outside of Beau and myself makes it even more real than it already is.

Tears leak out my eyes now for a totally different reason. Fighting this is going to be the hardest thing, but I have to do what is right for my babies, and that is staying strong, and not falling into the pile of lust I feel for my best friend.

26

BEAU

"Happy Thanksgiving, Ma," I say, squeezing my mother tightly with one arm.

"Oh, Happy Thanksgiving, honey," Mom replies. She takes the small platter from my hands, setting it down on the counter behind us. "How are you?"

"I'm good." I run my hand through my hair, hoping she doesn't see the shell of anxiety that I am. I'm not lying, I am good, but I'm anxious that I'll let it slip that Marley is pregnant. In the last three weeks since her appointment, things have been tense. Not as tense as they were before Josie and Andrew's wedding, but still, tense.

I know I pushed her too hard that day when I leaned in to kiss her. I couldn't help it. There's been this constant pull toward her, and it's only grown stronger now. Between the proximity, and the knowledge that she's pregnant with our children, it's been torture trying to keep my hands off her.

"Where's Marley?" Mom asks, unwrapping the plate of deviled eggs I brought. Marley made them, then promptly threw up from the smell. She opted to stay behind and shower again. She said it would be better for us to arrive separately, as it's less suspicious. I'd scoffed, and the death glare she'd given me shut me up immediately.

"Not sure," I lie. "I talked with her earlier, and she said she'd be here."

Jason arrives just then, saving me from further interrogation. Lennie runs through the living room into the kitchen and straight into my mom's arms. The two of them have such a special bond. The realization and hope that soon enough my kids will be running to her for hugs and kisses is like a sucker punch to the gut. I can't wait for that day.

My mom watches Lennie nearly every day, saving Jason from the costs of daycare until Lennie goes to school. He's been a single dad now ever since Lennie was just about one. His ex, Talia, was addicted to drugs, and shortly after Lennie was born, she picked up the habit again. She left just before Lennie's first birthday. He hasn't seen, or heard from her, since. He says it's for the best, but I know he wishes that Lennie could know her mom.

"Hey, man," Jason says, giving me a quick one-handed hug.

"Hey," I greet. Thomas follows close behind, with Gramps in tow. Gramps tosses his cane to the side as soon as he's in the door, making Thomas groan.

"Gramps, the whole purpose of this thing is to *use it*," he says.

Gramps waves him off. "It gets in my way." He looks spiffy in his dress pants, button down shirt, and wool sweater.

Thomas grunts, picking up the cane from where it was discarded. Gramps makes his way to the couch, joining my dad in watching the football game. I don't have time to greet him or Thomas, because Josie and Andrew are walking in, followed closely by Marley.

Josie has Marley pulled into a side hug, giggling as she whispers something in her ear. Marley's cheeks are flushed and she looks so happy. It would sound cliché to say she's glowing, but she really is. I can't help but react to it, I smile as I watch her, not caring who might see me staring.

She's in different clothes than when I left, now in a gorgeous moss-green sweater dress. It hugs her soft curves, and when she turns to the side, I swear, I can see the tiniest hint of a baby bump. I have the strongest urge to run to her side, hold her close, and rest my hand over her stomach, protecting her, protecting *them*, but I tamp it down.

She says hello to everyone, then comes to stand by my side. I'm under very strict instructions not to give anything away, which unfortunately includes touching her in non-platonic ways. To be honest, I think it's stupid. I've always touched her and hugged her, but now I have to stop?

Oh well. I'll do anything for her.

Her parents arrive, and shortly after, we all sit down to eat. The food is passed, plates are filled, and things are perfect. It's weird to think that next Thanksgiving, we will have two more to add into the family.

I reach over, squeezing Marley's thigh softly. I offer her a smile, thankful I get to share this with her. Instead of the happy face I expect to see, she looks miserable, and if I'm right, she's about thirty seconds away from puking.

Shit.

27

MARLEY

Hold it in. *Hold. It. In.* I swallow down another gag, pretending to take a bite of my sweet potatoes. I've been looking forward to Nikki's sweet potatoes all week, and the second Beau scoops a heaping pile onto my plate, I'm ready to upchuck all over the table.

Beau squeezes my thigh, and when he looks down at me, he has the sweetest look on his face, and I can almost read into it, read into his emotions, except I can't react, because I'm bolting up from my chair, muttering *"excuse me"* as I run through the dining room down the hall to the bathroom to puke.

I hear footsteps following me, but I slam the bathroom door shut behind me, needing the moment alone.

"Marley." Beau's voice is strained, worry etched into his tone.

"I'm fine," I bite out between gags.

A few minutes later, I finish. I didn't even puke. Just gagged and heaved up nothing. I wash my hands, and make sure I didn't ruin my makeup.

I open the door, and Beau is there, leaning against the

wall on the opposite side of the hall. His arms are crossed across his chest, giving me a glimpse of his forearms. He must've rolled up the sleeves to his sweater, because my eyes immediately dart to the extra bit of skin. His right arm is covered in tattoos, some of them similar to mine, but every single one is something we discussed together. The forest scene wrapped around his wrist is one of my favorites of his. We came up with the idea together.

Most of our tattoos don't even have meaning, except for our "Dead Sea" tattoo, and my butterfly tattoo. Though, Beau doesn't know the meaning of that one.

"We might be outed," he says cautiously.

A sinking feeling hits my chest. I'm not ready, not yet. I don't know how they'll react, and some part of me fears my parents will be disappointed in me. I'm unmarried, not even in a relationship, and I'm pregnant. With my best friend's babies nonetheless. "Can't we just say I have the stomach flu?"

Beau looks unconvinced. "We can try, but pretty sure everyone has some sort of idea, and if not, they have questions. I can hear Gramps speculating."

I drop my head into my hands. "I don't think I'm ready yet."

Beau wraps his arms around my shoulders, pulling me into his chest. "I know. I know you aren't, but we have such an amazing support system. They are going to be so happy for us," he says.

I feel the tears instantly. "I just had this really cute idea of how I was going to tell everyone," I blubber into his chest. "I was going to tell them at Christmas, with the ultrasound picture. I was going to photoshop little Santa hats on the babies, and it was going to be so cute." I can't stop the words tumbling out of my mouth. "Now they are going to find out because I can't even look at food without hurling."

"Shh," Beau soothes, running his hand up and down my back. "We don't have to tell them. We can do the Santa hats. It will be perfect."

"No, it won't," I sob. "They already know, so how will it be perfect?" I know I'm being irrational and that I'm quite literally the definition of a hormonal pregnant woman, and yet, I can't stop. My emotions are all over the place.

I've worked so hard on my mental health the last ten years, and one night with my best friend has all my emotions in a tizzy. It's frustrating.

Beau leans back, moving his hand to tilt my chin up so I'm looking into those deep, all seeing eyes. "If you don't want to tell them, we won't, Marley. They will respect our boundaries."

"Maybe," I sniffle. "Maybe we just play it off. Say I have a stomach bug. If anyone questions it, or says different, we can just tell them. Yeah?" I ask, not really sure if this will work, but figuring it can't hurt to try. I know I have no real reason to lie, to not tell them this life changing news, but god, I'm just so scared. Scared of disappointment, judgment, all of it.

What if it causes a rift between our parents? What if they think we aren't good for each other, or won't be good parents? It's better if we get them excited about something first, I mean, who doesn't love a good Christmas surprise, right? That has to be better than finding out your daughter is pregnant from her nearly upchucking all over the Thanksgiving dinner table.

"We can," Beau agrees. "I'll do whatever you need, butterfly." He wipes my face, careful not to smudge I'm sure what is already destroyed makeup. With a shaky breath, I release myself from his hold, and turn to head down the long hallway. Beau walks by my side, a hand resting on the small of my back.

The room is deathly silent when we enter, everyone staring at us expectantly. Josie catches my gaze, a silent question in her eyes. I give her a reassuring smile that I'm sure looks more like a grimace and hope she doesn't see right through me. But Josie's too perceptive for her own good. Luckily though, she won't bring up her conclusions, at least not in front of everyone. My gaze travels to every face in the room, taking in their looks of concern, question, and confusion.

The only one not looking at me, at *us*, is Lennie. Though to be fair, she's four, so she probably only cares about the mashed potatoes and scalloped corn on her plate. I stop when I reach my mother's face, her eyes shuttered with a concern that only a mother could bear. Looking away, I catch Gramps' eye. He has a knowing gleam there, a sense of mischief bordering on humor in the wrinkles on his face. He's just about to say something, I know it. Something that will surely be damning, and make me say the truth that everyone already knows.

And that is when I crack.

"I'm pregnant," I blurt, and all hell breaks loose.

MARLEY

Beau whips his eyes to mine, wide with shock.

"You're pregnant?" About seven voices shriek, laughter and screams of joy bursting through the room. Beau is shoved aside as arms wrap around my shoulders, bundling me in tight hugs. I don't even know who's hugging me, but based on the perfume, I can tell my mom is somewhere in there.

Pulling away from the hug, I'm met with the watery eyes of both my mom, and the woman who has always been my bonus mom, Nikki. "Yeah," I murmur through tears. " About eleven weeks."

"Oh, sweetie!" Mom cries, her joy sending waves of happiness straight through my heart. I haven't really given myself space to feel happy about the pregnancy yet, too afraid of others' reactions, too afraid to *feel* at all. "When did you find out? How? Who?" Her eyes flick back and forth across my face, as if I'll be able to reveal all the answers within a second.

Josie's next, but she's not questioning, because she

knows. "Oh my god," she says, her voice high, and full of realization.

"Yeah," I reply. I step backwards, giving Beau a moment to step closer to me again.

"We're having twins," Beau says, and another round of shrieks fill the room. I can't help but laugh, the pure joy of my loved ones something I never expected.

"It's about time," Gramps calls from across the table, scooping another bite of potatoes into his mouth. "Congratulations kiddos, I always knew you'd end up together."

"Oh," I start to correct him but Beau pinches my side. "Ow!" I swat at his arm.

"Don't," he threatens, not really menacingly, but I can tell he doesn't want to open that can of worms right now.

The questions continue, but Beau leads me over to our seats at the table. I eye my plate carefully, my stomach still uneasy. An almost awkward silence descends on the table, and I can tell everyone has about a million questions they want to ask us.

Beau, thankfully, is the one to speak first. "We are taking things slow, focusing on keeping Marley and the babies healthy right now. She's due June 21st, but the doctor says it will more than likely be earlier."

My mother clasps her hand over her mouth, emotion raw on her face. My dad hasn't said a word, but the wide, giddy smile on his face is enough to know how he's feeling. I look around the room at these people, my family, and I simply can't wait for our babies to be a part of this.

"SO…" Josie slyly pulls me aside after dinner, hiding us away in one of the guest bedrooms. "No wonder you've been acting so weird lately."

I shrug. "Things have been… interesting, to say the least." Almost unconsciously, I rest my hand on my still flat stomach. Josie's eyes track the movement, the soft smile on her face growing wider.

"How did it happen?" she asks, sitting down on the full size bed in the room. She pats the empty spot next to her and I sit, resting my head on her shoulder as she wraps me in her embrace.

"Well, Josie, when a man and a woman…" I trail off, teasing her.

"You little shit," she says, flicking my forehead.

"Hey! That hurt!" I cry.

"I'm sitting on pins and needles over here, Mar."

"Fine," I grumble, not all that upset. "It happened the night of your wedding. We danced together, and things escalated."

"I need more details, girl. I've been waiting for this for you two to get together for over a year now, and when it finally happens, you don't even tell me!"

I wince, feeling guilty. "I'm sorry. I just… I'm so scared," I mumble, turning my face into her chest as she hugs me tighter.

"Marley," Josie says, rubbing my back. "I'm sorry, I'm just teasing you. I mean, it's *Beau*. You two are meant for each other."

"And that's exactly why I can't let myself go too far with him," I say, letting myself sink into her. "One of us needs to stay level-headed. The stakes are higher than what they would be if it were just him and I, but now I… *we* have two babies to worry about. I'm trying to focus on being the best mom for our kids, and right now, that means co-parenting with him instead of dating him."

Josie squeezes me softly. "I get it, and I will only say this once. You and Beau have a history. You know each other. Regardless of the fact that you're pregnant, that man is in one hundred percent. He is ready to start a life with you, and I think if you give in to your heart, you would never regret it."

My mind strays as I sink into my best friend's embrace, letting her words comfort me. I know that what she's saying is more than likely true, and yet, I can't let myself do it. I can't put my guard down. Not now, and maybe not ever. Not after how he's saved me. And I know I have to tell her why.

The memory floods me before I have a chance to stop it.

My professor hates me. I know he does, and yet, he doesn't seem to care that I'm willing to put in the work, willing to do anything to be better.

Maybe things would be better if I just... quit. It's not like I need a degree to be a photographer. I have the talent, Professor Johnson has told me that more than once. The business end of it though... I'm struggling. My classmate and friend, Kylie, is convinced that Professor Lee has it out for me. We even tested a theory and gave the same answers, just different wordings, for our most recent written assignment. I got a D+, while Kylie got a B-.

I know that I'm not great at explaining things in writing, but still. I know my work wasn't that bad. Which brings me to my dilemma. Do I quit? Give up on it all? School, new friends, everything?

My chest sinks. I'm a failure. I've always been the failure of the family. Kenny and Prescott went on to do amazing things. My brothers never wanted anything to do with me, so it makes sense. I can't even keep my weight down, steadily gaining constantly. I'm probably known around our small town as the fat member of the Bell family. The only true person, only one I trust with my whole being in my life is Beau, and he's... drifting.

My traitorous brain tries to tell me he's just friends with me out of obligation now. He's made new friends at his university. Our conversations are shorter, more... awkward. I know I couldn't have him forever, but stupidly, I thought I would.

Rubbing my finger over the tattoo we share, I lose the grip I had on my sense of reality. I can't do this anymore. I can't be the failure everyone knows that I am. My fingernails dig into my skin, hard enough that they surely are breaking skin, but I don't feel it. I'm going numb, blank. Empty.

My roommate, who also hates me, is out of town for the weekend, leaving me completely alone. I could just... disappear, and no one would know. At least not for a few days. My hands shake, the pain of my fingernails breaking skin slowly creeping to the surface. I drop my hands, gripping the blanket underneath me instead. I need to feel. *I need something to pull me out of this.*

My cellphone is on my nightstand, taunting me. Do I call someone? Call my mom and tell her it's happening again? That this time I really need help?

This has happened before, but never this bad, and I've always been able to pull out of it. Beau has always been my constant, the person who can tell when I'm drowning on dry land. The one to know what I need before I need it.

It's like he knows I need him. Because even though my brain is telling me that he hates me, that he is sick of me, my phone vibrates on the rickety wooden night stand, his name on my screen. Gasping, my body suddenly feeling everything,

I burst into painful, soul burning sobs. I can't catch my breath. Can't focus on reaching out to grab the phone.

The vibrations stop for only a moment, before picking right back up as he calls again. With shaky hands, I reach out, sliding a finger across the screen to answer the call. I tap the button to turn on speaker.

"Hey, butterfly," Beau's voice fills my small room, and I choke out another sob, my tongue unable to form words right now. "Marley?" his voice is gruff, and I hear movement, the jangle of keys, and a door opening and closing.

"Beau," I cry. "I need you."

"I'm coming, Mar. Stay with me. I've got you."

I sob, his voice grounding me more than I ever knew it could. He talks to me the entire forty-minute drive from his campus to mine, telling me stories about something stupid his brothers did as a prank. How Andrew is graduating next spring, and he's probably going to take over the family wood-craft business. I listen, letting his voice keep me present, keep me here. I already knew everything he's telling me, but it doesn't matter. He doesn't even realize it, but he's saving me. Saving me from myself, from the harm that I was so willing to impart upon myself.

The minutes fly by as I listen to him talk, then the sudden silence of his car turning off, the pounding of his footsteps up to my second-floor dorm room. "I'm here. You gotta let me in, Mar."

I fly off my bed, leaving my phone on the nightstand. Opening the door, I see the person—my person—in front of me. His brown hair is a mess, eyes terrified and blood shot. He's in a pair of ratty pajama pants, ones he's had since we were sophomores in high school, and a University of Minnesota tee.

His arms wrap around me in a second, and I collapse

into his embrace, letting myself go fully. The feeling of safety in his arms is so unexpected, and so needed that I don't feel anymore. I just... am. I'm with him, and I'm safe with him. He lifts me, my legs wrapping around his waist, arms around his shoulders as my head rests in the crook of his neck. His fingers grip my thighs tightly, like he's afraid to let me go. Tears soak his skin, and he whispers soothing reassurances to me. He's been to my dorm before, so he knows which side is mine. He sits down on my bed. My legs move from around his waist so I'm now straddling him, my knees against the firm mattress.

"What happened?" he asks, but I shake my head. I can't, I can't tell him yet, can't tell him how much of a failure I am, how I always will be.

"Okay," he murmurs into my hair. "I'm here, I've got you. I'll pull you out."

I sob harder at his reminder. The reminder of our tattoo. He will always be there to save me, I will never sink when I'm with him. He adjusts so we're lying side-by-side. I'm settling now, crying into his chest with less emotion, because he's here. He knew what I needed before I did. Yet again.

With stuttered gasps, I tell him what happened. How I let myself sink. I didn't even give myself a chance. He gives me time to cry, to feel, and when I finally tire, I allow myself to fall asleep in his arms.

I'll never forget the next morning. Beau woke me, and together, we called my parents. He stood by my side while I told them I was ready to give up, and that I needed help. I upped meds and therapy the next week. I will never be able to repay him for that, and that's why I can't lose him. I've already changed our relationship so much that if I make one misstep, I'm sure he will run out the door.

Josie lets out a stuttered breath as I finish telling her

exactly why I'm so hesitant to move forward with him. "I can't risk it, Josie," I say, my own tears freely falling down my face. "I love him, I know I do, but he can't always be there for me. He won't always be there for me. That's why I need to make sure I can do this on my own, no matter how hard it is. I can't lose myself to my own mind anymore. Not if I don't have him to fall into."

"Oh, Marley," she croons. "That boy is always going to love you. I know it's hard for you to look past, but he's never going to let you go. I think you both need to give up on this notion that you aren't good for each other or that you would lose him if something went wrong, and just... fall headfirst into it. "

I nod into her chest. I need to try, for him. For us. I just don't know how.

29

BEAU

"Are the sellers motivated?" my client asks. She's a young woman with a toddler clinging to her leg and a large pregnant belly. Her husband glances around the room with a look of disdain, even though this house is everything they are looking for.

"Very." I gesture for them to follow, leading them down the hallway toward the bedrooms, giving lots of information on all the updates the sellers have done. "It's all within your budget, and has plenty of room for a family," I say with a gentle smile. The toddler stares up at me with wide green eyes, his bright blonde hair matching his mothers. "What do you think, buddy?" I ask him.

He doesn't reply, just burrows into his mother's leg. I chuckle, fully expecting that response. I haven't been around many kids in my life, only Lennie. I'm sure having two at once will be a rude awakening, but fuck, am I excited. I get a little giddy anytime I see a parent pushing a stroller down the street, because soon, that will be Marley and me.

She's officially in the second trimester now, and I've

been living with her for over a month. She tried to put up a bit of a fight about it, worried about the fact that my house is empty across town, but she's gotten used to it now and isn't complaining much. I think she secretly likes having me around. She's still nauseous, but not nearly as bad as the first few weeks. She's keeping food down now and has a bit more energy. I was getting worried when she was sleeping so much, but when I brought it up at her last appointment, Dr. Ness said I had nothing to worry about.

I still worry, though, not because of the sleep, but every-thing in general. I can tell she's getting sick of me hovering around her, but I can't seem to help it. I have this urge to be at her side as much as possible. Hell, if I thought I could get away with it without seeming like an utter creep, I'd sleep on the floor in her room just to watch her sleep and make sure she's okay.

My phone vibrates in my pocket, and I discreetly pull it out while the couple converses about the house.

MARLEY

Hey.

ME

Hey. What's up?

A giddy excitement bubbles in my chest while I wait for her response. Seeing her name on my screen has always given me a burst of excitement. On a second thought, I ask how she's feeling.

ME

How are you feeling today?

MARLEY

Good! Finished up a few sessions and
Andrew stopped by.

Ah. What did he have to say?

My favorite band is going to be at Blue Ox
tonight. Can we go?

You don't have to ask permission to go,
Marley.

I know that. I wasn't asking permission,
weirdo. I was inviting you.

Can't say I'm mad about that. Does this mean we're making progress toward her letting me back in?

ME

Oh. Yeah, I'll come. No showings after this
last one, so I can swing by and pick you up
from the studio if you want.

MARLEY

Nah, I can drive.

Would make more sense to have just one
car, though.

Fine. But I am capable of driving myself.

Never said you weren't. What can I say? I
want to spend time with you.

Oh okay. Text me when you're on your way.

I pocket my phone, checking the time as I do.

The couple is still looking intently around the kitchen, the toddler giving me side-eyed glares.

"How are we feeling?" I ask. This house is literally

everything they've been looking for, so I'm curious to see if they'll make an offer.

"I love it," the woman replies, her eyes full of light and ideas.

"Do you have any questions for me?" I ask, starting my process of finishing up the showing.

The woman asks a few more questions, clearly invested in this process. I answer them and then, thankfully, a few minutes later we are saying goodbye at our vehicles. They leave before me, but I sit in my car and stare at the house.

It's cute, a two-story house with four bedrooms and two baths. Tucked away in the woods, it has more privacy than what can be found in town. It has plenty of room for kids to play and grow up. An idea starts to form in my head, though I know Marley will never go for it.

I type out a few needs and wants in a note on my phone, and then I'm heading off to pick Marley up.

30

MARLEY

The brewery is crowded, but I wouldn't expect anything less. One of the local bands is playing tonight and they always bring out a crowd. I spot Josie at a corner table with Andrew. He's leaning down, whispering something in her ear, and she blushes hot red, shoving his chest to push him away.

They're so freaking cute, it makes me sick. But in a good way. Not like the nausea that I've been dealing with the last month.

Josie spots me, immediately standing and pulling me into a hug. "Oh my god, you totally popped this week," she sings.

"I know, it's crazy. I had the tiniest bump last week, and now it's like *bam*, there's babies," I reply with a laugh. I noticed this afternoon after I finished a session that my once soft stomach was no longer just my normal curvy bumps, but an actual baby bump. I pretty much made every excuse to look in the mirror the rest of the day, even making sure to take a few pictures to document it.

"Can I?" she asks, gesturing down to my belly.

"Of course." I step back, giving her better access to rest a hand on my bump. "Oh my god," I say, my eyes suddenly filling with tears.

"What?" Josie almost shrieks, her hands fluttering up my body as if to find something physically wrong.

"You're going to be their aunt," I say, my voice watery.

"Well, duh, we already knew that," she replies with a laugh.

"I just never thought about it. I mean I knew you were going to be their aunt, but like... you're their *literal* aunt."

"You're being dramatic," Josie says, but I can see the little hints of tears in her eyes.

"I can't help it," I say, tears sliding down my cheeks. "Everything makes me cry right now. I cried yesterday because my studio is so pretty."

"Oh, sweetie," Josie croons, pulling me back into a hug.

A hand rubs up and down my back soothingly, but it's not Josie's. When we release each other, I see Beau standing right behind me, ready to care for me if I need. I hate that he feels like he has to be at my beck and call at every moment, worried I may pass out or something again.

"Andrew, look at Mar's cute little bump!" Josie pulls her husband toward me. The man who was more of a brother to me than my own brothers smiles sweetly, his gaze full of affection.

"Look at you," he states.

Before he can get another word out, Beau is turning me to face him, glancing down my body.

I let him stare, taking it in. He doesn't do anything but stare until Andrew breaks the silence.

"Dude, why are you staring at her like you want to eat her? It's weird."

Beau is shaken from his stupor. "Sorry, just kinda crazy. I didn't notice this morning," he says, his voice quiet.

I nod. "It really is crazy."

Thomas arrives at the table next, greeting everyone, and giving out hugs. He smiles brightly when Josie points out my bump, kissing me on the cheek. Beau has his arm wrapped protectively around me, and I swear he tightens his grip when Thomas does that, which is ridiculous. Thomas has been, and always will be, like a brother to me.

The band plays loudly in the background, so Beau leans forward to speak into my ear. His voice is low, tickling the shell of my ear. "Do you want water? Or maybe a pop or something? I bet if we coerce Jason enough he would give you something from his fridge."

I chuckle. "Think he has juice boxes?"

Beau smiles. "I'm sure he does for when Lennie is here," he replies. "I'll go ask."

I reach out, grabbing his arm as I laugh. "I'm kidding. I'll just take some water, please."

"You got it," Beau answers with a wink. He squeezes me softly, kissing my temple before leaving Josie and I alone at the table.

"Alright, you gave me the bare minimum of information about the 'how' a few weeks ago, but I need more," she says, pulling her hair up into a claw clip.

"I would expect nothing less," I answer. We haven't had any one-on-one time since the announcement and the chat we had that night and I know it's been killing her.

"What finally broke the dam?" she asks. "Last I heard was how he almost kissed you at the rehearsal dinner."

"Yeah... We danced at the reception, and he looked over at you and Andrew dancing, and said something along the lines of, 'Did you ever think that would be us?'"

Josie practically swoons. She clutches a hand to her chest, jaw dropping in awe.

"From there, I actually ran, but he followed me. Wouldn't let me get any farther, and followed me to my room. Then he just... kissed me. And we didn't stop."

"God, that sounds like something straight from a movie." Josie's listening intently.

I shake my head. "I avoided him for almost two months. I was scared, but what's new? I didn't want to lose him, but I guess I already lost him in that time."

The fear of losing Beau inevitably made me distance myself. A self-defense mechanism that always seems to backfire when it comes to him. I'll never forget the look on his high school girlfriend's face the day after he broke up with her.

Her face was pale as a ghost, thick black bags underneath her once bright shining eyes. She'd asked me if I knew why he ended things with her, or if I knew of a way to get him back. I've seen first hand what it looks like to lose him, and I know I wouldn't survive it.

"One day we will get it through your thick head."

I don't get to reply. The men are returning back to the table, setting their glasses down in front of us. Beau passes me my water, and I sigh discontentedly.

"What?" he asks, instantly wary.

"I just miss their ales," I reply, glancing at Josie's drink.

"You'll be able to have one in a few months," he says, attempting to appease me.

"Yeah, six-plus months. If I breastfeed, I won't be able to drink much then either, cause we can't have drunk babies, Beau," I snap. I can feel myself becoming irrationally angry, yet another perk of the mood swings I've been experiencing.

Beau covers his mouth with a slap, holding back a laugh. "No, we can't have drunk babies."

"It's not funny, Beau!" I shriek.

"I know!" he crows. "I'm not drinking either." He points to the table, but I'm focused on his face. "If you can't drink, I figure I won't either."

"Don't be ridiculous," I scoff, but when I look down at his drink I see that he, too, has a glass of water. "Stop, you're being dumb."

"No, I'm not. I'm trying to do whatever I can to make this easier for you, and if me not drinking makes it easier, then I'll do it."

Tears prick my eyes. "Go get a beer," I answer. When he doesn't right away, I start to stand and head to the bar. "Fine, I'll get one for you." I'm fully aware of how ridiculous I'm being, but he's breaking down my walls, one crack at a time, making it harder and harder to keep my ground around him.

Beau stops me with a hand to my waist, setting me down in my chair. "Fine," he mutters.

I sink into my chair a bit, happy that he finally listened to me. "Thank you," I say.

"Whatever you want, Marley, you tell me, and I'll do it," he says, turning to head back to the bar.

A few minutes later, Beau is back, and we rejoin the conversation, laughing and all around having a good time. I notice that Beau hasn't had more than a sip of his beer, but at least he got one. We haven't gone out like this in a long time, not since before Josie and Andrew's wedding, which may be partly my fault. I was avoiding him at any cost.

A hoot of excitement leaves Andrew's lips as his best friend, Isaac, and his wife, Megan, appear at the table.

Megan sits down on my other side, pulling me into her grasp. "I've missed you," she murmurs into my ear.

"Sorry," I say with a slight wince. "Things have been… hectic." We haven't told anyone outside family yet, but Megan is also one of my best friends, so after I spilled the beans at Thanksgiving, I told her I was pregnant. She almost burst my eardrum out with how loud she screamed on the phone.

"You don't need to apologize," she says. "Things have been nuts for us too. Isaac's been prepping for all the holiday events and weddings, and I've been picking up some extra call shifts, so don't be sorry."

I nod into her embrace.

"I invited Fallon too, I hope that's okay. She was able to get a babysitter tonight, which never happens."

"Of course," I say. "It will be nice to see her again."

Fallon arrives a few minutes later, sitting in between Josie and Megan. "Hey, everyone," she greets almost shyly. Her honey blonde hair is down in loose waves past her shoulders, and she's in a deep green sweater and leggings with the cutest pair of boots.

We chat off and on for a while until Jason pops in from the back. "Hey," he greets. His eyes scan the table until they land on Fallon. For a brief moment, they hold on to her, but she's engrossed in a conversation with Josie, so she doesn't realize.

Everyone else does though. Thomas coughs, clearly trying to gain his brother's attention. It pulls him out of the trance, and he goes back to making conversation. *Interesting.*

My eyes start to grow heavy as the night continues, and soon it's nearing nine-thirty, and I'm ready for bed. I poke Beau in the side when there's a lull in conversation.

"Beau?" I ask, almost worried he's going to be disappointed.

He turns on his stool, shifting his full attention to me. "Yeah, butterfly?"

I giggle, remembering how he used to call me that when we were kids. I've always loved butterflies and what they represent. "Will you hate me if we go home?"

His brows furrow. "I could never hate you. Are you okay?" His concern is so sweet.

"Yeah, just really tired," I say, a yawn escaping me as if my body needs to prove its point.

"Why didn't you say something sooner?" he asks, standing immediately.

"Cause, we're both having fun, and I wasn't ready to go until now," I explain.

He narrows his eyes like he needs a moment to convince himself that I'm telling the truth. When he's content, he stands from his stool, grabbing his phone off the table. "We're heading out," he announces, offering his hand to me, helping me stand from my own stool.

We say our goodbyes, getting hugs and promises to do this again sooner rather than later. Beau helps me into my winter jacket, and leads us outside to his car.

The brisk air sends a shiver through my body. I huddle into my jacket a little more, cursing myself as my nipples pebble from the cold. They've been aching so bad, but I wanted to try and keep them for at least another week or two, but I think I'll have to take the piercings out when I get home. They're killing me.

Beau curses under his breath. "Shit, I should've started the car to warm it up before bringing you out here."

I laugh. "You're ridiculous. It's winter, Beau. Things are

going to be cold no matter what. I can handle it. We've lived with it our entire lives."

"I know we have, but still. I want to take care of you," he grumbles.

"You are," I reply honestly. He's been almost smothering me with how attentive he is, but I would be lying if I said I didn't like it. Well, depending on my mood that is. Every morning he makes sure my water bottle is full of ice cold water, and he's held my hair back as I puked more than once. It's sweet, if not a little gross, that he has to see me puke so much.

I shift uncomfortably in my seat as each bump rubs the sensitive peak of my nipples.

"You okay?" Beau asks, glancing over as he continues to watch the road.

"Yep." I shift in my seat, tugging at my nylon jacket to adjust the fabric underneath that is making me so unbelievably uncomfortable.

Beau, of course, doesn't reply, because he knows me, and he knows that I'm not okay. "I'm fine," I reiterate, my irritation only growing.

"No, you're not."

"Yes, I am."

Beau pulls over, shifting the car into park and turns his body, narrowing his eyes on me.

"Marley," he scolds.

"Beau," I imitate his voice with an almost nasally tone.

He stares me down, not giving in. After a beat, he raises his brow, and I crack. "God, why do you have to be so freaking irritating?" I mutter, crossing my arms over my chest, and immediately regretting it. I let out a pathetic sounding whimper at the contact.

"Marley," he repeats my name. "What is going on? Are you in pain?"

"I don't want to tell you," I murmur, dropping my chin to my chest in my embarrassment.

"You know you can tell me anything. That doesn't change because we had sex, or because you're pregnant."

My cheeks heat to an absurd degree, and I give up the fight. "My nipples are really sensitive, and they hurt," I mutter, speaking fast and low.

"What?" he asks.

"My nipples are really sensitive, and they hurt," I repeat, practically yelling now.

"Oh," is his only response.

"Yeah, but you're the one who made me say it, so you can't be uncomfortable. You did this to me!" I lean over, poking him in the middle of his chest.

He runs his hands through his hair, tugging at the strands. He swallows thickly, and if I didn't know any better, I'd say he's turned on. His cheeks are flushed, and he's shifting in his seat. His eyes have the same glazed over look from the night of the wedding.

When he speaks, I shudder at the deepness of his voice. "Do you need to take them out? Dr. Ness did say if they made you uncomfortable that you should."

I sink back, resting my head against the headrest. "I probably should, but I love them so much." A hint of sadness creeps in, but Beau surprises me.

"I do too," he says.

I feel my eyes widen, and I do whatever I can to *not* look at him. I cough slightly, shifting in my seat again. A low pulse thumps between my thighs, a burning ember of heat rising up my core.

"I just mean," he stammers. "I mean... I don't know

what I mean, or what to say, because I'd be lying if I said I didn't love them."

I ignore him. Can't process thoughts. "Anyway, things are really really sensitive nowadays, and I don't think the piercings are helping. I'll probably take them out tonight."

He nods, and thankfully sits straight in his seat, pulling the vehicle back out onto the road toward home. After a long minute of awkward silence, he speaks. "I saw a really nice house today while doing a showing."

"Cool," I mutter, not really focused on the conversation, as I'm still trying to get over our last one.

"It got me thinking. We should really look into getting something bigger."

I sigh. I know this isn't an easy topic. I need to stay strong on this, before I hit the point of no return. I'm losing the battle, letting myself get closer and closer to giving in, to just letting myself fall into this. But I need to be the one to control the situation. "Why? We both have houses, and I have the guest bedroom we can put the cribs in," I deflect, because deflection is my greatest skill.

"When you bought your house, we didn't know what we do now, and we didn't know that in just under six months we'd be bringing two babies home to it. It's too small, and so is my house. We need something bigger, something that will fit all four of us." He tries to reason with me, but I can't do this right now.

"No, it's fine. You can sell your house and get something bigger if you want, but I'm keeping my house," I reply stubbornly, ending the conversation.

When we arrive home a few minutes later, I'm so ready to get these piercings out it's not even funny. I shuck my jacket onto the couch, kicking off my shoes and heading down the hall to my room.

"Marley?" Beau asks, confusion thick in his voice.

"Fine!" I call back. I cannot have him bear witness to this. Once my door is closed, I whip off my black long sleeve, and unhook my bra, shimmying it down my arms.

The relief of not having my breasts condensed into the bra is palpable, but it only lasts for a moment. My nipples are swollen and red. They've been gradually getting more and more sensitive, but I'm at a breaking point.

I try to twist the little ball to loosen it from the curved barbell, but I can't get it. I huff out an irritated noise as I step forward to the long mirror hanging from the back of my bedroom door to get a better angle.

I take a deep breath, and try again, this time looking in the mirror as I try to twist. When it doesn't budge, I try the other side, only to have the same result. I groan, my irritation growing higher and higher with each passing moment. I flop down on my bed, staring at the ceiling. I don't want to ask for help, but I might need it. I can't get the angle right, and every brush against my nipples is like a mix of pain and pleasure.

A knock on the door answers my internal struggle. "Marley, I can hear you muttering to yourself from the hall. What's going on?"

I curse myself for always talking out loud. It's time to bite the bullet. "I can't get my nipple piercings out. The ball is too tight."

The door cracks open slightly, but not enough to where he can see in. "Can I help?"

I think for a moment, knowing fully that I need him, but also knowing that I'm going to have to give up a shred of dignity. I stand up, grabbing my cotton robe from where it's laying on top of my laundry basket. I wrap myself in it and stride over, opening the door to Beau. My heart is pounding in my chest with a weird sense of anticipation on what's about to happen.

I open the door slowly, and Beau is standing there in only his low-cut black sweats. I swear, he's been trying to smoke me out the last few weeks, walking around shirtless. Nevermind the fact that my hormones are all over the place, —it's making me horny as hell.

My clit thumps in agreement as I take in Beau's many tattoos. He side-steps into my room, closing the door behind him, as if we have to maintain privacy from someone, but it's just us here. No one else to see what he's about to help me with.

"Are they stuck?" he asks, eyes blazing with concern.

I shake my head. "No, I just can't get it loose."

He stands in front of me, eyes blazing as he focuses his gaze on my still covered chest. "I just need to unscrew it, right?"

"Yes, then I can take it out."

Beau sighs, stepping toward me. He reaches out slowly, hesitantly to the tie around my waist. Eyes lifting, he arches his brow. "Ready?"

I nod, turning my face away. I don't want to see his reaction to seeing my bare breasts again. Our night together lives in my mind on a constant loop, so I don't need to add another moment to my personal spank bank.

I feel the tie come loose, the cool air wafting against my skin. Beau inhales sharply as he takes in the swollen tips of my nipples. He tries to cover it with a cough, but I know what it was.

"Ready?" he asks yet again, his voice low and gravelly.

I say yes, and then Beau's fingers are on my right breast. He tries to twist the ball, but it doesn't give. I yelp at the sensitivity, cringing at the way it sounded more like a moan than anything. Beau lowers himself slightly, now eye-level with my breast.

He focuses intently on trying to get it off, but it's not working. Every touch is sending zings through my body, straight between my legs. My pussy is pounding, and I can feel my underwear getting wet. Why is this so fucking hot? This shouldn't be sexy, shouldn't be turning me on, and yet, it is.

"Fuck," he curses. His hands shake ever so slightly. "Why is this so hard?"

"I don't know," I whimper.

"Lay down, I might be able to get a better angle that way."

I do as he says, laying flat on my back on top of my comforter. Stupidly, I look at Beau, and holy fuck. His eyes are glazed over as he rakes his gaze across my body. I want to hide for just a moment, but I'm locked, unable to move from the intensity.

"You're so fucking beautiful, Marley," he utters, his voice cracking.

I flush, turning my face away, but not before I see the tent in his sweats. He's hard.

I feel the weight of his body as the bed dips, and I inhale, trying to get my body to calm. My nipples are tingling again, but not from the sensitivity, no. They're aching to be touched.

Beau's fingers caress the skin of my breast softly as he slides up to the barbel again. After a long moment of twisting and gentle tugs, I feel the rod slide free. A sense of relief rushes through my body, similar to the release of an orgasm.

I moan as Beau slides his hand to the other breast. It's not a clinical touch, it's sensual, and it's everything I need right now. The pressure between my thighs is building, and I feel so empty, so needy for him. My eyes are closed tight, trying to memorize each moment, each feeling and fleeting touch.

Beau gets to work on the other barbel, and with each graze of his fingers over my nipples, I yearn more and more for his touch.

It's only when I feel the stubble of his beard across my nipple that I realize what's happening.

His lips take my nipple into his mouth, the one with the piercing still in place, and he sucks gently. His tongue flicks the piercing as he nips at my skin. My hips involuntarily roll into his body, my mouth dropping open.

It's such a mix of pain with the best kind of pleasure that I don't know how to react. "Beau," I gasp his name, my hand reaching up to wrap in his hair, clutching him to my chest.

"Please don't make me stop," he murmurs against my skin.

"No," I cry as he flicks his tongue again. His free hand reaches up, cupping my heavy breast in his large hand, fingers toying with the other nipple. "Oh god."

He groans into my chest, kneading my breast in his hand. My eyes fly open and I turn my head to look at him. Consequences be damned, I need to see this moment, need to sear it into my brain. Beau opens his eyes at the moment I do, and he lifts his mouth off me with a pop. When our eyes meet, it's like a frenzy begins. Beau lifts his body to straddle my hips, being mindful of my small bump.

"Holy fuck," he mutters, and then his mouth is devouring mine. His tongue slides into my mouth, moving together. His erection is hard against my stomach, one hand tangling in my hair as the other continues to cup my breast.

My body is hot, his touch lighting up all my senses and every ounce of neediness that I've withheld for weeks.

Beau kisses down my neck, between my breasts, then is back on my nipples again. I moan with every touch, my body so desperate for him. He glances up as he slides his fingers down to my leggings, I nod frantically, giving him the go ahead.

In the back of my mind, I know this is bad, that I should be keeping my distance from him, but I don't want to stop. I *can't* stop. My leggings are down and on the floor in an instant, leaving me shaking in only my granny panties. I should invest in better underwear, but these are just so comfortable, and finding things that are comfortable lately is hard.

Beau groans when he sees the wet spot in the center. His finger slowly traces the outside of the fabric, feeling the wetness I've made. "You need this, don't you, butterfly?"

I'm nearly quivering as I nod. "Please," I groan. Beau's eyes soften, taking in my body in front of him. He slides his hand up to rest on my stomach. He's never done this, never touched where our babies are, and the love and adoration in his eyes is so pure and raw.

He bends down, pressing two soft kisses to my bump. "Gorgeous," he mutters. Then he's moving again, sliding my panties down. I haven't shaved since I found out I was pregnant, so things aren't exactly prim and proper down there.

"Sorry," I say, hiding my face in embarrassment.

"Don't you fucking dare," Beau states, using his hand to softly guide my face to look at him. "I fucking love your body. Every inch, every curve, dimple and soft edge. I love every single thing about it. I don't care if you haven't shaved, I will still devour this pussy like it's my last day on earth. I. Love. It."

To further prove his point he latches his mouth to my soaked cunt, his tongue hitting all the right spots. When he slides his fingers inside, curving and pumping them in and out, I'm gasping his name, writhing into his touch.

He works me over and over, giving me everything I need until I'm coming, my pussy clenching around his fingers, fluttering and aching for more even as I'm still coming down from the high.

I'm gasping, sucking in long gulps of air and shivering as Beau continues his delicious torture on my body. One finger from his free hand moves upward, and traces the outline of the tattoo across my ribs, the stem of the flower, the butterfly, the leaves, the petals.

"That's my girl," he says so quietly I'm not convinced I heard him. There's movement across my stomach and skin, then a soft tug and twist on my left nipple pulls me out of my haze. Beau slides the other piercing out, dropping it onto the bed next to me. I can't move, my limbs and body so exhausted and wrung out from pleasure.

Beau takes my robe, covering my body with the fabric as I shiver. "Can't have you cold," he says with a soft chuckle.

I nod, words not computing in my brain yet. I feel more relaxed than I have in months.

31

BEAU

Marley lays before me, her chest heaving as she catches her breath. I can still taste her on my lips, feel her wetness on my fingers. I genuinely could not hold back from touching her more, especially not after hearing her gasps and seeing the ways she reacted to my touch on her nipples.

"You okay?" I ask, laying down next to her, pushing her hair from her face. She trembles under my touch, her eyes falling closed.

"Mhmm," she mumbles. "Tired."

"I bet." I laugh. "Come on, let's get you to bed, butterfly."

I help her sit up and adjust her robe again so it's covering her, even though I want her to be bare and open to me. Marley stands, a totally blissed-out look on her face. I hand her the piercings I took out, and she glances down at them and sighs. "I'm going to miss them."

"Me too," I grumble.

"Oh, are you?" Marley teases almost flirtatiously.

"Yep," I reply. Deciding to tell her the truth, I continue,

"I think about them all the time, especially the way they felt in my mouth, and the way you gasped every time I flicked my tongue over them."

She gasps sharply.

"I've said it before, and I'll say it again. I'm in this, Marley."

She nods, and I can tell she's losing herself to her thoughts yet again. I reach down, clasping her hand in mine. I don't say anything, just squeeze her three times. Something we've done since we were kids.

I walk her to the bathroom, then leave her to clean up. I get her bedroom ready, pulling down her comforter, adjusting her pillows and plugging in her phone.

Marley walks back into her bedroom, her eyes drooping. Her face is washed, and she's in a comfortable pair of sleep shorts and a t-shirt. Her bump is so cute and now so visible that I can't wait to see what it looks like as the pregnancy continues. I have a feeling she's going to be the definition of glowing.

She sits down on the edge of the bed, avoiding my eyes. "Thanks..." she murmurs.

"For the orgasm? Or for the piercings?"

"Both?" she winces. "I don't think we should have crossed that line, Beau."

I don't agree, but I don't say anything. Sitting down next to her, I rest my hand on her thigh. Gently rubbing her smooth skin, I try to soothe her.

She sighs, leaning her head down onto my shoulder. We leave the words unspoken, at least for now.

"SHIT." Marley's voice carries through the thin walls of her house. There's a grunt, and then a thud as she drops something on the floor.

I sit up in bed, trying to wipe the grogginess from my eyes.

"Marley?" I call as I swing my legs out of the bed. She must not hear me, because there is another thud and an irritated curse.

Crossing the hall, I knock softly on her door. I open it, stunned at the sight of the chaos before me. Marley is standing in front of her closet, clothes strewn around her on the floor, shoes and all.

"What are you doing?" I ask gently.

She's wearing only a sports bra and underwear, and I have to fight to keep my gaze on her face and also keep my cock from reacting. She's flushed, bangs strewn as she runs her hands through her hair again. "I can't find a shirt that fits right," she murmurs, her voice cracking.

I stride toward her, leaving the door open behind me. "What about this?" I pull a shirt of hers off the hanger. It's one of my favorites, a long-sleeved burgundy sweater. "I love this one."

"I don't want to wear that today," she says, her voice wavering.

I rush to put it back on the hanger, not wanting to upset her. An idea pops into my head. Her emotions have been all over the place lately, and I definitely don't want to make things worse. "What are you doing today?" I ask.

"You don't remember?" she nearly scolds.

"Uh..." I hesitate. "No?" I wrack my brain for knowledge of when she told me what she would be doing today and come up with nothing. I even remember asking her last night if she had plans this weekend, though that conversation was interrupted when Thomas asked if we were going to find out the gender of the babies.

Marley sighs, her irritation only growing. "I am meeting up with Josie and Megan. We're going shopping."

"Oh," I reply, completely dumbfounded. Maybe I missed that part of the conversation last night.

She continues before I can get another word in. "And now, I can't find anything that fits. I swear in the last three days I've grown three sizes. None of my jeans fit and all my shirts are too tight."

"That's not a bad thing, Marley," I say, hoping I don't say the wrong thing. "It means the babies are growing."

"I know!" she shrieks. "But it also means that I'm getting fatter than I already am, and finding cute clothes is a pain in the ass."

Without a thought, I'm taking her chin in my palm, forcing her to meet my gaze. "Don't you dare say that about yourself. You are fucking perfect, Marley Bell. And you are growing our children. I can't wait to watch your body change and grow. Can't wait to see how you carry them. Can't wait to see how incredible of a mother you are." Her eyes widen, those brown orbs dilating at my words and the intensity of my gaze. "Do you understand?"

She slowly nods. Then she cringes. "That doesn't change the fact that I can't find something to wear right now, though."

I can't help the burst of laughter that bubbles out of my chest. "Come on," I say, dropping her chin and taking her hand. "You keep looking, I'll be right back. I need to use the restroom."

Marley nods, not really acknowledging me, too lost in her closet. I drop her hand, and dart across the hall to my room and pull a few things from my own closet. Cozy tops, like a worn sweater I know she's complimented before, an old tee from college, and a long-sleeved Henley.

I cross back over to her room with my haul, and tuck them into her pile of things as she continues her search through the closet.

Twenty-five minutes later, we have an outfit picked out. I never knew just how much went into picking her clothes, but every option she declined had a reason. Too hot, too itchy, not stretchy enough, will make her bump look weird, doesn't fit her boobs right, and so on.

She opted for leggings and one of the old college tees I threw in the pile, with a cardigan to wear on top. That way she can take a layer off if she needs. A burst of possessiveness hits me with the knowledge that she had so many choices and ended up choosing mine without even knowing.

She finishes getting dressed while I head into the kitchen to get myself a cup of coffee. I make her a cup of decaf, throwing in some cream and sugar and putting it into a to-go cup for her. I expected for her to be awkward in front of me this morning, especially after last night, but she hasn't brought it up at all. I hope she doesn't pretend that it didn't happen, that's the last thing that I want.

Marley strides into the kitchen, her hair in a ponytail with the ends curled. "Adorable," I state. She blushes slightly, then moans when she sees the travel mug I'm handing her.

"Thank you," she gushes.

"Anytime," I reply.

A honk from her driveway sounds. "That's Josie," she stammers. "I'll see you later?" she asks, voice hopeful.

"I'll be here," I reply, taking a sip of my coffee. "Hey, before I forget to say something, we should get a registry set up," I tell her, having thought of it when she mentioned shopping.

She misses a step, stumbling slightly. "You want to do that?"

"Of course," I say. "Why wouldn't I?"

"I... I figured you wouldn't be interested in doing that with me."

I withhold my irritation. I'm really going to have to beat it into her that I'm all in. I'm not just going to be a co-parent. I'm their dad, not just the guy they see on weekends. "Yes, Marley. I want us to do it together. Is that okay?"

"Y-yes," she stammers. "Maybe tomorrow we can go to the store and set it up."

"Perfect," I say. There's another honk. "Go, have fun." I lean toward her, kissing her cheek. "Call me if you need anything."

She steps away, eyes slightly widening at my show of affection toward her. I'm glad she's getting out of the house, because I have plans of my own today.

On cue, my phone buzzes on the counter, Thomas's name on the screen.

32

MARLEY

"How are you feeling?" Megan asks. We're in a small boutique in the Twin Cities, shopping for maternity clothes. I haven't bought anything yet; I'm mainly looking for now. Josie keeps throwing things into the cart though, and I'm a little worried about what the total might be.

I sigh, unsure of how I want to answer the question. "Depends on the hour," I reply with a soft laugh. "I'm not as nauseous lately, but I still feel like crap, and I'm exhausted more often than not."

Megan rubs my shoulders. "That makes sense. You have a lot happening in your body right now."

"When I was pregnant with Presley, I was sick the entire pregnancy. I had something called hyperemesis gravidarum. It was torture. I spent more time in the hospital than out toward the end of pregnancy. I constantly needed fluids," Fallon says.

At the last minute, we called her and invited her out with us. It ended up working out amazingly. We dropped her daughter off with Nikki on our way out of town. Lennie was already there, so the two girls get to have a playdate.

"Thankfully, my morning sickness seems to have lessened. Now I only get sick maybe once a week. But none of my clothes fit anymore, so that's fun." I gesture to the shop around us. "Hence the shopping trip. I had a meltdown this morning in front of Beau, and he had to help me find something to wear. It was so embarrassing." I cringe even remembering it.

"I'm sure he doesn't care," Josie says, holding up a forest green onesie with a baby fox on it. She points at the onesie, clearly obsessed with it. "I know we are shopping for you, but I can't help it. I'm buying this."

I chuckle. "I don't think he minded, but he was so jumpy, like he was waiting for me to start screaming at him."

Fallon laughs. "Oh he probably was. My ex was terrified of me, always scared I was going to freak out or start crying. Especially those first couple weeks when things stopped fitting the way they should."

"My moods have been pretty unpredictable," I agree. Josie throws the onesie into the cart, which definitely needs to be thinned out a bit. There's no way I need all of these clothes.

"He's probably treading carefully," Josie says. "He wants to take care of you."

I sigh. "I know. I just... I'm so all over the place. I don't know what to think."

Megan continues to rub my shoulders. "I'm sure he understands."

We let the conversation die, and Josie changes the subject. "Fallon, how are you liking working for Meadow Grove?"

Fallon smiles widely. "I love it, and it's been so fun

working with Isaac. Even if I'm not working an event, he's always finding things for me to do or giving me errands to run, and it's amazing. I love keeping busy."

"Good," Josie says. "Isaac was saying that he and Jason are working on a contract to get Blue Ox served at the bar, that would be cool."

"Wow, yeah, that would be awesome," I interject.

"Isaac mentioned that to me last night actually," Fallon says. "Definitely would be good publicity for both of them." She turns her face away as if to hide a reaction.

"I agree," Megan replies. We wander through the store, chatting about the winery, and how Josie will be extra busy next summer. The winter is slower for her—less weddings and more store front action, especially with Valentine's Day.

My feet ache and my head pounds by the time we are finished shopping. We make our way back with way more bags than necessary in the back of the car.

"You okay, Mar?" Megan asks from the back seat.

"Tired," I reply. "Pregnancy is annoying." I rest my hand on my small belly and I suddenly get excited for when I can feel them moving inside me.

Fallon chuckles. "As the only one in the car who has been pregnant, I have to agree with you. It's a pain in the ass, but the end is worth it. Presley is the best thing in my life." Her voice turns melancholy.

"How old is she?" I ask.

"Six," Fallon replies. "She'll be seven in May. She's such a good kid, and has taken all the drama from the last year in stride."

I don't ask her to elaborate. I know the minor details, but it's not my place to ask for her to give the nitty gritty information on her personal life. We aren't that close, though I hope someday we can be. I love her and the energy she brings to our little circle so far. She also seems like she's going through a lot in her personal life. Though, she also gives me the impression that she's not the type of girl to take any shit.

I watch Megan reach over and squeeze Fallon's hand. Josie's phone starts to ring as we make the final turn into town, of course, it's Andrew.

"Hello?" she answers.

"Petals, when are you coming home?"

"Soon," she says with a soft laugh. "We're just getting into town, and I have to drop everyone off."

He sighs heavily through the phone line. "Fine."

"Why?" Josie chuckles.

The line is silent for a moment. "Velma and Travis miss you."

Megan barks out a laugh, and I chuckle to myself. "Who are Velma and Travis?" Fallon whispers to Megan.

"Their dog and cat," Megan says through her laughter. Even I'm laughing because Andrew is so head over heels for Josie. He is the definition of clingy.

"Are you sure they miss me?" Josie teases. "Or is it you?"

"What if it's both?" he replies.

"I'll be home soon, honey. Go work in the shop, and I'll be there before you know it." They finish up the call, and then my own phone is buzzing with a text.

BEAU

When are you going to be home?

ME

Soon, why?

Have you eaten today?

I roll my eyes. Is he asking to be sure I don't pass out, or is he asking if I'm hungry? He answers my question before I can even come up with a snarky reply.

BEAU

My question is twofold. I need to know if you're hungry, and if you have been keeping hydrated. Can't have you passing out.

ME

We had a late lunch in the city, but I'm definitely hungry again.

I check the time on the dashboard, seeing that it's not even five, and we ate around three. That's annoying. I shouldn't be nearly starving.

BEAU

Craving anything specific?

His question makes me pause. Am I? I haven't had many cravings, but it's like his words flip a switch.

ME

I need pizza, but not from a chain place. I need the good homemade stuff from Pizza Palace.

BEAU

You got it. Any special requests?

Pepperoni.

No, wait. That gives me heartburn.

Chicken Alfredo.

> Fuck, I don't know. It all sounds good. I want it all.

lol.

> Sausage, pepperoni, black olives, onion and pineapple. I'll take an antacid. Please don't question my choices.

Never. I'll pick it up and be home soon.

> I'll be home in twenty.

I slide my phone into the pocket of my purse as we pull into Nikki and Richard's driveway. The lights are on next door at my parents' house, and for a moment, I consider having Josie drop me off too. I miss my parents, even though I saw them just about a week ago. I need to make sure I spend more time with them.

We say our goodbyes to Fallon, then run across town to drop Megan off before heading to my place.

When we pull into my driveway nearly thirty minutes later, the kitchen light is on, and I can see Beau walking around inside. He must have just gotten home. My stomach rumbles with the promise of pizza.

Josie puts the car in park, and I groan when I remember all the bags. I didn't buy nearly anything today except a handful of maternity items I insisted on purchasing myself, but the other girls did. They didn't hold back from buying me clothes, a pregnancy pillow, and all sorts of other goodies. They even bought clothes, stuffed animals, and things for the babies, too. "You have to help me bring all this in," I say with a huff.

"Duh," she replies. "I totally went overboard, didn't I?"

"Just a bit," I chuckle, holding my fingers up and pinching them together.

"Worth it, those two are going to be spoiled rotten. I already spoil Lennie, so get used to it."

I laugh, pulling my best friend in for a hug. "I love you," I say, my voice thick with emotion. "I'm sorry I'm a mess right now, but I appreciate you more than you know. I needed this day."

She squeezes me tightly. "I did too. We haven't spent much time together lately, and that isn't going to happen anymore. You're going to get sick of me."

"Deal," I reply.

Together, we grab the abundance of bags and head inside. Beau's standing in the kitchen in a pair of sweats and a short-sleeved shirt, plating the pizza. The wonderful aroma makes my mouth water and I have to stop myself from running across the room and swiping the plate from Beau's unknowing hands.

"Jeez," he says in lieu of greeting.

"It wasn't me," I defend myself.

"I can attest to that," Josie says. "It was all me and some of Megan."

"What is it?" Beau asks. As he turns, I see a layer of thin bandage on his upper arm just under the hem of his t-shirt. *Did he get a tattoo today?*

"Clothes for Marley, toys, the works," Josie responds, walking down the hall to my room. "Marley, should I put this bag in the guest room? Is that where the nursery will be?"

I'm so distracted by the potential of Beau's new tattoo that I don't interrupt her to tell her to put it in my room. "Oh." I hear her pause. "Nevermind!"

I groan, walking through the kitchen toward her. "Just throw it in my room for now," I say as I get closer. "It's a mess from this morning, but I'll find a place for it all."

I swing open my bedroom door, shocked to find it spotless. All the clothes that were strewn across the floor from earlier are now hanging in my closet or folded and placed neatly on top of my dresser. Beau must have cleaned it while I was gone.

"If this is your version of messy, we need to have a conversation," Josie teases.

I shake my head. "No, uh. Beau must've cleaned up the clothes after I left."

"Ahh," Josie murmurs, as if that explains everything. "Should I put these in the closet for now?"

"Yes, please," I answer. She puts the bags in a corner of my already stuffed full closet and pulls me in for a quick hug.

I lead her out into the kitchen, where we say a quick goodbye. Beau nods at Josie, mouth full of pizza. When the door clicks shut behind her, Beau steps over to me, taking my hand and leading me to the counter, sitting me down on a stool. He slides a plate with two slices across the counter to me.

"Thanks," I murmur, picking up the slice and taking a huge bite. I feel awkward as I remember last night—the way his mouth felt on my breasts, the gentle tugs as he pulled the barbell free.

I moan around the mouthful of pizza.

"Good?" Beau asks, sitting down next to me.

"So good," I mumble. I bet I look like the definition of a train wreck right about now, but I could care less. This pizza tastes like it's my first meal in days. We eat in silence, and when I'm so full I can barely breathe, I wipe my face, tossing my napkin onto the plate. I look to my left and my eye catches on Beau's upper arm again.

"Did you get a tattoo today?" I ask.

He glances down where I'm looking, as if he forgot, then replies, "Yeah. Thomas finally popped his tattoo cherry, so I figured I might as well get one too."

I reach out, lifting the sleeve of his t-shirt up. Under the clear bandage is an intricate work of art. A large roman numeral clock takes up most of his upper arm, with three butterflies flying from twelve o'clock position.

My finger reaches up, lightly trailing over the bandaged skin. "Wow," I breathe. "It's beautiful."

Beau takes in my reaction. I can feel his gaze on mine, watching closely as I try not to cry at the beauty of it. "It turned out really well. Something I've been thinking about for a while, but the timing never felt right. Until now." He tilts my chin up so I'm looking into those brown eyes.

I can't do this, not right now. If the butterflies now permanently etched on his skin have anything to do with me, or the butterfly on my forearm, I'm done. I'll fall head first into the hole that has been tearing through my heart and into his waiting arms. Clearing my throat, I lean back. "What did Thomas get?"

Now that I've thoroughly ruined the moment, Beau clears his throat. He stumbles over his words, like he forgot what Thomas got. "Just a few trees on his back."

"Did you take a picture?" I ask, already reaching out my hand. If there's one thing Beau and I do best, it's talk tattoos.

"Shit, no," Beau mutters. "I'll have him text me a pic though."

"Why doesn't that surprise me one bit?" I laugh. "You always forget to take pictures."

He laughs in response. "True story."

Now that my stomach is full, I'm left with a bone deep exhaustion. "I'm off to bed, unless you need anything?" I ask.

"Not a thing. Let me know if you need something," Beau says, the same thing he says to me every night before I go to bed. And every night, I think of the same thing as I lie alone in my bed, wishing I could ask him to climb in next to me and hold me. When I'm yearning for him to tell me that he's going to be there, no matter what. No matter when things get bad for me, and I try to ruin us, the way I've effectively done so far. I want him to hold us.

33

MARLEY

A slice of pain makes me hiss as I slide my finger under the wrapping paper. "Shit," I curse. I watch as the small bead of blood pools on my fingertip. I'm sitting on the living room floor, wrapping Christmas presents for the late family Christmas this afternoon. I call out, "Beau?"

"Yeah?" Beau's voice calls from the guest bathroom. I hear his footsteps as he strides into the living room. His toothbrush is hanging from his mouth, white foam spilling out over his lips onto his freshly groomed beard.

I chuckle softly. "I got a papercut. Can you grab me a Band-Aid, please?"

Beau sighs in relief. He stands before me in his dress pants, hanging low on his hips. Toothbrush still sticking out of his mouth, he settles his hands on his hips. "You can't scare me like that, Mar."

"Like what?" I joke. "I called your name, Beau. If that was scary, we need to check your blood pressure."

His eyes narrow as he pulls his toothbrush from his mouth. He runs back to the bathroom without another word, and I can hear the water run, then the cabinet door opening and closing before he's running back toward the living room. Beau kneels next to me. With him this close, I can practically taste his sharp cologne.

"Hand," he commands, holding his own hand out expectantly.

I chuckle when I realize that not only did he bring a Band-Aid, but he brought the whole damn first-aid kit. "Oh my god, are you going to give me stitches?" I gasp in mock horror.

"I'll do what I need to do, butterfly," Beau says, his irritation clear as he gently takes my hand. He takes a cotton ball, dabbing at the tiny amount of blood. With careful dexterity, he applies a dollop of antibacterial ointment, and wraps my finger in a Band-Aid.

"Am I going to live?" I tease.

"Ha ha," he laughs humorlessly and then gives me a playful scowl. He stands, taking in the mess of gift wrapping and packages around me. "What is all this anyway?"

"Do we need to get Dr. Ness to check your memory at the next appointment?" I joke. "Christmas presents, Beau. Remember?"

"I know that," he scoffs. "I mean why are there so many?" He gestures to the piles in front of me.

I shrug, feeling a touch embarrassed. "I went a bit overboard for both of our parents, but that's just because I love them so much, and I needed to get them presents from the babies."

"*From* the babies?" he asks incredulously. His brows raise and he pulls his long hair into a bun. "Mar... they aren't here yet."

"I know that. I just... I wanted them to be excited. It's not much, just a lot of little things."

"Did you get everyone presents from the babies?"

I hold my breath, anxious to reply, but I think he takes that as my answer.

"You did, didn't you?"

"I couldn't help it!" I squeal. "And of course I had to get Lennie some extra things, since this will be her last Christmas as the only grandchild. She needs to feel the love." I gesture to the small—*okay large*—pile of things for Lennie. I made sure to get her everything *but* toys. Books, coloring pencils, crafts, movie tickets for just us two. Things that won't break in twenty-four hours or send Jason into a fit of silent rage at me when he finds out the toy makes a screaming noise, or something like that.

"She does feel the love." Beau tries to bargain with me, but it's already done.

"It's happening, so you can either help me put all this in the car, or you can watch your pregnant girlfriend struggle herself."

As soon as the words leave my mouth, I freeze, my face heating in pure mortification. "I, uh—" I stammer, trying to correct myself. Shit, shit, shit. Why did I say that? I'm not his girlfriend.

"You name it, and I'll do it, butterfly."

I don't reply, silently relieved that Beau isn't going to make a big deal. I nod, focusing my attention back to finishing the last few packages. Beau takes my silence as an answer, grimacing slightly as he heads back to the bathroom to finish getting ready.

Crap.

"LOOK," I say, pointing to my feet sitting currently perched up onto the ottoman. "I've spent most of the day off my feet, and they're still swollen. I've got cankles."

Gramps chuckles next to me. "Now, kiddo, you haven't seen swollen until you've seen these ankles." With great effort, Gramps uses his pant leg to lift his leg up next to mine on the ottoman. He shifts his leg, tugging his pant leg up to reveal his tight, knee-high, white stockings. "Now, *these* are swollen."

I can't help but giggle. Gramps isn't technically my real grandpa, but he is in a sense. Our two families have always considered each other as more than just friends, and now, with my pregnancy, we will actually be connected by blood. Not that it matters. Family is family, no matter if you're blood or not.

"I think those are a good look for you, Gramps," I tease. "You're going to walk during the next fashion week, aren't you?"

"You know it, kiddo." I love that even at thirty-two years old, he still calls me kiddo. It makes me think of a time when things were easier. When I wasn't pregnant with my best friend's baby. Or when I just accidentally referred to myself as his girlfriend, when I know I can't be, when I know I need to keep a distance.

"Can you feel 'em kickin' yet?" Gramps asks, poking a gentle finger at my belly.

I rub my hand over my bump affectionately. "Not yet, but probably in a few weeks."

"Hmm," he mumbles. "So, you still giving my grandson a run for his money?" He nods his head toward Beau, leaning against the countertop. He has a pale gray sweater on and is drinking a glass of punch.

"Always," I reply. Though if anything, Beau is giving

me a run for *my* money. I'm losing stamina. You know what they say about the second trimester of pregnancy, right? Horny. All the sex dreams. All the porny thoughts every time Beau walks in my front door, or steps out of the bathroom in only a low slung towel over his hips. I swear to god, I almost propositioned him to play a pizza delivery boy the other day when he walked in the door with a pizza box. *I. Am. Losing. It.*

Just thinking of it now has my pulse climbing, my cheeks flushing, and a damp sweat breaking out on my brow. We haven't done anything since the night he took my piercings out and gave me the most incredible orgasm, and I've been aching for him since.

"Good," Gramps says. "Now, help me up. I need to take a leak." He scoots forward on the deep couch.

"Shouldn't you be helping me?" I laugh, gesturing to my now obvious baby bump. "I'm just as slow as you are nowadays, Gramps."

"Oh, hush," he grumbles.

I sit forward, standing from the couch slowly, making a dramatic show of it, resting a hand on my lower back and groaning. "Alright," I say. "Here we go." I hold out my hand, and help him stand from the couch.

He's not as tall as he once was, with aging and his posture changing, but he's still much taller than me. Gramps leans forward, kissing my cheek. "Thank you, kiddo."

My heart clenches as I remember how we almost lost him last year. The way Beau's voice cracked as he told me he needed me, the way he sobbed into my chest as I held him in that small waiting room. The fear of the unknown, not knowing if Gramps would be okay, if the center of our little combined family would make it.

Gramps leaves the living room, heading toward the kitchen. We had a late lunch about an hour ago, and I'm sure he's on a mission to get some dessert from Nikki.

I chance a glance across the room, seeing Beau sitting on the floor in front of the fireplace. His legs are out in front of him, crossed at the ankles. He sits next to Jason, and they talk about upcoming changes to the brewery, and what Jason has planned for the summer.

Josie is sitting next to Thomas on the other couch, so I decide to sit next to her, and join their conversation, rather than attempting to sit down on the floor. When I flop down next to her, she wraps her arm around my shoulders. "Hey, you," she greets.

"Hey," I answer.

Thomas leans over, greeting me as well. "How are ya feeling?"

I shrug. "Good, my hip joints have been kind of achy lately."

Thomas nods. "I don't know anything about babies or pregnancy, so… cool?" he replies, offering a thumbs up.

I chuckle. "Yeah, I mean, it means my body is adjusting to the pregnancy, so I guess that's good."

Josie shakes her head. "Don't worry Thomas," Josie says with a smirk. "You'll get it figured out soon enough."

He laughs. "Right, like I'm going to have kids anytime soon. I remember when Lennie was little, though. Man, she was cute." He pauses. "I can't wait to see what your gremlins look like. I bet they will be the perfect mix of you and Beau."

My throat tightens. Anytime I've pictured the babies, I've imagined them as little boys that look identical to Beau. Dark hair, dark brown eyes. "I think they're going to look like Beau," I reply.

"You do?" Josie asks. "Do you know if you're going to find out what they are yet?"

I shrug. "Not sure. My next scan is in a few weeks, but I keep forgetting to ask Beau if he wants to know."

"I think they're both girls," Josie announces.

Thomas shakes his head. "Nope, both boys."

They look at me expectantly. "I..." I hesitate. "I don't really know. I keep imagining them as boys."

"Do they feel like boys?" Thomas asks. He has a silly grin on his face, showing the gap between his front teeth.

"Thomas, you can't 'feel' what gender the babies are," Josie responds.

"I know that, I just meant like do you have a feeling? Like you know, when the weather changes, Dad can feel it in his hips."

"No, Thomas," I say through laughter. "I can't *feel* what they are. At least not yet. I know some people have said that they can, but right now, I don't have a gut feeling. Just imagination."

He nods. "Man, I think it's great though. You and Beau, together at last."

"We're not really together, Thomas. You know that," I say pointedly. I know he knows, because we made sure to tell our family recently that just because we were having the babies together, didn't mean that *we* were together. Beau was pointedly silent during that conversation.

He doesn't reply for a moment, only shrugs. "We've all been saying it for years. Clearly..." He eyes my stomach. "Something happened to crack the dam, we just need to break it down completely."

Josie squeezes my shoulder.

"It's a pretty strong dam," I mutter. "Might take a lot for it to crack again."

"I bet we can find a way," Thomas says almost conspiratorially.

The conversation is effectively ended when Lennie runs screaming into the room.

"Present time!"

MARLEY

"Have you decided if you want to know the gender?" our nurse, Mallory, asks as I step onto the scale.

"Umm," I murmur. "We haven't really decided yet."

"That's okay," she replies. "My husband and I waited for our first, and I don't regret it, but some of our friends have found out with their pregnancies, and that was also a lot of fun."

I let myself think for a moment as I step off the scale. It would be fun to know, especially in terms of preparing clothing and things. Beau is behind me. "What do you think?" I ask.

He presses a hand to the small of my back as I slide my shoes back on.

"I don't care either way," he says. "It's up to you, butterfly."

I huff as Mallory walks us down the hall toward the exam room. My ultrasound is right after we visit with Dr. Ness, so we need to decide quickly. I'm irritated, because yes we aren't together, but he still is an equal part in this.

Mallory asks me the standard questions, checking my

blood pressure and pulse, before letting us know that Dr. Ness will be in shortly. I get settled on the exam table, eyeing Beau as he sits in one of the chairs against the wall.

"Beau, you have a say in this, you know. They're your babies too," I try to explain.

"I know they are, but Marley, this is your body. You're the one growing them. I don't need to have a say in something like this. If you want to find out, great, we can get matching sets of clothes, or not. I really am fine either way." Beau stands, stepping up to the table to my side. He pushes my bangs out of my eyes, locking my gaze with his golden brown ones.

"I don't know what I want," I reply, my mind overwhelmed. "There are too many choices. I can't decide."

"Okay, well let's break it down," he says. "For the nursery, do you want it to be one theme, or are you okay doing neutral until the babies are born?"

I bite my lip, trying to think.

Beau continues. "Is it going to stress you out, not knowing what to plan for? Or are you okay to go with the flow?"

He says the last part pointedly. As much as I pretend to be, Beau knows that I am not a go with the flow type of girl. I like to have things planned, so all of the unknown is killing me.

"I think..." I say, biting down on my lip again. "I think I want to know. So we can be ready."

"Then we will find out," he says. He drops his hand to my lap, squeezing it. "There, easy. It doesn't matter to me what they are. They're going to be the perfect mix of us, and I cannot wait. All I want is healthy babies that take after their strong, confident, and beautiful mom."

My breath hitches. "Really?"

"Really." He drops his head, resting our foreheads together.

Dr. Ness arrives, her smile widening when she sees us. "Well hello, you two. And how are things going?"

"Well," Beau replies. "Marley?"

I nod. "Yeah. I've been feeling much better lately. More energy. High..." I trail off. I almost say I have had a high sex drive, but that will not be leaving my lips with Beau in the room. Absolutely not.

"High?" Dr. Ness asks with concern.

Immediately, I realize my error. "No, sorry, I meant to say high spirits. Not like alcohol spirits," I stammer, knowing I've been making it worse. "Like, happy. Happy times," I say, lifting both my hands in an awkward thumbs up.

Dr. Ness laughs. "Good, I'm glad to hear that. Have you felt them move yet?"

I shake my head. "Not yet, but sometimes I feel like a little bubble, or a swishing feeling. Does that make sense?"

Dr. Ness guides me to lay down to measure my belly, an excited smile forming on her face. "That is the babies moving! With twins, you can feel things a little sooner, since there is less room for them in there, their movements are more pronounced."

My mind stutters. "Really? That's them? I just... I thought it was my food digesting or something."

"Nope, that's them!"

"Woah," I mutter. I withhold the urge to caress my belly, as she's currently measuring me.

She finishes her exam, and Beau steps out, stating he needs to use the restroom. I'm grateful for the time alone with her, because I do want to mention something.

"Dr. Ness?" I ask before she finishes up.

"Yes?"

"Earlier... when I said I was having high... I was going to say I have a high sex drive." My cheeks flush a bright red, and I want to die inside. "Do you... do you have any suggestions on how to lower that?"

Dr. Ness's expression softens with understanding. "Having a high sex drive in this time of pregnancy is normal with all of the hormone fluctuations going on in your body. I know you mentioned that you and Beau aren't together like that, but it is totally safe to use toys to help relieve the tension. Or, you could ask Beau to help."

I cringe. I'm avoiding doing that very thing, but it's like my body is in agony. I want him, *need* him so badly, and yet, I keep denying myself him. I know if I were to ask, he'd be willing. But, I just can't bring myself to do it.

"Right..." I drag the word out.

"Do you have any more questions for me, about pregnancy and sex? We glossed over the subject at your first appointment, but I want you to feel comfortable and confident."

I swallow hard. Might as well get it over with. With that, I ask her all my questions, asking in depth about what I can and cannot do, with or without Beau.

BEAU

"Alright Mom and Dad, are you ready to find out the genders?" The tech asks, guiding the wand over Marley's belly. In the last few weeks, the babies have grown so much. I can tell that Marley's discomfort is growing. It can't be easy being pregnant, let alone being pregnant with twins.

"Yeah," Marley says. She looks over to me for confirmation.

I nod in agreement. The wand moves, a whooshing sound accompanying it. "Baby A..." she slowly says, "is a boy!"

My heart thumps wildly and I look down at Marley, tears in my eyes. "We're having a boy?" I confirm.

"Yep," the tech responds. Marley smiles, and I lean down, kissing her forehead. I have my arm wrapped around her shoulders, holding her hand in my free one.

"Oh my god," Marley laughs. "I can't believe it."

"We've still got one more baby," the tech responds with a laugh. The wand moves again, the picture on the screen morphing to the other baby. She studies it for a moment, then announces, "And Baby B is a girl!"

Pure shock runs through my veins. My eyes lock with Marley, and tears stream down both our faces. It didn't matter what the genders were, but it doesn't change the excitement. Now we can plan names. Marley can decorate however she wants.

My arm is still wrapped around her shoulders, my head resting on her forehead. "I can't believe this," I murmur, kissing her cheeks, the tip of her nose, her forehead, her lips.

"I know," she replies, eyes still watery.

I glance back up to the screen where we have a view of our daughter and son. "How is it possible to already love them so much?" I ask.

Marley softly laughs, leaning into my touch. "I feel the same. It's such a deep and raw feeling."

I nod, because that's exactly how I feel. Not only for them, but also her. I want to say it. I want her to know how much I love them.

"I love you," I say. "All of you." I press another kiss to her lips, not really giving her a chance to respond. I know she's not there. I've always told her I love her, so that's nothing new. I just don't think she knows that this time, I mean that I'm in love with her.

We bask in the excitement for a few more minutes, and the tech prints off some pictures for us, giving us an extra glimpse of the babies. Baby Boy is proudly showing off his gender, while Baby Girl looks like a little blob of black and white.

It's crazy what you can see with an ultrasound, even in black and white. I guess in a few more weeks, we can do a 3D ultrasound, and really see their faces. Marley wasn't sure if she wanted to do that, but I told her we should.

We walk side-by-side out of the clinic, and I resist the urge to reach down and hold her hand.

"It feels so surreal," Marley states as she settles into the passenger seat. "It makes me want to go shopping, and buy all the things." She laughs.

"Let's go," I say, pulling out of the small clinic parking lot. "We already have the day off work, may as well have some fun."

Marley turns. "You'd do that?"

"What, go shopping?"

"Well... yeah."

"Of course. I want to, Marley. I want to be there to help pick things out."

"Okay," she says with a renewed excitement. "Let's go."

"Where to, butterfly?"

I THINK I greatly underestimated just how much stuff we needed. My vehicle is packed full, and that doesn't even include the two cribs we ordered to be shipped to the house. Nevermind the fact that we need two of everything, babies need a ton of shit.

I'm more determined now to get Marley into a bigger place, though. In fact, the house I showed to that family a few weeks ago is still available. Despite the wife wanting the house, the husband wanted to keep looking. Sure, there are a few minor things wrong with it, but those could be easily fixed on a weekend with my brothers.

Marley's phone buzzes in the center console. We sent a mass text a few hours ago with the babies' genders, deciding not to do the whole gender reveal thing, and our phones have been blowing up since.

Marley is fast asleep, her head leaning back on the headrest, breathing hard. She's worn out from the busy day. My own phone buzzes as well, the group message acting up again.

THOMAS

What are you naming them?

ANDREW

I vote for Andrew for the boy. Or you could name the girl Andrea. That's close enough to Andrew.

JOSIE

Oh my god, you did not just say that.

ANDREW

Why? Is something wrong with Andrew?

JOSIE

face palm emoji

JASON

Some people are trying to work.

THOMAS

Turn your phone off then, grumpy pants. We're having a conversation here.

JASON

*Leaves Chat *

THOMAS

*Adds Jason to chat *

JASON

Seriously?

THOMAS

This is the family chat man, you can't just leave.

ANDREW

I'm offended.

JOSIE

Guys, leave him alone. He's got stuff to do.

ANDREW

Ugh fine. We haven't even heard from Marley and Beau since they sent the message. I think they're purposefully ignoring us.

JOSIE

I can't imagine why.

ANDREW

Was that sarcasm?

JOSIE

How did you ever guess?

THOMAS

fight, fight, fight.

JASON

I'm out.

I pulled into Marley's driveway a few minutes ago, and I've just been watching the messages roll through. My siblings are weird as hell. Marley gasps, startling herself awake.

"We're home?"

"Yep, and my siblings are on a rampage," I say with a chuckle.

Marley stretches, lifting her arms over her head. "Lovely."

"Andrew wants us to name our children after him."

She scoffs. "Right. Like that will happen."

"Pretty much." I shut off the car, and climb out, rounding the vehicle to her side. I open the door, and offer Marley my hand.

She shakes her head. "I'm fine, just taking a minute to wake up."

"I know, I'm just doing my partner-ly duty." She slides her hand into mine, and I help her out of the car. She's right, she doesn't necessarily need help, but either way, I'm happy to be of assistance.

She groans. "I just remembered we have to bring all that stuff in."

"I'll get it. Then what do you think about watching a movie and relaxing?"

"I'd like that," Marley replies, the softest hint of a blush on her cheeks.

MARLEY

Beau strides out of the guest bedroom into the living room, totally shirtless. He has his hair up in a half ponytail bun, and I swear to all that is holy, my mouth actually waters. Fucking hell, why is he doing this to me? Doesn't he know how attractive he is?

I squeeze my thighs together as I sit on the couch, growing irritated rather than more turned on. Beau grabs a glass from the cupboard, filling it with water from the sink. He drinks long gulps of it until it's empty, then sets it in the sink. He glances over at me, and gives me a look of total innocence.

"What?" he asks. He steps toward me, into the living room. When I don't say anything, he climbs onto the couch next to me. Though, I'm currently laying across the length of the couch resting my book on my baby bump. He lifts my legs in order to sit down, then plops my swollen ankles down on his lap.

"Nothing," I grumble. To be honest, I really don't know why I'm irritated with him. I flip the page of my book, realizing that I didn't actually read anything on the previous page. Well, it's not like I'm going to turn back the page. He'd notice.

Beau, clearly having a death wish, starts to massage my sock covered feet. He raises his brows. "Marley. I know you. What's wrong?"

I slap my book shut, resting it against my stomach. "You're shirtless." I use the book to point out my words.

"And?" he questions. "I was hot."

Jesus Christ. I clear my throat. "It's ten degrees out. It's March, in Minnesota, Beau."

He gestures for me to continue, and when I don't, he repeats, "And?"

I drop my head onto my throw pillow. "It's cold, Beau!" I'm completely exasperated now, and I myself don't even know why. "You—" I stutter over the word. "You're going to get sick or get hypothermia!"

Beau looks at me as if I've grown two heads. "Marley, we're inside. It's like seventy seven degrees inside, because you've been cold this week. Next week, I'm sure you'll be hot all the time, so I'll be lucky if the heat is on."

He's got a point. My internal thermometer has been all over the place, though that is not what I'm mad about right now. "You can't just walk around shirtless."

"Why not?"

"Cause, I can't, so therefore you can't. It's only fair."

"I never said you couldn't."

My cheeks burn. My heart pounds. And my vagina clenches around nothing. I barely register the fact that he's still massaging my aching feet.

Beau winks. *He winks.*

I yank my feet from his grip, setting them solidly on the ground as I attempt to move myself to a sitting position. It's quite fumbled though, since I have a volleyball attached to my gut. "Stop it," I groan.

"What?" he mumbles, feigning innocence. "I'm telling the truth."

Exasperated, I groan, deciding to give up on the subject. "Nevermind. I'm crazy."

"Marley," Beau says slowly. "I was teasing. If you want, I will go put a shirt on right now."

"No," I reply. And then I feel my throat tightening, and my eyes sting. "Don't."

He stills. "I... I don't know what to do. Will you cry if I put a shirt on?"

I attempt to scoff, but it comes out a choked sound. "No. I won't cry."

Beau sinks back into the couch, but not before leaning forward to grab my legs. I follow his movements, slowly laying back down onto the couch. He scoots closer to me so that his hip is against my butt, my thighs covering his. Reaching out, he grabs the hand I just rested against my belly. Squeezing gently, he says, "I'll wear a shirt from now on."

Shaking my head, I feel overwhelmed. "No," I reply. "Don't. I'm just being silly. I don't even know why I did that. I'm so all over the place. I like..." I trail off, because I don't know if I want to admit that I thoroughly enjoy him being shirtless.

"You like?" Beau says teasingly.

I groan, shutting my eyes. "I like being able to see your tattoos." I can't see his reaction, but he squeezes my palm again.

Neither Beau, nor I have brought up his new tattoo again. It's not like it's a taboo subject, but to be honest, I'm a little scared to do it. Scared to confront the emotions that I'm sure will come with it. When I got my own butterfly tattoo, I was at a low. I got it because butterflies have always signified change for me. A metamorphosis. I was ready to let go and start over, morph into something new, and let the flowers of my life bloom. I felt like I'd lost Beau, the one person I could always lean on. I knew my life was going to change, it just changed in a way I never would have expected.

But Beau's tattoo... it has to mean something. He's called me butterfly off and on since we were kids, and more frequently since I've gotten pregnant. And now, he has a beautiful antique clock, with three butterflies flying out of it. I can't think about it or I'll get choked up. I can't think about the fact that maybe those three butterflies signify me and the twins. Our babies and the life we've made.

"I like seeing your tattoos, too." He uses the hand he had on my leg, to rest on the swell of my stomach. "Do you think you will get a tattoo for the babies?" he asks, rubbing soft circles over my sweatshirt.

Opening my eyes, I shrug. Beau is glancing down at his hand. The babies aren't super active right now, probably sleeping. I've been able to feel them pretty frequently, but Beau hasn't been able to catch it yet.

"I'm not sure. Probably. I don't know what, though." I hesitate, then ask, "Will you?"

Beau's hand stills on my belly. He doesn't say anything for a long moment. "I..." he starts speaking slowly. "I already did."

My heart clenches tightly in my chest at the subtle confirmation of what I already knew. "You did?"

Beau shifts, angling his arm so I can see his shoulder clearly. He lifts his palm from my stomach, and gently traces the three butterflies. "This one," he says, pointing to the one closest to the clock, "is you. The other two are the babies."

As I process his words, confirming what I already suspected, he keeps speaking. "The clock... The clock is obviously a symbol of time, but the hands point up, toward you. To me, it means that there is never going to be enough time with you. With the family we are making."

"Beau..." His name cracks as I speak, every wall I've built crumbles down into rubble at our feet. I sit forward, doing my best so I don't look like a beached whale in this pivotal moment. Reaching, I brush my fingertips over the tattoo. It's so detailed, the butterflies so perfectly symmetrical. If I look close enough, I can make out the shape of an M in the wings of the butterfly that represents me. "I... thank you."

Beau shrugs. "You mean more to me than anyone in this world, and now the babies will be the center of ours."

I don't know why it's taken me so long to really understand, but he's in this. He's really in this, really there for me. For our family and this life that we've created. Without a second thought, I lean forward, cupping his cheek in my palm, and press my lips to his.

37

———

BEAU

arley's lips are against mine. Her soft, plump lower lip parts, and I take that as an invitation to take control of the kiss. Her hand cups my cheek, and I reach out, doing the same to hers. Her bump is in the middle of us, proof of the beautiful things we created. My other hand trails down her neck to rest on her breastbone. Her sweatshirt is thick between us, and while I don't want to rush it, I want it off her. I want to feel her soft skin underneath me again. To feel the curve of her breasts, the peak of her nipples in my mouth.

I let my teeth gently nip at her lip, loving how pliant she is. She isn't fighting this, isn't drunk, isn't doing it to prove anything. She's giving herself to me willingly. She hasn't let me kiss her for more than a peck every so often, and fuck if I haven't missed the way she tastes. More so, she hasn't taken the lead on a kiss, touch, or even second glance with me, so this feels different.

"Marley," I groan into her mouth. She arches her neck, leaning away from the kiss, but giving me more access to her. The hand I had on her cheek moves down, sliding

212

down to her waist, to those thick and ample curves that I fucking love so much. I lift the band of her sweatshirt up so my hand is on her bare skin. The touch gives her goosebumps, and I press kisses to her neck, accentuating my touches.

"This isn't going to work," Marley breathlessly whispers.

And just like that, my chest squeezes. "Don't say that," I murmur with conviction. "This will work. It *is* working."

"No, Beau," Marley reiterates. She pushes against my chest with her palm. "I mean like, literally. This," she gestures to her swollen bump. "This is too in the way."

Realization dawns. "We can adapt," I murmur, kissing her again. "For now, I just want you to lay back and enjoy. Can you do that?"

Marley darts out her tongue, swiping it over that bottom lip of hers, now swollen from my kisses. Her eyes are glazed over, eager for what will happen next. She nods, letting me tug her sweatshirt up and off her body.

She's bare underneath. No t-shirt, no bra. Just her beautiful skin. Her nipples have darkened and her breasts have grown even more since the last time I had my mouth on them. I have to hold in the feral moan I feel rising up my throat.

My head drops, and I take one of her nipples into my mouth. Marley jolts underneath me, her hands threading into my hair. I multitask, using my tongue to flick at her nipples, while one hand pinches the peaked bud of her other nipple, and the other hand slides down her skin to her pants. The leggings cling to her body, accentuating every curved and rounded edge. I let my mouth continue its work while I shimmy her leggings down. I free her nipple to lean back and watch what I'm doing.

When I reveal her worn blue cotton panties, I let out a moan. Don't get me wrong, I imagine this woman in lacy panties and lingerie nearly every day, but there's something so real about this moment. It's unplanned, unprompted, and just... real.

"Goddamn, butterfly." I groan, eager to have a taste of her. I scoot down the couch, pulling her panties down her legs as I do. When I get a glimpse of that pretty pussy, I nearly lose it. My dick throbs in my sweats, like it's reminding me that it needs attention, but it will have to wait. My focus is on Marley, and to be honest, I could care less if I come or not. I just want to make her feel good, to make sure she knows how much I want her. "I can't wait to feel you come on my mouth again."

Marley shivers in anticipation. I lower my body, my aim directly on her clit. When my tongue makes first contact, swiping up the length of her slit, she jerks under the touch. She sucks in heavy breaths as I tease her with my tongue. She tastes so good, like everything I've ever needed. I move to her clit, swirling and flicking at it, trying to learn what she likes.

Her grip on my hair tightens, giving me some insight that she's enjoying it. I don't have much room on the couch, but I'm making it work somehow. Next time—because there *will* be a next time, and soon—we do this, I'll make sure we have more room.

My fingers find her soaked entrance, and I slide one finger in, pumping slowly.

"Beau," Marley says through shuddering breaths. "I-I need you," she cries.

I lift myself from her cunt for one quick sentence. "You have me."

Adding another finger, I curl upward, putting a slight

pressure in my movements. She writhes, one leg sliding off the couch so her foot is flat on the floor. I hook the other leg up and around my right shoulder, angling her ass up slightly. Marley is moaning incoherent words and sounds, her pussy clenching tightly around my fingers.

"I'm," she stammers. "I'm coming, Beau," Marley shrieks, the sounds of her pleasure loud in the quiet living room. My hips grind against the couch, seeking any sort of friction.

I don't stop until her pussy stops fluttering around my fingers, then I'm scooting up so I can kiss my way up her belly. I press kisses across the tight skin of her bump, all the way up her breasts and neck until I reach her mouth. I cup her cheek, kissing her deeply, trying to convey my love for her into every touch. I don't think I'll handle it if she pushes me away again.

I know she's trying to protect her heart, to protect our babies, but she doesn't need to, because I'll do it for her. I'll hold her heart for safekeeping until she allows herself to fully lean into this relationship.

Marley's tongue tangles with mine, and she presses her hand against my chest, sitting forward.

"I can't breathe when I lay like that for long," she murmurs against my lips. "Or when you make me come so hard I see stars." She laughs, and I allow her to sit up, rocking back onto my heels.

Marley reaches forward, her palm cupping my hard-as-steel length through my pants. She squeezes it gently, my body spasming under her touch. I groan into her mouth, eager to have her bare hand on me.

Using the hand on my chest, she pushes me off her again. "Beau," she says my name in a voice so sultry it sends a shiver through my body. "I need you. I need this." Her fingers caress my bare chest as she adjusts her body to a more comfortable position.

"Tell me what you want," I say.

"I need to feel you inside me again."

I'm standing before she finishes the words, my head frantically searching the room for something, though I'm not sure what. I drop to my knees in front of her, turning her body so she can lay back, but she doesn't let me. "No, wait," she says.

"What?" I ask. My brow raises as I take in every single thing about her. I am putty in her hands, eager to do anything for her.

"Stand up," she tugs on my arms, prompting me to stand. She fingers the hem of my sweats, tugging them down. I don't have boxers on, so my cock bounces free as soon as the fabric is off. Her fingers wrap around the base of my cock, squeezing gently as she moves up and down my shaft.

"Marley," I groan as she moves. "Fuck, butterfly don't stop." I watch her eyes, the way her pupils dilate and take in my body. They scan up my chest, lingering over my tattoos until she reaches my face. Her brown eyes are round when they meet mine, continuing the tortuously slow movements on my dick.

"I haven't had time to fully appreciate you," Marley says. "That night..." she trails off.

"Was the most incredible thing to ever happen." She nods, her cheeks flushing scarlet. I cup her cheeks in my palms, noting how large my hands are compared to her small, round face. Her bangs are hanging in her eyes, so I brush them aside with my thumbs, and press quick kisses to her lips.

Marley continues to pump my dick with her hand, her

other resting on my thigh. Her warmth enraptures me, tethering me to this moment. I can feel the moment when she lets go, when she gives into this feeling. Her entire body relaxes, sinking into my touch. I lower myself down to kneeling again, and she lets me, releasing her fingers from my cock.

"Come here." I take her hands, pulling her from the couch. She sinks to her knees in front of me, so we are chest to chest. I quickly kiss her. "What will be most comfortable for you?" I ask, resting my palm on her stomach.

Marley's cheeks pinken again. "I... I asked Dr. Ness about this one of the last times we were in. I knew it was only a matter of time, and I wanted to be prepared."

I nod, loving that it means she has been quietly accepting this for a while.

Marley chuckles. "Nothing like talking about your doctor when you're about to have sex."

I kiss her forehead, no longer ignoring my constant need to be touching her at all times. "If that's what it takes for you to be comfortable, we can talk about it."

She shakes her head. "No. She just said as long as we don't put pressure on the babies, it's fine. So... like, from behind, or laying on my side, with you behind me is probably easiest."

I nod. I run my hands up and down her bare arms, feeling her goosebumps. "I have an idea. Turn around."

Marley shuffles so she's facing the couch. Moving so my body is nearly flush with hers, I wrap my arms under her breasts, while kissing her neck. Leaning forward, I guide her so that her chest is down on the couch. Her elbows prop her up, but when I lean back, I get the perfect view of her back and ass. Trailing my fingers down her back, I grip her waist. My cock nestles against her warmth, her soaked pussy so fucking ready for me. Marley twists just a bit so she can look back at me, while also staying in the position I settled her in.

"How's this?" I ask. My hands roam, unable to stay still with her beneath me like this.

"It's good," she breathlessly replies, and I can tell by the look in her eyes that she's telling the truth. I lift one knee up, the other resting on the carpeted floor. Her legs are between my thighs, perfect for what I want to do.

"Are you ready?" I ask, taking my hard cock into my palm. I slide it up and down her slit, gathering the wetness there. It glistens on the head of my cock, just waiting for her approval.

"So ready. Fuck me, Beau," Marley says. I line up my cock and thrust in. I slide in until I'm fully seated, my hips flush against her round ass.

"Fuuuuck," I groan. She's tight, soaked, and so fucking mine. With every movement, I can feel her wetness growing, dripping from her entrance. She meets me with my pace, her hips rolling into mine.

Only, it's not enough, I need to be deeper. It's as if she knows, because Marley stops me. "Wait," she groans. "I need you closer." She pulls her right leg forward, trying to lift it to hook up and around my knee, and drape over my thigh. She can't get the angle right until I lower my leg, and when she has hers draped over, I lift it back up. The new angle instantly allows my cock to slide in deeper. Marley's hips drop, her ass popping out and up.

"Yes," she hisses, and I pick up my rhythm again, knowing that I'm not going to last very long.

My fingers dig into her ass cheeks as she grinds against me. I do my best to lean forward and kiss her, but with the new position, I can't. Marley's breathing quickens, her back glistening with sweat under the exertion. I grit my teeth and bite the inside of my cheek, trying to do anything to hold myself back from coming. She feels too fucking good that I'm about to lose it.

"Beau," she cries out my name, her head dropping forward onto the couch. With one arm, she tries to reach her clit to give herself some additional pleasure, but can't reach it with her belly.

"I got you," I groan, leaning forward best I can to reach down and strum my fingers across her clit. It doesn't take long, between my pace and the movement of my fingers, to feel her coming around my cock.

It feels like the first time, only better, because I know that no matter what, I'm never letting her go.

38

MARLEY

My pussy clenches around Beau's cock as he pounds into me from behind. His fingers are still rubbing my throbbing clit, and if he keeps up the pace, I might come yet again.

"Oh god," I cry, my body tingling and alive with heat.

"I'm going to come, Marley," Beau groans, his shaft filling me with each pulse and press of his body into mine. His movements become harsher and faster until he stills, thrusting only slightly as he empties himself inside me.

His warmth leaks from me, dripping onto the carpet below us. I don't care, though. This moment is pure bliss. My head drops onto my arms on the couch, my breath coming stuttered and fast. A bead of sweat drips down my forehead and onto my arm. Beau's hands drag up and down my back, soothing an invisible wound.

Words fail me. I thought that our first night together was the best sexual experience of my entire life, but I was wrong. Or maybe it's because I was drunk, that I thought it was so good, but this just beat it tenfold.

Beau leans down, kissing my back and up my neck. His

rapidly softening cock slides out of my soaked pussy, and I immediately miss him. A shiver wracks through my body as he shifts my leg off his thigh. There's an ache in the muscle, but not enough that it's painful. It's a good reminder of what we just experienced, the way it felt.

I knew I needed to have him the moment he explained his tattoo, and I knew I would be waiting for that regret to hit after, but... it hasn't. If anything, it feels right, like things are settling into place, the last piece finally clicking.

As if to agree with my internal line of thinking, both babies kick on opposite sides of my stomach. I gasp, their sudden movement a jolt of reality. "Woah," I breathe.

"What's wrong?" Beau asks, his voice suddenly panicked, all previous relaxation gone. I shiver as the sweat dries, my body no longer heated and moving.

"It's okay," I chuckle. "I think we woke up the babies." I lift my head, and sit back on my heels, shifting so Beau can see that I'm really okay. "Here." I reach out, taking his hand.

He scoots closer, but not before taking two blankets off the couch. He wraps one around my shoulders, and lays the other across his lap. I take one of his palms, resting it on the side where Baby Boy is kicking the shit out of me, and then take the other, to rest on the opposite side, where Baby Girl is. I lay my hands over his, and through his palms, I can feel the subtle bumps of the babies.

Beau's eyes glaze over. He hasn't felt them kick until today. They are asleep most of the day, only waking in the night when I'm in bed and he's fast asleep. Beau is completely enthralled at the feeling, and it's something I've gotten so used to that I forgot how incredible it is.

In my small living room, with his hands on my belly, our babies moving inside me, I allow myself to fall deeper in love with Beau Cunningham. For the first time since we found out I was pregnant, I really let go, and don't fight my feelings.

WE STAY in the living room for far longer than necessary, only cleaning ourselves up after the babies' movements slowed. We take turns showering, since my shower is not built for two people, especially when one is a plus-sized pregnant woman carrying twins.

I make Beau go first, since he'll be quicker After I climb out, I do my best to dry myself with the towel that doesn't quite wrap around my body anymore. Beau is standing in the open doorway of the bathroom, watching me with interest.

"Uhh, whatcha doing there?" I ask, my wet hair dripping down my back.

"Bringing you clothes," he replies. He's wearing a tee shirt now, and a pair of sweats. It's highly unfair that he's already in his cozy clothes.

"Oh," I murmur, seeing the pile of clothes he's laid out on the counter for me. "Thank you." Again, here he is, meeting my needs before I realize them.

"I'll let you get dressed," he says, an almost sheepish grin on his face. He turns, closing the bathroom door behind him, and I let myself take an extra breath. I throw my hair up into a towel to wring out some of the extra water in it, and work to dry the rest of my body. Before dressing, I lather some sweet smelling lotion all over, internally cursing the Minnesota winters for making my skin so dry.

As I rub the lotion over my stomach, one of the babies kicks my rib. I wince, and press my fingers down on the spot. "Stop it," I scold, as if they know what they're doing to me. Like they're responding, they kick back. I shrug the shirt over my body, cringing when it's tight across my stomach. It used to be a loose tee on me, and now it barely stretches across my large stomach. I sigh, mournfully, knowing I still have weeks of pregnancy ahead of me.

I leave the bathroom, heading toward my room. Thankfully, I'm not quite at the waddling stage of pregnancy, but I'm sure it's only a matter of time. Seems like time has sped up since the day we found out I was pregnant.

Beau stands in the hall between my room and his, leaning against the wall as he scrolls on his phone. When he hears me coming, he slides it into his pocket, looking up with a glint in his brown eyes. It's surreal to me that the man I've called my best friend my whole life—the one I've trusted with everything, the one I've pushed away more than once out of fear of getting too close—is here, and this is the path our lives have taken. I'm standing here, swollen ankles, huge pregnant belly wearing a shirt that no longer fits, no makeup, and my hair up in a towel atop my head, and he's still looking at me like I hung the moon. Like I'm the one he would sacrifice everything for.

I swallow the sudden lump in my throat and step closer to him. He reaches out his hand, taking mine without question. He leads me into my room, and unwraps the towel from my head. My damp hair falls down my back, bangs strewn across my forehead in what, I'm sure, is a ridiculous style.

"Where's your brush?" Beau asks. He makes his way toward my dresser, where I have a random collection of things. "Nevermind, I found it," he says, holding it up like a trophy.

"Thanks," I say, holding out my hand to grab it from him.

Beau holds his finger up in between us, shaking it back and forth. "Nuh-uh."

I raise my brow, confused, until he guides me to sit on the edge of my bed. He climbs onto the mattress behind me, fingers already gliding across my shoulders.

"I can do it, Beau," I try to reason, but he gently squeezes my shoulders.

"Let me, please," he murmurs in my ear, and I catch the scent of his body wash. The clean, familiar smell of him makes me pliant and agreeable.

I nod, leaning back slightly. Beau starts by separating my hair into sections, then slowly runs the brush through the pieces of hair starting at the bottom. The touch is so soothing and relaxing, I find my eyes falling shut. When the brush reaches my scalp, I open my eyes.

"I think I'll have to cut my hair once the twins are born," I confess, voicing something I've thought about for the last few weeks.

"Why?" Beau asks. His tone is curious. "Not that it matters to me, you're beautiful with long or short hair," he rushes to clarify. I reach behind me, squeezing his leg.

"I know what you mean," I say. "Babies are grabby, and sometimes, hair is the closest option."

Beau scoots off the bed, ready to head to the dresser with the brush. I snap my fingers. "Hey, it's my turn," I scold.

He turns, brows pinched. "Your turn?"

"To brush your hair." His hair is still in a knotted mess after showering. I gesture to the floor, and he smiles, handing it over, and sitting down between my legs. With one hand holding the brush, I run the other through the damp waves on his head. "You might have to cut your hair too." The thought makes me sad, because I love his long hair.

"Nah," Beau says. I can see his face in the mirror, and he's all smiles as I run the brush through it. While his hair is long, it's still much shorter than mine, and less tangled, so it takes just a few strokes of the brush before it's done. "I think I'll keep it."

"Yeah?" I ask. "Babies can be really strong."

"There's no way they're that strong," he tries to say, but I narrow my eyes at him through the mirror.

"Whatever you say," I tell him. He stands, taking the brush from my outstretched palm. "I won't cut it right away, but it might have to happen once they're a few months old."

Beau nods. He stands in front of me, almost awkwardly now, as if he's waiting for something. I slowly stand from the bed, and pull back my sheets and comforter. My trusty pregnancy pillow is strewn across the middle of the bed. I feel some of the awkwardness radiating from Beau, and it's making me uncomfortable, because... what now? We still aren't together... at least I don't think we are. It's not like we had a conversation about it while he was inside me. Does he want to sleep in here? Do I *want* him to sleep in here?

My internal answer is almost an immediate resounding yes. *Yes*, I want to fall asleep with Beau's arms around me, around our babies.

"You're thinking awfully hard." Beau rounds the bed to the other side, and pulls the sheets down.

I stare down at the pillow. "It's just..."

Beau interrupts me. "Marley, I want to sleep in here. Is that okay?"

I nod. "I want that too," I reply instantly, looking up at his handsome face.

"Then what's wrong?"

"It's... I take up a lot of space."

His eyes narrow.

"I mean... I tend to sprawl out. And the pillow is the only way I get any sleep, so I'm just worried I'll kick you or something."

He chuckles under his breath. "Love, if you kick me in your sleep, I'll consider it payback since you have to deal with the twins kicking you all day. I want to hold you. I need to be close to you."

I nod, and do my best to climb into bed without looking like a flopping fish out of water. Apparently I'm not successful, because Beau snickers. "Hey, you try getting in bed with two babies in your belly. It's not easy!" I roll onto my right side, and try to adjust myself again. Now that I think about it, maybe we should tape a watermelon to his stomach so he can know what it feels like. I've seen videos of that on social media.

I reach out, grabbing the pregnancy pillow and shoving it between my legs. I roll onto my back, sliding it under the bump and then roll back to my side. My face is toward the wall, my arms cradling the pillow. I hear the shuffle of sheets, feeling the mattress dip as Beau climbs in.

It feels... weird. The last time we cuddled, we were drunk, and I was convinced I'd just made the worst mistake of my life. Now, we're thrust into this life together, something we have both wanted for so long, just not in the way we expected it. It makes me wonder if I can do this, if I really can let myself go, the way I slowly have been, to give us the best chance at a life together.

Beau's arm wraps around my waist, cradling me against him. He scoots himself closer to me, instead of having me move myself after I just got comfortable. The small—

minuscule, really—gesture is enough to have tears sliding down my cheeks.

I sniffle. "Thank you."

"Thank you," Beau replies, and like always, he knows what I need. He holds me close and whispers all the exciting things that are coming for our future. Meanwhile, I lay there, feeling more connected to him than I have in my entire life.

My phone vibrates on my desk as I edit some photos from an earlier session this week. The couple I did the shoot with is sprawled across the bed, a tangle of sheets, skin, and expert angles so you don't see everything, just enough to make you curious.

I did the wedding photos for this couple last year. I love getting to see both sides of them, on the biggest day of their lives, and then in a more natural, comfortable setting.

I finish the final edits of the photo, ignoring the ideas that pop into my head when I think about doing a shoot of Beau and me. What positions would I put us in? Would I have him between my thighs? Would I make it appear as if he's eating me out? Or I'm riding him?

A pulsing settles between my thighs at the mental image. In the weeks since we were together again, I thought maybe my constant horniness would get better, but it hasn't. If anything, it's worse. I should try to take care of myself, especially since I have the A-okay from Dr. Ness, but I can't find the time, and I'm definitely not about to ask Beau. What if he says no?

My phone vibrates again, re-notifying me of the message I'd forgotten about. I tap my screen to see who the text is from, not really surprised when the message is from Beau.

BEAU

Hey butterfly, what are your plans after work?

ME

Hmmm. Probably sit on the couch with my feet up in your lap since they're swollen again. I wouldn't be opposed to one of those foot rubs you gave me a few weeks ago. ;)

Haha, you got it. What do you think about going out on a little dinner date first?

My stomach flutters, and one of the babies kicks me at the same time, so I get a double whammy of butterflies. It's like they're telling me, *"do it, Mom!"*

ME

I'd love that. What time?

BEAU

Six?

Sounds perfect. Where to?

I was thinking something more casual, unless you really want to go somewhere fancy, then we could head into the cities?

I scrunch my nose. While a fancy dinner date sounds fun, the thought of doing that tonight does not.

ME

Casual is preferred haha. I'm not sure I'll be up for a fancy night until long after these babies are no longer occupying my uterus.

BEAU

You got it.

I should stop getting so excited every time I see his face on my screen, should stop the butterflies I get every time I see his face, and avoid the inevitable hurt, but I don't. With a sigh, I lock my computer, vowing to finish the edits tomorrow morning, and head out of my studio, waving at Josie in her shop next door as I leave.

Beau arrives to my house around the same time that I do, and after a shower and a fresh set of clothes, we decide on one of the our favorite places in town, a classic bar and grill..

"I thought now would be a good time to iron out some details," Beau says. He's sitting across from me in the small booth, a glass of ice water in front of him. The waitress has just left to put in our orders: a cheeseburger for me and a BLT for Beau.

"What kind of details?" I ask.

He takes a deep breath. "I don't want you to get defensive about it, but... space. We're going to need more of it."

I sigh, a slight irritation blooming. He's just trying to help and be proactive, and yet, I can't stop the feeling. "I like my house, Beau."

"I know you do, but we're going to be bringing two babies home now. Not just one. It's barely big enough for two adults, let alone two adults and two infants who require a ton of stuff."

I take a sip of my water. Deep down, I know he's right,

but my house is one thing that I can control. My life is changing drastically right now, between a not-really relationship with my best friend and being pregnant with his twins.If I don't have the place I feel most comfortable, then what do I have?

"I know I've been staying with you, but I wanted to formally ask you." Beau pauses, as if waiting for some sort of reaction. I don't speak or react, so he continues. "Are you comfortable with me moving in and putting my house on the market? It doesn't make sense for me to have my place and live with you and the babies."

"Yes," I say without a second thought. I might not know what will happen between us, but I know that I don't want to do this without him. "Put your house on the market."

The smile that breaks out on his face is reminiscent of the smile he gave when I told him I was starting my own photography business. Proud, excited, and so much life in his eyes.

"I'll get a storage unit and really downsize, but I do think we should talk further about a bigger house." Beau reaches across the table and I rest my hand in his, squeezing softly.

"One step at a time. Okay? I'm not saying no, I just... I need time to acclimate."

He nods and a flicker of heat passes between us. I find my mind straying to the feeling of his mouth on my breasts, tongue caressing over my nipples as he eased the discomfort of taking my piercings out. My cheeks inadvertently heat at the memory, and I can tell that Beau must be having a similar thought cross his mind.

The waitress arrives with our food a few minutes later, startling us as she sets the baskets down on the table. We rush to pull apart and I lean back against the leather of the booth. I scrub my hands up and down my thighs, my hunger overtaking the moment.

WHEN WE GET in the car after dinner, the atmosphere is quiet. We haven't talked much more outside of selling his house, but there's been a continued, undeniable tension between us, albeit not a bad kind.

Beau reaches across the console, taking my hand in his. He squeezes three times, and my heart flutters. That low heat starts to simmer low in my belly, and I think of my earlier conversation with Dr. Ness. She basically told me to enjoy myself and to listen to my body.

However, what my body wants is Beau. I know I shouldn't want him. I should be keeping a distance after my slip up a few weeks ago, but apparently, my mind and body are on two completely different train tracks.

Beau runs his thumb over the back of my hand, talking about things we still might need before the babies arrive. I'm not paying much attention though, too focused on the way my clit is practically pulsing. I can't stop thinking about the way his thumb felt brushing over my sensitive nipples instead of my hand. Or the way he will gently caress my cheek with the same thumb.

My heart thrums in my chest, my body aching with the need to be touched by him. I must be completely lost to my own senses, because we're pulling into my driveway a moment later.

"What are your plans for the rest of the night? Want me to give you that foot massage?" Beau asks with a small waggle of his brows. He turns off the car, letting go of my hand. A shiver rolls up my arm at the loss of his warmth and I shift in my seat, squeezing my thighs together.

I look at my phone, checking the time. It's just past seven, but pitch black outside, no thanks to it being the dead of winter. "Rain check? I might go to bed early. It's been a busy day. What about you?"

Beau nods. "That's fine. I need to catch up on a show so Andrew can finally talk to me about it without spoiling, but then I won't be far behind you." He opens his car door, and the frigid winter air seeps into the once warm car. I brace myself before opening my own door. The air is like a near literal bucket of ice water dumped over my head. It cools my heated body, but only momentarily, because Beau is striding up to stand beside me.

Beau has slept in my bed since that night a few weeks ago, and while I love it, it hasn't exactly given me much time to take care of things myself.

He reaches out, pulling me in close, his arm around my shoulders. "Come on, let's get you in where it's warm, butterfly."

I let him lead me inside, allowing myself the freedom to sink into the embrace. The snow crunches under my feet, giving away just how cold it is, and thankfully, we're inside quickly.

Beau helps me slide my jacket off, hanging it on a hook on the wall. I rest my hand over my belly as I kick off my snow-covered boots. I wobble slightly as I'm taking one off. Beau reaches out, clasping his fingers around my upper arm. "Don't want you falling," he murmurs.

When I look up, his brown eyes are dark, hair falling into his face.

"I'm okay," I say, my voice breathy, almost needy. I tear my gaze away from his, and head further into the house. I shake my hands out, trying to get my head to clear, and my body to get with the program. I need to get out of Beau's vicinity, because I need to take care of this needy feeling.

All I want right now is to ride Beau till my bones are mush. I cringe at my own thoughts. *Did I really just think that?*

"I think I'm going to go to bed," I squeak, waving behind me in Beau's direction. I don't look back at him, out of fear that I may maul his beautifully handsome face if I look at him once more.

"Okay?" he says, more so as a question. He's probably confused by my abrupt exit, but I need to get away.

I rush down the hall toward my bedroom, and when I get a whiff of Beau's muted cologne wafting from the guest room, I'm a goner. I need a release like I need my next breath. I nearly fly into my bedroom, closing the door as gently as I can behind me, and shimmying my leggings down to the floor. I kick both the leggings and my under-wear off as I make my way to the bed.

"Fuck," I curse as I feel just how needy I am.

I flop like a beached whale onto my bed, blindly reaching into my nightstand for my trusty toys. I grab the first one my hand touches, my free hand already reaching between my bare thighs. Wetness has gathered there, and I let out a low moan, biting down on my lip to silence myself when my fingers make contact with my clit.

My hand brings forward the toy I've grabbed, the one that focuses on my clit. Perfect. I hold down the button to turn on the suction, and ramp it up all the way. Just the way I like it.

All the repressed tension starts to release from my body as soon as it makes contact with my clit. "Oh, god," I moan. I lose myself to the sensations, my hips rocking at their own rhythm. The hand not controlling the toy slides under my shirt, pulling my bra cups down. My fingers skate over my nipples, teasing them gently. I miss my piercings, but my nipples are just as sensitive now without them as they were with them.

Thank you, pregnancy.

I tease myself, adjusting the vibrator slightly. I try to shut off my mind, to just give in, but I can't. I can't stop thinking of Beau. Of the way he felt inside me, his fingers, and his cock. The way his weight felt over me, the way he kissed me.

My cunt clenches around the emptiness, and I yearn for more. I already can't get the best angle with the vibrator due to my stomach, so I can't imagine that trying to multitask with my dildo and my vibrator would end in anything other than frustration.

I turn my head, unknowingly turning my face into a leftover hit of his cologne from the close contact I had with him throughout the night. I inhale, sucking in that perfect scent of him. My clit thumps, a low heat rumbling through my core. My pussy tightens, taking me closer and closer to an orgasm that I so desperately need. I twist and pinch my nipples, giving into the temptation, remembering his mouth on them.

With that, I explode, coming hard and fast. My entire body shakes with the release, my legs unable to stop moving. I let out a loud string of curses, grateful that I'm alone, and can let myself go, can let myself feel every breathtaking moment of this incredible orgasm.

The vibrator moves just a bit, but it spurs another round of pleasure. My heart pounds, body going limp, only jerking every other second as I try to compose myself.

I needed that. I shift the vibrator from my now over-sensitive clit, holding down the button to turn it off. I flop my hand onto the bed next to me, the vibrator landing beside me on the comforter.

With a heavy sigh, I allow the endorphins to run through my body, giving me that natural high I've been craving.

An eerie feeling washes over me though, and I get the sense that I'm no longer alone.

Sure enough, when I open my eyes, Beau is standing in the now open doorway, leaning against the frame, his arms crossed, and his eyes hungry.

40

———

BEAU

I knew it. As soon as we walked in the door, I knew something was up. I had a feeling she needed me, and... she did, just not in the way I expected.

I watch as Marley tenses, her body cresting through what appears to be an incredible orgasm. Her legs shake, hand holding the little blue toy tightly to her soaking clit. From here, I can see how wet she is. Her pussy glistens in the dim light of her room, and my mouth waters. *Literally waters.* Because I know what she tastes like, and I'm ready for another hit.

She moves the toy from her pussy, turning it off and flopping her arm to her side. My dick strains in my pants, aching painfully. I lean against the frame of the door, crossing my arms as I watch her. Watch her as she catches her breath, and when she opens her eyes, she freezes.

"Butterfly..." I drag out the word. "What are you doing?" She sinks further into the bed—if that was possible —sliding her legs closed. She doesn't say anything, but her cheeks grow hot. "Because it looks like you were taking care of something that is my job."

Marley scoffs indignantly. "It's not your job."

I step forward into the room, taking the elastic from my wrist and pulling my hair back into a bun. "Yes it is. It is my job to take care of you in any way you need, pregnant or not."

She scoots up, sitting cross-legged on her bed. "I can take care of myself," she murmurs, tucking her hair behind her ear. She looks down, spots her vibrator on the bed, and quickly shoves it under the covers. "You shouldn't have seen that."

"I beg to differ. It seems like you might need some help."

"I already came, Beau," she says with an embarrassed look. "I don't need your help."

"Yeah, once. And my butterfly needs more than one to be *truly* satisfied."

She is still refusing to look at me. I sit down on the bed in front of her. My hand reaches out, covering hers where it rests on the bed. I trail my fingers up her arm over her shirt, only stopping when I reach her neck. Goosebumps erupt on her skin.

"Beau," she breathes my name, sending my own trail of shivers over my body. She's not flat on her back, as she isn't supposed to anymore, but sort of... half sitting. I lift my hand, cupping her cheek, and lean forward. My lips take hers in a harsh kiss. I need her to feel all my pent up emotions. The way I feel about her. The way I need her *so desperately*.

Marley tangles her hands in my tied hair, holding me to her mouth. Her teeth graze against my bottom lip, and she does something totally unexpected. She bites. Not a soft nip either, it almost feels like she's trying to mark me.

I groan into her mouth, scooting up so I can get onto my

knees on the bed. Our mouths stay locked together as her hands slide under my shirt. Her fingers trail over my stomach, my chest, then back down, nails scratching delicately over my goosebump-covered skin. I groan against her lips when her fingers lift the bottom of my shirt, and I drop my hands from her face, allowing her to take my shirt off. We part with heavy breaths, and I take in the sight of her—lips swollen and wet, eyes glassy and round as she takes in my body.

Marley reaches out her hand, caressing my shoulder and sliding her pointer finger over the details of my tattoo. She traces the wings of the butterflies, then the arms of the clock. I shudder at the gentle touch, but instead of letting her continue, I stop her, using my hand to guide hers off my shoulder. I slide it down until she's resting over my heart, where she can surely feel the rapid pace.

I lock my eyes on hers, taking in the moment again. The world slows, giving me just another second to be just us two. Just two people who don't know what is going to happen next, but at least we have each other to hold.

I lean into her, pressing kisses across her jaw, then her lips. I move so I'm kneeling beside her, cupping her cheek in one palm, and using my other hand to hold her smaller hand against my pounding heart. I pull away so I can tell her how I want this to go.

"I need another taste of you, Mar." Marley lets her hand fall from my chest, and I rock back on my heels. "You're going to ride my face."

Marley's eyes widen. "Right," she scoffs.

I take her soft hips in my hands, gripping slightly. Rolling onto my back, I take her with me, gently so she doesn't get hurt, but also in a way that shows her I'm not fucking around. I land with my head on a pillow, and

Marley adjusts so she's straddling my chest. Her wet pussy is warm on my chest, and fuck, I can't wait to feel her thighs around my head like fucking ear muffs. I would die a happy man if I could taste her, and make her come like this every day, but I get the feeling that this moment may be fleeting, so I fully intend to not take a moment for granted.

My hands slide down slightly so they rest on her thighs, squeezing the dimpled yet smooth skin. With one hand, I push up her shirt so I can get a full view of her slightly rounded stomach, and her full breasts. Marley reaches back, unhooking her bra and letting it fall from her arms after her shirt is off.

Her breasts practically topple from the shelf of her bra, her nipples dark pink and tips swollen. My hand runs over her bump, cupping one of her breasts with one hand.

"Oh," she sighs, when I pinch her swollen nipple. "Beau."

"It's my turn to make you come, butterfly." I move both hands to her hips, and pull her up my chest.

Once I've arranged her where I want her, and she's hovering over me, I lift my eyes to hers. She looks concerned, and I think I know why.

Winking, I'm about to settle her on my mouth, when she stops me.

"Do you…" she hesitates. "Are you sure this is a good idea?"

I raise my brow, not bothering to answer. My mouth attacks her clit with eagerness, flicking and swirling. She bucks over me immediately, leaning back, resting one hand against my stomach. She's holding back, not settling her full weight on me, though.

I pull back. "Marley," I groan. "This is a fucking fantastic idea, so I'd really appreciate it if you give me a set of ear muffs, courtesy of your thighs. Give me all of you, and I'll make you come so hard you'll forget all about that fucking toy of yours."

She sits forward, eyes wide. She chokes out a stuttered word, but doesn't get far with making a fight of it.

"Hands on the wall, butterfly."

She does as I say, and then I'm enjoying my meal only a second later.

Marley groans, letting her weight settle on me. I trail my hands all over her body, cupping her ass and squeezing, rubbing her thighs, reaching up and tweaking those pointed nipples, granting me the cries I've so desperately wanted to hear for the last few weeks.

I don't let up, not even when I feel her try to lift up off my face. She hasn't come yet.

Marley rocks her hips over me, giving herself the extra friction that she needs. I'm still doing everything I can to get her to come all over me. Her body pulses, and I can tell she's getting close.

"Beau, oh my god, don't stop, please don't stop," she chants, giving my ego a slight boost. Her warm wetness coats my lips, beard and tongue, as she comes all over my mouth with a long, breathy cry. Marley's orgasm lasts twice as long as the one she got from her vibrator, her thighs shaking until she's nearly prying herself off my mouth.

With a cocky grin, I look up, and her eyes gleam with her release. "Fuck," she breathes.

I chuckle under my breath as she scoots down my body, her breasts swaying with each movement.

"How did you know?" Marley asks.

I shrug, sitting up. I'm trying to ignore the hard-as-steel cock in my jeans, but it's nearly throbbing, yearning to be inside her. "You've been on edge all week, Mar. I knew you needed a release, and I'm more than happy to be the one to give it to you."

She simply nods, then glances down at the tent I'm currently sporting. I don't say anything, figuring she might ignore it, but she doesn't. She reaches down, unbuttoning them with quick fingers, and pulling both my jeans and my boxers down.

41

MARLEY

I slide Beau's pants down and off his legs, freeing his cock. Drops of moisture sliding from the swollen, red tip, and fuck, if I didn't want him inside me so badly, I might lick each drop until he's coming down my throat.

I should have known Beau would have known I needed the release, should have known he'd hear me. I was just so desperate for it that I wasn't thinking with my head on straight. This might not be the best idea, but I'm past caring and past giving a shit about anything but this current moment.

I rise up, moving forward until my entrance is poised right over him. With one glance, I know he's just as hungry for this as I am. When he was making me come ten times harder than my vibrator ever will, all I could think about was how empty I felt, how much I needed to have him inside me, needing *more* of him. *All* of him.

Beau's strong fingers grip my hips again, this time helping me hold steady as I hover over him. I reach down between us, gripping his warm length and sliding it over my soaked pussy. My wetness coats his cock, and helps him slide inside me easily.. My hips are flush with his, my hands resting against his chest.

Mouth falling open, I revel in the feeling of him inside me. No barriers, no restraint, just *full*. He's hitting in deep—deeper than I've ever felt—and it's so good. I don't want to move.

Yet, Beau's guiding my hips up and down, my body moving at its own rhythm as I ride him, exactly the way I wanted to earlier.

"Christ, Marley," Beau says through gritted teeth, a bead of sweat dripping down his brow. The bed shakes underneath us with the movement of our bodies. "You're so fucking tight."

My head drops back, a long guttural cry sliding from my lips at the sensations of him. He's lifting his hips, meeting the motions of of my hips and body rocking against his.

"I need to—" he chokes out. "Fuck, I can't think."

I can't help but laugh at his words. There's a deep furrow in his brow as he tries to verbalize another set of words.

He bends his knees, letting me lean back against them. "Need to take over," he groans. "Yeah?"

"Yeah," I say with a groan as he hits that deep spot again.

He thrusts his hips up, fingers digging into my hips. Faster and faster until I feel him jerking underneath me, hips bucking and cock filling me with his cum.

"Ah," I cry. My legs go limp, my head dropping forward as he jerks a final few times inside.

I can't hold myself up anymore. My arms give out and I'm landing on Beau's chest, my body completely and totally sated, exhausted, and ready for bed. Beau rolls us so that we're both on our sides. He's still inside me, and I let my eyes flutter open.

Reality starts to creep in as I take in his face, but I push it away, not ready to let go yet. I'm not ready to yell at myself for giving into my feelings again. He's breathing heavily, sweat dripping down his brow, hair a disheveled mess.

I laugh, pushing his damp hair from his eyes. "Thanks. I needed that," I tell him. Then shyly I add, "I needed you."

"Same," he responds, pushing my own damp and sweaty hair from my face. Beau leans forward, kissing me deeply. "Stay here. I'll get you cleaned up."

I do as he says, for once, not letting myself overthink and choosing to enjoy this moment.

42

BEAU

Thomas climbs into my car, slamming the door behind him. "Where we going, little bro?" he asks, turning in the seat to click his seatbelt into place. He's still in his uniform, just finishing a shift.

"I'm hardly your little bro," I scoff as I reverse from his driveway. "But, to answer your question, I'm taking you to see a house."

Thomas turns his head toward his house behind him. "Dude. You do know I already have a house, right? Like... we just left it. It's still there. I don't need a house. I have one."

"Not for you," I tell him. I take a turn that leads out of the main drag of town. "For Marley and me."

Thomas's eyes widen. "Wait, is this that house you sent me a link to a few weeks ago?"

I nod. "Yeah. We thought it was going to sell right away, but it hasn't. I told myself if it was still on the market by the time Marley hit twenty-seven weeks, I would get pre-approved and put an offer in."

A realization dawns on Thomas's face. "So... how many weeks is she? Does she know about this?"

"Thirty, and no."

"And did you put in an offer?"

"Yep."

"Dude, you gotta give me more than that. What now?" Thomas fidgets in his seat. This is the first time I'm saying it out loud. I haven't breathed a word of this to Marley. Things are slowly settling into place between the two of us and I don't want to create a rift.

"They accepted. Closing is in a month."

Thomas is silent, which doesn't happen often with him.

"Well?" I prompt.

"Well, this house better be fuckin' awesome, or Marley's going to kill you," Thomas says, his laugh relieving some of the tension lingering in my shoulders.

"It is awesome." I list off all the important information, giving Thomas a little bit of insight to the house as we drive toward it. It's just about ten minutes from town, so not a bad drive at all. After my conversation with Marley a few weeks back, my brothers and I spent a weekend at my house, clearing it out and getting it ready to go on the market. I listed it a few days ago after a few repairs, and I already received an offer for just over the asking price.

We pull into the driveway of the two-story home, and it's as perfect as it was the first time I saw it. I had a small fear that when we arrived it wouldn't be like I remembered, or I would panic, realizing I'd made a mistake. Only, the fear's not there, and I'm not panicking. I only feel pure joy, excitement, and a sense of peace over the next chapter of life.

Turning my car off, I climb out, and Thomas follows. The driveway crunches under my tennis shoes as I squint into the early spring sun. It's "fake spring" right now, which really means that in about a week, we will get another cold blast, and a foot of snow. Right now, it's forty-three degrees, which is T-shirt weather.

The front porch steps are sturdy as I climb them, no warping, or visible damage. The front door is locked, but I have the key code to get into the lock box. Once it's unlocked, I open the door to the now empty home.

Our footsteps echo off the hardwood floors and high ceilings. Thomas whistles lowly. "Damn. You sure I can't buy this?"

I glare at my older brother. "Yes, I'm sure."

He chuckles, holding his hands up in surrender. "I'm just giving you shit. Honestly," he pauses. "It's perfect for you guys. Does this mean you two are..."

Thomas doesn't finish his sentence, but it was obvious what he was going to say.

I sigh. "To be honest, I don't know what we are right now. But I have made my intentions clear from the start. I don't want to start a life with her only because she got pregnant. I've wanted it for a long time, I was just too cowardly to do something about it."

"What was holding you back?" Thomas asks as he explores the kitchen. The appliances are all updated, which is definitely a plus.

I scoff. "When I was eighteen, shortly before we went to college, I kissed her. The day we got our 'Dead Sea' tattoo, actually." I lead Thomas up the stairs to the second floor.

"You kissed her? Why didn't you start dating then?" Thomas glances into the first bedroom off the stairs, the room I imagine might become the nursery.

"She shut down right after. Told me we shouldn't continue if we wanted to keep our friendship. At the time,

I agreed, figuring I'd convince her one way or another. So, I went over to her house one day when I knew she was working. I had plans to ask Gabriel permission to date her."

"No way, you did?" Thomas sounds incredulous.

"Sure did."

"Obviously, he said yes," Thomas says.

"He actually didn't. Dad was there too, and they both agreed it would be best for us to stay friends. I took it as they didn't think I was good enough for her, so I shut down, and never brought it up again."

"Shit," he says with disbelief. "I can't believe they said that."

"I couldn't either. But, long story short, after things went down at the wedding, and before I found out she was pregnant, I went to Gabriel again. He laughed, told me it had taken long enough."

Thomas laughs wholeheartedly. "I coulda told ya that. We've all been waiting for this forever."

"Something is still holding Marley back, though. She's keeping a bit of distance, claiming it's for the babies, but I think it's something else."

I flick off the light as we move down the hall toward the master bedroom. It's a huge room with built-in bookshelves lining either side of the large window on the far wall. There's an attached bathroom with a large bathtub I know Marley will love.

"I'm sure you two will work it out. You've got a lot to look forward to, and this house... It's perfect." Thomas claps me on the back. "You're lucky, man. I'm excited to watch you be a dad."

My throat tightens. "Thanks. That really means a lot." I take one last look around the master bedroom, before turning away. "What about you? Any girls on your radar lately?"

He chuckles, running a hand through his hair before hooking his thumbs in his vest. "No girls. The drug trafficking investigation has been taking up a lot of space in my mind—as well as my actual time—so I figure it's best to keep my focus in one place for now. But soon, I'm sure. I'm ready to settle down."

"You'll be a good dad, too, if that's what you want."

"Thanks." Thomas smiles, showing the familiar gap in his teeth. "So, when are you telling Marley you bought her a house?"

I run a hand over my scruffy beard. "Probably next weekend. Her baby shower is then, and I figured I would bring her out here after."

"Smart. She will be all happy after the baby shower, that way she won't be as mad at you."

"She won't be mad at me," I reply, though to be honest, I'm not totally positive of that.

Thomas doesn't give me another answer, just continues to explore the house. After I show him the deck, he's completely sold on this crazy idea I had. I point out the far corner of the yard where I want to have Andrew help me build a swing-set.

After I lock the house back up, and we're heading back into town, my nerves start to kick in. In ten weeks, more than likely less, I will be a dad.

43

MARLEY

Surprisingly, the third trimester has been treating me wonderfully. I didn't expect to feel as good as I do, and I know it won't last, so I'm taking advantage of it. I decided against doing a maternity shoot. My brain is so scattered when it comes to Beau and me, that the thought of taking maternity photos with him, sends me into a spiral.

Therefore, I'm doing my version of a maternity shoot, a boudoir shoot. I have my camera set up on a tripod in the center of the room, and have a beautiful white lace with floral accents bra and panty set on. My breasts are almost spilling out of the top with how much they've grown. Thankfully, they aren't as sensitive anymore, but I know they're going to grow even more when I breastfeed.

I dim the lights so the room is left in a warm glow. It's early evening, and with it being spring now, it doesn't get dark at four o'clock anymore. Instead of using the camera's self-timer and getting all hot and sweaty from running back and forth, I have a small remote I can tuck into my palm, or hide behind my belly.

With the room ready, I check my camera lens one last

time, and then position myself in front of the frame. I pose, clicking the button a few times before I change the way I'm standing. While I take the photos, I let my mind wander a bit, falling into the muscle memory of the boudoir shoot.

Beau has spent every night in my room now for weeks, and while I know I should fight it, or work harder to keep things separate, I can't seem to do it. Every night when we lay in bed together, he talks to the babies. He tells them all the things we will do together, the places we'll go, and every night, another crack in my armor appears.

I've loved Beau for so long, and now, he's offering me everything I've ever wanted on a silver platter. Himself, a future, a life together. And yet, I hold back, just enough to make sure that I'm protecting my heart.

He is my reason for breathing. I should know by now that I won't lose him, regardless of our children. Beau will always be there for me. I wish I knew what I needed to let go of my fears, to stop worrying so much and just... be. I wish I knew what I needed to fully entrust him with my heart and with my future.

I've always loved Beau. I've never questioned that. But now, I'm learning what it feels like to be *in love* with him. What it's like to wake up every morning in his embrace, even if I'm sprawled across the bed like a starfish, or with smelly breath.

He proves to me every day that he is there for me and not just because I'm pregnant. Why do I let my stupid brain take the front seat, telling me that we aren't ready to give in, even though I know I can, that we have, and that I want to? He makes me feel beautiful, confident, and happier than I ever thought I could be. I love the body I've been given. While I've had moments during my pregnancy, overall,

Beau has made me feel like the most gorgeous woman on earth.

This maternity shoot is for me. I want to memorialize the way I look right now, the confidence I have in myself. And also... I want to feel sexy, to show myself that even though my ankles are swollen, and I've gained more weight than I have in years, I can still be sexy.

With that, I take off the bra. My breasts are heavy on my chest as the fabric falls to the ground, and I hook my thumb on the waistband of the panties, shimmying them down to the floor.

I adjust the lights again until the room is swathed in a deep glow. There's a sheer sheet hanging off the side of the chaise lounge, so I grab it, carefully draping it over my body.

Clutching the fabric, I lay it across my breasts. Since the fabric is sheer, it is easily seen through, but the illusion will be gorgeous in the photos. The rest of it hangs down my side, the ripples of fabric settling against my thigh. My nipples begin to pebble under the cool breeze in the room, and I have a feeling Beau would be dying if he were here.

I pop one leg, and rest my free hand over my stomach. Still holding the small remote, I click the button a few times, then slowly adjust my pose.

After a few more poses, some more risqué than others, I decide to move to the bed. I drop the sheet onto the flat bed, and arrange the camera where I want it. It's a bit of a challenge to climb onto the bed, given that I'm nearing eight months pregnant, but I make it. I'm slightly out of breath, but hey, I have two babies pressing against my lungs.

When I catch my breath, I move to the position I'm imagining, and get to work taking the photos.

I'm unsure of how much time has passed when the front door to my studio unlocks. Only two people have keys, so it has to be either Josie or Beau. I still panic slightly, as I'm totally naked underneath the sheer sheet I'm still using as my prop.

"Marley?" Beau's voice calls from the entryway. Thank god. I stop my attempt in rushing to get up, instead turning onto my side and adjusting the sheet to cover me.

"Back here."

His footsteps move closer, then halt as he takes in my prone form on the bed. "What are you doing?" His voice is tinged with confusion.

"I was taking some maternity photos." I chuckle softly at the look of awe on his face.

Beau nods, and I really am able to take in his appearance. His hair is down today, hanging in loose, wavy curls on his shoulders. He has on a pair of dark jeans, and a white button-down shirt. His eyes rake up and down my body, like he isn't sure where he wants his gaze to land.

Brown eyes rest on my face. "Fuck, I don't deserve you, Marley Bell."

"I think it's the other way around," I reply with a breathy voice. My heart rate slowly picks up with each passing second, a raving heat passes through my blood down my limbs. Warmth spreads between my thighs, and I shudder.

"You deserve every good thing in this world, and if I'm what you want, then I'll work to earn your love every single day for the rest of my life."

His proclamation comes from his lips so easily that I can't bear not touching him for a moment longer. "Come here, please," I murmur.

Beau crosses to me in two steps, already working down the buttons on his shirt. I sit up—awkwardly—and take his cheeks in my palms so I can feel him. Our breaths mingle as our lips crash together, and a rush of emotion floods my chest. He is mine, my person, my best friend, the father of my children.

His shirt falls to the floor, leaving him in only his white undershirt. I practically rip it from his body, so desperate and eager to have him right now.

My fingers move around his inked chest, feeling the trembles and goosebumps that follow my path. My legs wrap around his waist as I pull him closer to me. His hands are moving up and down my back, til he reaches the bottom, squeezing my hips. "I need this," I say breathlessly against his swollen lips.

His cock swells against my stomach, hardening further with each passing second. "Tell me what you need," Beau says, kissing down my jaw.

I don't reply, just tangle my hands in his hair, and pull him to my lips again. "You. I need you," I murmur.

Beau shifts us, scooting me further onto the bed. "Let's get you comfortable then."

He adjusts me so I'm leaning against the headboard, my body propped up with pillows. He takes gentle care in making sure I'm comfortable with every passing breath. I'm already completely naked for him, my belly completely on display. I love how sexy this man makes me feel. Beau's tongue darts out to wet his lips, and he quickly unbuttons his jeans, shoving them down his legs. The way his cock is so visible even in his boxers makes me want to skip whatever he has in mind, and get his cock in my mouth right now.

Beau slides his boxers down his legs, freeing his cock and giving me a little taste of what is to come. He settles onto the bed between my thighs, eyes rampant and eager.

He lays down so his chest is flat against the bed, face

lined up with my pulsing cunt. "I could spend every hour of every day between these gorgeous thick thighs. Every taste of you has me instantly craving more, Marley."

Beau gently kisses the inside of my thigh, sliding one hand underneath my knee to hook it around his shoulder, opening me up further to him. My walls clench around him, as I anticipate his next move. My hands clench the sheets beneath me, the constant yearning for him only growing stronger as he sits between my thighs.

His lips make contact with my slit, tongue swirling and circling my clit in a delicious form of torture. "Beau," I gasp his name, my heart pounding rapidly.

Just his tongue is enough to build the heat inside me, bringing me closer to a mind blowing orgasm, but he doesn't stop there. He moves his chin slightly, and I'm sure I'll have beard burn between my thighs, but it will be worth every ache, because I'll be reminded of this moment.

Beau's large fingers slide into my soaked, waiting pussy, and the first curl and twist of his fingers sends a jolt of pleasure, making me writhe against his touch. He works me with practiced skill, like he knows my body better than I do.

He probably does, to be honest. We've been together less than five times, and yet, he knows exactly how to make me come, knows exactly what feels good to me.

Tongue flat against my clit, he curls his fingers inside me again and pumps in and out. An extra gush of pleasure soaks his fingers, and he groans into my clit. The tickle of his beard and the vibration of his mouth sends me spiraling to the edge of a mind numbing orgasm, but when his fingers slowly slide out, I nearly curse. "What are you doing?"

"Can I try something?" Beau asks.

"What?"

"Do you trust me?" His gaze is so pure with lust and heat.

"Of course," I tell him. "I trust you." *More than anyone in the world. More than I even trust my own mind.*

Beau's answering smile gives me a new sense of joy. His mouth is on my pussy again within a moment, and the pleasure builds once more.

His fingers circle my entrance, but never enter. They slide lower until they contact the tight ring around my back entrance. He circles there, applying only the slightest amount of pressure.

"Beau!" I gasp. It's a completely new sensation, something I've never thought about doing before, or truly even considered.

"Is it okay?" he asks, backing away for just a moment.

"Yes," I cry, shivering with anticipation.

Beau grins, and then his mouth is back, tongue tracing designs and patterns around my clit.

His finger never passes the entrance, just applies a torturous pressure. Two fingers slide back into my pussy unexpectedly, encouraging the heat to build again.

With one finger pressing on my ass, two others curl inside me, twisting and thrusting, my walls clench around him, and I'm hurtling toward an intense orgasm only moments later. "Oh my god," I cry out, my body eager and pulsing.

He murmurs something against my clit, and the subtle vibration is the final push I need. My orgasm shocks me, my body jolting and jerking into the bed with each pulse and movement. My other thigh clenches against him, and the fingers not inside me squeeze the outside skin of my thigh, giving me a slight bite of pain with the deep, bone-rattling intensity of my orgasm.

His finger increases the pressure against my back hole, but it's enough—a delicious hint of what could be.

When my body relaxes and I'm no longer shuddering and jolting under his touch, I release my clutch on the sheets and let my legs fall to rest on the bed. "Holy," I can't even finish my words.

Beau slides his fingers out and my walls clench once more around him. When he rocks back onto his heels, his cock is still proudly waiting for what is coming.

"My turn." I sit up, moving over to the side, and pushing Beau down onto the pillows. He tries to fight me, but I rest my hand on his chest, kissing his wet, swollen lips. "You like tasting me?" I ask.

He nods.

"I like tasting you, so let me have my taste."

Beau groans, reaching back and pulling at the roots of his hair.

I slide my hands down his chest, pressing open mouthed kisses as I do. His cock is still rock hard, the tip red and eager for my touch. When I reach his thighs, I use one hand to stroke up and down his cock, and then I take him in my mouth.

The instant taste of precum spurs me on. I squeeze the base of his dick, sliding my tongue slowly up the shaft as I suck hard on the tip. When I reach the back of my throat, I let it relax, opening further to him.

One of Beau's hands leaves from behind his head to cup the back of my head, hands tangling in my hair. He tightens his fingers at the root, guiding my head as I move up and down.

He tastes so good, and I'm so eager to make him feel as good as he made me feel.

When I gag slightly, my eyes water, and I feel Beau's

hand leave my head to slide down my back and cup my round ass. He squeezes hard, fingers digging into the soft, ample flesh.

My pregnant belly makes the angle awkward, and I'm short of breath within moments, but I don't want to stop. I want to feel him coming down my throat.

"Marley," Beau groans, squeezing my ass harder. His other hand pulls me up and off his cock.

I pout as I pop off his cock, eager for him.

Beau shifts so he's sitting, rock hard cock ready for whatever is next. He cups my cheek, kissing me softly. "How you doing?"

"So good," I reply. I'm still catching my breath, my eyes watering. "Next time, you're coming in my mouth," I tell him.

"You won't hear me complaining," he says with a chuckle. "Lay on your side."

He helps me lay down on the pillows still on the bed. Adjusting the pillows under my head, he asks, "Are you comfortable?"

I nod. "Yes," I say, telling him the truth. I love how he always takes the time to make sure I'm comfortable and content before doing anything.

Beau slides down behind me, his chest pressed against my back. Both of our bodies are hot and sweaty, but I feel whole and complete next to him.

His length is pressed against my back, giving me a reminder of what is soon to come. With one arm, Beau slides under my thigh, lifting it up to hook on his thigh, opening me to him. He adjusts my hips, pulling me up and back.

His cock settles at my entrance, pressing slightly, just enough to give me a little taste of what's to come.

"Please, Beau," I cry, and he slowly thrusts inside me. The tension that has wrapped around my heart, the barrier I've held deeply between us starts to crack and fall to the floor in shambles. I'm giving myself over to him with every passing second.

His breath shudders against my neck. I feel so full with him at this angle that I can hardly form a coherent thought. His hips thrust in a leisurely pace, his arm wrapping around my body to cradle me to him. Beau kisses my neck, gently nipping and biting.

"Beau," I cry. This moment is intimately tender, leaving me at a loss for words..

He groans into my neck, clearly feeling the same as I do. I can't reach my clit to give myself more friction to achieve another orgasm, but I don't care. I feel incredibly connected to him right now, that it's the best possible feeling. My hand reaches behind my head to twist my fingers into his hair, clutching him to me.

"You feel so good, Mar," Beau groans. "Fuck, I—" he cuts himself off, instead kissing my neck and thrusting harder into me. His voice is thick with emotion, and it makes me wonder what he might have wanted to say.

I'm holding back myself, the words resting on my lips, because for the first time in our entire friendship or relationship, I feel at peace with my decision, with the choice to let go for once and for all.

My walls clench hard around him, and he pulses inside me. Beau's hand squeezes my tits, paying special attention to my nipples. "I'm so close," he says in my ear, and it's overwhelming, having him like this, feeling this connection to him. I cry out as he thrusts two final times, coming inside me with a low growl.

"Oh my god," I say through heavy breaths.

"Yeah," Beau repeats the sentiment. His cock twitches inside me as his head flops onto the pillow. "You okay?"

I sigh in delight. "Yeah. I'm so good."

"What happened?" Beau asks.

"What do you mean?"

"You kinda pounced on me." He rushes to add, "Not that I'm complaining, just... surprised."

"Just... realizing some things."

"Like?" he presses.

"How much you mean to me, how much I..." I hesitate. "Care for you. You've done so much for me, and I don't think I'll ever be able to thank you." I want to say more, but the words don't seem to come.

Beau pulls me closer to him. "You have nothing to thank me for, Marley."

Throat tightening, I nod. "If I weren't carrying a beach ball around my belly I'd turn around and hug you, but that will take five business days."

He laughs, and I feel the vibration in my back. "I'll come to you, love."

Beau slides out of me, our mixed wetness sliding out onto the sheet below me. I adjust a bit, and Beau quickly rounds the bed to my other side. He lies down beside me, and cradles my head in his hands, kissing me softly all over my face. I giggle with each kiss and movement until he lands on my lips. He kisses me slowly, as if trying to convey so many words in the action.

44

MARLEY

"What do you think about alliteration?" I ask Beau as I scroll through my Pinterest board.

"What the hell is alliteration?"

We've been going back and forth on baby names now for a few hours, with no luck at all. I've had a list in my phone for years, but none of them feel right now that I'm faced with the decisions. I'm sitting in bed with no less than three pillows propped behind my aching back. Beau is sitting beside me, wearing only boxers, getting some work done on his laptop. He has his blue-light glasses on and his hair in a mussed bun. He looks even sexier than normal, if that were even possible.

Last night after Beau helped me get cleaned up at my studio, we threw the dirty sheets in the wash and wiped down the bed before putting fresh sheets on. Then, Beau drove us home, but only after stopping by my parents house for a quick dinner. My mom was so excited to show me all the decorations she's made for my baby shower this afternoon.

My mom, and Beau's mom are hosting in the Cunningham's house, and while I'm excited, I'm also exhausted. The babies kept me up most of the night, and I had to get up four times to pee.

"Alliteration is…" I try to think of a way to explain it. "Tasty tacos."

"You want to name our babies 'Tasty' and 'Tacos'?" Beau questions. His thick brows are raised. "Do I need to run and get you some tacos before the baby shower? Are you craving them?"

"No," I laugh, reaching over to smack him in the chest lightly. His bare skin is warm under my quick touch. "I was just using it as an example, dumbass."

He laughs, shutting the lid of his computer. "Fine, what are some name examples?"

"Hmm," I say, using my pointer finger to tap at my chin in dramatic thought. "Tucker and Taylor?"

"Hard pass," Beau says with a wince. "Remember Tucker Hillbrand from high school?"

"Oh, yeah," I answer, a shudder rolling down my spine. "He was a jackass."

"He was. What about Leah and Luke?"

I ponder for a moment. "That could work." I type the names in my notes app, then promptly delete them. "Nope, nevermind."

"Why not?" Beau asks, leaning over to peer at my list.

"Leah was my roommate in college, remember?"

"Shit, yeah she was a bitch."

I laugh, and delete the names. "We will think of something. They don't have to alliterate either, it was just a suggestion."

Beau reaches over, taking my hand and squeezing gently. "We have time, no matter what your mom says."

"She acts like the babies have been born for months and

have no names," I mutter. I love my mom to pieces, but she's shocked we don't have names picked, or even narrowed down. For some reason, I feel like I have to meet them before I can know for sure. I won't be getting the cute pre-made blankets or hats with their names stitched in them, but I don't care. They'd only wear them for one photo anyway, then likely be shoved into a bin for special keeping.

"She means well," Beau says. He lets go of my hand to rest it over my stomach. Baby Girl is kicking me like crazy right now, and Beau starts to murmur in hushed tones. I can't always understand what he's saying in these moments, but the fact that he's so unabashedly connecting with them before they're even born makes my heart flutter.

I rest my hand over top of his, squeezing it. "I have to get ready," I say. Beau groans, moving his hand from my belly. "Are you still okay to bring me?"

"Of course," he replies. I haven't been wanting to drive if I don't have to, since my bump is getting to be more in the way.

I climb out of the bed and head to the bathroom to get ready. As time goes by, and the end of my pregnancy looms closer, I'm starting to realize that maybe I am ready for this. Ready to give myself to Beau, completely. Every piece of my soul wants him and wants the future he's painting for us. There's still a piece of me holding back, though. Still a younger version of me afraid of that chance that he won't be there to answer my call when I desperately need him, or will look at me in disgust when my name comes across the screen. I don't want to go through that feeling again, only this time, it's not just me who would be at risk in the fall. I want to be in this, to be *together*, not just as parents, but as a unit, as a pair.

I want the life I dreamed about with him, and I'm so close to getting it, I just need to get over myself.

I shove the feelings down for now, plugging in my curling iron to fix my hair.

I'M EXHAUSTED, my feet are doubling in size every minute, and I'm over this. Josie keeps giving me side eyed glances like she knows I'm going to blow, and yet my mom and aunt just aren't getting the hint. They mean well, I know they do, but a girl can only handle so many baby shower games, and we are currently on game number four.

I didn't realize how many people they'd invited, but it's been a revolving door of extended family, my mom's church friends, and people I haven't seen in years. My only saving grace is the fact that I've had either Josie, Fallon, or Megan at my side at all times. They've helped deflect many questions about my relationship status, whether the babies were planned—apparently joking that you only signed up for one and got a bonus baby isn't as funny as I thought—whether I plan to breastfeed, or have a natural birth.

All way too intrusive questions, if you ask me.

Nikki has been making sure I'm hydrated and fed, handing me a glass of water or sparkling punch anytime my hands are empty. She pops another plastic cup with red liquid into my waiting palm, and sits down next to me on the couch. I'm not participating in the game, really waiting for the moment I can text Beau to help me make my escape. He will have to help us load all the stuff into his car anyway, so maybe I should text him sooner rather than later.

A bounding figure to my right makes me jump slightly. Lennie crawls onto the couch between Nikki and me, curling her small body into my side.

"Hey Lenners, what's up?" I press a kiss to the top of her head. For being only four-years-old, and the only kid here, she's been doing so good.

"Is Grandma Jane going to be done talking soon? Miss Fallon said I could come over and play with Presley after this, but Grandma Jane keeps telling me it will be over when everyone leaves, but Auntie, *no one* has left." Her chocolate brown eyes are round as saucers as she peers up at me.

"Hopefully soon," I whisper. "Auntie is ready to take a nap."

"I don't take naps anymore. Daddy says I'm a big girl now." She gazes up at me with such a proud look on her face.

"You are a big girl," I tell her. She takes her small palm and rests it on my stomach. "You're going to be the best cousin ever." As if responding to my sentiment, one of the babies kicks in the exact spot where Lennie's palm is placed.

She jerks away in a panic. "What was that?"

I smile, laughing softly. "That was one of the babies saying hello to you."

Lennie's smile grows, and she leans down, cupping her hands around her mouth, pressing them on my belly. "Hi, baby," she says, then looks up at me. "Can they hear me?"

I nod. "Yes, they can hear you."

"Cool," she murmurs, bending back down to keep talking to my stomach. The babies move around to the sound of her voice, clearly enjoying it.

My phone buzzes at my thigh, and I grab it, choosing to snap a few pictures and videos of Lennie talking to the babies before reading the message. I send them off to Jason, knowing I won't get a reply for a few hours. If he's working, he's more than likely busy.

I read the message on the screen, noting that it is now just past two o'clock.

BEAU

Wasn't it supposed to end at two?

ME

Yep, but try telling my mom that. We haven't even opened presents yet. I'm exhausted.

Should I come and steal you away? I have something I need to show you tonight anyway.

What do you need to show me?

Surprise.

Really though, want me to come get you?

No. I think your mom is about to push things forward, so maybe an hour? You're going to have to load all the presents into the car.

You got it. I'll be there in an hour, and if you're not done, I'll rush it along.

I owe you.

Not a chance.

Nikki stands from next to me on the couch, clapping her hands together. "Jane, I think it's about time we open presents, yes?"

My mom smiles, adjusting her short gray hair. "Oh yes,

I think you're right! I didn't even realize the time. Megan, can you help me move the gifts over to Marley?"

Thank goodness.

45

BEAU

The peals of feminine laughter are loud as I walk up the front steps to my childhood home. I got slightly sidetracked by Gabriel, sitting in a lawn chair in his front yard, so I'm five minutes later than I'd promised Marley.

I don't bother knocking, it is my house in a sort of way. I nearly stumble on the many pairs of shoes scattered in the front entry as I walk toward the living room. The laughter and chatting grows louder with every step I take.

When I reach the living room, I see Marley sitting in my mom's favorite rocking chair, with people gathered around her in a large circle. I spot a few extended family members, but mainly, I'm focused on Marley. She's smiling, eyes bright and excited as she pulls a pajama set from the gift bag on her lap, but I can see how tired she is. She was up most of the night, her body aching more and more with each passing day.

There are dozens of bags and boxes around her feet, some open, some still pristinely wrapped. My mom sits on one side of her, with a little notepad, and a garbage bag filled with discarded tissue paper. No one seems to have noticed my arrival, except for Josie. She sits next to my mom, and gives me a small wave. Lennie's sitting in her lap, and when she notices who Josie is waving at, she practically falls out of Josie's lap to run to me.

It makes my heart burst a little to see how excited she is. She launches herself into my arms, climbing up my body. "Uncle Beau!" she squeals. "Auntie Marley said the babies like me!"

"Oh yeah?" I answer, my heart clenching again. "I'm sure they do. You're going to be their favorite cousin."

She beams, squeezing me tightly.

Squeezing her back, I turn my eyes toward the rest of the women. "Ladies," I say in lieu of greeting. "I'm here to kidnap my girl."

All of the older women croon in delight, and Marley's face turns red. I carry Lennie through the small circle to set her back in Josie's lap. With her out of my arms, I walk over to Marley, and lean down, kissing her soft lips quickly. The ladies all croon again, but I pull back, only to ask Marley a silent question with my eyes.

She nods slightly, letting me know she's okay. Knowing she's good, I step back. "Should I take a few loads out to my car while you finish up?"

My mom, and Jane both nod. "Lennie, why don't you bring some of the bags to the door so Uncle Beau can put them in the car?" Mom says.

Of course, Lennie is more than willing to help, so we are up and moving within minutes while everyone continues to chat. While I load the vehicle with more bags and boxes than I can count, an anxious stirring grows in my gut.

Closing is in three weeks, and I have that much time to

convince Marley that this is the right choice for us. That this is what we need.

Once the last of the presents are in my—full to the brim—car, I head back inside. Women are slowly heading toward the entryway, giving Marley long hugs and caressing her stomach in a way that makes even me feel uncomfortable. She's masking her discomfort, though, because I know her so well, know her tells and body language. I can sense by the shift of her weight back and forth and the hand resting on her lower back, that she's in pain.

I cross to her in a few steps, standing behind her and wrapping my arms around her so she can lean on my chest. Her body relaxes slightly, but she's still uncomfortable. I lean down so I can murmur in her ear. "Ready?"

She nods, and thankfully, the person that was talking to her says goodbye, finishing their conversation. In just minutes, the room has cleared of everyone but my mom and Jane, Josie, Megan, Fallon and Lennie. I can feel the almost instant relief in Marley now that we are surrounded by only our closest family and friends.

"I have plans for Marley and me, but if you need help cleaning up later, I'm more than happy to swing by," I offer to my mother.

She waves her palm at me in a dismissal. "We've got it. Don't keep her out too late, I think she's pretty tired."

Marley smiles sweetly, giving my mother a tight hug. "Thank you for hosting," she says into my mother's embrace. They say a few more words of love and appreciation, and Marley hugs her mother and friends, and soon we are heading out the front door.

"WHAT IS this surprise you're taking me to?" Marley asks as I take the road leading out of town.

"You'll see," I say, my voice shaking slightly. Marley raises her brow. I reach over, resting my hand over her thigh. "It's nothing bad. I promise."

"What are you nervous about then?" she asks in return.

"It's more of a nervous excitement," I try to explain. Luckily she accepts that as an answer, and watches the trees as we drive.

When I turn down the gravel drive and Marley sees the house, her eyes widen, jaw dropping open. "Beau... What is this?"

I stay quiet for a short moment, pulling up to the garage and putting the car in park. I get out, rounding to the other side to open her door. Her mouth is still agape, emotion blurring behind her eyes. Unsure of whether it's a good or bad emotion, I tread carefully.

"Remember how we both agreed we needed more space?" I slowly start.

Marley doesn't say anything, darting her tongue out and biting her lip.

"I saw this place, and it had so many showings, but no one ever snatched it up. I told myself that if it was still on the market by the time you hit twenty-seven weeks, and we hadn't found a place, I would put an offer in." Her face goes blank, leaving me no clues on how she feels. "They accepted my offer."

I give her a moment to process, then I speak again. "It's got four bedrooms, two baths. There's even a soaking tub in the master bath. The basement has plenty of room for guests, or more kids," I joke.

Marley still hasn't said a word, and my gut starts to churn. I reach down, taking her clammy hand in mine to lead her up the front steps. I use the key in the lock box to open the door, leading her into the empty house. Her face remains stoic, but eyes scan the room, taking in every single feature.

She drops my hand, walking out into the open area kitchen, trailing her hands over the countertops and cabinets. I follow behind her, giving her little tidbits of information as I do, panicking only slightly at her complete lack of reaction.

I guide her up the stairs, showing her the master and two other bedrooms. After, I show her the guest bedroom downstairs, and the swing-set out back. The entire time, she's quiet, but her face grows more and more red with each passing moment. I can't tell if it's from the exertion of the stairs, or... something else.

When we reach the front entryway again, I shove my hands in my pockets. "Well?" I ask.

Marley takes one final look around. "I don't know whether to strangle you or be excited."

"Preferably the second option," I chuckle nervously.

"You bought a house without talking to me? I know we said we needed more space, but I figured maybe we'd have a conversation, and not make any rash decisions at the end of my pregnancy."

"I know, I just... It's just so perfect for us, and the first time I was here, I imagined us in it, and... I had to make it a reality." I do my best to explain, knowing she's not pleased with me, or this idea I had.

"Can you take me home, please?" She strides out of the front door without a second glance in my direction.

I knew it might take a bit of coercing, but I didn't expect her to ice me out like this. My heart aches at the not-so-subtle rejection, at the fact that instead of holding her in my arms in the house where I want to give us a new beginning, she's turned her back on me. Turned her back on what I thought could be, and I'm the reason why.

46

MARLEY

He bought a house.

He seriously bought a fucking house without talking to me about it. If I weren't so hormonally cranky, I'd probably swoon from the sweet and thoughtful gesture. Yet, I can't find it in myself to behave rationally right now. He did something so huge, something that people usually discuss for months—even years—on his own, and without consulting me. It hurts knowing that I was so close to handing my heart over to him, only for this to take me back so many steps.

The only consulting we did was a brief mention over a month ago.

Beau and I aren't together, well, not officially at least. This is not something that people who aren't really together do. They don't buy each other houses to co-parent their children in. Right?

I climb into the car, slamming my door shut behind me. I watch as Beau carefully locks the house up and saunters over to the car. He looks defeated, and it kills me that I put that look on his face, but one of us needs to be smart so we both don't get lost in our feelings.

Beau gets into the car, and I turn my gaze away. I can't look at him right now, and I can't look at the beautiful house in front of me. I rest my hand on my curved stomach, willing myself to be strong.

As we drive, I feel myself slipping. Slipping into a place I know all too well, and the person that I usually trust to get me out of it is the one who put me there. When we pull into my driveway, I remember all the stuff we have to bring inside. I drop my head back against the headrest, withholding my groan.

Beau reads my mind, looking behind him at the stuffed vehicle. "I'll bring everything in, and we can sort through it tomorrow. Go take a shower and relax."

He doesn't mention talking about the house, and for that, I'm grateful. I don't know that I have the emotional capacity for a civil conversation tonight. Nodding, I unbuckle my seatbelt, gasping slightly at a tightening, cramping sensation across my stomach. I clutch my hand to my bump, wincing at the discomfort. It's not horrible, like a strong period cramp, but it's definitely not comfortable. It eases within a moment. Beau must not have realized since he was already out of the car when it happened, or he likely would have lost his mind, worrying something was wrong.

Beau opens my door, and I try to pretend like everything's normal. He helps me out, and I grab my bag from the floor, heading toward the house. Beau takes a load of things and follows.

I hold open the door for him, and then I'm heading down the hall toward my room. I need to get out of this bra, out of this dress. I'm overwhelmed, and just so freaking over this day. Am I being ridiculous? I don't really think so. This is why I've been so hesitant, so careful with my heart for all these years. I'm overstimulated, hot, tired, and frustrated and ready to be asleep and done with this day.

I hear Beau bring load after load of things into the guest bedroom, which used to be his room. He hasn't slept in there for a while, and the small, petty part of myself wants to make him sleep in there tonight, but I won't. Because even though I'm mad, and essentially breaking my own heart, I can't bear to have him away from me. Again, I need him more than he will ever know, than I will admit to anyone. If I can't have him in my corner, I'll lose myself.

I strip out of my clothes, throwing on my comfy sweats and shirt that I had to buy just to fit me. None of my actual clothes fit anymore. I draw back the covers of the bed, ready to be done with this day.

The babies are active, kicking and punching my ribs, stomach, and bladder. Almost like they are trying to get me to see reason—that Beau wasn't thinking maliciously when he did this without me, he's doing this *for us*. To provide for the family we are making, our future.

They are always more active when he's around. They recognize his voice, know that their dad is there and he'll protect them the way he's always protected me. The man himself enters the room. I keep my eyes closed and my hand resting on my stomach, feeling them kick and assault me from the inside. The mattress shifts behind me, and Beau's warmth rests behind my back. Every night, he holds me until I fall asleep. Of course, it doesn't last long because I'll usually wake up soon after, having to pee or take a layer off since I sweat through the first one.

His palm splays over my belly the same way it does every night. Tonight, no words pass between us, just silence while I lose myself to my weary thoughts.

BEAU WAS STILL ASLEEP when I woke up for the day an hour ago. I wasn't ready to get up by any means, but the babies were. I'm snuggled into the couch, trying to read a book but failing. I've read the same passage about four times now, and I can't seem to process the words. My mind feels like an endless black hole, unable to crawl out, this constant negative loop of feelings about Beau, all the conflicting feelings of loving him and the idea of a life together, or keeping my distance, afraid to be burned.

"Hey," Beau greets as he saunters into the living room.

"Hi," I reply, slamming my book shut and setting it onto the table beside me. Beau sinks onto the couch, scooting close to me. Now that I've had some time to think, I have come to a few conclusions. "We should probably talk."

He nods, starting, "I should have talked to you first. I know that. I regret not including you in this decision, but I don't regret doing it. I think you will love the house, and I can't imagine not living there with you, raising our children there together." He finishes with a long exhale.

"You should have talked to me. How did you expect me to react, Beau? I told you I needed to take things one step at a time, and instead, you jumped in head first, buying a house. Your house isn't even on the market yet!" My voice is rising as well as my frustration.

"My house already has a contingent offer," he refutes. "I tried to take the thinking out of this for you, Marley. I tried to make this easier for you, but yet, I'm still getting the third-degree."

"You can't blame this on me!" I yell, trying to sit up now,

and move away from him. "What part of this being a part-nership don't you get?"

"Oh, so we *are* partners now? Every time someone brings our relationship status up, you shut down. Yet, in private, it seems like you're more than happy to have me play the part of your boyfriend." Beau stands from the couch, rubbing his face in irritation.

"How is this on me?"

Beau groans. "I'm not saying this is on you. I'm just... Fuck Marley, can't you see how much I love you? How much I want this for our future? I feel like all you are thinking about is the right now, instead of planning for our life together."

It feels like a serrated knife has just been stabbed into my heart and twisted, shredding the muscle and every piece of me with it.

"We both know that we have been fighting feelings for each other for so long, but why? Why can't you just give in and let me love you?" His voice is strained, the pain visible in his face.

I shrink back into the couch, wiping a tear that has slid down my cheeks. "What happens when you get sick of me?" I ask.

Beau scoffs, not getting it. "You've been my best friend for nearly twenty years, Mar. If I haven't gotten sick of you yet, why would I now? I've been trying to make you see that I'm all in, since day one. What do I have to do to prove it to you? To get you to believe me for once?"

"I don't know," I shout. "But what if you do! I don't want to lose the one person who really knows me. You are the one person I can rely on when I fall into that dark hole. You've single handedly picked me up more times than I can count. The playing field is always uneven. You're always the one helping me, but when have I ever helped you? What do I bring to this relationship?"

"You!" Beau cries. His face is red, eyes glassy as he steps back toward me. "You bring yourself to the relationship, and that's all I've ever wanted. You keep me sane, you're the one I tell all my secrets to, the one I will love until my dying breath. I love you, Marley. I've loved you since we were kids, swimming in the lake, riding our bikes to school every morning. I've loved you every day since the day we met. And I've lived every day, in pain, wanting you with every fiber of my being, but never letting myself have you, because I couldn't. Do you know why?" he asks.

I shake my head, dropping my gaze.

"Our dads."

Confusion rattles in my brain. What do our dads have anything to do with this? "What?" I ask.

Beau rests his hands on his hips. "The day after we got our 'Dead Sea' tattoo, the day I kissed you..." He pauses for only a moment. "I went to ask your dad permission to date you. I wasn't going to let you shut me down like you had. I was ready to fight for you."

I remember that day vividly, how I shut him down, how I was so convinced he was going to tell me we couldn't do that again. I built the walls before we even had a chance. "What happened?" I ask.

Beau chuckles. "My dad was there too, and they both told me no. That we shouldn't, not if we wanted to keep our friendship. Me, being the dramatic eighteen-year-old that I was, took it personal. I thought they meant that I wasn't, and would never be good enough for you. It hurt, but... in retrospect, maybe we weren't ready."

My heart hurts for the younger version of the man standing in front of me. It seems that we have both been our own worst enemies. Both of us are fighting something that seems to be so inevitable. So clear to everyone around us, but both of us so blind to it.

"The morning we found out you were pregnant, I went over to your parents' house. Gabriel actually laughed at me, told me it'd taken me long enough. Don't you think we've waited long enough? Why do we have to fight this?"

"I'm scared," I admit. "I'm a lot. You of all people know this. You're the only one I call when things get bad, when I'm low. I can feel myself slipping, even now, and I don't know what to do."

Beau moves to sit back down beside me, the heated argument seemingly done, for now at least.

I continue as he sits by me, "Neither of us have been in a successful relationship before. To be transparent, I don't think I've ever even been in a real one. I've watched, as both of us have failed with others throughout the years. I've watched you end relationship after relationship, leaving the person gutted and yearning. I can't let that be us, I can't give myself over to you completely, knowing that we both aren't ready for this, for a future that we are together, and not just together for our children." My voice shakes, and I can feel the steady stream of tears as they fall down my cheeks.

Marley," he croons, "The reason I've never been in a successful relationship, the reason I am always the one to end things, is because *they weren't you*. They were never the one person I wanted. I'm here, Marley. You are who I live my life for. And now, these babies are a part of that too. I want to be the best partner for you, the best dad for our children."

I lean into him, letting myself fall into his familiar warmth. "Where do we go from here?" I ask.

"I guess that's up to you," Beau says. "We can set up a

meeting with one of my co-workers, Jake, and he can talk us through everything, the offer, the closing date, everything. Or," he pauses, like he really doesn't want to say it, "I can look over the contract again, and see what will happen if I back out." What he doesn't say is that by doing so, he'd likely lose money, maybe more.

"No," I tell him, squeezing his hand where it rests on my thigh. "Let's... let's set up a meeting. I need to look at things from a technical standpoint. I mean, Beau, can we even afford this house?"

"We can," he says. "The house is priced really well, and with the money I'll make on the sale of my house, we can put that toward it." He stops, clearing his throat. "And if you choose to sell this house, we might be able to make some money on it as well."

I glance around my living room, and the home I've made. Deep down, I know that what he's saying is true, we *can* do this. I just have to get my brain on board with my heart.

Rolling my lips, I pause, choosing my words carefully. "I love the house. I really do. I just don't like that you made this huge decision without me. I'm thirty-one weeks pregnant with twins, Beau."

He nods, grimacing. "I shouldn't have done it. I regret that I did it without talking to you, Marley. I thought if I could eliminate the hard part for you, it would make it easy for you to say yes."

"I get it, I really do, and I appreciate the thought." I pause, trying to gather my next words. "I want to be your partner. I want to not be scared, and I want to be all in with you, the way that you are with me. But for me to do that, we need to communicate, and clearly, we haven't been doing that."

Beau nods, squeezing my leg. "So, we communicate, we work through things together. No more buying houses without talking to each other," he jokes.

I chuckle, and repeat, "No more buying houses without talking to each other."

47

MARLEY

For it being early May, it's excessively hot. Though, maybe it's just me being in the third trimester of pregnancy. Josie seems to be handling it just fine, though, she won't stop hovering over me.

She's been asking me what feels like every thirty seconds if I'm staying hydrated, offering me sports drinks, or making sure my water bottle is close by. Marissa was more than willing to help me with this wedding before my maternity leave, and most of my clients I had booked for the summer ended up switching to her, which I'm grateful for. She's so talented, and deserves to have a steady clientele.

It's about time for the ceremony, so we head towards the building. After doing countless weddings here, I know this place like the back of my hand, and it's always nice when there is a last minute need and the wedding planner is busy, I can just run and find it, or call Isaac. Today has gone off without a hitch.

Marissa is walking beside me as the bridal party all separates to do a few last minute tasks before the ceremony. "So, getting close, huh?" she asks.

"Thank goodness," I mutter. My back is absolutely killing me. It doesn't help that my camera harness is not cooperating today, putting more pressure on my shoulders and lower back than there already is.

"Third trimester sucks. In the early weeks of it, you feel great, but then, those last six weeks hit you like a freight train, and everything makes you uncomfortable and pisses you off."

"You've got that right," I reply.

"I can't even imagine doing it with twins though. On the bright side, if you have another kid, chances are you'll have only one baby, and it will be like a totally different experience I bet."

I groan. "The thought of having another baby right now makes me want to vomit. I haven't even had these ones yet."

Marissa chuckles. "Fair."

We make it into the ceremony area, where guests are finding their seats. I gratefully take a seat in the back of the room, my backache easing a bit. I spot Josie in the front making final adjustments to the flower arch, and Fallon, running around with her trusty clipboard.

Marissa is going to be taking a majority of the photos of the ceremony, and I'll take the secondary duties, giving myself a little bit of a break before the reception, and portraits. I rest my body for a moment, then I'm up and taking pictures again as soon as the ceremony starts.

About halfway through the ceremony, a tight pain like the one I had a few weeks ago bands across my stomach. The pain stays, and I fight to breathe through it, knowing it's more than likely just some Braxton-Hicks contractions. Dr. Ness told me I would more than likely experience them now, but only to come in if they develop a pattern in timing, or the pain gets worse.

The pain evaporates, and I get back to work, all thoughts of pain and preterm labor fleeing my mind. The babies are as active as always, with Baby Girl pressing on my bladder more often than not.

The rest of the ceremony goes by quickly, the bride and groom bringing nearly everyone—myself included—in the room to tears with their love story.

The Braxton-Hicks continued off and on throughout the ceremony, but never enough to conform to a pattern or make me question if I was in preterm labor. Josie has been watching me the entire time, and I suspect she's going to make her way over to me within minutes. I take a few pictures of the receiving line and watch as Josie does exactly what I thought.

As soon as she reaches me, she speaks. "Are you okay? You winced a few times and you look like you're in pain."

I wave her off. "I'm fine, just some Braxton-Hicks contractions, and they're irregular."

Josie furrows her brow. "No, I don't think you should be working anymore. Especially in this heat. I can call Beau to come get you," she murmurs, already pulling her phone out.

I swipe her phone from her palm without thinking twice. "I'm. Fine."

She narrows her eyes. "I'm watching you, Momma." To drive home her point, she holds two fingers to her eyes, then moves them to me, and back again.

"If anything changes, I'll tell you. But this is normal."

"Right," she murmurs, and I know she's not convinced. "Can I at least have my phone back?" She holds her open palm out.

"Only if you promise not to text Beau."

She begrudgingly agrees and I hand over her phone.

Marissa saves me from the moment, thankfully. "Ready

for portraits? The bride really wants some photos in the cellar."

"Yep, let's go." I fully expect Josie to hover and follow along with us, but instead, she waves at Marissa.

"Hey, she's having some Braxton-Hicks contractions. Watch her. If they get more regular, call me." She points at me again. "The babies need to cook longer, so don't push yourself."

I sigh, knowing she's only trying to take care of me. "I won't. I promise I'm okay."

She throws her arms around me in a tight hug. "I'll be up here if you need me." I nod into her embrace, the babies kicking at my stomach. "Woah, was that them?" Josie asks in surprise.

"Yep," I say with a small laugh. "They love their Auntie Josie. Every time they hear your voice they get excited."

"Really?" she says, her voice squeaking. "Hi, Babies, Auntie Josie loves you!" She bends down, resting her palms on my stomach. Of course, she feels the moment my stomach tightens, and hears my sharp intake of breath at the sudden pain. "Marley..." she warns.

I can't say anything, because the pain doesn't lessen this time, it gets worse. I hold up my finger, trying to breathe through the wave. Less than a minute later, it's done, and I'm working to catch my breath. "All good," I say, with a pursed smile, trying to convince both myself, and Josie.

"Not good," Josie replies.

Marissa furrows her brows. "I think Josie's right, Marley. You should go get some rest, and maybe call your doctor."

I huff out a breath, and tears fill my eyes. I know they're right. With a shaky voice, I say, "Can you call Beau to come pick me up?"

"Yes," Josie breathes. "Marissa, what do you need from me?"

"Not a thing. I'll go update the bride and let her know you're okay, but you need to go home. She's so sweet, I'm sure she won't mind at all." Marissa takes my hand in hers, squeezing my palm. "You need to take care of yourself."

I nod in reply, my throat tightening. Josie's already got her phone to her ear, and I can just barely hear Beau through the phone, his voice is edgy and concerned. I don't want to be so emotional right now, but tell that to my hormones. Marissa tells me she will update me later on the rest of the event and that she wants an update from me as well. She gives me a quick hug, and then she's off, heading down to the cellar.

Josie takes my hand, still on the phone with Beau, and leads me to the front lobby of the venue. There's a few leather couches against the walls, and Josie deposits me in one. She finishes the conversation with Beau, and then points her finger at me. "Don't move. I'm going to get you some water and find Megan. Put your damn feet up, please."

"I will," I agree and do as she says. She nods when she sees me following directions, and then she hurries out of the room.

My own cell rings in my pocket, and I pull it out, adjusting myself so I can take my camera harness off my shoulders. Unsurprisingly, Beau's name is on the screen.

I swipe my finger across the screen to answer the call. "Hi," I say.

"Butterfly, are you okay?" Beau asks, his voice is thick, and I can hear the sound of a car door slamming in the background.

"I'm fine, really. I just pushed myself a little too hard,

and I'm having some Braxton-Hicks contractions. Nothing major." I lean my head back onto the couch, closing my eyes. The heat from outside is making its way in, forcing the air conditioning to work overtime to keep up. Luckily, I'm right under a vent, so I have a nice cool breeze on my sweaty skin.

"Don't downplay this, Mar. Call the nurse line, and tell them what's going on. If you need to go in, I want to know right away so we can stop by on the way home."

"I will. I'll call as soon as we hang up," I tell him honestly. I have another contraction right as I finish my sentence and I inhale sharply.

"Shit," I hear Beau murmur. "Are you having another one?"

I nod, but he can't see me, obviously.

His voice is panicked. "Just breathe, I'll be there as soon as I can. It's okay," he repeats, over and over until it passes.

"I'm good now," I say on a heavy breath. "Just wasn't expecting that one."

"I'll be there soon."

"Thank you," I murmur. "I'm in the front lobby." We say goodbye, and I immediately pull up the phone number for the nurse line.

Halfway through the conversation and endless questions, Josie strides back into the room, this time with Megan and Isaac in tow, and Jason, who I'm surprised to see. Megan and Josie sit on either side of me on the couch.

I finish the conversation with the nurse, who has determined I should come in, just to be monitored for a little bit to make sure it's not active labor.

"Well?" Josie asks when I hang up the phone.

"They want me to come in. Just for evaluation though. She doesn't think I'm in active labor, but since things are a bit more risky with twins, she wants to be sure." I rest my phone on top of my bump. Jason sits on the coffee table next to my legs, hands clasped in his lap.

Megan nods. "After Josie told me what was happening, I figured that would be the case." As a family medicine doctor, Megan has a bit of experience in all ends of the spectrum, including a bit of women's health and obstetrics.

I rest my hands over my lap, tilting my head back to let the cool air hit my face and neck. I take a steadying breath, unsure of why I feel like crying. Is it nerves? What if I'm really in labor? I'm not ready.

"Marley," Jason's deep voice pulls me out of my internal panic. I raise my head to look at him. Jason has always been the big brother I needed. My own older brothers didn't seem to care about me or our family. They didn't even have a reaction to finding out they were going to be uncles, other than to ask who the father was, and give a disgruntled groan when I told them it was Beau. Jason's brown eyes look so much like Beau's that my heart squeezes. "Do you need anything? Hungry? Thirsty?"

I shake my head. "I'm okay, really. I'm tired, but otherwise, I think I'm okay." He pats my legs that are still resting on the coffee table. Isaac is hovering behind Jason, eyes round with worry.

"You sure?" Jason asks. "I can always get Thomas to give you a police escort. You know he'd do it."

That elicits a small laugh from me. "No, I promise I'm okay. If things get worse, I'll let you know."

He nods. "I'm sticking around until Beau gets here." Like I said, big brother.

The tears that went away are back now, this time streaming down my cheeks. "Why are you even here?" I ask, my voice shaking as I come to the realization that I don't know why he is here.

Jason chuckles. "It's the first wedding we are serving Blue Ox at. I was over at the bar when I caught Josie running like a madwoman through the reception area."

Josie leans forward, smacking his bicep. "Hey now, I was on a mission. As soon as I told you what was happening, you were running faster than I was."

"I'm not denying it."

As he speaks, Fallon rounds the corner, her face red and flushed. "Josie!" she calls across the lobby. "We need you, one of the drunken cousins knocked over the flower arch."

Josie huffs out a sigh. "Call me with an update or if you need anything. Okay?" She pulls me into a quick hug. "Keep those buns in the oven."

"I will," I tell her with a nod.

She runs off toward Fallon, Isaac follows, explaining, "I should check on things if there's already a drunken cousin."

I wave him off. Jason stands from the coffee table, sitting next to me on the couch. Megan stays by my side as well.

Jason is typically not a man who brings up his past or his ex, but for some reason, he does. "When Talia was pregnant with Lennie, she got those early 'practice contractions' all the time." He uses air quotes over the words. "She had a super low pain tolerance, so we were going into the hospital every other day, it seemed."

The words ding like a light bulb in my brain. "Oh yeah. I remember that now. How did she do during her actual labor?"

Jason rolls his eyes. He leans forward so his elbows rest on his knees. "Lots of screaming. Lots of begging for drugs and lots of curse words."

"That's usually the norm, though," Megan tries to say.

Jason shakes his head. "Not like this. The doctors struggled with how to tell her no, that she was maxed out on her meds, and there was nothing else they could do. I knew she'd had a problem with drugs in the past, but never realized it was that bad. She swore she was clean and ready to be done with that life. I should have seen it coming. Three months after Lennie was born, she fell off the deep end."

I reach out, squeezing Jason's arm. "It's not your fault. You couldn't have known, Jason."

He shrugs. "Lennie is safe, and that's all that matters, right?"

I nod. "Yep." My stomach tightens, as well as my grip on Jason's arm. Leaning forward a bit, I close my eyes. I squeeze hard as the pain wraps around my belly, stronger and longer than any other one I've had. Taking my hand, Megan coaches me through breathing. In the distance, thundering footsteps sound, and then Megan's hand is replaced with a familiar one, and Beau's voice is murmuring reassuring words into my ear.

It passes and I pry my eyes open. Beau has one hand in mine, one resting on my round stomach. "Hi," I whisper. His eyes are dark, worry evident on his face. "Should we go?"

"Probably," he says. "I didn't even turn the car off, and I left my door open. It's a good thing we know the owner or I'd probably be getting towed right now."

I chuckle softly. "Probably." I let go of Jason's arm, noting the red marks on his skin from my fingers. "Sorry," I say, gesturing at his arm.

Jason laughs. "Nothing to be sorry about, Mar. If you guys need anything, let me know." He stands, making a show of rubbing his arm. I swat at his leg and he chuckles.

Beau stands from where he was kneeling in front of me, giving his oldest brother a hug.

Megan stands, reaching out her hand to me again, and I take it. I already know that getting out of the deep leather couch is going to be difficult. Beau turns his attention to me and takes my other hand.

They help me up, and I cringe slightly in embarrassment at just how much help I need. Beau grabs my cameras and harness from the coffee table, and leads me toward the automatic doors of the lobby. Megan helps get me in the car despite my protests, and thankfully with the car still running, the AC is blowing cold right in my face. I sink into the cloth seat as Beau gets in the driver seat.

As soon as he's buckled, he's driving. "Are they happening in more of a pattern?" he asks.

I shake my head. "No, still inconsistent, but getting a bit stronger."

Beau's hair is a mess, like he's been running his hands through it every five seconds. "Okay. And they want you to come in?"

"Yeah. They want to monitor for a bit, even though she thinks it's just Braxton-Hicks."

"Good."

Beau reaches over, taking my hand in his, his thumb drawing circles on my skin as he drives. We're nearly to the birth center when I'm hit with another contraction. I squeeze his hand involuntarily, trying so hard to focus on my breathing. If this isn't real labor, I'm terrified of what real contractions feel like cause these are a pain in the ass. They aren't world ending, but they definitely aren't comfortable.

Beau coaches me through it, and when it's done, I lean

back, taking deep breaths. "That one didn't seem too bad," Beau says, squeezing my fingers.

I turn my gaze toward him, my eyes wide and irritation flooding through my body, because oh my god? This man is telling me that it "*didn't seem too bad?*"

"Are you serious?" I ask.

He spares a glance at me, and I see the shift in his demeanor. "No," he stammers. "I just mean... Shit. I mean that compared to the one at the winery, this one wasn't as long. It didn't seem like it hurt as much." I can tell he's regretting his words, but fuck, I'm irritated.

"Do you have two babies suddenly occupying your ball sack, and squeezing the shit out of it every twenty minutes? If so please enlighten me on how I'm feeling right now." I pause, waiting for him to give me some sort of answer. Unsurprisingly, he doesn't. "No? That's what I fucking thought."

I don't let him reply. I turn as best I can in my seat, and watch the scenery as we make the last bit of the drive toward the birth center.

48

BEAU

Just over two hours after arriving, Marley and I are back in my car, heading toward home. The babies are both active with strong heartbeats and the contractions have ceased. They gave her some fluids and that seemed to help overall with how Marley was feeling.

Dr. Ness put Marley on bedrest, which I am secretly grateful for. She needs to rest, especially in the last few weeks of her pregnancy. Which means no sex, no extraneous activities, nothing.

We are meeting with Jake, a realtor I work with, tomorrow, to go over all the things about the house. We're also going back to the house, so Marley can get a good look at it, and really make an informed decision, rather than the decision I made for both of us. I'm definitely going to be keeping an extra watchful eye on her tomorrow, and until the twins arrive. I don't want anything to go wrong, and I want her to be as comfortable as possible.

I've been reflecting a lot in the last week since Marley and I had our argument. We've both been treading carefully, but I think things are better. Marley seems to be a bit more sure in where we stand, and I get that she's not totally ready to go full-steam ahead with a relationship, but fuck, am I ever. I laid all my emotions and words out for her, told her where I am at. The ball is in her court now. I need her to be the one to take this next step, to tell me she's all in, too.

I pull into her driveway, looking over at her sleeping form. She's been exhausted lately, and I'm sure all the contractions from today didn't help. I reach across the car, using the back of my knuckles to brush softly across her cheek. "Mar, we're home."

She wakes slowly, eyelashes fluttering open.

"Want to get into the cool air?" I suggest. The heat is nearing unbearable levels today, so I'm eager to get into the house too.

"Hmm," she murmurs in agreement.

I get out and head to her side. She's still sitting in the same position when I open her door. "Ready?" I offer her my open palm. She takes it, letting me guide her out of the car. She's moving slow, like her entire body is aching, and I'm sure it is. Between the pregnancy, the wedding, and the minor scare today, she has to be exhausted.

I keep her hand in mine, leading her into the house. She breathes a long sigh when the air conditioned air hits her. "That feels so good," she murmurs. I watch as her shoulders droop, no longer tense and tight.

"Want to shower?"

She nods. "That sounds amazing."

Twenty-five minutes later, she's walking into the bedroom in only her robe, her hair piled up in a towel on her head. I'm not ashamed to admit that I stood outside the bathroom door the entire time, making sure she didn't need anything, only leaving when I heard her brushing her teeth.

There are dark circles under Marley's eyes, showing me just how bone-deep her exhaustion runs.

"Sit down," I tell her. She does so without complaint, and I grab a pair of underwear, cotton sleep shorts, and a t-shirt of mine from her drawer. I kneel before her, gazing up into her eyes.

She turns her face away, a red flush creeping up her chest and neck. Lifting her feet, I slide her underwear up her legs, then do the same with her shorts. The moment feels intimate, almost sensual, but in a comforting way. I rise from my knees, taking her hands to help her stand. I pull the underwear and shorts up underneath her robe, settling them on her hips. She lowers herself back to the bed, untying her robe. Her breasts fall from the fabric, her dark pink nipples hard and peaked under the cool air. It kills me, knowing that I can't touch her, can't make her feel as good as I know she deserves.

I help her into the baggy shirt, forever loving seeing her in my clothes. My cock grows achingly hard underneath my sweats, but I can't do anything about it. I help her lay down, silently getting her comfortable with her pillow.

"Are you still wanting to go by the house tomorrow?" I ask, climbing into the bed behind her.

Marley reaches out, searching for my hand. "Yeah, I am. I want to see it again, and really start to plan things out." I clasp our hands together, and she squeezes back gently. "Today scared me. I feel really unprepared."

"Hey..." I murmur, scooting in closer. "What can I do to help? Do we need to push this off?"

She shakes her head. "No, surprisingly it's not that. I mean like... a hospital bag. A plan. Who's going to be at the birth center with us? My mom has been pressing me to come, but..."

I shudder softly. "I love your mom, and it's totally up to you," I tell her. "But... I wouldn't mind it being just us two."

"Oh thank god," Marley sighs. "I don't want her in the room. She can be in the waiting room. I figured you were going to be surprised, and be on her side, saying I need my mom there."

I chuckle. "Butterfly, that is up to you. If you want her there, then she can be, but, if you don't, I will help you tell her that."

"She's going to be so upset," Marley whispers.

"Well, it's a good thing she isn't the one who's pregnant," I say, kissing the side of her neck. "So, we need to pack a hospital bag. We can do that tomorrow, after the meeting?"

"Yes, please," Marley hums. "I know it sounds stupid, being that I could go into labor tomorrow, but if all goes well, can we make a plan for the next few weeks? What, with moving, and everything?"

"Absolutely," I reply. "I'm happy to do whatever you need to make you comfortable."

THE MEETING with Jake goes well, with Marley getting excited at the prospect of the nursery, and what will be our room. The possibilities are endless with the house, and I could see the wheels turning in her brain, this time for a good reason, rather than the anger that was welling up last time.

We're back home now, sitting in the living room as we pack the hospital bag. Apparently there are all sorts of posts on the internet about what is totally necessary, and what isn't, so Marley is treating the information like it's a bible. The bag sits nearly empty in front of us, while we talk.

"If we decide to keep moving forward," I say, swallowing a lump down my throat, "Closing would be in three weeks. You'd be about thirty-five weeks. We can either stay here until you're comfortable and healed enough to move, or we can try to get as much done before the babies come."

Marley folds a soft pastel-green onesie, and lays it in the bag as she thinks. "Right now, I feel okay with packing. I feel good about the house. I want to move forward. I almost want to try and get in and settled before they come."

I nod, the feeling of everything coming together grounding me. I fold a baby blanket and put it to the side so Marley can put it in herself. I don't think she's realized it, but her nesting instincts have started to kick in. Just the other day, she had to rearrange the kitchen storage, and when I asked her why, she couldn't give me a solid reason, only that it didn't feel right the way it was.

"We can do that," I say. "But if at any time, you change your mind, you have to tell me." I raise my eyes, staring down at her intently. "You are going to be going through a lot of changes in the next few weeks, and I want to make sure you're most comfortable throughout this."

Marley looks up from the second onesie. "Thank you. I will. I promise. We're working on communication, right?"

"Right," I say.

She pauses for a moment. "I'm still working on it, I promise. But... I'm in this, Beau. I want us to be together, not just as co-parents. I want to be your partner. I want this."

I reach out, taking her hand. "I want that too."

49

MARLEY

I feel good. Better, more... stable. Every day this week, Beau and I talk, and not just about the weather, or how I'm feeling physically, but we *talk*. He holds me every night, and I think the fact that we can't bury our feelings in a physical act, instead having to verbalize them has been a game changer for us.

He, of all people, knows how bad I can lose myself to my depression, but I don't know if he realized how well I've gotten at masking it, to not only myself, but to him. I've been clawing my way out from this hole for years, only to dig it deeper and fall back in. I'm terrified for after I have the babies. I've read some of the information on postpartum depression, but I'm going to try my best to stay on top of things, no matter how hard it gets.

I won't lie, I miss the physical intimacy we had, but I think this is for the best. I haven't had a contraction now since the day we went to the hospital, and I feel good. Dr. Ness told me at my appointment this afternoon that I don't have to be in bed twenty-four seven, but to still take it easy. I was starting to go a little stir crazy, and Beau was only letting me go from the couch, to the bed, or to the bathroom. Until my appointment today, I hadn't left the house in nearly a week.

My mom and Nikki were here to visit everyday, helping me organize all things baby. We separated things into totes, labeling the sizes and whether they would be for Baby Boy, or Baby Girl. A majority of the items I've got can be worn by either baby, and are more neutral colors. As expected, my mom has hounded me on names, continuously. Beau and I have talked, and added, then erased so many names, that at this point, I'm sure we won't decide on something until they are here.

Josie, Fallon, and Megan were here too, helping me pack up the rest of the house. It probably sounds crazy, moving into a new house when you're pregnant with twins that could arrive at any time, but that's what my instincts are telling me. The packing has almost helped with the nesting instinct though.

Beau is trying to get the closing moved up on the house to give us more time, and we should know by tomorrow if we can. The house is already empty, so it's just a matter of the inspection and appraisal being cleared.

I'm sitting on the couch, folding a newborn onesie on top of my bump, when Beau comes into the living room. He's been working outside for the last hour, since we got back from the clinic, and he's all sweaty. His hair is tied back, but he looks like sin. The droplets of sweat running down the side of his cheek has me feeling almost animalistic.

I bite down on my lip as he strides toward me. "Hey, butterfly," he greets. I release my lip when he bends down to peck me on the lips. "How are you feeling?"

"Fine," I reply. "Packing, nesting, the usual."

He nods, taking in the disaster in front of him. "Is there a method to this?"

"Yep. I don't know what it is yet, but I promise it makes sense to me."

"That's all that matters," he says with a chuckle. "I'm going to shower, and run to the store. Do you want anything specific for dinner?"

I shake my head. "Not at the moment, but give me twenty minutes, and I'll think of something." He's been busy the last two weeks. On top of helping me around the house, he's been working extra hours at the office to help his co-workers when he's gone for paternity leave.

"Let me know," he says, turning and heading down the hall. I hear the shower turn on, and my body starts to ache, but not in a bad way. It's like I've just remembered that he's naked in the shower, and my body wants him.

I wouldn't have guessed that I'd be so horny at thirty-four weeks pregnant, but I am. I want this man so fucking badly, that it hurts. Dr. Ness didn't give me the all clear for sex today like I'd hoped, but there's always next week. Right?

I focus on folding and refolding the tiny outfits and blankets, my eyes filling with tears when I think of how small they will be. How much they will probably look like Beau.

I stand from the couch to put some things in the tote next to me, cringing internally at how long it took me to stand.

Beau walks back into the living room with damp hair, making his way to me immediately, stopping behind my back. His arms wrap around me, resting at the top of my belly. "Bye," he murmurs, squeezing me to his back gently. I don't know why he's doing this to me, but he needs to stop. It's like he's purposely rubbing his cologne over me, marking me with his scent. Maybe it's some primal thing. Marking his territory. Or maybe he knows how much I love the way he smells, and he's trying to drive me crazy. That seems like the more logical option. Right? A low pulsing in my groin picks up speed, leaving me aching, yet again, for him. I scold myself. I need to knock this shit off.

"Bye," I reply. He reluctantly pulls back, but not before I hear him take a deep inhale.

"I'll be back in an hour or so." He steps away, and I hear his footsteps as he walks out the side door, locking it behind him. A moment later, his car starts, and he rolls out of the driveway. I try to focus on the task at hand.

Put the clothes in the tote, Marley. Just... put the onesie in the tote.

I let the small piece of fabric slide from my fingertips into the tote, and grab the lid to seal it. It's completely full now, and ready to go into the garage.

My mind can't seem to focus on the baby clothes, or the totes anymore. I can't stop thinking of the way it feels like when Beau is inside me. I shake off the temptation, and head into the kitchen. I need to do something else with my hands, to keep me busy. I take a sponge and get a mug soapy and wet, and start to scrub it. But I can't stay focused. Not on the mug at least.

No, it's thinking of other things. How it would feel to wash Beau. To get him all soapy and wet in the shower. To land on my knees in front of him, and...

I drop the mug, and it clatters into the metal sink. Thankfully, it doesn't break, but it startles me. Okay. Maybe washing the dishes is not a good idea when I'm distracted like this. The last thing I need is to drop a knife or squeeze it and slice my hand open. I shut off the water, and dry my pruny hands on the towel next to the sink.

I glance around the kitchen. I need something to do with my hands, to distract me from the thoughts of Beau. Of naked Beau. Of the way he felt inside me. So thick, so full. *So…*

"Oh my god, Marley," I say out loud to my empty house. "Knock it off."

Thankfully, my house doesn't reply, or I would really be concerned about my mental state. I rub my hands over my bump, further drying my hands on my shirt.

A strong whiff of Beau's cologne wafts over me as I walk down the hall toward my room. It halts me in my tracks, right in front of the guest room's half open door. Even though he hasn't slept here in a long time, and it's full of baby things, it still is full of Beau's personal items. He has a scattered stack of business cards on the dresser, the bedsheets are rumpled and half open. A pair of sweats is on the floor next to the laundry hamper. Typical man.

But it's not the pants that catch my attention most. It's the books on his nightstand. My interest piques, and I push the door open the rest of the way. The scent of him slams into me like a brick wall, heavy and unfiltered. I swear, he has never smelled this good before. Is it the pregnancy hormones that are making it stronger? I'll have to ask Dr. Ness.

I stride over to the bed, sitting down on the edge of it. The mattress sinks under my weight, enveloping me in a cloud of comfortable foam. My eye catches the books again, and my heart leaps.

Oh my god. He has pregnancy books. And not just one. He has a whole pile of them. Multiple books. One about twin pregnancy in specific, one about how to be the best partner during pregnancy, one about labor and delivery. And they aren't untouched. The pages are crinkled, with tabs sticking out in random spots. I open the top book to the first tabbed page, and my eyes fill with tears. He's reading about pregnancy. For me. For us.

I shouldn't be crying, yet here we are. This realization hits me deep. I put the book back where I found it, making sure it doesn't look out of place. I stand, with effort, off the bed and see a worn sweatshirt hanging off a chair in the corner. Without second guessing it too much, I swipe it off the chair, throwing it on over my body. It fits me well, even with my large stomach, and the scent of him envelopes me almost immediately. I grab the books off the nightstand again, deciding I don't care if he knows that I found them. I want to look through them.

I waddle—because I'm officially in the waddling stage of my pregnancy—down the hall to the living room again. It looks like a war zone here, the totes scattered and clothes everywhere. I sit down on the couch, flipping one book open to the first tabbed page. The chapter is labeled as *Morning Sickness.* He has passages highlighted with possible remedies, or signs that your partner should go to the doctor.

The next tab marked is labeled *Mental Health.* He has highlighted the subheading *Depression,* and even has a few notes taken down. There is a passage with ideas on how to assist with mood swings and depression, and Beau seems to have read every one. There is a pen dot next to each sentence and suggestion.

A stray tear slides down my cheek. He did this for me. I didn't ask him to, and yet, he's doing what he can to take care of me, and our twins. A notecard falls out of the next page, Beau's handwriting filling the lines.

Questions for Dr. Ness

Monitor her moods. Is she sleeping more than normal?

What is normal at this stage in pregnancy with twins?

Can she continue to take her medication?

*Sex can help mood swings. *release happy hormones**

Cuddling also helps

Is that why he's been so cuddly? Or is that just him? Either way, my eyes are steadily streaming tears. Has it really been this way all along? How did I not realize how in tune he was with me the whole time, masking or not?

I flip through the rest of the book, through every tabbed page, highlighted passage, and note card taped to the pages. I read through every note, and learn things that even I didn't know.

I don't even hear the door open and close until Beau is standing in front of me, his face a mask of pure distress.

50

BEAU

The sound of stifled sobs is the first thing I hear when I make my way through the door into the kitchen. I'm on edge instantly. I stalk through the kitchen to the living room where I find my girl sitting on the couch. Her feet are propped up on the cushions, her rounded stomach covered by a sweatshirt of mine. A burst of possessiveness runs through my veins. Knowing that she's mine, that she's carrying my children, that one day I will put a ring on her finger, and give her my last name, makes every bit of pain from the last fifteen years worth it.

"Did someone hurt you?" She doesn't respond. "Marley, who hurt you?" I let my voice deepen.

"No one hurt me, you caveman," she finally replies. "I found your books."

"My books?" I reply, at a loss. I can't recall what books she's talking about, until I look at her lap to find the pregnancy books I've been reading. I ordered them the day we found out she was pregnant.

"Yes. I can't believe you paid so much attention, learned

so much for me." Her voice is tight, like she's holding back her emotions.

I'm confused by her reaction. I guess I assumed she knew, but maybe not. "Of course," I reply earnestly. "I am here for you, no matter what. Marley, I've wanted to make this as easy for you as possible."

She nods, her bangs falling into her eyes. I push the hair away, cupping her damp cheek in my palm. "Hey," I croon. "I've got you."

Nodding again, she mumbles something under her breath.

"What?" I ask, leaning forward.

"I know that now," she murmurs. She leans into my touch, tilting her head to rest on my shoulder. I wrap my arms around her shoulders, pulling her into me. Her entire body relaxes, fingers gliding around my neck to tangle in the hair at the nape.

I hold her, letting her get out her emotions until she's only sniffling.

When she pulls her head back, I smooth her hair away from her face. Her eyes are red and watery, but they're bright, and happy at the same time.

"What happened?" I ask her.

"Seeing that... your notes, how invested you are, it helped put some things into perspective for me." She wipes the last tears on her cheeks. "I love you. I won't lose you."

"You won't," I reiterate. "Honestly, you're kind of stuck with me."

"You're mine, right?"

"Of course I am," I reply. "Just like you are mine. I love you, Marley"

"Calling you my boyfriend feels insignificant for how much I love you," Marley says.

I can't even begin to explain how much her claim on me means. I've been waiting for this day, this moment. I've watched her acclimate to it over the last few weeks, but watching her have the full realization in real time is so fucking incredible. My heart wants to beat out of my chest. I'm so proud of her, of how far we both have come, to get to this moment. "Is that what I am?" I tease.

"Yes," she replies, "but you're so much more, and you know it."

"I do." I lean in, kissing her deeply. The saltiness of her tears mingles with the taste of her, but I know now that it's good tears. Her lips move against mine, her tongue parting my lips to dart in and taste me.

When I pull away, she whimpers.

"Why?" she moans.

"We can't get carried away," I say. "No sex, remember?"

She groans, dropping her forehead against mine. "I know."

"Want to know something exciting?"

She raises her brows. "That's a stupid question, I always want to know something exciting."

"We get to close on the house in the morning," I tell her. "I know I took the wrong path toward getting the house, not including you in the decision, but I think this will be good for us."

"We get to close?" she asks.

"Yep." What she doesn't know is that I've been working at the house for the last week, with the previous owner's permission, to get a bonus surprise ready for her. Everything was ready to go, it was just the title company that was busy, and couldn't fit us in until tomorrow.

Marley leans forward, squeezing me tightly into her embrace. "Thank you. I don't think I've said that yet. I know

I was angry, but I get it. You were just trying to provide for me and for our family."

I nod into her neck. "I was, but I also know I went about it the wrong way."

"It's done now," she murmurs. "We've worked through it, and I'm ready to put it behind us."

"I talked with my brothers and our parents. While we are closing they are going to load up vehicles with furniture and boxes."

She nods, listening closely.

"Then, we'll get to the house, set up the couch for you, and you get to watch us all make the house a home for us."

Her eyes well with tears again. "I feel bad," she says.

"Why?"

"I won't be able to help. I'll be sitting there, like the beached whale that I am, watching everyone do all the hard work."

"Butterfly, you have the best job, and honestly, the hardest of them all."

"How?" she says with a laugh.

"You have to tell us where to put things, all while growing two humans."

Marley shrugs. "When you put it that way, you're probably right. With how crappy I've been sleeping lately, I'll probably end up falling asleep."

I kiss the tip of her nose. "Even better."

51

MARLEY

We've dotted every *i* and crossed every *t* possible, and are signing the last sheet of paper. Beau has his hand resting on my thigh, fingers splayed. Every few minutes when the babies move, causing me the slightest discomfort, he moves his hand to rest on my stomach. Baby Boy is right under his palm, and it's like he knows his dad is here, because he stops kicking me instantly.

The woman sitting across from us smiles sweetly as she finishes explaining what's on the last page. Beau, of course, already knows what is on each page, and doesn't need explaining, and honestly, my mind is elsewhere. The twins could come at any time now, and it's a little nerve wracking.

I'm going to try to deliver them vaginally, but if something happens, I'd rather get a C-Section, to ensure that all three of us are as safe as possible.

The goal is to keep them in for another few weeks. I'll be thirty-six weeks in a few days, and to be honest, I don't know if I'll make it til thirty-seven, which is Dr. Ness's goal. I don't know where they're going to go. I'm rapidly running out of room in my uterus, and my body is rebelling. Beau had to help me in and out of bed last night, totaling a whopping five times to get to the bathroom.

He didn't seem to mind, but I felt guilty waking him just to pee. He reminded me every time that we'd be getting up with the babies more often when they arrive, so it was practice. Didn't help me from feeling guilty, but at least it made sense.

Beau slides the last sheet of paper toward me, showing me where to sign and initial for the final time. As I do, the biggest grin appears on his face. "We did it." He kisses me quickly, and takes my hand.

The woman offers us her congratulations, makes us a copy of the title, and then passes us the keys, sending us on our way.

Beau leads me to the car, and helps me in. Once he's in and we're both buckled, he heads off. The drive goes by quickly, and when we pull up the long driveway to the house, I'm in awe. There's something so special about seeing it again, knowing it's ours. Knowing this is the house we will bring our babies home to.

It's perfect. Quaint, two-story house with a deep blue siding and crisp white trim. There is a connected two-stall garage, and a front porch with fresh potted flowers on each windowsill and a few hanging from the overhanging roof.

Beau parks the car in the front spot, glancing over to take in my reaction. I'm trying my best not to cry, but I know it's inevitable. We're the only ones here, and I'm grateful. I want this to be ours, just us.

Silently, Beau helps me out of the car, and leads me up to the front porch. The flowers are varying colors of purples, pinks, and blues. "Josie?" I ask.

Beau chuckles. "Yep. I asked her to make me a bouquet for you, and she insisted on this."

"It's beautiful," I say.

"It is." Beau reaches into his pocket, pulling out a small silver key. "Ready?"

"Ready," I reply. He slides the key into the lock, turning the key and pushing the door open. The house is filled with natural light from the front picture window, and my eyes widen. It's just like I remember it, but now, it feels even more special. It's ours, and it's where we are going to raise our family.

Beau guides me carefully up the stairs, and down the hall toward the bedrooms. When we reach the closed door of the room we designated, he stops. His hand rests on the handle, and he takes a deep breath.

"My brothers have been helping me with this all week, but I wanted it to be just us when I showed you."

Heart pounding deep in my chest, I nod.

"I wanted a way to show you that this is for us, for our family, and our future." He pushes the handle down, opening the door into the nursery.

The once bare white walls are now a perfect sage-colored green. Two white cribs are lined against the far wall, with one solid sage sheet on one, the other patterned with green foliage. Hand-crocheted blankets rest over the rails, and I instantly know that my mother made them. She loves to crochet, and I asked her months ago if she would make the babies blankets, and she said yes, but then I never heard anything of it.

Photos of their first ultrasound are framed in a light wood frame, as well as photos of baby animals. There's a dresser and changing table to my right, perfectly matching the color scheme. I have no idea how he knew exactly what I wanted, but he did. It's perfect.

Empty hangers await in the closet, just waiting for the

totes of baby clothes to arrive and be filled. A handmade rocker is in the corner, clearly Andrew's work, with a soft cushion in the seat, and fluffy blanket hanging off the back.

My jaw is certainly on the floor, my entire being filled with so much love and affection for Beau. He did this for me, without me knowing, and I couldn't be happier. One of the things I told him I was worried about most with moving during the end of my pregnancy, was not getting a nursery done and ready before they were born, and he did it. He didn't even hesitate to take one of my biggest concerns and eliminate it completely.

When I glance over at Beau, I can see the fear underneath the emotion all over his face. "You…" I start, having to swallow the thick lump in my throat. "Beau, I can't believe this."

He gazes over at me. "I knew this was the thing you were worried about most with moving."

I nod. "It's perfect."

"You like it?" he asks hesitantly. "I wasn't sure. I know you mentioned wanting a sage green palette, but I wasn't really sure what else you'd like. Did you know that Fallon is really good at interior design, too? I think we should have her do the rest of the house," he babbles, but I stop him, wrapping my arms around his waist.

My belly stops me from getting as close to him as I want to, but I still have contact with him, and that's most important. "Thank you," I say, looking up. "It's everything. *You* are everything."

Beau tilts his head, resting his finger under my chin to keep me looking at him. "I love you, Marley. I'm in love with you, and I'm in love with the life we are going to have."

A choked sob escapes my lips. "I love you, too, Beau.

You've proved to me that I can have both sides of you. My best friend and the man I love."

"Always," he tells me. His brown eyes are searching mine, and I wait, eager for the moment our lips collide. He doesn't make me wait long, kissing me deeply. One hand cups the nape of my neck, fingers tightening in the roots of my hair. We make out like teenagers, making up for lost time. It's not until there's a loud whoop that echoes through the empty house that we pull apart.

Beau laughs. "There's Thomas." He pulls me in for one last kiss, and then with a final glance at the nursery, he leads me down the hall to the master bedroom.

"We don't have much time, but I wanted to see your reaction." I quirk my brow as he opens the door. Covering the far wall are picture frames, varying in shapes and sizing. I step closer, my heart soaring when I see them.

Pictures of us. From the first summer we met. In one photo, we're both soaking wet after swimming in the lake on the Fourth of July. My shoulders are sunburned, and Beau's grin is cheesy, but his arm is wrapped around me, keeping me close.

Another depicts our eighth grade snow-ball dance. We decided to go as friends, but that night was unbearable, trying not to show him how big of a crush I had on him. Beau has the same grin on his face, but this time, his mouth is full of braces, the neon green bands so vibrant they nearly glowed in the dark. I'm wearing a zebra print dress with a hot pink sash. My hair is teased within an inch of its life, and I have a thick layer of eyeliner on. I don't know how my mom let me out of the house like that, but that was the trend.

Junior Prom is the next photo. I went with my friends, and Beau took his on-again-off-again girlfriend. We took pictures together and they turned out horrible. We look awkward as hell, almost like we were afraid to touch each other for fear of outing our feelings to the other with a simple touch.

Those aren't the photos displayed though. There's one where I'm getting my corsage placed on my wrist, and Beau's looking at me like I'm the most beautiful thing he's ever seen.

Senior prom, high school graduation, tattoo shop selfies, college graduation. You name it, and it's up there. Our entire friendship scattered over the walls of our room, to show me how much we've been through.

The picture I spot last is one I've never seen. It's a photo of us at Josie and Andrew's wedding. The night our lives changed. We're dancing, my head is resting on his chest, his cheek on top of my head. Both of our eyes are closed, and it's like you can see us trying to live in the moment, both unwilling to leave yet scared to stay.

We've come full circle.

"Thank you," I tell him. I've said those two words so often in the last fifteen minutes, but it will never be enough. I have a lifetime to show him how thankful I am for him saving me, and for giving me this life with him, but it will never be enough.

52

MARLEY

"You're almost there," Dr. Ness says, patting at my knee as she finishes my vaginal exam. "Things seem to be right on track. Both babies and you are healthy. You're about two centimeters dilated, so things are starting to move along."

"Does that mean we can try to induce labor?" I ask eagerly.

She chuckles. "Yes, you can. Nothing too crazy, though. I wouldn't recommend doing curb steps, with the way you're carrying, but everything else is fair game. Spicy food, nipple stimulation, sex, all the things."

Beau's brows raise in surprise. I watch him swallow thickly. It's kind of a crazy realization that we can start doing things to get them out.

With my luck, they will probably make us wait another two weeks, but I hope not. I don't think I can make it that long.

Dr. Ness helps me sit up on the exam table, which is no longer an easy feat like it once was. After asking us a few more questions, she finishes up and leaves me to get dressed.

Beau is still standing beside me, seemingly running on autopilot. "You good?" I ask with a laugh.

He laughs in return. "Yeah, just all kind of hitting me. They could be here soon. Like, really soon."

His realization is adorable. "Yeah, they could," I say.

WE STOPPED at a bar and grill on the way home, and got a to-go box of spicy buffalo chicken wings. I'm not a huge fan of spicy things, but I'll do anything at this point. I'm desperate.

As if to drive home my point even further, Baby Boy kicks at his cramped living space, hitting my lungs. I gasp, then poke at him. "Knock it off," I say.

"Little man giving his sister trouble?" Beau asks. He has an amused smirk on his face, one hand on the wheel, the other resting on my thigh.

"More like giving his mom trouble," I say. "Kicked me in the lungs."

"Stinker." Beau turns us down our driveway, parking in the garage. "Have you thought any more about names? We are kind of running out of time."

I shake my head. "Not really. All the names I have on the list don't feel right. Do you have any?"

Beau shakes his head too. "Nope. But I don't know them as well as you do, at least not yet."

"I still like the idea of having their first initial be the same."

"Me too," Beau agrees. "I think that's a good idea." He helps me out, taking the bag of to-go boxes from me.

Once we are inside, I settle in at the kitchen table with

my napkins and glass of milk. I'm not messing around. I'm going to eat the spicy stuff, but I will do whatever I can to not be miserable the entire time.

Beau sets the box in front of me, taking his own box and sitting down next to me. Beau isn't huge on spicy stuff either, but I'm making him eat a few out of solidarity. Team-work, and all.

"Here we go," I say. I open the box and take a chicken wing out, my fingers already getting covered in the neon orange buffalo sauce. "Cheers." I hold out the wing to Beau, who taps his wing against mine.

MY MOUTH IS STILL BURNING, and there are no signs that I'm any closer to going into labor. My stomach hurts, and I've got a killer case of heartburn, but that's more than likely from the wings and extra hot sauce I slathered all over them.

I took an antacid, but it hasn't quite kicked in. Beau is pumping up my exercise ball, and I'm ready to start bounc-ing. He comes in from the garage, ball in tow, and sets it down in front of me.

After he helps me stand, I lower myself on the ball. The pressure decreases slightly on my hips and back, helping ease the ever present ache.

Beau sits down on the couch in front of me, holding his hands out to take mine. Setting my hands in his, I rock back and forth, bouncing slightly.

"What exactly will this do?" Beau asks.

"Honestly, I'm not sure. Irritate them?"

He chuckles. "Sounds about right. How long does it take for things to start working?"

"I have no idea," I reply. "I wish it was instant."

"Well, maybe they just aren't ready."

"Maybe. But I am."

"Same."

53

MARLEY

"Beau?" I call from where I'm currently rotting on the living room couch. It's been a full week since Dr. Ness told us to start attempting to induce labor, and while I've had a few contractions now and then, it's been nothing consistent, and nothing strong. I was still four centimeters dilated at my appointment this morning, and Dr. Ness said to keep doing what we were doing, that they would come eventually.

Beau strides into the living room from where he was organizing the kitchen pantry.

"What's up?" he asks. He runs his hand in his strewn hair hanging loose on his shoulders. "Contraction?" He has his phone out of his pocket, ready to time at the drop of a hat.

"No," I laugh. "I was going to see if you could get me another glass of water."

"Oh. Well, sure."

He heads back into the kitchen. As if his words triggered it, I have a shockingly strong contraction. "Beau," I gasp, only it comes out as a sort of squeak, because it's like all the air has been sucked from my lungs. The pain is so much worse than any Braxton-Hicks contraction from weeks ago. I squeeze my eyes shut, trying to breathe through the pain like Dr. Ness told me.

"Oh shit," Beau's voice reaches me through the mind-numbing pain, and I hold out my hand, a small sense of relief hitting me when his warmth clasps mine. "Did I speak that into existence?"

I nod through clenched teeth.

Distantly, I hear the cup being set down on the coffee table, and wait for the pain to cease.

Finally, it eases off, giving me a moment to catch my breath.

"I'm good." My eyes open, and I see Beau, his own eyes soft and worried as they look over me.

"Think this is it?" Beau asks.

"I'm not sure." My heart starts to stammer in my chest with anxiety. "I guess we need to time them, and see what happens."

"I'm trying so hard to be chill right now, and not imme-diately drag you to the hospital," Beau says with a slight laugh.

I laugh. "Give it time."

He checks the time, and types it into his notes app. "How long do you think that lasted?" he asks.

"Five minutes," I say. "Well, it felt that long at least."

"So... a minute?"

"Yeah, probably."

He nods, typing that into his phone.

Barely eight minutes later, another one starts. Beau coaches me through it, starting the timer when I tell him to, and letting me squeeze his hand. It feels different. This feels like it could be real, like I could actually be in labor.

Once it's done, Beau enters it into his phone. "Should we call the nurses? Check in?"

"I've had two contractions, Beau. We need to give it a little longer."

"How much longer?" he nearly pouts. "I don't like this. Seeing you in pain is hurting me."

"You're in for a long ride then, sweetie," I say, my voice thick with condescension. "Sorry, that was mean."

He only laughs softly. "Butterfly, that wasn't mean. You're in pain. I'm in pain, watching you in pain. Say whatever you need to say, and I'll be here for you the whole time."

"FUCK YOU, Beau Cunningham and your magical sperm!" I shout.

Yeah, I'm *really* in labor, and this *really* fucking hurts.

"I know, love, I'm sorry," Beau says as he drives us toward the birth center.

My contractions have been strong and steady for two hours now, getting closer together with each one. We called the nurses to let them know we were heading in, and they told us they would be ready.

I'm probably going to lose a few teeth with how hard I've been clenching my jaw, but I couldn't care less right now. All I know is that I'm in pain.

Another contraction rips through me as we whip into the parking lot of the birth center. Beau turns the car off, grabs the bags out of the backseat and practically runs to my side of the car. When the contraction finishes, he helps me out and then attempts to rush me inside. I can only waddle so fast, especially when it feels like there is a baby trying to press down on my bladder.

We make it inside and I see the familiar face of the receptionist there to greet us. When she sees me gripping Beau's hand hard enough to cut off his blood supply, she bolts into action, running to get me a wheelchair.

"Here, sit down," she offers, and I gratefully take it. Beau tries to subtly shake out his hand, and I smack him in the stomach.

"Sorry," he says with a wince. "Just getting the blood moving, that's all." He switches the bag to his other shoulder, offering me his other hand.

I take it with a glare. He better not pass out on me or he is going to have hell to pay. The woman pushes us down the hall, leading us toward the delivery unit rather than the clinic side. When the locked unit opens, the nurse we've come to be well acquainted with greets us at the door.

"Ready to have some babies?" Peyton says with a smile. Her short blonde hair is half up in a bun on top of her head, and the pearl necklace she always wears glitters on the gold chain.

I glower at her. She doesn't react though, only smiles back at me, stepping behind me to push the wheelchair down the hall. Beau keeps in step with us, my hand still gripping his. Peyton turns into a room right off the nurses station, and it's like all of the emotion and reality of this situation hits me.

In the far corner, there are two baby warmers with stacks of baby blankets and other tools ready for us. A cart is next to it, topped with a blue covering. The bed is turned down, with a hospital gown laying on top of the sheets, and an IV pole sits next to the bed, ready to be used.

A burst of anxiety hits me and I sink into the wheelchair. Peyton starts to rattle off instructions, but I don't hear anything. Because I'm about to lose it. She leaves the room after rubbing my shoulder gently, leaving Beau and I alone.

My breaths start to come in rapid succession, the reality of this hitting me hard. "We should go home," I say without thinking. "I'm probably not in labor, they're not ready to come out yet. We aren't ready."

Beau sets our bags on the small couch beside me and crouches down so he's at my level. "We're ready, Marley. You've got this. You are the strongest person I've ever known, and if anyone can do this, you can."

His words ease my anxiety but don't completely stop my spiral. "What if something happens to them?" I squeak. "They could get stuck, or have the cord wrapped around their neck, or—"

"Then we are with a group of amazing doctors and nurses who know exactly what is best for them, and you." Beau interrupts my spiral. "I'm scared too, but we just have to put that fear aside and go all in." His fingers entwine mine.

"You're scared too?"

"Butterfly, I'm terrified. I hate seeing you in pain, and I know that you're in for a lot of it, and there is nothing that I can do to help you."

"Don't leave me," I tell him. "That is how you can help me."

"I won't leave your side, I promise." He presses a gentle kiss to my forehead, my nose, then finally my lips.

54

BEAU

We've been at this for hours, and don't seem to be any closer to delivery. Marley's exhausted, and I'm exhausted watching her. She's been sitting at seven centimeters pretty much since we arrived, but her contractions are getting closer and stronger each time. Her water broke shortly after we got here, which I guess means things are way more painful now.

There's a quick rapping knock on the door, and Dr. Ness and Peyton come in. Both are wearing bright smiles, a contrast to the frown marring Marley's beautiful face.

Marley is standing in front of me, her body bent, elbows and arms resting on the bed, with her head on her hands. I've been massaging her back between and during contractions as she sways her body back and forth to try and ease the pain.

When they enter, Marley slowly straightens, giving them the fakest smile I've ever seen on her face. If I weren't so anxious, I might laugh at her attempt to be kind while she's this uncomfortable.

Peyton chuckles. "Dr. Ness wants to see how you're doing. It's been a while since your last check."

Marley nods, sighing softly. "Beau?" she asks, gesturing to the bed.

I help her get in and attempt to get her in some semblance of comfort. Dr. Ness gets a set of gloves on, and sits down on the rolling stool.

They adjust the lights, and Peyton throws a blanket over Marley's lap to cover her as Dr. Ness adjusts her hospital gown. She starts her examination, something Marley seems to have gotten used to, since she barely reacts.

"You're ready," Dr. Ness practically exclaims. "You're at a nine, so by the time we get everything ready, you'll be ready to push. One of the heads is sitting right there, just waiting. Peyton is going to coach you through a few practice pushes, while we get the rest of the crew. It's about to get real crowded here."

I look down at Marley who is mirroring my reaction. Both of our eyes are wide, mouths agape in shock. "You're serious?" Marley asks.

"Honey, if I lied about that, I would get into a lot of trouble," she replies with a chuckle. She snaps off her gloves, and pats Marley's bare leg. "I'll be back in about ten minutes, then we are going to have some babies!"

I think my brain is in a state of shock. Marley gazes up at me, brown eyes filling with tears. "I'm so scared," she whispers.

Her fear knocks some of mine out. I need to be strong for her right now, I can't show her how scared I am, afraid that something will go wrong. "You can do this," I tell her, wiping her sweaty bangs off her face. "You've made it this far, and you're going to run to the finish line."

She nods, the tears falling down her cheeks. "We should

probably send a text update, our moms are probably losing their minds. Oh, and can you text Marissa to come in?"

I'd completely forgotten that Marissa is in the waiting room, ready to come in to take pictures of the delivery. She offered to do it as a gift to Marley, and I'm glad, because now I can be present, and not have to worry about taking my own photos, and then we don't need any of our family in the room. Don't get me wrong, it would be amazing to have them here, but also, I want to have this moment for just Marley and I.

I nod, pulling my phone from my pocket and texting Marissa first. Once the message is sent, I pull up the group thread with everyone in it. Ignoring the previous messages asking for updates and how things are going, I send off a message.

ME

Almost time. Nine cm dilated, doing practice pushes. Will update later.

I put my phone away before any additional messages come through. I'm not going to worry about them right now. Focusing back on Marley, I notice that Peyton has her legs up in stirrups now, a bright light beaming down on her. I shudder. I can't imagine what it must feel like to be so... displayed.

I look down at her, and help her adjust her pillow. "Feeling okay, love?" I ask.

"As good as I can be," she replies. I kiss her swiftly, cupping her cheeks in my palms. When I pull away, she glances between her legs to Peyton, who smiles sweetly.

"Ready to practice?" Peyton asks.

Marley nods, and Peyton gives her some instructions on what to do. Right before she's about to push with the next contraction, Marley looks up at me. "This is really happening."

"It is," I say. The contraction hits her, and Peyton starts to count to ten. Marley squeezes her eyes shut, her brows furrowing, face growing red with each passing second.

"Actually," Peyton stops counting after five, her brows furrowing. "Stop pushing."

Marley does with a heavy breath. "Why?"

"You're a really good pusher, and I'm not about to catch my first baby. So, you're going to hold them in while I go get Dr. Ness. Got it?" Peyton holds up her gloved hand, pointing at Marley.

Marley nods, eyes growing wide in shock. "Okay."

Holy shit.

The room is suddenly full of people. All Peyton had to do was open the door and wave, and what feels like twenty five people are now crammed into the small space.

Marissa is ushered in, camera in hand. She comes to the head of the bed, and Marley reaches out. Marissa squeezes her hand, offering her a smile. She has a few kids of her own if I remember correctly, so she's been on this end of things before. I wave at her, and watch as she steps back, allowing us to focus back on the nurses in the room. I notice that Mallory has entered the room now too, and is helping Dr. Ness get gowned and gloved up.

"There's a lot of pressure happening down there," Marley squeaks, her brows arched in confusion.

Peyton glances down, and Dr. Ness hops into action. "You would be right, Marley," she says. "Baby is coming, so once you have another contraction, you're going to start pushing, just like you practiced."

My heart is thumping hard, because holy crap this is really happening. Marley nods, taking a deep breath. I kiss her forehead, taking her hand in both of mine, and I watch the monitor behind us spike, something I know now signifies a contraction. She bears down, tucking her chin to her chest and starts to push.

I'm completely in awe at this beautiful woman, the one who owns me, heart, body, and soul. She squeezes my hand at the same time, and I feel my knuckles crack, the muscles tightening, but I ignore the discomfort, because it's nothing compared to her pain right now.

Marley lets out a low guttural moan as Peyton reaches ten, taking a deep breath before pushing again. Dr. Ness praises her, marveling at how well she's doing.

This isn't like the movies or shows I've seen. Marley isn't screaming bloody murder, or crying out for drugs. She's focused, bearing the pain with an insane amount of grit and tenacity. The only noise coming from her is the low groans that almost seem to be aiding in her ability to push.

"Good, the first baby's head is out, Marley. Shoulders are next, then the baby will be out. You've got this," Dr. Ness says with awe.

"I can't believe I have to do this twice," Marley groans. The contraction ceases, giving her a moment to catch her breath.

Peyton softly laughs. "You're doing so good. Most people take a long time to get to this point."

"I don't know whether to smack you or thank you," Marley says.

"You can do both, I don't mind," Peyton says.

I run my thumb over her hand, leaning down to rest my head on her shoulder. "You're incredible, I can't believe you're doing this," I tell her. "I love you so much, butterfly."

Marley's eyes soften, and she turns her head so our eyes

meet. "I can't believe this is real life. Are you sure this isn't a dream?"

"Positive," I say. She tilts her chin, searching for a kiss. When I press our lips together, her body relaxes. As we pull apart, Dr. Ness grabs my attention.

"Dad, do you want to see?" she asks from between Marley's legs. I'm about to say yes, when Marley pinches my hand.

"Don't. Even. Think. About. It," she mutters, her voice murderous.

"Please?" I ask. "I won't look at anything else, I just want to see the baby."

She sighs. "Fine, but you can't tell me anything about how it looks."

I chuckle, kissing her again. I decide to look quickly so she doesn't think I'm staring at her bits.

I glance quickly, seeing blood and goop covering the head of dark, thick hair. "It's got our hair," I tell her.

"Dark and thick?" Marley asks with a chuckle.

"Yep," I reply. Another contraction starts as settle back in at the head of the bed, and she starts to push. This one is accompanied by another low moan, and my hand being squeezed into oblivion.

"Good, good," Dr. Ness says. "Shoulders are out."

And then our first baby is being placed on Marley's chest, bright red and covered in white gunk, but screaming like no other.

"Baby boy!" Peyton says with glee, wiping him down and suctioning out his mouth. He screams, lungs clearly working. His hair is so dark, sticking down to his head, and his eyes are squeezed tightly shut, mouth open wide as he adjusts to life on the outside. "Congratulations, Mom and Dad!"

My eyes lift to Marley's, tears streaming down my cheeks, as her hands fret over our son. "Oh my god," she murmurs over and over again. "I made you. Hi, baby, oh hi. It's okay, I know, baby. It's so hard, you're okay. You're okay." Both of us are crying.

"You look just like your daddy," she cries. "Beau, he looks like you." I nod, looking between our son, and this beautiful woman.

"He looks like us," I say. "You're so amazing."

I kiss her quickly, almost unwilling to take my eyes off either of them for more than a second. "Want to cut the cord?" Mallory asks.

I nod, taking the scissors from her. I follow her instructions, cutting the soft cord between the two clamps, a burst of pride carrying though my body.

They clean him up a bit more for another moment on her chest, and then Mallory lifts him up off her, telling us she's bringing him over to weigh him and get him wrapped up.

"I hate to be the one to tell you this, Marley, but we have one more baby to get out," Dr. Ness' voice is almost apologetic. "Baby Boy is doing great, so I want you to give me a really good push here."

Marley obliges, pushing hard and long again. I can see how tired she's getting, but she's doing her best not to show it.

"Good. Again," Dr. Ness says. Our son is crying over on the warmer, and it's hard not to go to him, but I know he's in the best hands right now.

55

MARLEY

Right now, all I know is pain. This is so incredibly painful that I don't know how to process anything else. It feels like half of my heart is across the room, being swaddled and cared for by other people, and yet, I can't move, can't do anything but sit here and try to push my daughter out.

She's stubborn, not moving down like she should. My body and mind are so exhausted, I don't know how I'll continue, but I know I have to. I'm nowhere near the end. Nowhere near holding both of them in my arms. When the next contraction hits, I put my all into it, willing her to move farther down.

"Good job, here she comes, Mom," Dr. Ness says. There's tugging and movement.

Beau stands strong and steady next to me. He hasn't dropped my hand once, has given me constant encouragement, strength and power when I need it most.

"Is she coming?" I ask, my voice hoarse and breathless.

"She is, but her cord is wrapped around her neck. I

need you to push hard, so I can get it off." Her voice is serious, worrying me even more than I have all day.

"Is she okay?" I cry. She has to be okay.

"She will be, but you need to push, Marley."

I bear down with everything I have in me, feeling the pressure and tugging like I felt with Baby Boy. It feels like my vagina is shredding in half, and someone lit it on fire with how much pain I'm in, but I'll bear it if it means my baby is safe.

"Cord is off, one more big push, and she'll be here," Dr. Ness says.

I do what she says, and there's another blast of pain and pressure, and then just as fast as it came on, it's gone. My daughter is placed on my chest, much like her brother was, but she's purple and not moving, not crying.

"She's not crying," I cry, my voice shrill and high. "What's wrong? Why isn't she crying?"

Peyton moves up the bed, roughly rubbing her back with a blanket. Her mouth is open, but she's still not crying. It looks like she's trying to, trying so hard. Peyton uses the bulb to suction her mouth, and finally, a gargled cry escapes her mouth.

Tears stream down my cheeks as I listen to her cry. "Good job, baby, you're breathing," I say to her. Beau leans down, resting his head to look at our girl.

She's still purple, and not crying as hard as our son did. "Marley, I need to take her to the warmer, we need to check her out, and get her breathing better," Peyton tells me, and my heart nearly stops.

"Okay," I say. I unwillingly let her take my girl, and watch as she rushes her over to the warmer next to her brother.

Beau stays by me as we both watch Peyton and the

other nurses work on her, calmly calling orders and getting the pediatrician on call in. Anxiety burns my veins, and I can feel myself following Dr. Ness's instructions as she helps me deliver the placentas and get me cleaned up.

Mallory brings over my son. "Here, let's get you some time with Baby Boy. Baby Girl is already doing better, she just needed a little help." I nod, my mind not totally believing her. I won't be okay until I know for sure she's okay.

"Do you want to do some skin to skin? Try breastfeeding?" Mallory asks me.

"Yes, please," I say. I need the contact with him, to know he's okay. She and one of the nurses help me get into a better position now that Dr. Ness is done, and then Mallory unclips my hospital gown at my shoulders, pulling it down so it's just barely covering my breasts. She sets him on my chest, his warm, soft skin immediately relaxing me. I'm not totally appeased, but this is helping more than I knew it could. I look up at Beau, who is now taking a few pictures on his phone. Marissa is still here, but I can tell he also wants the memories for himself. Baby Boy settles into my skin, his small fingers grasping and searching for me. My emotions are so conflicted, because there is so much joy in me at having him close by, but also, so much fear that my daughter isn't okay.

"She's doing fine, Momma," Peyton comes over, my daughter in her hands. She has on a little pink hat with a bow, and there's a small oxygen tube underneath her nose. "She just needs a little help adjusting. She inhaled some fluid and the cord around her neck didn't help."

My daughter is laid on my chest for the second time, and my fear vanishes. She's no longer purple, but a healthy pink. Her eyes are closed as she sleeps, her breathing even and steady. She's okay. She's here.

Beau is giving me the biggest smile, his eyes completely awestruck. To be fair, I am right there with him. I can't believe this is our life.

"You're so amazing," Beau says for what feels like the hundredth time today, but I believe him, because I did that. I made and grew two humans.

"Thank you," I tell him. "For this, for being you. For loving me."

"I'll never stop," he says.

"WE STILL DON'T HAVE NAMES," I say to Beau as he folds a blanket, putting it in a bag. Baby Boy is latched onto my right breast, and Baby Girl, freshly off any tubes or monitors, is in a small bassinet beside my bed. We're being discharged in a few hours, and we're determined to name them before we leave. It's been a long two days, but our girl is a fighter. She had a few rough hours when she was needing more oxygen and care, but overall, she's doing great. Breastfeeding is a challenge, especially with two, but I want to give it my best go. I'm planning on pumping, that way Beau can feed one with a bottle, and I can feed the other with my breast.

It's nice being just the two of us today. Ever since we knew that Baby Girl was going to be fine, it's been a revolving door of our parents and family. Not that we've minded. It's been so nice to see how much love everyone has for them, and us, but it's good to have a break. I'm ready to get home and figure out our new normal.

"What about Arlo for him?" he asks. He steps forward, reaching down and lifting Baby Girl from the bassinet. She squirms, letting out a whimper of displeasure, but calms immediately when she feels the warmth of Beau's chest. He's been walking around shirtless ever since they were born, determined to have as much skin to skin time with them as possible. I don't mind. Seeing him shirtless, with the tattoo he got for us on his shoulder, makes my heart jitter every time I see it. There's also nothing sexier than seeing the man I love, my best friend, being a father to our children. Watching him do it shirtless is just a bonus.

I look down at the little pink cheeks of our son. He looks so much like Beau, it's crazy. He's right, though. He does look like an Arlo.

"Arlo Earl Cunningham," I say, never taking my eyes off him. It feels right.

Beau stands, cradling Baby Girl in his arms. I gently scoot over in the bed, well aware of my sore and battered vagina. I wince slightly, but Beau doesn't notice, thankfully. He would immediately demand to try and help me, but there isn't really much he can do.

He slowly sits on the bed beside me. He gazes over at our boy, and nods. "Yeah. That's it." He kisses me quickly. "Now we just have to name this hell-raiser."

The nickname might stick. Since birth, she's been nothing but trouble. Arlo—it feels weird, in a good way to refer to him as his name—has been nothing but calm. Only crying when we take him out of his blankets to change him. The complete opposite of what he was like during my pregnancy.

"What about Ariel? Arlo and Ariel," I offer.

Beau glances down at the bundle in his arms, and I do

the same, looking at my sweet girl. Her cheeks are chubby and flushed pink, soft blush lips opened in a small *o*.

"Yeah. That feels perfect. Ariel Ruby? For your grandma?"

"Ariel Ruby Cunningham." I smile. "It's perfect. They're perfect."

I rest my head on Beau's shoulder, glancing down at the little ones who helped make us a family.

"Fuck, I love you so much," Beau says with a gust of air. "I can't believe this."

"I love you so much."

56

MARLEY

Beau flops down on the couch next to me, having just set Arlo down in the bassinet beside us. Ariel is latched onto my breast, suckling happily. This has been exhausting, but we're doing it. We are successfully being parents. They had their two week check-up this morning, and are both gaining weight as they should be.

My mom is asleep in the guest bedroom down the hall, having spent last night here, taking a shift so Beau and I could sleep for longer than two hours at a time. Everyone has been so incredibly helpful, but also giving us our space when we need it. Ariel slowly falls asleep, her mouth falling off my nipple.

I adjust her, and cover my breast with my nursing bra. Beau takes her from my arms, resting her on his shoulder to pat her back and burp her.

A few pats and a large belch later, she's sound asleep, and Beau places her in the second bassinet next to me. I lean back onto the couch, giving myself a minute to breathe before I do my evening pumping session. One of my breasts hurts and I'm worried I might be getting mastitis. It's achy and hot, and the thought of anyone touching it right now hurts more than anything. When I pumped earlier, almost nothing came out, making me think there's a clogged duct. Beau scoots in close, pulling me against him. I let myself sink into his embrace, needing his touch.

"I can't believe asking you to dance at a wedding would bring us here," he murmurs, pressing kisses to the top of my head.

"Pretty sure it was you chasing after me that changed the path of our lives, but yeah. You're right. It's pretty crazy."

There's a soft knock on the front door, my dad's voice softly calling as he enters the house. "Hey Dad," I greet him as he walks up the stairs.

"How ya doing, kids?" he asks. He glances at Beau and me, snuggled up on the couch, and the babies in their bassinets beside us. He smiles softly, a knowing affection in his gaze.

"Good," I say through a yawn. "Mom is sleeping in the guest room."

Dad nods. "I'll let her sleep for a bit. Do you guys need anything?"

I shake my head. "Not right now."

"Why don't you two shower and take a short nap while I stay here with the twins? I'll get your mom if I need anything."

I look up at Beau, waiting for his agreement. He nods eagerly. "You're sure, Gabriel?"

"Positive. I need some time with my grand-babies, anyway."

Beau shifts before standing, offering me a hand to help me stand as well. The soreness between my legs has eased, but it's still present.

I'm nowhere near being cleared for sex, or even wanting or craving it, but I miss the intimacy between Beau and me. Sure, we snuggle and he shows me love in other ways, but I miss that connection with him.

Beau leads us down the hallway after I give my dad a brief rundown on when the babies will need to eat next, and what has been working best to soothe them lately. "I don't dare sit down," I tell Beau. "If I do, there's no chance you'll get me up."

He chuckles. "I was thinking we could shower together. No funny business of course, but I need some closeness."

"Can it be a hot shower?" I ask. "My boob hurts. I think it's getting mastitis. Dr. Ness said heat and warm compresses could work so it doesn't get too bad."

"Why didn't you tell me sooner?" Beau asks, stepping closer to me.

I shrug. "It wasn't too bad until this last feed. I want to try and loosen it up before I try to pump the clog out."

Beau hums to himself, then takes my hand, leading me into the bathroom. He starts the shower, letting it warm up as he helps me undress. I'm more than capable of doing it myself, but it feels good to have him assist me. He lifts my shirt off me, leaving me in only my nursing bra and granny panties. My nursing bra is scattered with milk stains, and I still have on disposable underwear, as I'm still bleeding off and on.

Beau gazes down my body like it's a rare gem. He doesn't gawk at my many stretch marks, or the way my stomach is still deflating after carrying twins. He stares at me like I'm a gift. Like I'm something special, meant for him, and only him.

He shrugs off his clothes, leaving him naked before me. I take off my bra, and slide down the underwear, trying to discreetly hide the blood in the center. Beau doesn't seem to care, though. He just tosses the disposable underwear into the garbage. Holding out his hand, I take it, and he helps me step into the steaming shower. The water beats down on my aching body, the mental and physical tolls of postpartum life weighing me down. For the first time since the twins were born, I feel like I can breathe.

Beau is the only person I've let see, but my anxiety has ramped up. Even when the babies are sleeping, I'm barely sleeping. I'm watching them non-stop, worried that Ariel will stop breathing, or that they missed something in the hospital. What if her lungs aren't strong enough, and they give out?

When Beau steps in behind me, he wraps his arms around my chest, letting me sink into his embrace. I haven't had time to really process anything, the feelings that I have, at least until my appointment today. Dr. Ness upped my medication, and gave me something to help when I start to spiral.

Tears stream down my cheeks, blending in with the water cascading down my body as I let myself feel it all. The exhaustion, the anxiety, the constant fear that Ariel will stop breathing. Being a new mom is weighing on me.

My dad showing up and offering to watch them means the world, but yet, I don't know if I'll be able to sleep still, not having my eyes on them.

It's been hard, trying to verbalize the things in my head, but Beau listens to each fear, and helps me rationalize them. I broke down the first night we got home, away from the constant monitoring of the nurses, and he made me tell him every thought I was having. He was ready to drive us right back to the birth center, scared I was having some sort of reaction, especially when I wouldn't give Ariel to him. I couldn't put her down. I made him call the nurses, just to be sure she was really okay. They probably thought I was crazy, but they were sweet about it.

"I'm sorry, I'm such a mess," I cry, letting my head fall back onto his chest. Beau repositions us, his body directly under the spray now so it's no longer hitting me directly in the face.

"Shhh." He tilts his head so he can whisper in my ear, "I've got you, remember? I'm here to catch you when you fall. I'll be the one to watch you get back on your own two feet when you feel strong enough."

I nod, words failing me. I know he has me, but I'm so scared that I'll end up in that dark place again. I want the medication to work right away, even though I know it won't. I wish that I wasn't like this, that I didn't have to take medication just to feel like a normal human, but Dr. Ness told me that I am normal, that these feelings are normal, especially with how out of sync my hormones are.

I let the warm water soothe my body and mind while Beau holds me. When the water starts to run cold, I let my arms drop, and Beau steps back. My right breast throbs while my left leaks milk like a faucet.

I grab a towel, and work on drying my body. Beau holds open my cotton robe when I'm dry enough, and I slide my arms in. When Beau is dried off and has a fresh pair of boxers on, I ask, "Are you willing to grab my pump and everything from the living room? I don't really want my dad to see this." I gesture down to my left breast, already creating a damp spot on my robe.

Beau nods. "For sure." He leans down, kissing my cheek. "Go sit in bed, I'll be back in a minute. Want something to eat?"

"Please," I say, not caring what he brings me, but

knowing I should eat something. "And my water bottle, too!"

He offers me a thumbs up on his way out the door.

I climb into our bed, adjusting my pillows so I can sit comfortably. The room feels so empty without my babies in it, and I stop myself from changing my mind and going out into the living room anyway. It's okay to need a break. I love them, and just because I'm taking a little bit of time to myself doesn't mean I'm not a good mom.

Beau walks back in moments later with what we call my milking cart. It's a rolling cart with my pump on the second shelf, with extra tubing, bottles, nipple cream, and anything else you might need. The top shelf is usually where I put my phone, water, and snack, so it's easily within reach.

My nipples hurt just thinking about what's to come. I'm still getting used to the whole breastfeeding thing and working on getting my supply up. We've supplemented a few times with formula and I don't mind. All that matters is that they are fed.

Beau hands me the already connected pump. I connect my left breast first, knowing that at least that side won't be painful. I adjust my right breast, getting the nipple in the flange correctly, and then nod at Beau to flick the power on.

The suction starts immediately along with the burning pain in my right breast. I hiss, trying to fight through it. Beau sits down next to me, running his palm up and down my legs, the ones that I haven't even considered shaving in the last two weeks. Not that it matters, he's seen every inch of me at this point, and not in a sexy way. I mean, my boobs are hanging out, being tugged within an inch of their life right now, and he's cuddled up next to me without a care in the world.

After fifteen minutes, my left side is drained, and I have

five ounces to show for. My right side however, has barely an ounce, and it hurts like a bitch. Beau's been scrolling on his phone most of the time, and my mind has been focused on not crying from pain.

"Did it work?" he asks.

I shake my head, wanting to cry in defeat.

"Hmm." he ponders. His brows crease downward. "I found a couple things online while you were pumping, can we try them?"

"You... that's what you were doing?" I ask, my voice full of surprise.

"Yeah? Is that okay?"

"It's fine," I reply. "I just thought you were on Facebook or something like that."

"No," he says with a small laugh. "I could tell how uncomfortable you were. Do you have one of those suction cup thingies?" He gestures at his chest, like I'm supposed to know what he's talking about.

"Um, no? What is that?"

"You didn't get one at the baby shower?"

"Beau, I have no idea what you're talking about."

He pulls his phone from his shorts pocket, taps on his screen a few times, and turns the phone to show me. It's a manual silicone breast pump, but instead of the pump, it's just natural suction. "I read that these can be really helpful, you can put hot water and epsom salt in it and suction it on there. It's supposed to help loosen it up."

"I don't think I have one."

"We could try another way, then. You have those hot packs, right?"

"Right..." I don't quite know what else to try, besides pumping again.

"Why don't you put the hot packs on your breast, and

then I can kind of try to massage and suck it out," Beau says with complete certainty.

"Suck it out?" I squeak. "You want to *suck it?*"

"*That's what he said,*" he jokes.

I narrow my eyes, glowering at him. "Not the time, Beau."

He chuckles. "Sorry, but really. I read that it can help, and a lot of the online forums say that the pumps don't have strong enough suction."

"But... what if you taste it?"

"Then, I taste it?" He shrugs. "I've heard it's sweet."

"I can't believe you're offering to do this."

"You're in pain, love. I just want to help. Please?" He gives me his best attempt at puppy dog eyes.

"Fine, but we won't speak of this, ever again."

He rolls his eyes. "Sure, Mar."

He grabs the hot pack, reading the directions before popping the tabs. He wraps it in a cloth and passes it over to me. I uncover my breast, resting the warmth on it. It helps to relieve some of the ache immediately. Beau comes over to my side of the bed. "Where do you want me?"

Embarrassment washes through my body. I shouldn't be embarrassed, but this feels... almost taboo. I scoot more toward the middle of the bed, so Beau has space on my right side to kneel.

He does so quickly, getting close to me and leaning down to kiss me. "If it's too much, just let me know, but Marley, I want to do this. I want to help you."

I nod, kissing him back with everything I have. How did I get lucky enough to have him? How is he so willing and open?

He adjusts his body so he's flush with my swollen nipple, opening his mouth and closing his lips around it. I close my eyes, leaning back into the headboard. It takes him a few tries to get used to it, but then he's got a good latch, and is suckling at my breast, alternating between hard pulls, and short staccato ones. He's trying to help get the clot loose and out. I look down at him, and he's focused so intently, brows furrowed and grooves lining his forehead. His still wet hair is hanging across my lap, dampening my robe.

This goes on for a few minutes, and then it's like a dam bursts. Pain flares through my nipple, and my breasts let down the milk, and Beau nearly chokes at the sudden rush of milk into his mouth. He lets my nipple free, swallowing a few times before his eyes widen.

"I think I got it," he says, beaming with pride.

I laugh. "Yeah, you definitely did." I gesture down to where my nipple is steadily leaking milk.

"I kinda wanna do it again," he says, face flushing red. "It tasted good once I got a bit of it. It was also kind of relaxing."

"It was?"

"Yeah. I mean, are you really surprised? I've always loved your tits."

He's got a point.

The ache now relieved in my breast, I know I'll probably have to pump this side so I don't get clogged again. I reach out for my pump, ready to hook back up, but Beau reaches out, stopping me. "Can I do it one more time? Just a little?"

"You really want to?"

"Obviously." He doesn't hesitate to lean back down. He does give me a moment to decline, or tell him no, but when I don't he latches back on to my breast, suckling the dripping milk. I give him a minute or so, but then I'm pushing his head off.

"I need to pump now." I'm not about to tell him how sad I am to have him stop, because I'm loving the intimacy of it, how it feels different than when the babies do it, more sensual, like I have more ownership of my body, but I also need to collect as much as I can for them.

"Fine, but I want to do that again sometime. Okay?" he nearly pouts.

"Okay," I say, kissing him. I can just barely taste the sweetness he spoke of, and I love how much he loved it.

57

BEAU

THREE MONTHS LATER

Ariel screeches in my arms, completely and utterly pissed at me. I shush her, rocking her in my arms, knowing exactly why she's mad. I don't have boobs, and I'm not Mom.

Marley is back at work for her first shoot today, just a quick mini boudoir shoot for Megan. She's not fully back to work by any means, only planning to do one shoot a week. Until the twins are a bit older, she's working very part time. I wish I could be home with her every day, but I unfortunately need to work. Luckily, my mom, or Marley's mom, or one of her girlfriends are here to help her if she needs. Though, she's got a pretty good routine, and doesn't need help everyday. She's such a badass.

Marley took Arlo with her to the studio, mainly because he's the chill one. Ariel has been dealing with a lot of colic and tummy issues, pretty much since day one. She's a trouble-maker, but we love her all the same. She's the spitting image of her mother, and has a lot of her spunk. When she's happy, and gives us one of her smiles, it makes me feel like I climbed a mountain. It's a huge accomplishment.

I'm meeting Marley and Arlo at the studio in about an hour, and we are going to do a quick photo session. What Marley doesn't know is that I also have something else up my sleeve.

Ariel finally settles an hour later, with a few extra ounces of milk in her, and enough bouncing to make her turn into a milkshake, and we are heading out the door. I get her carseat locked into place, and make my way into town.

I'm dressed casually, but still nice, and in an outfit Marley picked out for me. When I make my way into the studio, I can hear the familiar sounds of Marley singing to Arlo. He loves when she sings him nursery rhymes, or more often than not, she'll sing Taylor Swift songs, or showtunes.

Arlo is cooing happily, staring up at her in delight. She's stunning. Her hair is curled in long, loose waves that fall past her shoulders. Her lips are painted a stunning maroon, accenting her soft silver nose ring, changed from the usual golf hoop, and she's wearing a soft white cotton dress that is cut in a deep v, giving me the perfect view of her beautiful breasts.

If I thought I loved her tits before she started breastfeeding, I was sorely mistaken. They're insane. Not only because they feed and provide for our twins, but because they make an incredible pillow. She's gotten a few more clogged ducts, and I've happily helped her with them, but that's not the only time I get a little taste of her milk.

We have only started having sex again recently with the blessing from Dr. Ness at her six week appointment, but also waited until Marley was comfortable. I didn't press the subject, not wanting to pressure her, and wanting her to want it.

One day, she literally just jumped on me after we put

the twins to bed. She started leaking in the middle of her orgasm, and I was more than happy to help clean her up.

Marley spots me as I carry Ariel's car seat over to her. "Hey, how was she?" she asks, cooing at our daughter.

Ariel squawks when she hears Marley's voice, her little face immediately turning bright red. She starts to cry, and Marley winces. "Like that," I say, tilting my head down to look at her. "She wants your boobs."

I set the car seat on the bed, unbuckling her from her seat and lifting her out. Marley sets Arlo down in the bouncy seat she brought with, buckling him in before heading over to the chaise lounge to feed Ariel. I bring her over, and Ariel roots at Marley's chest until she finds Marley's nipple. Immediately, she starts to suckle, making happy whimpers as she fills her belly. I head over, picking up my son from the bouncer.

"Hey, big man," I say, helping him form a little fist to give him a fist bump. "Were you good for your mommy today?"

He coos at me in response, and I take that as my answer. I sit down on the couch next to Marley, and we chat a bit about the shoot, and how both our days were.

When Ariel is done, we get her cleaned up and burped, and then get the babies in their outfits. A little onesie with a skirt for Ariel, and a pretend dress shirt with khaki pants and suspenders for Arlo.

Marley gets her camera all set up, and my nerves slowly kick in. I've thought this through, asked her parents, hell, we've even talked about it, but I'm still worried she's going to say no. I check my pocket for the hundredth time, making sure the small box is there.

After everything is ready to go, I adjust Arlo so he's resting against my chest, facing the camera. Marley takes

Ariel from the bouncer, shoving it off to the side. The small remote is in her hand so she can continuously take photos. We did a shoot when the twins were small, but I asked to do this one specifically. I want to commemorate their growth, as well as the growth in our relationship.

"Ready?" she asks, reaching out to fix a piece of my hair with the hand holding the remote. Her left hand.

"Yep," I say, bending down to kiss her cheek. "I love you."

"I love you too," she says. On her arm, I see the spot directly underneath her large butterfly tattoo. Once she's done breastfeeding, she plans to get three additional butterflies, one for me, and one for each of the twins.

The last three months haven't been easy, not by a long shot. For every three good days, Marley has a bad one, where her anxiety is out of control, and her depression makes her question her worth, our relationship, or her ability to be a mother. She's found a good medication though, and that has seemed to help. I'm so proud of her. It's a hard road, but I'm staying by her side through it all, the way I have always tried to be. I don't think I will ever forgive myself for the night I didn't answer the call, but she's here. She chose to stay, and chose to live this life with me.

Marley gets us into a few poses, and I smile down at her, so fucking proud that she's mine, and will be until the day I die. I follow her directions, taking picture after picture, and when I notice Ariel making her irritated face, I decide it's now or never.

"Oh no," Marley says, looking down at our daughter. "I think she's about had it."

She's not paying attention to me as I slide down onto one knee, cradling Arlo to my chest, facing him out so he can see her. I set him on my outstretched knee, and reach into my pocket to grab the box. Ariel starts to fidget more, and I silently will my baby girl to hold out for three more minutes.

"Marley?" I ask, trying to get her attention.

"Hmm?" she tuts at Ariel, only glancing at me briefly. She does a double take, jaw dropping as she realizes what's in my hand. She fixes Ariel so she can see me, and Ariel coos happily at seeing her brother and dad in front of her. "Beau, what are you doing?" Marley asks, though I know she already knows exactly what I'm doing.

I clear my throat to rid the anxiety building there. "Marley, I love you. I think I've loved you since you moved in next door to my family. Throughout everything, you've been the one person I trust, the one person I know will always have my back, and always love me. I promise to do the same for you. I promise to pick you up on the bad days, to always answer the phone, and to always be the man and father that you and our children deserve. I love you with everything I am. Marley, will you marry me?" My eyes are full of tears when I finish, and Marley is nearly sobbing.

She bends down to her knees, holding Ariel to her chest, not even looking at the ring. Her brown eyes are solely focused on me. "I love you so much, Beau. Yes, yes, I will marry you."

I take her lips in a rushed kiss, unable to do anything but kiss her, as my son is in one hand, and the ring is in the other. The babies are between us, giggling at each other and their sudden proximity.

When we pull away, Marley's cheeks are flushed red, eyes watery and cheeks tearstained. The remote for the camera is tossed onto the floor, but thankfully, I have my phone in the corner. I recorded the whole thing.

I glance down at the ring box, waiting for Marley to look

at it. When she does, tears fall harder down her cheeks. Nestled in the velvet is her grandmother's ring. With her dad's permission, he gave me the ring to use when I asked for her hand in marriage, shortly after the twins' birth.

It's a classic solitaire diamond, set in gold with intricate engravings around the band. It's perfect for Marley, delicate, but so strong and bold like her. She shakes as I one handedly take the ring from the box, and slide it onto her finger.

"Is that my Grandma's ring?" she asks in awe.

I nod, tears filling my own eyes.

"Thank you," she murmurs, looking down at the ring.

"Anything for you," I say earnestly. "I love you so much, butterfly. I can't wait for our life to really begin together."

She nods, kissing me hard as our babies try to bat at each other in our laps.

MARLEY

As a little girl, I was always obsessed with my grandmother's ring. I never knew my grandpa, but the stories she told me was a story of true love, and I wanted that for myself. I haven't seen the ring in years. Honestly, I assumed it had been buried with her after her death.

It took me a moment to recognize it today, but when I did, something settled into my chest. Beau and I had talked about getting married, and he'd even talked about proposing, but I never saw it coming today. It was intimate, just our little family, and just the way I dreamed it would be.

My life is slowly settling into the place I never thought it would be. A year ago, I was still pining after my best friend, still so desperately in love with him, but so afraid to tear down my walls and let myself love him the way we both deserved.

Beau drives us the short distance across town to Jason's brewery. "Jason closed for the night, so it's just our family and friends."

"He did that for us?" I ask in surprise.

"He did. Only took a little bit of bribing."

I chuckle. Jason is a surly man, but he has such a soft spot for his younger brothers, and for me. The babies are fast asleep in the back, and I almost regret that we are going to wake them up the minute we go inside. Though, I think it will be worth it.

Beau grabs Ariel, and I grab Arlo, and we meet at the front of his car, reaching out and entwining our hands together to make the short walk inside.

The door is open, letting the warm September air into the brewery. Gramps is the first one I see, sitting in the chair closest to the door, his cane at his side. "Well hey, kids," he says in his gravelly tone. "I hear you got somethin' to celebrate."

Beau chuckles. "Yeah, Gramps. We're getting married."

"Took you long enough," he teases. "You better get married fast. Took you nearly twenty years to get the girl, who knows if I'll make it to the wedding."

"Stop that!" I say, giving him a teasingly—*gentle*—tap on the shoulder. "You can't say that stuff."

"Eh, I know, I just like giving the boy crap." Gramps smiles at Beau, always so full of humor and mirth.

Before we can continue a conversation, the room erupts in cheers when they see us. Everyone rushes over, my mom throwing her arms around me. It's a tight, loving embrace, and my dad is next.

We are both passed around from person to person, and somehow, the twins remain calm the entire time. To be honest, I'm sure they are just confused as to what the heck is happening.

Jason hands me one of his fruit ales, and I take a large drink of it. I can always pump and dump later. Josie and Andrew are giddy as they watch us, having only just celebrated their one year anniversary. It's been a crazy year, but through it all, I ended up with the best person, and the most incredible future that I never would've believed would be mine.

Beau tugs me over to the front of the room. He holds my hand, as he starts to speak loudly. "Thank you all for coming, and Jason, thanks for letting us have the brewery for the night."

I spot Fallon in the corner with Presley, and offer her a small wave. Beau lifts his glass to her. "And to Fallon, for whipping his ass into shape long enough to help plan the event."

The room erupts into laughter, and I wonder what that might be about. Jason doesn't look over to Fallon, rather looking down at his feet and kicking at an invisible rock. Fallon glances at me and shrugs. I make a mental note to talk to her about that later. I knew she'd been doing some event planning for the brewery, but didn't think it was that much.

"It took us a long time to get to this point," Beau continues, ignoring the laughter and jeers from his brothers in the crowd. "Just a year ago, I was still fighting my feelings for this incredible woman, and now, we are here. Two babies that changed our lives, and an incredible group of family and friends who helped us every step of the way. Please, raise your glasses to my beautiful fiancée, and the love of my life."

Everyone cheers, and I notice Thomas striding in from the far entrance. He has a stricken look on his face, and Arson is clinging to his side like glue. He's still in his uniform, and he must have just come off shift. We all take a sip of our beverages, and then we're bombarded with more people.

Ariel loses her shit this time, probably a little overwhelmed, and hungry. There hasn't been enough time for the alcohol to get into my breast milk, so I decide to feed her. Beau grabs one of the bottles of breast milk from the little cooler we cart along with us, and sends Jason to the back to heat it up.

I find a quiet corner, and get myself ready, laying my nursing cover over my body. When we are at home, I usually just free-boob it, letting it all hang out. I don't know if the crowd here would be as appeasing to it as Beau is though.

Once I'm all arranged, I let Ariel latch on. Beau is carrying Arlo around, glancing at me every few seconds to make sure I'm alright.

Josie sits down on the cushioned bench beside me. She plays with Ariel's socked feet poking out from the blanket. "So, did you know this was coming?" she asks. Her eyes are bright and happy.

"No idea," I say honestly. "We'd talked about getting engaged, but never really anything major. I never would have guessed this was happening tonight."

"He did good," Josie says. "Not that we weren't pretty much sisters before, but now, we get to *officially* be sisters."

My heart clenches. "Holy shit, you're right. I've never had a sister before," I say with tears filling my eyes. "I can't wait."

"I'm totally telling Beau you're more excited to be my sister than his wife," she jokes.

"You do that," I reply sarcastically. She stands, saying a quick "talk later," when Andrew waves her over to him. He's sitting at a small table with Gramps, and they seem to be discussing something intensely.

A soft wet nose nuzzles at my leg, and I look down. Arson is booping at me, trying to get my attention. "Hi, buddy," I croon. I reach out with my free hand, scruffing the fur on top of his head. Thomas is two steps behind him, sitting down next to me with an exhausted huff.

He leans over, resting his head on my shoulder. Thomas is a bit of a flirt, but for us, it's always been more of a bantering siblingship. "Hey, lil' sis," he says through a yawn. "I hear you're officially joining the Cunningham crew."

"I guess so," I reply.

He raises up his left arm, giving me a quick high-five. "Heck ya."

"You alright?" I ask him. He's way more subdued than normal. I've seen him after rough shifts, but not like this.

"Mmhmm," he mutters. "Tired. Long day. We caught a lead on the drug circle, but it ended in finding a teen OD'd on fentanyl laced marijuana. Couldn't get him back."

"Oh, Thomas," I breathe. "I'm so sorry."

He shrugs. "Part of the job, Mar. Just wish we could find a concrete lead. Everything turns into a mess with each potential string."

I pat the top of his blonde head, feeling bad for him. It's got to be exhausting working the way he does, and seeing all the horrible things he sees.

"I'm happy for you two though," Thomas says, pulling me out of my silent thoughts. "Only took you nearly twenty years."

"That seems to be the phrase of the night," I reply, mirth filling my voice. "I'm just glad we made it."

"Me too, sis." Thomas stands. "I need a drink. You need anything? Which one you got under there?" He points to the bundle under my cover.

"Ariel," I tell him. "And, I'm good. Thanks." I adjust her foot, waving at him with it.

He bends down, taking her small foot between his

larger fingers. "Hey Lil' Mermaid, Uncle Tommy will come get some snuggles later, kay?"

She wiggles at the sound of his voice, and Thomas chuckles. "I'm totally her favorite uncle."

"Time will tell," I say in return. He strides off, leaving me alone for a few minutes.

I spot Beau crossing the room toward me, giving me a smile that makes my panties ever so slightly wet.

"Hey, you," I say, leaning over to kiss him.

He kisses me sweetly, tasting like the hoppy beer he's been drinking. "How are you, love?"

"I'm amazing," I honestly reply.

"Me too," he says. Arlo is passed out in his arms, a small dribble of milk falling from the corner of his mouth. Beau wipes it up, and I lean over, resting my head on my future husband's shoulder. I look around, taking in our family and friends, my sweet baby boy in Beau's arms, and Ariel falling asleep in mine. We did it, and I'm so ready for the future.

I glance down at the shimmering ring on my finger, feeling so content, so happy and whole. It's been a long time since I've had this feeling, and I know it won't last forever, but for now, I'm going to keep it as long as I can.

ACKNOWLEDGMENTS

How are we already at book five? It feels like just yesterday I was writing Tip of My Tongue. This journey has been filled with so many ups and downs, but I wouldn't be here with out any of these people.

Aria Harding, my author bestie. You've talked me off so many ledges, hyped me up, read my panic messages when the characters aren't cooperating, talked me through plots, edits, and Taylor Swift Clown theories with me. I wouldn't be here without you, and I'm forever grateful for you.

The Indie Author's Unite Group Chat, I love you all! I will never take for granted the little group that we have.

My Beta Readers, Emily, and Brittany, your kindness and suggestions are so incredible. I appreciate you taking the time out of your busy lives to read and make this book better!

My ARC and Street Team, thank you for taking the time to read my books, and hype me up. You are all the best.

My family and friends, for listening to me gush about my characters and stories, and being my biggest supporters.

Victoria, for answering my calls, and listening to me talk through book ideas and telling me when a certain position definitely would not work.

And lastly, to my readers. Thank you for making this dream of mine a reality.

Cinder Valley Series

Tip Of My Tongue- Lainey & Colin

How Do I Tell You?- Mallory & Tyler

Give Me A Minute- Theo & Peyton

Ivy Ridge

Flowers in Your Hair- Andrew & Josie

Never Really Mine- Beau & Marley

Can't Let You Go- Jason & Fallon

In Plain Sight- Thomas & TBA

Minnesota Blue Herons Hockey Series

TBA-Grace & Adam

ABOUT THE AUTHOR

Alice Daniels is a born and raised Minnesotan who loves to write books based on the small town she grew up in. Her books are sweet, heartfelt, and sexy, with relatable characters.

As a child, she was an avid fiction reader, which evolved into a deep love for romance novels and the community surrounding them. She recently discovered a passion for putting her ideas into writing and decided to pursue her childhood dream of becoming an author.

She spends time with her family and friends when she's not writing, especially on the lakes or outdoors in the summer.

Follow Alice on Facebook, Instagram, and Goodreads for book updates, teasers, and future releases!

Join her Facebook Group, Alice Daniels Reader Group to get all the insider info, sneak peeks, and more!

https://alicedaniels.com/

amazon.com/author/alicedaniels

facebook.com/authoralicedaniels

instagram.com/authoralicedaniels

goodreads.com/authoralicedaniels

bookbub.com/authors/saylor-ann

www.ingramcontent.com/pod-product-compliance
Lightning Source LLC
Chambersburg PA
CBHW061109310726
48974CB00002B/463